Usha K R is the author of the novels *Sojourn* (1998), *The Chosen* (2003), *A Girl and a River* (2007), and *Monkey-man* (2010). Her novels have been listed for several awards including the Commonwealth Writers' Prize, the Man Asia, and the DSC Prize for South Asian Literature. *A Girl and a River* won the Vodafone Crossword Award, 2007. *Monkey-man* was shortlisted for the DSC Prize for South Asian Literature, 2012. Her short story *Sepia Tones* won the Katha Award for Creative Writing back in 1995.

Usha K R attended the International Writing Program at the University of Iowa in 2011. She lives in Bangalore.

PRAISE FOR USHA K R

Monkey-man (2010)

'Like an experienced angler landing a difficult catch, Usha KR keeps her line taut all the way through this elegantly plotted novel. Not till the end do we get to see the whole thing as it lies panting and struggling, revealed at last in all its oddity, neither a mystery nor a romance but a story of people caught in the embrace of a complex and hairy *otherness*.'—Manjula Padmanabhan in *Biblio*

'... weaves an intricate patchwork quilt of lives over many decades and political persuasions to hover between a mix of a strange mystery, a tale of old stereotypes and newfound opportunities, and modern day India's work-centric culture ... The descriptions in the book sometimes take on a deeply poetic even philosophical twist.'—*The Hindu*

'No shortcuts, no slang, hers is a celebration of language. Every sentence is pregnant with meaning, the mundane comma could mark a passage of time, and time itself becomes secondary as the narrative leapfrogs back and forth.'—*Hindustan Times*

A Girl and a River (2007)

'*A Girl and a River* is a book to be relished ... written ... with shrewd wit and a rich regional flavour.'—*Outlook*

'This is an intricately plotted and beautifully written novel that moves between an intensely imagined past and an uncertain present ... The happenings ... are narrated with a quiet mastery that is the signature quality of this book ... *A Girl and a River* does that rare thing: it creates a world so discreetly furnished with historical detail that it seems alive.'—*Citation, Vodafone Crossword Award, 2007*

'*A Girl and a River* makes excellent reading and Usha keeps the plot so well in control that not one but two lines of suspense are running together at the same time; try as you may, it's difficult to guess ahead or to draw a logical conclusion as to the surprising turn of events in either narrative strand.'—*The Hindu*

BOYS FROM GOOD FAMILIES

Usha K R

SPEAKING TIGER

SPEAKING TIGER BOOKS LLP
4381/ 4, Ansari Road, Daryaganj
New Delhi 110002

First published in paperback by Speaking Tiger Books 2019

ISBN: 978-93-89231-70-0
eISBN: 978-93-89231-71-7

10 9 8 7 6 5 4 3 2 1

Typeset in Garamond Premier Pro by SÜRYA, New Delhi
Printed at HT Media Ltd, Gr. Noida

Contents

The Daily Things We Do

The daily things we do
For money or for fun
Can disappear like dew
Or harden and live on.
Strange reciprocity:
The circumstance we cause
In time gives rise to us,
Becomes our memory.

—Philip Larkin,
from *The Daily Things We Do*

Prologue

He woke up to a heavy head, a ferrous tongue and a room full of the morning light. During the night, between bouts of fitful sleep, he must have willed his exhaustion. He had dreamt that his body lay limp on the bed, his limbs falling away, his manhood splayed to one side, futile. He had tried to conjure soft hands to massage him, to leaven his tiredness, but they weren't willing; he had woken up a log of wood.

The fan above him was still, its blades edged with grime, its small pot belly telling its vintage make, unchanged perhaps from the time the room was built, forty years to the least. The electricity must have gone off at night, stifling the room, leaving him in a sweat—there was a rational explanation for everything, thankfully, even bad dreams.

It was cooler on the balcony. But the monsoons could be temperamental. The day could begin well but get gloomy and oppressive. A glint of silver blinded him for a moment—the sun off a dish antenna on a nearby roof. They sprouted roof after roof after roof, like mushrooms after the rains, ears turned upward to the sky. One of those roofs was his, for he was a man of substance, owner of property, a house; but here he was in a hotel, a transient, a man invisible even to himself. And therein lay his tale, his destiny even, if he would allow it.

In the adjacent building, at right angles to his balcony but much lower, two storeyed to his fifth floor, was a large terrace, partially covered with a roof of old-fashioned Mangalore tiles. The previous night, men had congregated there, stripped to their waists, lounging around, smoking, chatting with each other or just standing close, looking into the night, relaxed as men are when they know they are not being watched. Later, they had fitted a trestle table against a wall, brought in two blackened aluminium tubs of food, and heaped their plates with yellow rice and red gravy. In the morning, a young man, his torso as tender as a leek, had swept the place, whisked the washing off a line at the far end, prodding with his foot, even as he did, a mate who still slept, all flung out on a straw mat. Within minutes, he and two others had set up chairs and tables, stacked potted plants between them, cordoning them off into aisles, and watching from his balcony he had recognised the laminated tables and plastic chairs and the space itself as the outdoor 'open to the sky' café of the hotel he was staying in, where he had dined the previous day, and the men as the waiters and the room service boys who had brought him his food and refilled his water jug. Some were very young, fair-complexioned, bright-eyed, with a ready smile, up from the coast, brought by a relative who was already working here in the city. He knew those boys. At one time he had been one of them, sleeping on a mat, bent over a plate, spooning mouthfuls, not so much out of hunger but out of a strong feeling that he was undeserving in some way, that he should finish quickly before the plate was taken away from him.

He poured himself a glass of water to ease his parched throat. His calf throbbed. He must have run a fever at night. The jug clung to the table top and he had to prise it off. There was a tiny insect struggling in the slimy ring the jug had left behind. He edged it out, allowing it to dry itself. There had been a buzz around the tubelight at night and in the quiet he had heard them strike the tubelight intermittently—after a while he had been able to empty his mind of all thoughts and listen only to the buzz—the music of the death of insects. In the morning, usually a fresh-faced boy came with a dustpan and swept them off, a small grey heap.

The room was small but full of light in the daytime. There was a bed with a hard mattress—free from bed bugs—a table and chair, the laminate on the table worn down in several places. He recognised the colour and pattern of the laminate—one of the earliest concessions to 'unclean' modernity his father had allowed. A man had come home with a length of brown-and-white-flecked 'Decolam', cut it to shape and glued it with a thick white gum to the surface of the table that would now become the dining table. His sister had been ecstatic—she could now wipe the table clean of meal-debris with a wet rag; no more sitting on the floor to eat.

The bathroom had a bucket and mug—grimy, plastic—but he was glad of it; after years of battling with complicated shower contraptions, he was glad to have just the one tap to turn on and off. (The squat-style toilet had also eased his constipation.) The large mirror over the table—the silver eaten up at the edges—and the wrought iron furniture in the balcony spoke of grander times, of more genteel ambitions; the noisy tubelight was a later, cost-cutting addition, a contrast to the fluted lampshades on the walls, empty of bulbs.

The room was small, yes; it took him back to his lean days, his really lean days, in his single room occupancy off North Broadway Street. There had been two trees outside his window. The sugar maple, quiet in the summer, had caught fire in the fall, the upper leaves turning red, the air turning smoky around it. Often, he had brought the leaves home, caught in the hood of his fleece, and lain them out on the dresser—leaves like the webbed feet of birds, in shades of red, pink and brown. The honey locust on the other hand, he had taken for the tamarind, misled by its compound leaves and chambered seed pod, and its false featheriness, but he found it soothing, even as he knew he was mistaken.

He had seen the trees summer after summer, fall after fall. Eventually he had moved, rolling up his mat, taking down his washing, leaving the room as he found it, stripped bare to its mattress, dresser, table and chair, to the next of his transient homes, leaving no sign of his habitation.

He had tried for the power of discrimination, for harmony, balance and equanimity as enjoined by his daily prayers. Of the injunction to modest possession, the one that he had followed faithfully, equally by circumstance as will, was the one to live in a retired cell with a low door; also the command to be celibate—he had needed little persuasion there. He had resolved to strive for that state of calm reflection, where he could look equally upon a learned man, a cow, an elephant, a sugar maple, a honey locust, a dog and a dog-eater, and he was sure they would look upon him with equal non-attachment when it was their turn.

I

One

The garden was over-run with rats. No ordinary rats, the gardener said, these were bandicoot rats, regular little pigs. They eluded his traps, baited with tough bits of dry coconut. And you won't let me poison them. The gardener threw up his hands. They can tunnel into foundations, into stone, into anything, and this is an old house. Better get the boys to attend to it.

The fullgrown trees, the mango, the jackfruit and the jamun, were safe from them, but every new sapling and tender root had been attacked and destroyed. Even his mother's precious tulasi plants had not been spared. There were burroughs all over the garden, with tell-tale dunes marking them, perfectly shaped, the soil friable and light, as if it had been sieved. They were remarkable feats of construction, when you thought of it—a warren of tunnels extending for miles perhaps, a few feet below the ground on which the house stood. The garden had turned into a conviviality of squirrels, crows and rats. And monkeys, when the fruit ripened on the trees. The boys had to be called. His father had taken a decision. And his father's word was law.

Theirs was a complicated household, the chain link of tasks, responsibilities and supervision as complex as the warren beneath the ground. From the street you could see a large house, old, commanding still but a little shabby, just beginning to crumble round the edges, hostage to the monsoon moss, set in a compound full of trees. His grandfather had built it fifty years ago, sometime in the 1920s, and named it Neel Kamal—Blue Lotus—apparently after the lotuses that had been in bloom in a nearby pond that afternoon when he had bought the land on an off-chance. His grandfather, a lawyer of eminence and a grandee, with a presence in the Mysore court, had had many properties but Neel Kamal had become the family home. The house had come to his father, as part of his inheritance, and it still remained the family hub, with a regular traffic of relatives and a retinue of servants to maintain it.

This house is too large. There are too many people coming and going, no privacy, he had said to his mother once and she, who was used to pulling out mattresses into the large hall when they had guests, and chatting with them late into the night, had looked at him in surprise. Be glad of it, give thanks to God. If people stop coming and going, a house would turn into a tomb. He had not pressed the point, for technically there were just four of them in the house, after his grandfather had passed on, not counting the cousins who stayed for extended periods of time, sometimes lasting years, when they were studying in the city.

The gardener, known simply as Old Man, too old to do any heavy work, but as eternal as the trees he tended to, was now loping off to the back of the house to see what the kitchen would yield, one eye out for the boys for whom he had contempt but edged always with curiosity. He had to clear out by the time the kitchen top work help—a redoubtable woman of large proportions—came in the mornings for she did not like outsiders in her pantry. Then there were a series of odd jobs men and delivery boys, the experts who climbed the coconut palms, silvered the woks, and cleaned the well, who made their way to the back of the house and waited in the yard for top work Kaveramma to notice them.

And then there were the boys. They lived in the outhouse set off at the back of the compound. Several years ago, when his grandfather was still in charge, Sanjeeva and his family had been inducted into the outhouse. The head priest of the local temple had asked his grandfather. The man, newly come up from the village with his young family, had minor duties in the temple, so they needed to house him close to it. His wife would help around the house. They were a good family, the priest said, belonging to a community of religious mendicants with a long tradition of pledging the first-born son to religious service, so in a way, people of god. But of course, city life had unravelled everything. Where was it possible to follow one's traditional vocation strictly these days?

As far back as he could remember, Sanjeeva and Ramakka had lived in the outhouse, with their children. In the last two weeks of December and the first fortnight of January, as the sun transited through Sagittarius and entered Capricorn, Sanjeeva stood in the courtyard of the temple and blew on the long horn, every day, much before day break, to caution the devout that soon the sun would rise and they would have to be quick in their pieties before going about their duties. This was the month of Dhanur, special to Vishnu.

On certain auspicious days, Sanjeeva would go on his rounds collecting alms. He was a striking figure—tall, straight and impassive, and he looked the alms giver directly in the eye, as would befit a man who received alms in the name of god. All his children, including his daughters, had inherited his tall reed-thin frame and a certain distant air. The sound of the gong meant that he was on his rounds, and the long blast of the conch that he was standing at your gate. Oh that's the Dasaiah, the woman of the house would say to herself and hurry to the store room to prepare her offering. You poured the rice into the copper vessel strapped to his side and folded your hands briefly in front of the covered lamp he carried—conch, gong, bowl and lamp, each one a weighty symbol, an object of veneration, of which the bearer had to be worthy.

In the evenings, Sanjeeva sat in the dark on the steps of the outhouse, a single kerosene lamp burning inside, for the outhouse was still to be electrified, and warmed by a 'baby', a small sachet of arrack, enough to turn the water turbid and see him through the cold winter night, sang in a clear high voice, so plaintive that it could cleave the heavens, protesting his devotion. Ashwath's mother muttered under her breath, but who could say anything to the chosen of god. When his mother was laid up with post-partum weakness after he was born, so he had heard, Sanjeeva's wife had suggested a drop of arrack—just enough to cloud a glass of water. Drink it up, she said, to warm your insides, and to help you hold up.

And the household help bit did not work out as the head priest had said. For one, between her lay-ins for the many children she had and her ill-health in between,

Ramakka could not do much; she sent her daughters when they were old enough, but his mother complained that they were disorderly, they couldn't quite understand housework. Same with the boys—they weren't quite as biddable as his mother had hoped they would be. So, the girls were declared to be wild creatures and the boys elusive. But every week his mother sent over quantities of rice, oil and chillies to the outhouse. Sometimes the outhouse would send a covered plate of offerings to the main house. It disconcerted his mother, who did not know what to do with the coarse grain, the bits of root and resin, the betel nut and the coloured thread. It angered kitchen top work Kaveramma, who thought the gesture presumptuous. Drama, pure drama, his mother had said once after an energetic burst from Sanjeeva, and asked him not to sound his long horn and his gong till he was well out of range of their gate. His father took the occasional appeals for handouts—the straight back and the patient vigil outside his window—in his stride; in the periphery of his obligations, he included his servants as well.

*

The boys will deal with the rats. You supervise. I've spoken to them, his father said before he left for office.

Years later, he would use an egg-shaped object with a ruby eye to repel rats—an ultrasonic rodent control device—in a box-like room with a narrow window that looked out into a grey alley, and the rats would be Norway rats, not bandicoots, but that was much later, far removed from this life and all that it had made familiar.

The boys would give him a list of things and he should

procure them himself, his father said, not send them to the shop with the money. He had counted out the notes carefully and caressed the coins as if they were made of gold, before handing them over, looking distinctly unhappy as he always did when he was parting with money, especially to his son. A kilogram of red chillies. Coal. Mud pots. It was a curious list but there was no arguing with the boys, especially when his father had said so. In everything, he obeyed his father unquestioningly, that had become a habit. Try as he might, he could never please him. Every instruction was delivered with a severity of tone that seemed to belie his faith in his son; he seemed to trust the boys more. There were three of them—the boys—three of Sanjeeva's sons who lived in the outhouse. Whenever there was work of a heavy duty nature, furniture to be shifted, sacks to be lifted, a tree to be cut down, they were summoned. The older two were easy; they looked at the ground when they spoke to you and pretended not to hear you when they did not feel like, but they completed their tasks. The youngest one Srinivasa a.k.a Gunda, was the tricky one. He had a bold stare, and his manner, deferential enough, had an edge. Mud pots, with narrow mouths, you know where to get them don't you? There was an upward lilt to his voice. In the mornings, when Ashwath wheeled his cycle out of the gate, Gunda would sing out, to no one in particular—Here I go, shirt and pant, off to win the world. He always told himself that Gunda was full of beans. He meant no harm.

The plan was to put live coals into the mud pots, fill them with red chillies, put them into the burroughs, pack the entrance tight with mud, and smoke the rats senseless. The pots were perforated with small holes at one end, and the open end was sealed with mud, such that as the chillies burned, the smoke filled the burroughs. It was a slow process; the rats were to be taken by surprise.

It was a Sunday and they had an audience. Kitchen top work Kaveramma's son Prakash was there, lounging on the bars of his bicycle. He was in engineering college, senior to Ashwath, on a means-cum-merit scholarship. Kaveramma's exertions, her stepping out of the house to do kitchen top work, was only to make up the rest of his fees, she had let it be known. So Prakash the fee-guzzler, as he and his sister had named him, was there, ostensibly to pick up his mother after her work was done. In the eyes of his family, especially his uncle Suchi, there was no virtue that Prakash seemed to lack; they were always holding him up as an example of hard work, ambition and capability—a boy who had pulled himself up by his bootstraps. The unsaid thought hung in the air—he, Ashwath, should show himself to be a little more worthy of the advantages he had, more grateful for the family name he bore.

Gunda bent low on the ground to blow through the perforated end of the pot before burying it in the ground. Prakash edged closer, crouching next to Gunda, and Ashwath noticed, with a start of resentment, that both of them were wearing his shirts, castoffs passed on by his mother to theirs. Gunda looked up, his eyes bleary, his voice rasping with the smoke. You had better wait in the porch. The chilli smoke may be a bit too harsh for you.

No. I'll wait here, Ashwath replied. See that you finish your job.

It took all morning for them to set up the pots and fumigate all the rat holes, and he waited till they were done.

After the job was over, there was a convivial moment on the porch, where his mother had sent up buttermilk for all of them.

That should be the end of them.

What happens to the rats?

Oh, we dig them out and eat them—Gunda smiled, wiping his mouth with the back of his hand.

Not here. In the villages, in the paddy fields—his brother, kinder, said. Along with the grain the rats store in their nests.

I believe it tastes good. Chilli smoked rat meat, Gunda persisted. Prakash smiled up at him.

Not us, we don't eat it, the older brother said quickly.

My father will speak to you, he said, addressing the older brother.

And these—will you take them to the back of the house—he couldn't quite bring himself to meet Gunda's eye.

They broke up immediately. He went in through the front door, and the boys made their way to the back of the house, carrying a clattering tray of tumblers.

*

He sat on the terrace, waiting for his sister, angry with her for having escaped the morning's humiliations—every encounter with the boys, he felt he came off the worse, and Prakash's presence was an added irritant, not just an irritant, a provocation. And at the end of it, his father hadn't been happy.

He watched as Sanjeeva's daughter, the older one, came in through the gate, returning from the temple, holding a basket—her share of the offerings the priest had given her. He watched her walk through the garden, tall and slender, without turning her head to look at the house, at him, to her home in the outhouse. He heard the gate when Savitri returned—she threw it open, and it squealed, a painful high-pitched sound. She stood at the gate, looking up at him on the terrace, waiting for him to notice her, and then held her hands up at her shoulders and fired. Pshwaw. Pshwaw.

She came bounding up the stairs and as soon as she saw him she cocked her right hand at him and fired again. Pshwaw. Pshwaw. She was wearing khaki trousers and a khaki shirt and a cap on her head with a red feather sticking out—her National Cadet Corps uniform, which he knew she loved.

Today we had rifle shooting. I had an almost perfect score, better than anybody else, even the boys. I held it like this, pulled the catch back and pshwaw ... Next, we'll be trained in the lying down position. The paragliding trials are coming up after that ... If I do well, I'll be selected for the Republic Day Camp in Delhi...

Look—She was cradling a small shiny object in her palm, a narrow brass cylinder about two centimetres tall, a spent cartridge case. We weren't supposed to, but I picked it up ...

Savitri, he said, you had better get out of these clothes, and those heavy boots. And forget about paragliding and Delhi, you know they'll never let you.

Their mother disapproved of Savitri wearing what she called 'men's clothes' and did not share his sister's enthusiasm for the NCC. We'll see—Savitri was not to be repressed so easily. I'm not like you, scaredy-poo. Afraid of Amma, trembling in front of Appa. Okay, okay, calm down. Here, look what I've got for us—she pulled out a large paper cone. He caught the reek of raw onion and hot oil.

Savitri!

Amma will not come up the stairs, you know that. Come on, hurry.

They ate quickly, in large, ungainly handfuls. The bhelpuri from the roadside vendor was terribly spicy but it tasted good. Their mother had forbidden them from eating it.

Of course, today was your big game hunting day, Savitiri said. How did it go?

He was not satisfied, as usual. Said it had taken too long. That I should have also gone to the kirana store to settle the bill with the Shetty in the morning. And he wanted a paisa-paisa account of the purchases. Who gives a receipt for coal and mud pots! You know, sometimes I think he hates me. Who? Savitri looked startled. Don't be silly!

Well, he prefers you to me.

And his brother to both of us, Savitri laughed. Is he still going on about those khata papers? But in all fairness, you did lose them. And it put Suchi mama into so much trouble. Amma pacified him—Savitri slid a sideways glance at him as she did when she was about to parry. Said you lacked viveka buddhi, discernment, that means you're somewhat dull—she dodged out of his reach.

It was a simple errand. His father had asked him to deliver some papers concerning a piece of property to the lawyers. And he had lost the papers. He remembered strapping the file on to the carrier of his cycle but when he reached the lawyer's office, the file was gone. He had cycled back, retracing his route, even questioning the boys at the tea shop where he had stopped off but he couldn't find the papers. His father had been furious. Look at him, he had raged to his brother, their uncle Suchi. Grown so huge with the rice he eats in this house and can't be trusted with a job that a child could have done. How is he going to manage the really tricky cases?

They stood on the terrace, eating out of the newspaper cone in silence, sniffing occasionally and wiping their smarting eyes. They watched Sanjeeva's daughter come out of the outhouse, walk through the garden, and make her way out of the gate.

Yes, she is pretty, Savitri said.

I didn't ...

But I know what you were thinking, I always do. Her name is Tripura Sundari, after the goddess of unparalleled beauty, and she is very devout. Immersed in the temple.

But—he began, and stopped.

He realised that she was teasing him, and he must not rise to her bait.

Two

He was dreaming, surely, or perhaps he had already died and gone to heaven, for his brow was being smoothed by a goddess, her eyes large and calm, the ringlets of her hair springing away from the dome of her forehead. The blue sky stretched behind her, for an eternity, framed by a broad-leaved green, for she lived in a forest of Kadamba trees. How well her complexion became her, flushed with wine as the song promised, and he could smell the musk of her perfume. He knew her immediately from the hymn his mother sang to her in praise and in worship—more beautiful than the red hibiscus, her eyes, like freshly bloomed lotuses.

He heard his mother's voice, urgent, issuing commands, asking him to open his eyes. But his eyes were open, it was his head that seemed to have split and something warm and wet was crusting on his face. His white shirt, he could see, was awash in red, and the toehold of his slippers, bought just the other day, even the price printed in gold lettering had not worn off, had been wrenched out.

He had to have stitches on his forehead.

What a fuss, his father said.

You fell from your cycle, hit the kerb and were brought home by Thippy, Sanjeeva's daughter. I've told you before that you have to take the curve slowly. The road slopes downwards there.

Tripura Sundari—the goddess whose beauty ruled three cities—that was her name. Proof of her parents' delusions of grandeur, rather than their devotion, according to his mother. Ah those innocents in your outhouse, living in their own world, how long is it going to last, kitchen top work Kaveramma would smile in the rare moments of familiarity his mother granted her. But the girl was called Thippy, her given name all but forgotten. This, his mother approved; ironically, it meant 'she of the dung heap'—a name given to children born after a difficult birth or after a child was lost in childbirth, so as to mollify the fates.

His forehead healed quickly but he would retain the snaking scar complete with the teeth of the stitches; it would even come to be one of his identifying marks, along with his moles, on the countless official forms he would fill—a mark to identify his body. And her face, calm-eyed and beautiful, had branded itself on his mind's eye. But he didn't see Thippy the whole of that week. Unlike the boys and her sisters, there was no question of her coming to help out in the main house; the life of a domestic help was not for her. She assisted her father in his temple duties, and attended to all his instruments—keeping the lamp in trim, polishing the long horns and keeping the conch clean. She tended to his mother's tulasi plants in their enclosure, the jasmine and hibiscus bushes, the parijata tree—whose white and orange flowers fell in heaps on the ground. This was never discussed between them, no formal arrangement was ever made, but it just came about—so much so that his mother would not trust the gardener to tend to her grove that yielded flowers for worship.

*

A week of waiting, after which, on his way back from college, he hesitated outside the bangle shop in the corner of the bazar. The shop attendant, a keen-eyed Marwari boy, recognised him.

What happened to your forehead, the boy asked.

He went into the shop sometimes with his sister on the way back from her music class, never failing to be dazzled by the array of trinkets that blazed from the display shelves, and the stoic calm of the boys who stood behind the counters, small-made, with delicate features, from far-off Rajasthan.

I want to buy something.

For your sister? What do you want to buy?

Something. Anything. No, earrings.

Aaah ... I'll show you something special.

He reached out for a cardboard box on the top shelf and held his hand over the box for a moment.

Special item. I don't show to everyone ... They were works of art—whorls of filigree with stones embedded in claws.

Silver, the boy said, pure silver, and the stones are semi-precious.

He reached for a pair with red stones that stood out in a fan of filigree.

He imagined them against her face, flushed not from the wine of his mother's song but from the exertion of supporting him when she had brought him home. In his mind, he nuzzled against her cheek and rested his face in the soft nest of her hair.

I'll take these.

Good choice, the garnets. Thirty rupees.

He slipped the small brown paper cover into the pocket of his shirt, where it rustled like a mouse as he cycled back. He was dazed by his effrontery at having bought this at all, and then paying for it with the money meant for his examination fees.

He set off on his cycle, in no particular direction, not wanting to go home. The day turned to dusk. The streetlights came on—a single bulb wearing a tin hat, casting an orphaned pool of yellow light on the road below. He cycled on, the compound walls of houses, the peanut seller's cart and the people walking on the pavements turning into a hazy, jaundiced blur. He was at once restless, and also filled with a sense of calm, as if his brain had been lobed into two opposite halves. The wound above his left eyebrow began to throb—the stitches were yet to be removed—and he felt his tiredness overcome him. Then, he went home.

*

The house needed to be painted before the monsoons arrived and several 'petty works' as his father called them, as if they were neatly tied parcels to be delivered, had to be completed before the rains made inroads through the many cracks and crevices. It was his job to examine the walls, buy the cement and lime and rouse the handy boys to scrape the mossy patches, apply bandages of cement on the walls, and paint them over.

He could hear the drone of voices downstairs from the outer sitting room. His uncle Suchi was probably there, discussing how to manage the dwindling supplies of rice from their shrinking land holdings, or how to rescue a piece of property, stuck somewhere, for which a new claimant had surfaced. He would be expected to accompany Suchi to the mandi to fetch sacks of rice and coconut, he knew. This was not the way to spend a Sunday morning, wishing he could, like some of his friends in college, let off a stream of English language expletives to relieve himself.

But no, it was the priest, come to discuss the arrangements for his grandfather's tithi, the annual shraddha ceremony that his father performed. As ceremonies went, this was a big one, and his father was punctilious in its observance. He took the morning off from work, which was a serious matter in his father's workhorse book, but paying obeisance to one's forefathers was a debt that one owed to them. In his father's eyes, everything that one was, that one had—name, honour, prestige, one's standing in the world—flowed from family.

Of his grandfather's sons, none had risen to their father's eminence; neither his father nor his uncle had had the energy or his keen speculative mind which was intent on carving the most advantageous path for itself through the world. His grandfather had foreseen the sun of the British empire and the Maharaja's fortunes setting, and had managed the transition from princely state to independent sovereign republic well. The privileges of community, caste and family would erode quickly, he had sensed; they might hold in his lifetime, but not that of his sons, who were still blinking like newborns against the harsh light of day. He had, in the nick of time, managed to get his sons government jobs. Ashwath's father had risen to gazetted officer in the Accountant General's office. The others had started and retired in clerical positions while Ashwath's father had risen to Senior Audit Officer. We are like the Maharaja, his grandfather would say. Independence has been hard on us. The land reforms had depleted their fertile rice growing lands; now only a few handkerchief-sized plots remained scattered here and there, and the house—a crumbling edifice, a white elephant.

If there had been a Communist coup in their country, the thought crossed Ashwath's mind, as in Russia, they would have had to share the house with the peasants, as in the film *Dr Zhivago*. Then the people in the outhouse would have moved into the main house—for a moment he nursed the happy delusion. But the closest they had come to a coup was the Emergency, which had not demanded such drastic measures—only the closure of a certain students' union in his college. The Emergency, declared by Prime Minister Indira Gandhi in 1975, had been the source of much hushed conversation between his father and Suchi mama. On some days, they praised Mrs Gandhi, saying that the Emergency had flushed out the black-marketeers who had created artificial shortages of essentials like rice and dal and onions, and at other times, when they had to rush to office to be on time or when the newspaper had carried a blank centre page in place of the editorial, they grew sombre. Their sharpest attacks they reserved for the chief minister of their state who smiled from the newspapers—wily-eyed, crafty and handsome. Eventually, after two years, the Emergency was lifted, there was a falling out between Mrs Gandhi and their chief minister, and the shabby old bus of democracy wheezed and rattled on its way.

*

There was still the matter of the thirty rupees and the exam fees to be paid. The private moment that he sought with his mother was proving elusive. With his father, he did not dare. He might have to rely on his sister after all, as he did with most things.

By the time he woke up, his mother was well set in her day. She had bathed and was out in her grove to tend to her tulasi plants and offer her morning prayers. She would peep through her fingers to look at the eastern sun, for who can look the sun directly in the eye, and summon him by all his names. When he went to the kitchen, top work Kaveramma was already there and she had his mother's complete attention. Kaveramma had, strangely, spread out several clunky-looking gold ornaments on the kitchen counter, like a display at a bangle store. Lying on one side was a soft pouch, mouth agape, disembowelled.

This one, Kaveramma said, pointing to a fat pendant, more an encrustation than a piece of jewellery, a gift from my uncle when I got married ... this chain with gold coins, when my son was born ...

On the terrace, his father and uncle Suchi were standing at the parapet wall and looking at the garden. There was another visitor with them—his father's cousin, who was sitting on a chair, holding a walking stick, a fine rosewood specimen with a carved head. He was quite fond of this cousin, whose name he wasn't sure of, for his father and Suchi mama referred to him by an unflattering nickname. Of all his father's relatives, he was the one with some taste. He carried in the pocket of his silk jubba a tin of slim cigarettes and a silver snuff box, objects of endless fascination for Ashwath when he had been a boy. On Sundays the cousin went to his club to play billiards and have a drink. There was more than a tinge of disapproval when his father spoke of his cousin, which marked him out in Ashwath's favour. His father usually disapproved of anyone—any of his relatives that is, for people outside his circle didn't count—who had done better than he had, who hadn't followed the straight and narrow—a rank in engineering or medicine, a government job and marriage into a good family, and who marked all the regular milestones in life with ritual and ceremony. Anything outside the sanction of convention, an original thought, an exhibition of individual style, was taboo. His sister had found ways around his father's strictures, but he was clumsy and collided with them head on. Ashwath often boiled over at his father's parsimonious ways which reduced things to their shabby essentials—his anxious counting of every paisa they spent, the endless lists of expenses he prepared and his exhortations to Ashwath's mother to be careful. There seemed always a piece of property that was in peril, papers that were not in order, dues that did not measure up and rents that were not forthcoming. These were the only things he and Suchi mama discussed; Ashwath was sure his father actually enjoyed those conversations, that he had begun to nurture these anxieties and worries. He was a far cry from his openhanded cousin who was standing there, one beringed hand on the parapet wall, and the other holding a cigarette. Not once had his father taken them out on a vacation that did not involve visiting a crowded temple or had a celebration at home that was not a religious occasion.

Normally, he joined the conversation when the stylish cousin was there but that morning, he would rather not have met any of them. They caught sight of him though before he could retreat and Suchi summoned him over with a wave of his hand.

How is your head? Have the stitches been removed?

Oh it was nothing, a scratch merely. A tumble from the cycle is quite common. I've been going to college, he said.

He has a hard head, difficult to make a dent in it, his father said, without smiling.

Speaking of college, the cousin said, when are you going to America?

He has to finish his engineering first, get a degree ...

And for that you have to stop day dreaming—his father looked visibly put out.

That may be but you must plan right from now if you are thinking of your Master's.

The cousin's younger son had migrated to Canada, and was trying from there to get to the United States.

And why should every young man want to go to the US? Leave home and hearth and go to some unknown land, seeking a pot of gold? Isn't there life here? His father sounded pained.

The cousin looked surprised. Where are the jobs here, show me—he rounded on Ashwath's father. You know how my son struggled for years after his Master's as a lecturer in a college, being paid a pittance, before he went to Canada. That is the fate of our boys.

Nonsense, his father said. Nonsense—where is the guarantee that our boys will have a better life outside?

We must keep our eyes open to all opportunities—for once Suchi mama seemed to express an opinion contrary to his father's. Even the likes of Kaveramma know that. She is trying to raise hand loans now, preparing to send her Prakash abroad next year—Suchi mama said approvingly.

Suchindra, our case and Kaveramma's can hardly be compared. I could raise the money if I wanted. I don't need to pawn my wife's jewellery—his father stood up, making his displeasure clear, signalling that the conversation was over. Why don't you take Ashwath with you when you go to inspect the kharab land today, he said as he turned to go inside. We need to think of what to do with it. You could have your morning meal and leave. The cousin got up to go down to the kitchen to pay his respects to Ashwath's mother.

Morning show at Vijaylakshmi theatre—James Bond—he winked at Ashwath as he passed by.

But there was no escaping the job that had to be done. Every Sunday, his father thought up these errands. There was something or the other to be done, some chore lying in wait for him.

As his father's cousin sauntered past in a waft of scented tobacco, Ashwath remembered that the matter of the examination fees was still to be settled.

Mama, he said, I'll walk downstairs with you till the kitchen. You don't need that fine cane of yours inside the house.

*

That afternoon, that very Sunday afternoon, when he thought it was impossible, he ran into her unexpectedly. He was cycling home when he saw her standing on the footpath, halfway between the temple and the house.

What are you doing here? He did not mean to sound so masterful.

She was wearing a long skirt which ended at her ankles and a man's shirt—thankfully one he couldn't recognise. Her feet were bare. And then he noticed that she was holding something in her hands, covered with a towel, and the thing underneath the towel was stirring.

It was a baby owl, round-eyed and fluffed up in fright. She had rescued it from some boys near the temple. She had tried telling them it was a sacred bird, Lakshmi's vahana, but when they did not listen, she had thrown stones at them and driven them away. She now planned to take it to a safe place, in a small knoll of trees by a lake some distance away.

She hopped on to the carrier of his cycle with alacrity, legs astride. They put the bird in the cane basket attached to the front of the handle bars. She was so light, he could hardly tell she was there behind him on the carrier. It was getting on to evening and the sun—worthy of all twelve of his names—diviner of minds, the radiant one, slayer of darkness, blazed in the western sky. In minutes they were out of the city and the tarred road gave way to a narrow dirt track. The track led through fields, now lying fallow, the red earth turned up to receive the next round of seeds. A little further the track transformed into a bund, a brown lake spreading out on one side. The lake, more a muddy pond, was full of lotuses, the broad leathery leaves spread out on the surface of the water, the flowers drooping now at the end of day, the veined undersides of their petals showing, pink and white. The dirt track turned to slush and his tyres wobbled; he felt the drag at the back, light as she was, but carried on. He could ride endlessly, he felt, right through the strip of casuarina trees in the distance, and into the setting sun on the horizon.

There was a clearing at the edge of the casuarina standing, a small space with a sprawling banyan and a cluster of huts next to it. A dog barked a welcome and a woman appeared at the door of one of the huts.

He watched as she scooped the towel out of the cane basket with her long ladies-finger hands, thick at the wrists, nails edged with dirt. Her ankles flashed through the green grass, sinews strong and straining, heels bare. He dusted a space on the stone culvert built around the banyan tree and stretched himself out. There was an old temple somewhere beyond he knew, where a crowd gathered once a year at the time of the ooru habba or the local village festival, in which Thippy and her family participated and in which, apparently, Thippy had a stellar role.

The branches of the banyan spread above him, some with red fruits clinging to them. Above the banyan, the blue sky was turning pale and colourless before surrendering to the dusk, and he could hear the faint sounds of birds in the distance. In the casuarina grove, a chirruping began of wood insects, high-pitched and continuous, a hymn to the advancing night. He would come again to the casuarina pelt later, at a momentous time, to hear the wind sloughing through the insubstantial leaves, the bark peeling off, the flowers withered, the seed cones scattered on the ground. But that evening, the sky belonged to him; the trees, the land, the stone bench warm beneath his shoulders, the lake beyond with the drooping lotuses were all his—he held them in the scoop of his palm. Spread out at his feet were offerings of flowers—arresting splashes of red all around on the darkening ground, right up to the casuarina grove. They were flowers of the Bandhuka or the Dopahariya, which bloomed in the afternoon and all through the night, to close only in the morning. The god of love was supposed to be as beautiful as the Bandhuka flower, as brilliant as tens of millions of suns and as cool as tens of millions of moons.

*

It was dark by the time they set off on their way back. He cycled across the fields and on the bund by the quavering light of the dynamo, the only thing moving on the road.

He set her down on the footpath outside the temple, under the single lamp on the street. She stood for a moment in the halo of light, the sheen of sweat making her face glow, her eyes looking straight at him, the three dots tattooed on her chin in perfect symmetry. This was the moment he knew he should produce his gift; he should reach for the square of brown paper that had lain in his upper left-hand shirt pocket all week and burnt a hole no doubt into the extremely inferior vena cava of his heart, pull it out with a flourish and put it into her hands. But he could not do it. His hands lay inert on the handlebar of his bicycle.

In a moment she was gone. She smiled at him and crossed the road and was out of sight. He felt satiated, complete. They were already united—her limbs, strong, sleek and slender as the boughs of the guava tree against his, his lips first against the three dots on her chin and then moving to heal her rough chapped lips. He turned home, light-headed, a warm ember glowing within.

Where on earth—his sister began as soon as she saw him. She had been looking for him all afternoon and evening. Why had he disappeared without telling anyone?

He flicked the brown paper packet at her with an exaggerated twist of his wrist.

For me? She looked in disbelief at the intricate web of silver and the glowing red stones, at the sheer span of it on her palm. She smiled and laid it out on the parapet wall so that the light could catch the stones.

Just then the gate creaked open and they watched as Thippy walked through the garden towards the outhouse, a towel slung over her shoulder. Savitri caught his eye before he could look away, before he could school the expression on his face. She looked at the earrings again, and touched them cautiously, as if they were live things, and put them back into the packet. They walked back in silence to his room where she opened the drawer in his writing desk, the one where he kept his watch and his wallet, and slid the packet into the back.

*

Coffee?

He was surprised to find his mother at his elbow and not his sister. She stood by his side on the terrace and watched him sip out of the steel tumbler, saying nothing, pretending she had not noticed that he was staring fixedly in the direction of the outhouse when he should have been at his desk, studying.

Your father is in the puja room, and he'll take some time, so I thought I'd speak to you, his mother said. He did not turn to look at her for he could guess what was coming.

You've been asking people for money it seems—she came straight to the point.

It's only thirty rupees for heaven's sake, he snapped. It's not as if I borrowed a fortune. And I'm going to pay it back as soon as I get my scholarship money—

Your scholarship money is not due till the end of the year. You know you have to keep up the high marks. Finally, you will have to ask your father for it ... Whether it's thirty rupees or thirty paise, you know your father is a stickler for achara, for appropriate behaviour. Even with his own brother, he keeps such scrupulous accounts. He hates the thought of any one of us stretching our hands out. A begging bowl is a begging bowl all the same, irrespective of the money that's put into it. And why did you want so much money? Don't we give you all you need?

Again he said nothing, not turning to look at his mother. They stood in silence, looking out into the garden and watched as Thippy came out from the outhouse and walked out of the gate on her way to the temple.

Your sister tells me you bought a pair of earrings ...

So Savitri had told on him.

Yes. I bought them for her.

Silver and gold, you leave that to us. We'll take care of those things when she gets married.

His mother reached out and touched the scar on his forehead. He flinched and moved away, out of her maternal reach, for the wound had not fully healed.

I can understand that you are grateful, even to servants who do their duty. But there are ways, paddhatis to be followed. A gift of jewellery, gold and silver—it means something, it's a sign of commitment, apart from being an extravagance. So don't do anything foolish. And don't shame your father. Get back to your books, now. I'll tell him you needed the money to get your gooseneck lamp fixed.

I am not a child to be chided, he said, angrily.

Then prove that you are a man, that you can stand on your own feet.

He flung himself back on his bed and covered his eyes with his forearm in frustration. There was no way he could get those wretched thirty rupees, he knew. He would have liked to throw the notes into their face if he could. But his father calculated things so carefully that he gave him just enough for coffee in the canteen and the occasional movie. He had had to get his cycle repaired himself. His father had said that he would not pay for his carelessness. He couldn't ask his friend Satish again—Satish had already paid for his ticket the last two times they went to the English movies together.

He left without having his morning meal, without telling them where he was going, even without taking the blessing from the lamp that was placed before the icons and without the pat of vermilion powder on his forehead. He would not go to college, he decided. He would loiter, go where his heart took him, a free bird.

He cycled over first to Lalbagh and sat by the lake; he was cooled by the breeze though the waters looked green and scummy. There were a few men sitting on the banks, fishing rods in hand or watching their nets. They looked as if they had been waiting there forever. He spotted a young couple, tucked in a discreet nook under a tree, heads close together, lost to the world. He conjured Thippy beside him, her musk, that heady mix of a spicy, pungent resin and sweat, filling his senses. A stranger, a vagrant in tattered clothes and matted hair, came up and sat on the bench at the other end. The couple in the nook got up and left, disturbed by a persistent peanut vendor, and Ashwath too got up.

He felt in his pockets and came up with some loose change—a plate of idlis and a cup of coffee was all that it would buy him. He wandered through the crowded lanes of Chickpet—he had already seen the film on the morning show at Vijaylakshmi theatre, and in any case he didn't have the money for a ticket. By noon, he was hungry again. He considered his options—Suchi mama's house or any other relative's was out of the question and all his friends would be at college. The temple near his house, where

Thippy and her father worked, served free afternoon meals but that was unthinkable. His father was one of the main sponsors of those meals—it would create a scandal if he showed up there, lining up with the poor and the needy. He cycled back to Lalbagh, pedalling hard under the sun, up Krumbiegal Road, and stretched himself out on one of the hard cement benches to take a nap. The morning's vagrant was still there, asleep on an adjoining bench, his bundle clutched to his chest.

It was still early evening by the time he got home. He would tell them that the last class was cancelled, if they asked. He went up to his room and lay on his bed, his brow furrowed in thought.

This was no way to live—hostage to his father's strictures, his mother's goodwill and the largesse of relatives—which is what the grand terms of custom and tradition boiled down to, even as he was constantly reminded by Suchi mama that the house and all his father's lands would be his some day. For the rest of the evening he pondered on his fate, till sleep overcame him. It had been a tiring day after all.

Three

The monsoons came and went and the house held out without springing a single leak. The second year too, the house surprised them and his father grunted his approval. The boys had turned out to be good handymen after all.

Top work Kaveramma missed work one day, unexpectedly, regular work horse that she was, and came the next day with good news. Her son Prakash had got into an American university, whose name she could not remember right then. She had made something special in celebration. His mother served them all a bit of it, to be polite, and then put it away—a thick pottage of millets and molasses—to be dealt with later. Kaveramma had become thin of late, with dark pits under her eyes. She had taken on more houses, running around in a frenzy of work, so that she could send her son to America.

It was the season for America. Suchi mama brought his wife's nephew home, the investment banker from the US, and the cook and the girls dropped all work and gathered in the doorway to peer at him. He was wearing shorts—the half pants that you stopped wearing when you got out of junior school, and a sleeveless tee shirt—the gear of Olympic runners—and he did not remove his footwear at the door like everyone else. He sat on the sofa with his right knee stuck out, his foot resting on his left knee, sole facing out. He spoke loudly and continuously in English, about 'our' economy and what 'we' were doing in the First Bank of America, taking easy ownership of his organisation and the country of which he was now a citizen.

Ashwath's father tried to talk shop with him on the strength of his officer's grade in the State Accounts department, and produced a litany of complaints. He had to be alert to so many possible misdemeanours—people trying to collect salaries against false claims and documents, whole departments that were claiming funds which did not exist. These were familiar stories and situations, but that day, in contrast to Suchi's wife's nephew's account, they sounded sordid. Manohar—call me Man—for that was Suchi's wife's nephew's name—had just returned from Machu Pichu. It was really hot there, he said, and he was set to go on a skiing holiday in Aspen, Colorado, a mountainous place in contrast to the flat prairie Midwest where he lived. At that ski resort you could hope to rub shoulders with the likes of Goldie Hawn and Harrison Ford and even Lee Iacocca.

Manohar has helped Prakash, our Kaveramma's son, settle down in his college. He has been really helpful, Suchi mama said, looking pointedly at Ashwath. The names of the people and the places Manohar mentioned meant nothing to Ashwath. What he remembered was the confidence of Manohar's manner, surging forward as if he were the first to plant his flag in an unknown, uncharted land, and that there were no precedents he was bound to follow. It was as if he was led by his instinct alone, either in the way he had decided to fashion his life or in the smaller things, his clothes, and the assurance with which he had spoken to an elder, or waved away food and drink that was pressed on him, unmindful of the manners of a good guest.

That summer, the summer of his discontent, he had the impression that his uncle Suchi was trying to convey something to him, perhaps a disappointment of some sort—and Suchi mama was his father's agent. Suchi mama's hints that others, such as top work Kaveramma's son Prakash, and Harish, who could best be described as a poor relative, a boy who was being sheltered in their house while he completed his degree in medicine, were getting ahead of him and that he was in danger of losing the race, were too obvious to ignore. So he started avoiding Suchi, neglecting to meet him on one instance—the morning after a botched lab exam—at the land records office where they had to claim a certificate, wandering instead into the thick of

Chickpet till his feet found their way to a regular haunt, Vijaylakshmi theatre, which had reruns of old Hollywood films in the morning slot.

He bought a ticket and went in. Usually he chose films about cowboys or gangsters, but he liked the title of this one. *Breakfast at Tiffany's*. It was unusual, unlike the title of any other film he had seen before, compact and efficient, and yet descriptive. The words also appealed to him visually—two words of equal length separated by a preposition. He also liked the fact that it referred to an activity as routine as breakfast. He wondered whether the restaurant Tiffany's across Cubbon Park had been named after the film; it was quite possible.

He could not catch all the words—there were no subtitles—or all the threads of the plot, but he understood enough to make sense of the film. It was a love story. A simple country girl comes up from her village to a big city, attracted by the city lights, wanting a man to take care of her. There were some nice scenes in the film. A party going on in a crowded flat. A woman's purple turban was set alight by a careless cigarette, and a man casually poured his drink into it to put out the fire. The hero pressed his misted glass against a woman's bare back; startled, she moved and made way for him to cross the packed room. He also liked the scene in the girl's kitchen when the pressure cooker burst on the stove. That was a situation that he knew, an object he could recognise from his own life.

In the final scene, when the girl had decided to leave the man who loved her, and he was riding with her to the airport, she suddenly flounced out of the cab to look for her cat. The film ended with the two of them embracing in the pouring rain, with the cat squashed between them. Love, here, was different from what he imagined. The girl was not chaste, yet she loved the man, as she realised in the end. She was thin, with big eyes, and whimsical, and she called her cat Cat. Such a girl he could fall in love with, easily.

*

He was surprised that she accepted to come at all. He was sure only when he saw her across the street from the temple, although it took him a few seconds to recognise her. She was dressed not in her usual long skirt and man's bush shirt, but a half sari, a long pleated skirt in a black and white print with a white gauzy veil or davani, drawn across her chest like the pallu of a sari, her feet shod in slippers, her hair sleek and shiny with oil. No fuss with frills and lace and satin petticoats, or puffy hair that his sister created, standing in front of the mirror, her mouth full of hair pins, nor a face pink with powder. Without greeting or preamble, she stepped up and hoisted herself on to the carrier of his cycle.

It occurred to him that Thippy was the first girl—other than his sister who didn't count—to ride with him on his bicycle and to whom he had spoken at some length. In his engineering college, run by a monastic order, there were very few girls in his class and those that were there all sat bunched together in the first row, like horses with blinkers. There was a separate line for them in the morning prayer and in the canteen. Only Satish among his friends was courageous enough to speak to them, to say anything more than 'May I borrow your notes'. He doubted if he could recognise any of those girls if he met them outside college.

The class picnic was the sanctioned time for mingling but he had had to give it a miss since his scholarship money did not cover the cost.

But a vista had now opened up before him—a combination of Hollywood and 'Man' Manohar had made it possible. He was going on what the Americans called a date; if nothing, America was a place where you could hold your own and not defer to elders all the time, where you could have a party for no reason and where love was a real possibility, an actual thing, even when the chips were down.

They cycled through Cubbon Park where the gulmohurs were a blaze of red, and emerged opposite the stadium. There it was, a white building chamfered between two roads, set back in a garden, a ramp leading up to it. The name was up against the white wall, inscribed in a cursive hand in wine red letters, the large T balanced by the downward loop of the y.

There were several tables in the large high-ceilinged hall, covered in white table cloths, each bearing a vase with a single red rose. They sat by the window, with a view of the garden, and the island where the roads met. The waiter in white uniform, who had addressed him as 'Sir', brought them the menu, opened it and placed it in front of her. She closed it immediately and handed it back to him, with the scrupulousness of a person returning property that was not hers.

What will you have—He could not say her name.

Sweet, khara, coffee—I will have whatever you decide, she said.

Sweet, salt and spice, the flavours of a balanced palate, and the pleasantly bitter slough of coffee to wash it down.

Wherever she went, she would create the comfort of the familiar; he wondered if she would be fazed at all in any circumstance or situation.

The ridge gourd bajjis were hot and crisp, but the gulab jamuns, immersed in thick sugar syrup, were hard at the core—the syrup had not seeped through. She gave it the concentration of a ritual meal, solemn, eyes lowered, respectful of the receptacles in which the food and drink were served. She neither spoke nor commented on what she ate, eating in little bites, lips closing quickly round the spoon, embracing the coffee cup with both hands. Sweet, khara, coffee—I will have whatever you decide, she had said, in the assenting tone of a promise being given for life. It was the presence of the waiter, and the thrum of the traffic from the main road, he was sure, that prevented him from reaching out, uncurling her hand from the coffee cup, and taking it into his own.

I have been wanting to come to this hotel since I saw a film with the same name, he told her. The film is about a girl with a cat. At the end of the film she decides to leave town but the cat runs away so she stays back to look for it.

Does the girl find the cat, she asked.

Yes, she does. And the man who is in love with her.

That's only right, she said, looking at him with her steady eyes. A cat needs to be taken care of. It is a helpless thing. A mute animal. A mook prani, she called it. The phrase could well embrace a cat and a man in love.

*

One morning he found Thippy gone. The outhouse was shut, locked. It came as a shock to him, that they could leave, all of them at once, without a word, but it turned out his mother had known about it. They had all gone to their village for the annual festival, the ooru habba, that fell right in the middle of the monsoons. His mother grumbled but there was little she could do. The local festival was central to the life and well-being of the village. Three days of propitiating the village deity. Festivities at the temple, the presiding deity worshipped and dressed in new clothes and taken out in a chariot round the village. Fire-walking in the evening and a village fair. Three days of drunken revelry for the men, she said.

They returned after a fortnight, almost reluctantly it appeared, to their city lives. Thippy proved elusive. He caught glimpses of her—wan, pale, much thinner, her complexion seemed to have taken on a yellow tinge—but he couldn't speak to her. She stopped coming to him to fill out the bank pay-in-slip, apparently the temple accountant had started depositing the money in the bank himself. He was certain she had fallen ill.

Savitri, what has happened to Sanjeeva's daughter?

Which one?

The elder one, who else? She's the one I like—It slipped out before he could help it.

They were riding on Nanda Talkies road, one of the prettiest roads in the city. Flanked by a canopy of rain trees, there was a garden all along the stretch of the road, more than a kilometre long. In the right season, it was a garden of rose bushes, the air thick with the fragrance of roses. Three days a week he cycled down this road, escorting his sister to her music class and back—a task he looked forward to. He could have taken a shorter route home, but he liked ambling down the beautiful straight road, flooded with the scent of roses in the sharp heat of summer. Fresh from her class, his sister practised her song, humming the new notes, chasing the elusive swaras. Sometimes he caught the errant note for her and sang it in the right pitch. He had toyed with the idea of taking music classes himself but knew that his father would disapprove. Men appreciated music; women sang.

Stop, Savitiri cried. Stop right here.

He slowed down close to the kerb and came to a halt.

Do you know why they close the outhouse and go away whenever there is a festival? She had got off the carrier and was standing at the edge of the footpath, set at a considerable height from the road, and had turned the handlebars of the cycle towards her, both hands outstretched so that he was forced to look up at her. This was not a matter to be tossed in the air, from the back of the cycle, he understood, one of their conversations when he mimicked a relative or even their father—a word, a gesture or a sound—and they were convulsed with laughter till they reached home.

Of course I know why they close their house and go away, he said shortly, trying to free his hands. Savitri's hands were clamped down on his on the handlebars.

Ashwath anna—she addressed him formally, which distressed him somewhat. Have you seen the women the goddess takes over? They spin round and round—people ask them questions and they answer on behalf of the goddess. That's what Sanjeeva's daughter—she hesitated. Ask Kaveramma. She knows. Amma would not take us to the temple on those festivals when we were children. She said it was too crowded and noisy. She was scared we would get lost.

Kaveramma—he snorted. Everyone knows how that woman gossips.

But he remembered going with Sanjeeva and the boys to a temple up on a hill. The path uphill had been crowded with devotees, some with rough-hewn bamboo poles balanced across their shoulders with flower-bedecked pots suspended from them. Red was the colour in the air. The red of the devotees' clothes, the red of vermilion, the red of ecstasy, an excess of red.

The flag pole outside the temple bore hundreds of small lamps all lit with smoking flames. Inside, amidst the press of bodies, the harsh hack of incense and the distinct fragrance of sacred ash, he had seen a woman circumambulate the courtyard in a rhythmic ecstatic dance, accompanied by drum beaters who kept up the beat to which she danced. The crowd had been reverential and had kept a respectful distance from the spinning figure. Once or twice, someone from the crowd would dart forward to prostrate themselves at the woman's feet, moving out of her way quickly. The woman's head was shaven, her hair given to the goddess she wanted to propitiate, the new growth pixelling her scalp. Her eyes were closed and her face was smeared with turmeric. Her cheeks were pierced with a small spear—he could clearly see the shaft at one end and the arrowhead at the other. It was a clean incision, no sign of blood.

In the evening a group of young men were to pull the chariot with ropes attached to metal hooks which were impaled to the skin on their backs. He had not waited to see them pull the chariot, but Gunda had told him all about it later. In those days, the days of his boyhood, there was a kind of friendship between him and the boys, especially with Gunda who was closer to his age, before they grew distant, riven by the knowledge of their different destinies, of what they could reasonably expect, of the consciousness of giver and receiver.

But right then, on Rose Garden road, her eyes needle points of accusation and her mouth drawn in anxiety, his sister was trying to tell him something. That he should read between the lines and not have things spelt out to him.

There were no songs that evening, no humming, no small talk, no banter and repartee. He felt the pressure on his muscles as he cycled home, thinking perhaps his bicycle was not meant for two.

*

And sure enough, his mother was on the terrace the next morning. Only a matter of such monumental importance as peril to her son's soul would prompt her to risk her knees and come upstairs when her osteoarthritis was playing up.

I thought I'd made it clear—she huffed.

Made what clear?

He did not get up from his chair and ask her to sit down; he would let her stew. And in her bathed and 'purified' state, she would not sit on his unmade bed he knew, and risk contamination. But she pushed his bedclothes aside and sat down, facing him, ignoring his small act of unkindness, putting at risk her her accumulation of punya, merit.

Don't think people haven't noticed you mooning round the terrace and your sudden religiosity, your trips to the temple—even Kaveramma has commented on it.

What's the harm in talking to her, he said, taking the bull by the horns. Can't we be friends?

Friends? His mother choked on the English word as if it were an alien concept, something dangerous, a virus that could well cross the species barrier.

How could you be friends with people who were worlds apart, with whom you had nothing in common, his mother asked. A poor, uneducated girl, out of caste, whose family was dependent on their largesse, was what she meant though she did not say it.

You will have nothing to do with her.

But you yourself have made an exception for her, haven't you—he challenged his mother. She brings flowers for you in the morning. And incense to burn before your gods.

He knew his mother did not have an argument to that. She had bent her strict rules of madi, of ritual purity, to allow Thippy to pound bark and resin into incense, and to pluck flowers for her morning's worship. In fact she had given strict orders to the Old Man not to tamper with her tulasi plants—Thippy would look after them. He had heard his mother say to Kaveramma that Thippy was a good girl, that there was a glow of virtue on her face.

Yes, that may be. But we are not the same people. We have our ways and they have theirs. We follow our own destinies—

There were traditions to guide you, precepts to keep, a dharma to abide by, his mother said. There were restrictions on conduct that people were meant to follow, niyamas, for their own good. You had to develop a moral sense, know the difference between right and wrong, what was allowed and what was not.

Where is it written? Show me—he challenged.

The trouble with you is that you cannot understand

sookshma, subtlety—his mother said with something close to sorrow in her voice. Everything has to be spelt out to you—she leaned against the bedstead as if exhausted from her effort. That is why we ask you to listen to your parents, do as they do. You have to learn how to live the correct life, the life ordained for you.

You people think money is everything, he had thrown at Suchi mama once, after a frustrating day at the lawyer's office.

Suchi mama's face had had a similar expression as his mother's, as if he was astounded at Ashwath's inability to grasp the obvious. It is and it isn't, Suchi mama had replied. Even the flowers you offer in worship come from a tree that grows on the land you own. If not you'd have to go to the market to buy them. Money, as Ashwath had put it so baldly, formed the cushion for everything else. Family, community, inheritance, went together to form your social standing, to define who you were. Without them you would stand naked in the world.

Enough—his mother sat up. I have work to do. I can't sit here all day giving you advice. Remember, if your father even gets a whiff of this nonsense—she widened her eyes and spread out her hands in a helpless gesture, implying that there would be a pralaya, destruction of cosmic proportions and there would be little she could do to protect him. There was no saying how his father would react. Ashwath could well be packed off to the village to live with his father's cousin and take care of the lands. Could he not see the irony of it? Here they were, sheltering so many of their poor relatives, helping them get a better life, like Harish who had come there to become a doctor. And he, the son of the house, would have to be sent back to the village. Or even worse, disinherited.

Let him do his worst, he said recklessly. I will get a job soon. And not be beholden to him, to any of you.

That will be the day, his mother said, heaving herself off the bed. I hope I'll be alive to see it.

And there the matter rested. He had no wish to risk his father's wrath. But the worm had entered his head. 'Ajagajantara' was the word his mother had used—a jangly, dramatic word, to signify worlds apart—the difference between their world and that of Thippy's family was like that of a goat and an elephant. It could apply to him and his family too—he the nimble goat and they the elephant, static, lumbering, graceless, unable to put its weight on all four feet because its body was too heavy.

Four

In his final year of college, the cloud of expectation hanging round his head grew denser; any moment, there would be a deluge. He seemed to be disappointing his father in many, often inarticulate ways. For one, his scholarship was not renewed. His average over the last four semesters was not high enough to meet the requirements. It would be restored depending on his results in the next set of exams. News of it got round and at family gatherings his relatives commiserated with him as if someone had died. His father became more distant, icy, communicating only through Suchi mama. When there were things to be done around the house he spoke directly to the boys, not bothering to include Ashwath in the loop of commands.

On weekends he boarded crowded moffussil buses with Suchi mama to survey plots of land which were under litigation, or to visit distant cousins whose co-operation was required to rectify an error in land-related papers—journeys he undertook with reluctance, for meetings with people he had no wish to see. He was introduced as so and so's son or grandson and immediately their clouded expressions gave way to effusions of gratitude, even affection and he was greeted with folded hands and offers of tiffin and coffee. You look exactly like your grandfather, some of the older women offered, bashfully. In one household, the whole family crowded into their one room and said to him, your grandfather took our son in to Neel Kamal when we could not afford a hostel in the city; we owe everything to him and your father.

Things are getting tough for them, and they are not well off to begin with. You must be more obliging, Suchi mama said, when he grimaced at the prasada, a greying sludge of milk, yogurt, jaggery and bananas, that was offered to them.

As Suchi mama continued, his encouraging tone would acquire the edge of a harangue, a threat. You must make your way in the world, you know, make a mark. You must burn the midnight oil. Your father is anxious about you. Sometimes he would speak of other young men with enviable qualities, mainly Manohar and Prakash, go-getters who were enterprising and resourceful. Suchi mama spoke of their distant lives, full of glamour, like illustrations on the pages of glossy magazines—their cars, their houses, the cereal they ate for breakfast. At eighteen, the Americans get out of their homes and live on their own, they don't expect their fathers to support them—he said.

He grew weary of these conversations; he was defenceless against these thrusts and insinuations, not knowing how to respond. On Sundays, other than his fetch-and-carry tasks or his adjunct role in the pettifogging schemes that Suchi mama and his father constantly discussed, he was alerted to a new responsibility—that of finding a bridegroom for his sister who had now become a 'graduate'. The way Suchi pronounced the word, it could well be a physical ailment that had to be concealed, and she had to be married off quickly, before it was discovered.

My colleague Chandran knows the chairman of BEL, his father said. He knew what that meant. He could have a coveted public sector job as an engineer if he wanted. And as the future owner of Neel Kamal, slip into his father's mantle, the chain mail of a familiar life. Unlike Suchi mama, his father was not keen to see him go to the US. One more year. That was the time he had. And then the net would close in on him. The thought made him despondent.

From his mother's quarters, the kitchen and the extended yard, there came the offer of seeming neutrality—he had made reluctant peace with her; she could not sustain her anger against him for long, and he and his sister were natural allies, despite their fights.

Top work Kaveramma and his mother were often in a huddle; now Kaveramma was trying to sell what remained of her wretched jewellery—tangled strings and lumpy pendants of gold—it was difficult to believe that these were meant to adorn. Her son was having a tough time, working several jobs, some not quite legal he gathered, to meet his expenses. So Kaveramma had asked Manohar in Cleveland, Ohio, to loan her son some money, the rupee equivalent of which she would pay his family here in India. Only, the dollars worked out to a lot of rupees. It was so cold there, you had to keep your room heated all the time and heating was expensive; her boy was surviving on stuff out of tin cans.

*

He fled, that day, on the pretext of borrowing notes from a friend, to the refuge of a Raj Kumar film. On all counts, he preferred the familiarity, the intimacy even, of a Raj Kumar starrer, the reassurance of its sentiments and the plausibility of its thrills, to an English film. With an English film, you never quite knew where you stood. You were forced to dwell on the discomforts of other worlds and to consider that familiar things—friendship, love, family, villains and evil, the sky, the desert and even the motor car—could be so displaced.

Do you like Hollywood films, Satish, with whom he usually saw them, asked.

Yes, more than our local films, he said bravely, in full faith that his answer spoke of his ambition if not his actual taste. He had returned, pleasantly chuffed by CID Agent 999 of *Operation Diamond Racket*, whose appeal far outshone that of Roger Moore's 007, to find Suchi mama waiting at the gate, pacing up and down. Then he remembered. He was supposed to accompany Suchi mama to inspect a piece of land somewhere on the outskirts of the city. But now it was almost lunch hour and Suchi mama would not set out so late. Not all was lost though, Suchi mama said. The boys of the outhouse had hired a tempo van and were setting off on a jaunt, one of their periodic gadabouts. He could ride with them, survey the land, and catch a bus back. Suchi mama looked ominous; he agreed to go. The eldest of Sanjeeva's sons was summoned and informed that he would ride with them.

He was given the place of honour, up front, and there, sandwiched between the driver and one of the older boys, he caught her eye in the rear view mirror; she smiled, and a blue ray of happiness shot through him, travelling from head to heart, from limb to limb.

He did not catch her eye again, nor hear her voice in the rustic cadences from the back, but it buoyed him up through the heat and the smell of sweat, even the discomfort of the broken seat with bits of coir and metal springs sticking out. It was not just a boys' outing. The whole family was there—a multitude of women and children packed into the back of the tempo van.

They stopped at a cluster of shops on the highway, the last of the box shops before the countryside began in earnest.

One of the older boys hesitated. Would you like to wait here in the truck, he asked Ashwath. We are picking up some ... supplies ...

'Supplies' he understood was a code word, out of deference for him, his vegetarian sensibilities.

I'll come with you. Why not?

We will be cooking our afternoon meal when we stop next, the older brother said.

The women called out instructions from the back of the truck.

Ashwath anna can taste some of our mutton saru, a voice rang out cheekily. He recognised the voice—that was

Lingi, the youngest of the girls, before she was shushed by one of the women.

They walked into a side lane, a few metres from the main road, into one of the box shops. At the counter stood a handsome boy, perhaps in his late teens, fair-complexioned with light eyes and a generous mouth, his strong hands resting on the chopping block—the stump of a once gigantic tree. His shirt was stained dark down the front and at his open neck hung a silver amulet on a black thread.

Naveen Kumar, how are you—the brothers greeted him like an old friend and he seemed happy to see them.

See, we've had tiles put up behind the counter, like a proper shop.

The blue and white tiles on the wall behind him were spotless. Above the new bright tiles stood an array of gods, fresh flowers of worship in place around them.

Suspended from the ceiling were three skinned carcasses on meat hooks—pink, lean, headless—legs extended in yogic grace, genitals gravely in place.

Two kilograms of the best chest rack, and some off the legs. No stringy back, mind.

Gunda pointed not to the carcasses that were intact but to a partially dismembered one at the back, striated with threads of fat. It was smaller, a deeper red.

Here, Naveen Kumar turned it round and showed its tufted tail, kept intact to distinguish it from the sheep. He pointed to the two large glistening chocolate brown sheaths of liver but the older brother shook his head.

Goat mutton, he explained, was preferable to the lighter softer mutton from sheep. The goat was the tougher, hardier of the two and ate a variety of grasses and shrubs while the grazing habits of the sheep were tamer—it preferred meadow grass. The small plump animals, with thickening skin and yellowing bellies and their legs drawn up, those were chickens, the older brother said. He seemed to think disparagingly of chickens.

Naveen Kumar cut off a section of what looked like the rib cage, his cleaver moving like butter through the wattle of flesh. He placed it on the stump of wood and primed the cleaver against the shaft of a long metal probe. The cleaver rose and came down, a sharp thwack of metal on bone. He weighed out the meat, slid the pieces into a black plastic bag and tossed a spaghetti curl of fat into it. Naveen Kumar's forearms were tight, smooth and plump, and clean of hair—like a child's; a prominent vein ran up from his wrist and disappeared into the sleeve of his shirt. For a moment Ashwath felt envious of this handsome, strong, happy boy.

They collected their bag and turned to leave. He wondered for a minute whether he should offer to pay but put the thought out of his mind immediately.

Here, would you like this? I could discount it for you— Naveen Kumar reached below the counter and placed his offering on top. It was the head of a goat, small, refined, with delicate features and pleasing proportions—eyes evenly placed, ears tucked in, long stretch ending in a retroussé nose. Its colour verged on mustard, all hair on its skin burnt off. It would yield a perfect skeleton.

Gunda grabbed the head and pretended to make a shy at him. You want?

Ashwath stood his ground. Not today, he said.

Gunda shook his head and smiled. Naveen Kumar

tossed the head back into the plastic bucket under the counter. They heard the thud as it hit the bottom of the bucket.

The bone marrow, the older brother started explaining as they walked the distance to the truck, as a palliative perhaps to Gunda's excess of spirits, is very strong. You can boil the same pieces of bone again and again in water with a little salt, red chillies and coriander—the soup doesn't lose its taste or strength.

Ashwath anna has become one of us now, Lingi said. There was approving laughter from the back. The women were amused by him, he could see. And it was easier with the boys the rest of the way.

*

They pulled over into the courtyard of a large shambling building at the base of the knoll of hills that fringed the city, just before the road started climbing up. It was a chowltry or a rest house built by a local philanthropist whose name it bore, a place for weary travellers and pilgrims to break journey and rest before they set off again.The building was in a state of disrepair, the mortar eaten up in several places, exposing crumbling brick but the arc of the colonnade and the slim proportions of the pillars recalled a time of grace—someone with taste (and money) had planned and executed it all those years ago. If the plaque were to be believed, it was almost a hundred years old.

The boys set to cleaning the place and setting things up; the women got a wood fire going at the far end, in an enclosure without a roof—so they were open to the sky.

A few from the group wanted to go up the hill to visit

the shrine of the Plague Goddess. The temple had been built hastily when an epidemic had broken out, and now had several devotees visiting it regularly.

Would he like to come with them, Gunda asked. It was a group of boys and girls, a gaggle of children. Then, out of the corner of his eye, he caught sight of the hem of a skirt with a floral print that he recognised, and the bare feet with long toes and knobby phalanges, the tops flaring out into ragged mushrooms. He knew those feet. And Gunda seemed to be in a conciliatory mood.

They walked on a narrow beaten track for a stretch. The land was flat and the air was hot with the smell of dry grass and the buzz of insects. The voices of the little girls tinkled like cattle bells as they ran ahead. Gunda slashed at the yellow grass with a stick; the three of them walked in silence.

The temple to Plague Amma was soon discovered—a small shrine in plain sight, in the overhang of the rock. The group converged on the shrine like a flock of birds.

At the other end of the rock face, the implacable stretch of rock seemed to cleave to allow for a sloping upward path, complete with footholds.

I think I'll go up there, he said.

Up there is the forest, the trees are thick there, Gunda said. You have to follow the path. It leads to the Shiva temple.

The path rose upwards steeply, all rock and thorny thicket. But there was a path, a trail made by others who had gone before, and the trees beckoned from above.

He kept up a good pace despite the thorns and the scratches on his arms, glad he had remembered to wear his sandals. From time to time he stopped to catch his breath and wipe his forehead on his sleeve. On one side was the steep face of granite, and on the other, a gentle fall to the ground, where he could see the road, the arches of the chowltry and the splash of the yellow truck.

The track turned less steep but the rocks, bald and smooth, were more slippery and he had to grasp the bushes to get a purchase. Just as he was beginning to wonder what had possessed him to dart up the path, past the Plague Goddess temple, perhaps it was the hope that she would follow him which he now knew was misplaced, the path flattened out and led into a glen of tall trees. It was dark there, the evening sun barely filtering in through the dense canopy, the ground soft with a mat of fallen leaves. He heard a rustle behind him and turned quickly, thinking it might be an animal from the woods, when he saw the familiar leaf pattern of her skirt, her bare feet and then her flushed face. She smiled and walked past him, churning up the leaves and waited at the end of the path for him to catch up.

They were standing at the edge of a quadrangle but what hewed into view first were the banyan trees. The trees seemed to have broken through the ground with great force, violent eruptions, limbs flung out in all directions, ashen, rough of bark, gnarled, the trunks knotted into huge grey warts, twisting the branches into impossible shapes, reaching out to claw the sky. There were several of them, with spreading branches speckled with red fruit and small pale leaves. A grove wild enough to suit the temperament of the god it housed.

Amidst the branches, the curvilinear spires of the temple

came into view, fitted to a modest body, as if reluctant to compete with the spectacle of the banyan. In the middle of the quadrangle was a square of water—green, clear and tranquil. The temple tank.

Thippy smiled and came towards him. He saw grace in her gesture, mysterious intent in her eyes. Mad about that girl. That was an expression he would encounter much later, in a song, in a very different world. Right then, he wanted the courage to reach out and hold her hand.

A movement at the other end caught his eye. They were not alone. A dun-clad figure, the temple priest. They walked down to the temple in silence. He was closing the doors, done for the day. The time for worship is almost over, he said, smiling. He had white teeth and a thick, well-nourished moustache. A good-humoured man, still young. He opened the door for them. It was a small cell, unostentatious, with a stone linga on a pedestal, decorated with flowers. The fragrance of jasmine mingled with that of the sacred ash. A brass lamp, its flame steady, dangled from the ceiling. The priest rang the bell above the threshold of the cell, wove the arati flame in slow circular movements round the stone linga, reciting as he did the many names of Lord Shiva. Ashwath dropped a note into the plate meant for offerings, which had a few coins, and noticed the way the priest's gaze was arrested by the note.

Few people come up here these days, the priest said. Other than this main shrine those in the courtyard are almost in ruins. He lingered outside the door, waiting.

And where would you be from, he asked, the sweep of his glance taking them in together.

Just here, up for the evening. Ashwath waved his

hand in the direction of the city. You were saying about this place ...

Apparently there was a legend about this magnificent ruin. Centuries ago, a royal party, out on a hunt, had lost its way and chanced upon this grove of trees. The king, whose horse had been the first to crash through the bushes, had been struck by the place, and later in his life, had decided to retreat here to meditate. He was the one who had commissioned the temple complex, which was why it was so fine, the priest said, especially the sculptures that remained, and the temple tank, whose waters were destined to remain eternally unsullied. Eventually the king, whom history had crowned a philosopher, had moved here for good, relinquishing his throne to his younger brother, drawing around him a select group of followers.

You can still feel the power of their penance here, the priest said, the pull of their prayers. His eyes were solemn when he said that.

Do you believe that, he asked the priest, in the spirit of this place, in the power of someone else's prayers?

Of course—the man looked surprised. I've been coming here since I was a boy. I know this place well. I can feel it myself.

Look here, the priest walked with rapid strides to the side of the temple. He stood before a sculpture in relief on the side of the wall. Ardhanarishwara—the lord literally embracing his consort—man and woman together, the life force.

The figure stood in languid repose, a bejewelled thread running diagonally from shoulder to hip, marking man from woman. On the left side was sculpted the upturned breast, curved hip, a small swelling belly with three indentations—the three folds that were the hallmark of feminine beauty, centred by a deep navel. Low on her hip slung a belt ringed with bells, each one etched clearly in stone, from which flowed a garment that covered her leg. The right shoulder was all Shiva, matted hair, eyes sunk in bliss, his shoulders and chest as solid as the trunk of a tree, a serpent girdle—sarpa mekhala as the priest called it—at his waist.

There he is, the priest said, the Lord, Ishwara, the essence of life, reminding us that every divine form, all of nature, lives in us—the Sun in our eyes as sight, the Moon in our hearts as the mind, Agni, Fire, as speech, and Vayu, Wind, as breath, plants as body hair, and death—there is no escaping death, is there—is the breath that lives in the navel.

There was a fervour in the priest's eyes when he spoke, in the way he drew out his words, pronouncing each syllable, his lips parting when he finished, in thrall to what he had just said.

Ashwath was conscious of the moment, that he and Thippy were standing close together, contemplating this sculpture, symbol of the union of man and woman, the male and female essence, of all of nature, so casually poised on the wall of the temple, unmindful of its potency. What had the priest made of the two of them? Had he looked at them speculatively and had his eyes lingered on Thippy, perhaps to spot the black beads of matrimony, or the turmeric-stained thread? And then his thoughts went to the priest himself. Was he married—his face was youthful, there was a radiance there that could be ascetic, but the loose frame beneath the shawl, the rounded shoulders, suggested the well-being of a householder.

This place, the priest said, this temple, these sculptures, is the most beautiful ... no, the most—he searched for the word and said—the most happiness-giving place ever. Ananda, that was the word he used.

How do you know, Ashwath asked him. Have you been on pilgrimage to other places, other temples?

I have never left this place in all my life, the man said. Every day, ever since I was a boy, I have been coming from the village below, climbing up the hill with my father. He is old now—he comes in the morning and goes away at noon. I clean the place and light the lamp, see that it is lit morning and evening.

Look at this carving on the roof—he urged them to look at the ceiling of the porch. Notice the petals of the flower. You would expect a lotus, but it isn't. It is the ekka, the commonplace ekka that grows wild here ...

He recognised the flattened edges of the petals and the central whorl—a flower within a flower. On either side of the flower was carved its bud—plump, closed, the outlines of the five petals clearly etched. This was the milkweed that grew wild everywhere—on the roadside, in ditches, on sandy banks and in abandoned lots—leaves light green with a dusting of ash, thick-petalled purple and white flowers. When you plucked the flowers, the stem oozed a white latex. These were the flowers dear to Shiva, an easy god to please.

These have no fragrance. You wouldn't want to wear them in your hair. He smiled and pointed to the string of jasmine, now wilting and brown round the edges, in Thippy's hair.

The priest turned to leave. They stood side by side, watching him walk away quickly, out of sight.

They were alone now in the darkening grove, shards of the westerly sun knifing through the canopy, as if in defiance. Ashwath felt that he could reach for a blistering ray and break it off with his bare hands.

This was his moment, he knew. He turned to Thippy to speak—his Thippy, as beautiful and as precious as the ekka flower.

But out of the corner of his eye he saw Gunda approaching rapidly through the twisted banyans, charging straight at them. For a moment he was alarmed, imagining wildly that Gunda would challenge him to a fight. But Gunda strode past them and disappeared behind a rock. He re-emerged, clad only in long drawers, and jumped straight into the waters of the tank. Then he heard a second splash and saw that Thippy too had jumped in, from the top of the steps, skirt, blouse and all, her jasmine-strung plait floating on the water like a fat serpent.

Gunda looked up at him and beckoned but he shook his head. Come in, the water is clean, Thippy called. The tank is fed by a spring in the hill, so the water is always clean.

He watched them splashing around, rejoicing in their animal spirits. Then, even as he watched, they disappeared. The water was still and ripple free, as if it hadn't ever been disturbed. At the edge of the tank, there was a small structure, a stone umbrella that he noticed for the first time, a shrine with an idol—he could see the red flowers and the leaves that had been offered in worship. And that was all; otherwise the water was a stretch of languid green. And just as he began to panic, wondering if he should dart down the hillside after the priest, they surfaced, Thippy first, red in the face and bursting, and then Gunda, triumphant, clutching in his upraised hand a sodden mess of purple ekka flowers.

*

In the morning, he caught the first bus back to the city. It was not yet fully light, there was no one stirring on the streets, not even the newspaper boys or the milkmen. The gate screeched and he flinched—the perpetually unoiled hinge, a task that he had neglected to get done by the boys—it sounded like an animal being beheaded. The front door was wide open, the steps leading to it washed and still wet, the rangoli was in place—a flag that all was well within. He paused for a moment, and decided against entering his house through the front door.

He made his way past the side of the house, to the back. He stood at the threshold of the door, on the worn wooden band and finding her light blocked, his mother looked up. He saw the relief in her eyes and her shoulders sagged. She made as if to come towards him but her eyes grew hard and she turned to the kitchen instead. Then he saw his sister, coming in from the still dark hall beyond, rubbing the sleep from her eyes like a child.

So his highness has returned—her voice was thick with phlegm and insolence—And you thought she had spirited your son away.

He felt the blood rush to his head and his face grow hot.

I could marry her you know—he threw out at them.

For a moment his mother stood still. Then she resumed stirring the pot, savagely, the hot sound of metal on metal resounding in the kitchen. His sister set up a cackling laugh—he could hear her all the way down the corridor.

He stood at the door, seething, irresolute, as always.

When his sister returned, face wet, hair patted down, she went straight to the pantry and fetched herself a cup of coffee. Every morning, she boiled the milk and made coffee for both of them, and they sat together on the stoop, drinking their first cup of the day.

The pot hissed and threatened to boil over. A smell of burning filled the kitchen. But still his mother did nothing.

So, when shall we begin distributing the wedding invitations—his sister mocked him.

Savitri—his mother said at last.

What is this, Savitri, drinking coffee all by yourself?

His father stood at the inner door, newspaper in hand. And I had to fetch this myself. Your brother looks tired and hungry. Give him his coffee. Let him bathe and get on. He will be late for college. His father's voice had been unusually gentle, for which he was grateful. It was true, he had hardly slept a wink at night. They had come down the hillside in the gathering dusk and then the group had swallowed them. They had dried themselves off by the fire where the night meal was being cooked, and while they all feasted, he had been given fruits—two guavas, a banana, and water—an offering to a monk. He had stretched out on a straw mat, the stone floor hard and cold beneath him. He had left in the morning, while it was still dark, before anyone could stir. At night, across the bonfire, Thippy had met his eyes, her hair open and drying about her shoulders, her smile shy, her eyes complicit. Had he imagined that she had come to him later in the night, and engulfed him in the canopy of her hair, had he felt her breath on his face—gossamer-scented wings of sweetness flitting over his cheeks. Had her telltale anklets spoken and her glass bangles chimed in song? Had he imagined the cool softness that had burnt through him like a fire?

After his father left for work, his mother came up to his room, quickly, before his sister could. I will steel myself and ask you this, she said, without meeting his eye—Did anything happen? Did you ... have you—she choked on her words. I trust you have not done anything you shouldn't. That our honour, our maryade, is intact?

We stood side by side in the Shiva temple and the priest blessed us, like man and wife, he said.

His mother held her head in her hands and rocked on her feet, moaning as if in pain. Look what he does, she said. Look what he does.

And do you think she will marry you—his sister had flung at him later, when they were alone in his room on the terrace.

Thippy likes me, he had said. You should see the way she smiles at me.

A smile is a pleasant way to fill the gaps in the conversation—it's a way of making up when you have nothing to say.

The heart, you don't see her heart in her smile as I do, he would think to himself though he would not say it aloud. How can you think of her as a friend, his mother had asked. Friendship can exist among the like-hearted, the sahridaya. We are more than that, he wanted to tell his mother. We share the same heart.

An illiterate girl with a tattooed face, Savitri sneered.

You'll have to lock the shed each night so that the boys don't make off with the logs of wood. And you'll have to carry their father in to the outhouse at night when he's fallen in a drunken stupor. You'll have grand in-laws!

He heard a sharp rustle and a hiss, as if a snake had entered the room. He looked down to see a blood red eye blazing at him from a fan of filigree. The earrings had slid out of the brown paper packet and on to the floor where she had tossed them.

You did not give them to her, did you? Did you ever think why? There must be a reason why you did not give them to her. Ask yourself what it is and be man enough to admit it to yourself.

*

His mother would not talk to him. She served him his meals, as punctilious as always, but in silence. She made no demands on him, her usual peremptory inconvenient demands that he escort her to that relative's house or accompany her to this jeweller. His sister started taking the bus to her music class. His father behaved as if he had not spoken, as if his outburst had not taken place. He had patted him on the shoulder after the incident, a rare gesture of intimacy for him, and asked him to concentrate on his final exam and not get distracted. I have spoken to your principal, he said. We will appoint a tutor for your weak subjects.

He had done the unthinkable; he had made the thought word. In doing that, he had surprised himself. The thought itself receded in his mind. He could not remember his exact words, only the memory remained of the rush of unnamed feeling, the heat infusing his neck and face, spreading up from his chest. He had become a dangerous outcast, a man-eating tiger. A noble animal that had fallen into unnatural ways after tasting human blood, and now was neither this nor that, a creature to which no laws applied since it had lapsed into instinctive ways that were primordial. To him, the truth of a lifetime had been revealed in a moment. He saw his people for what they were; their faces grew grotesque and reptilian, like characters in an animated film, where gentle creatures morph instantaneously into their true misshapen selves. He contrived to be home only for his meals. In any case, college kept him busy, and the extra tuitions that his father had arranged for him. He had to prepare for his exams and his final viva. There was a flurry of recommendation letters, application forms and meetings with Chairs and committees. Satish, his classmate with whom he went to see Hollywood films and whom he envied his sideburns and bell bottoms—both prohibited by his father—had made it to an Ivy League college, and was going round, surrounded by a constellation of acolytes, bidding his goodbyes.

And you Ashwath, have you firmed up your plans, the head of the department asked him.

I don't know Sir, I haven't yet made up my mind. It was the one clear-headed thing he had said in a long time.

No Ivy League for him. He had received offers from a couple of private colleges in the US. There was also the prospect of a job in BEL, the engineering behemoth whose chairman was the friend of a friend. There was also, lurking between the lines, a reference to an eligible daughter, a graduate with homely ways. This, he knew, was what his father would prefer.

He had first thought of applying to the American universities after Suchi mama had brought Man-Manohar home that unexpected morning. Manohar had flooded the room with the lemony smell of aftershave lotion which remained long after he had left and which Ashwath would associate with a sense of resolve, of clean and fresh beginnings. He seemed like a man who had forged ahead and taken charge of his destiny. He had leaned forward and tapped Ashwath's father sharply on his dhoti-covered knee, cutting short his lamentations about the khata for his land not being clear and the unconscionable bribes being demanded by the clerks in the development authority office. This country will be mired in corruption forever, he had said briskly, a country that threw out companies like IBM and Coca Cola. I was here ten years ago, working in the public sector, an officer. It meant nothing to me. The union would go on strike all the time, and all work would stop. I felt like a free man only after going there. You know I wasn't given a passport here because I was a public sector employee. So I resigned, and then applied. They couldn't deny me my passport then. I took a risk and it paid off. I got my Green Card, and then my citizenship.

That day Ashwath had become aware that he had not travelled much—in his twenty-three years he had gone only as far as Madras, and once on a college trip to Delhi—and now he was convinced that his life was closed, confined, and that he lived in a small, mean place. The first stirrings had grown into a perverse desire to oppose his father, to break away, to turn his back against all that was familiar and which had tied him down, Over the past year he had come to realise that he couldn't continue in the gilded cage, weighed down by the family name, smothered by their concern. He would be ground down by the long established routine—like his father, if he had dosa for breakfast instead of idli, his taste buds would rebel. He would demand coffee at the right temperature and on the dot and make a virtue of his habits. He would wear a long coat and loose trousers and a cap on his head—sixty years already—and go to a nameless government office every day. He would marry the girl of his parents' choice—ah Thippy, my love—and the whole family, his parents included, would go to a temple after the wedding or to visit relatives. Maybe his wife and he would have one solo trip to Brindavan Gardens together before the children descended—a boy to bring fame, keerti, to the family and a girl who would ensure a lifetime of aarti—celebrations, festive occasions. And the chain would continue forever and forever. Every thought, every feeling would be as per prior sanction. A life filled with sameness, platitudes. Of what use was salvation if you had to follow the straight and narrow road to it?

Suchi mama informed him that his father had come around; he was ready to sell some land to finance his studies abroad. He mentioned the location of the land—it was prime irrigated coconut yielding land, which he knew his father was attached to. He would not have to struggle like Prakash, he thought, his mind filling with distaste as the image came to his mind, of Prakash hunched over a can, in a cold sunless room. But he still had to say the word to his father.

His evenings hung heavy after his exams were over. He had stopped taking his sister to her music class. He stayed back longer in college, loafing with friends, sometimes with boys he just knew by sight, sitting over coffee in the canteen. On weekends they played cricket on the college grounds. They ragged Satish, who was the opening batsman of the college team, that he would soon have to switch to baseball. Even as he joined in the chorus of voices around Satish he realised that he had yet to decide on how to act on his future, as Suchi mama put it.

*

He set out on an evening's aimless amble in the direction of the market, stopping at a cart heaped with boiled groundnuts. The man poured out a half pav measure and he stood by the cart, eating out of his paper cone, slowly, one peanut at a time, his foot hitched up against the compound wall of the nearest house. He saw his sister on the opposite pavement, hurrying to her music class, and from the way she averted her face he knew that she had seen him and had crossed the road to avoid him. He also knew that she was very fond of boiled groundnuts, and normally would have come running across to demand her share.

The streetlights began to come on. He stood about for a while and then turned in the direction of the bright lights of the market. He sauntered past the first few shops, looking around, pausing to see if he could find anyone he knew. As he approached the circle, he saw that a crowd had gathered there. There seemed to have been an accident. He could see somebody, a man, sitting on the footpath, leg flung out, chappal overturned by the side, dhoti riding up his thigh. It was a weak thin leg, the length of bone straining against the soft flesh of the calf. He moved closer to the crowd.

An elderly man ... seems to have fallen in a faint, a man in the crowd said.

When he moved closer, he recognised the man; it was his father's cousin, the stylish one with good taste, whose name was an epithet. It had taken him a few seconds longer to recognise him because the man's black cap had fallen off, exposing a vast bald head, which he was now mopping with a trembling hand. The cousin was a frequent visitor to his house; he may well have been on his way to visit them. Ashwath knew him to be a generous man, free with his hospitality, ready to make arrangements whenever a family gathering was planned. He reminded himself that he even owed this man his very first outing, as a boy. The cousin had piled all of them in his car and taken them to the Congress exhibition in the Majestic grounds. It had been an evening of extravagance. They had had rides on the giant wheel, and eaten a sticky, fluffy pink sweet wrapped around a stick. It was called Grandmother's Hair, and it was the first time he had eaten it. The cousin had bought him his first toy—a tiger whose head moved when you patted it. He moved to the front of the crowd and their eyes met. There was a moment of recognition, of relief in the fallen man's eyes, and he slumped back assured that help was at hand. But Ashwath stepped back and stumbled out of the crowd, walking away, towards the glare of the shops. He knew he should have helped the man up, dusted his topi off and put it back on his head, tucked his silk handkerchief back into his pocket, searched for his slippers, given him a drink of water and led him home. But he did none of these things. A thieving thought entered his mind. How would he have reacted if it was Suchi mama who had fallen there? Or his father? As he stepped away his eyes smarted with the truth that he would not admit.

He walked rapidly, past the sari shops where in the display windows the material strained against the impossible breasts of the mannequins, past the coffee works, the bakeries and the fancy stores, past the heaped vegetables and the glistening mounds of fruits, past the hiss of the petromax lamps of the flower sellers, the bright hot light picking out the tinsel woven into their garlands, past the throngs of shoppers, past the canopy of trees filled with the cries of birds returning to their nests, till he reached the small park with the taxi stand next to it.

Taxi Sir, taxi, the first one in the fleet of black and yellow topped Fiat taxis hailed him.

No, he shook his head. No.

The queue of drivers waited for him to make up his mind. For he had reached the end of the market. He could not walk any further. From the far end of the taxi stand there was a sound, a brief scuffle and a woman's voice broke out in a mocking cackle. He looked down at his hand to find that he was still holding the empty paper cone—a soggy twist of a page from a magazine. He flung it away from him, working off the bits of newsprint that stuck to his palm, like flowerets of fungus. He caught a whiff of boiled groundnuts, an overpowering briny smell, and he almost gagged.

He knew then that he had to leave. There was nothing more left for him here. He would tell his father in the morning that he had made up his mind to go to America.

II

II

One

The sky above was not the same as the one he had left behind. Here it was, the vast limitless Midwestern sky, a different blue, a whiter lighter blue, not curving overhead for there was no horizon to meet, sheltering alien trees—maple, oak, pine and elm, still names to him, except hickory, which evoked a meaningless line from a long-forgotten nursery rhyme—flooding itself with a 24-carat sunlight in the evening, in the August month that he arrived. He could imagine the terror that followed close on the heels of such majesty.

Nature alone seemed to hold sway here, in this glacier scoured plain, vast and flat enough to challenge the sky. The moraine had fed grasses for centuries, and now, endless fields of grain. Even the road—broad, asphalted and even-tempered—seemed born of itself—swayambhu. The road looped round gently rolling hills, clustered thick with trees, reminding him not so much of the landscape he had left behind but impressions of it by an old colonial master—views of outstretched plains from the crest of a small hill—so much so that he expected a flock of sheep to spring up with a shepherd leaning on his staff. In this place that nature had first groomed and then left to its own devices, the only signs of human intervention were the minatory signboards that appeared on the road from time to time—

Right-hand traffic must turn right—and the roadkills, large grey furry animals whose hair was still stirred by the breeze.

When he left home, at the airport, in the departures lounge, he had seen a young man, about his age, perhaps a student like himself, surrounded by members of his family, and he had felt a pang of sadness, for he himself was there alone. But moments later the young man was wiping the auspicious marks off his forehead, and had dumped his garlands and food packets in the dustbin before proceeding to the terminal from the lounge.

And then, just as he was about to board the plane that would take him to America, he had glimpsed another figure—a slim, vigorous figure with clean-cut limbs, in a long-sleeved white shirt. It had taken him a moment to recognise his reflection in the glass door, clad in the armour of new beginnings, and the flutter of trepidation at the pit of his stomach had given way to a surge of excitement.

Delhi-Beirut-Rome-London-New York. It was the cheapest ticket available but he did not find the journey tedious. The green arrow of destiny had mapped his route steadily on the monitor, moving across mountains and oceans and continents, which had been, till then, names on a flat map. As they left London, the friendly air hostess with a sing-song voice, her hair tucked into a cap, gave him pretzels and apple juice in a tin can; all firsts—his first glimpse of blonde hair, and with the food and drink of his new country. The pretzel, which was looped like a Kannada alphabet, was hard on his teeth, and the apple juice had a sweet-sour tang. The in-flight reading pouch had a copy of the *New Yorker*, which he tried to read. It puzzled him. He recognised the words but could not make sense of the language. It was much much later that he came across a famous critic's assessment of the magazine, whose language had been a black box to him, as high-class kitsch for the luxury trade. Kitsch was a new word to him, and he had to look it up in the dictionary. By then the pendulum of his fortunes had swung to the other side, and he had learned to love the elves-and-toadstools Thomas Kinkade print on his wall, and could stand and watch, like the camera-toting tourists in Pioneer Court, the larger than life Seward Johnson V-J day sculpture of a man in a sailor's cap bending a woman in a nurse's uniform backwards to kiss her. As for roadkills, he was to learn that roadkill cuisine was a practised culinary art, and as for pretzels—he could not remember eating another pretzel again after the one he was given on the flight by the smiling air hostess.

*

For the next two years, this lugubrious red brick building, built to house soldiers during the Second World War, with its uniform trim of white windows, set in a sorrowful grove of trees, was to be his new home. By daylight, the building had a worn nobility about it, accentuated by the tall, majestic trees. He learnt that the building was considered a historic monument and the stately elms amidst which it stood was the only grove for miles around that had been spared the devastating Dutch elm disease. But by the failing light of the evening, struggling with his suitcases—there had been no one to meet him at the airport or on the campus—still reeling from the twenty dollars, the one hundred and sixty rupees he had paid the taxi, his first home here had a touch of the portentious.

He was shown to his room on the eighth floor, at the end of a narrow corridor, the sound of his laboured breathing masked by the crunch of the floor tiles. By a stroke of luck he had been offered a single room, which he need not share with anybody else. The person at the desk had looked at him steadily, pen poised over the register—Did he want a small single room on the eighth floor or to share a large room on the ground floor? It was an American moment, a test of decisiveness, one of the many that he was to face. Single room, he said without hesitation and by the way the desk person nodded and snapped the register shut, he knew he had passed his first test.

On the eighth floor, he changed hands like a baton, and another person took charge of him. He gave him his key, showed him the way to the showers, shook his hand, wished him good luck and left. The door to his room shut with the finality of a lid closing on a coffin and he was alone. There was space just enough for a wooden bed, a desk and a chair, and a clothes cupboard. The white fangs of a large creature gleamed at him from the wall next to the window—it was only the room heater. He understood why this was a single room—the wall on the opposite side into which the bed was tucked sloped down to meet the window, cramping the space but giving it the look of a picture-book cottage.

It was too late for dinner in the dining hall. He felt in his pocket for the remnants of the pretzel that the air hostess had given him on the flight, and ate it quickly, bending over the newspaper he spread on the desk to catch the crumbs. It was a newspaper from home and already the headlines—the goings-on of a tehsildar, the failed monsoon and the pronouncements of the chief minister—seemed barely recognisable. Was it still August 1981? They seemed to come from an alien world, a world he had long left behind, though the newspaper was just a day old.

The first night, he slept on the bare mattress, fully clothed and with the light on. The staccato buzz from the fluorescent tube soothed him like a lullaby.

*

In the morning there was a pounding on the door, and rubbing the sleep from his eyes, he let in Sushil Khanna, the president of the Indian Students Association.

You should have picked the room on the ground floor, Sushil Khanna said immediately. Make sure you use the facilities on the ground floor, not on this one—

Sushil Khanna made him open his luggage and inspected it.

Ash, he said. Better call yourself Ash. No one here can pronounce your name.

So Ash he became.

We will go shopping this morning. You can't use any of the things you have in your suitcase.

Sushil Khanna owned a beaten-up blue Chevy Chevrolet and he drove like a maniac. Ashwath thought he recognised the road from his journey to the place—the gentle hills and wooded knoll, but he could not turn his head to look out of the window, not with the barrage of information, advice and opinion that Sushil Khanna kept up.

There aren't many Indians on the campus, Sushil Khanna said. And they have their own Indians, they're called Native Americans, more correctly. On the ground floor the facilities have doors, the stalls aren't open like on your floor. You should have gone there. I would have found you an Indian to share the room with.

Sushil Khanna was from Delhi, his parents lived there, but he had an uncle in Chicago. Actually, he lives quite far from Chicago, in the state of Michigan, but if you live within a hundred miles of Chicago, you can say you're from there.

Sushil Khanna lived in an apartment which he shared with two other Indian students and every second weekend he drove six hours in his Chevy Chevrolet to the place-near-Chicago where his uncle lived and brought back in an icebox the food that his aunt cooked for him—enough to last him till his next visit.

*

Within twenty-four hours of landing, he was laying siege to the fortress of America—he was shopping at Walmart. The lone grey building bloomed in the landscape like a rose in the desert. No dearth of parking, Sushil Khanna inflected his head briefly.

Inside, Sushil Khanna seized a trolley, wiped the handle carefully with a paper napkin that seemed to be kept on the counter for the very purpose—this was Ashwath's second learning moment—the need to be alert to sources of contagion which might strike from anywhere—and charged through the aisles pulling in a sundry assortment of goods, including an alarm clock, a plastic tub and mug, bed sheets and a handsome container with a lid. Your dustbin, he said.

At the checkout counter, Sushil Khanna watched him as he peeled off dollars from his modest roll, and for once said nothing.

Their next stop was a Goodwill store, which he understood was a store for second-hand clothes and other things that people no longer wanted.

Everyone shops at these stores, Sushil Khanna said, noticing his hesitation. We couldn't survive otherwise.

And sure enough, he himself would bring his clothes to give away at the Goodwill store and exchange them for khakis and tee shirts and a hoodie. When he had laid out his clothes on his bed—white shirts and polyester trousers, custom-made under Suchi mama's directions—he had seen how inadequate, how plain wrong they were for America. But right then, lighter by just one note, he was equipped with a jacket, a warm muffler and a pair of boots.

On the way back they stopped for petrol. He sat back and viewed the line of red and white filling stations—such plenty on a little-used road, theirs being the only vehicle in the petrol pump, or gas station as Sushil Khanna corrected him, no queues, no threat of shortage, no squabbling over a scarce resource. He pondered the quaintly misspelled name of the station Kum and Go—a name that suggested easy availability though Sushil Khanna grumbled that prices had suddenly shot up, a dollar and twenty for a gallon, thanks to a revolution in far-off Iran. That had affected their oil exports and the answering throes in the US had led to a recession. Ashwath tried to recall the price of petrol back home, but could not, for he had cycled or taken the bus wherever he went.

After the exertions of the morning, Sushil Khanna bought him a pizza. They went to an Italian pizzeria, a cheerful place with postbox red seats—the genuine stuff, Sushil Khanna said, and they sell by the slice. His voice dipped conspiratorially when he said that, and Ashwath filed away another leaf in his learnings notebook—that of the importance of thrift and the art of practising it skilfully.

No, pepperoni was not a variety of pepper, Sushil Khanna laughed. Let me order for both of us.

And there it was, the speckled wedge of Dagwood Bumstead's dreams, the black and white illustration of the daily newspaper comic strip come to life in technicolour. There were bits of vegetable, green olives and red tomato floating in a bed of white liquid. When he bit into it, the liquid solidified in strings down the sides of his mouth—but elusive as the thing was, he liked the taste.

Cheese, Sushil Khanna said. Bet it's your first pizza.

And watching his friendly, guileless smile across the table, Ashwath resolved to have as little to do with Sushil Khanna as was possible in the future.

At the door Sushil Khanna gave him his number and asked him to call if he needed anything. He then returned, halfway from the parking lot, to invite him to a cards party over the weekend in his apartment, a promise to drop off a spare electric coil stove—it's against regulations, but everybody has one, just be discreet, and an offer to help rent a fridge.

He had two calls that afternoon. Prakash, top work Kaveramma's son, called from Chicago. Welcome, you'll do great in America, he said. He shut his ears to the suggestiveness in Prakash's tone, to the triumphant chime that rang across the line. Manohar, Suchi mama's nephew called from Cleveland, Ohio. Sushil Khanna is a good guy, he said. His elder brother was with me in college. His uncle owns a factory somewhere in Michigan, so he could be useful. Why haven't you called home yet, Manohar asked. They are waiting for your phone call. And have you rented a mailbox?

He *had* rented a mailbox at three dollars a month at the post office, a mailbox to send and receive letters from home that he did not want. The previous night, his first night in America, after the Resident Assistant had bid him good luck and the door of his room had closed on him, he had stayed awake for a long time. He had stood by the sliver of a window that faced the street and watched the rain—the rain had come out of nowhere, the sky had been clear and infinitely blue. He watched the dripping branches of the majestic tree outside his window, that he would learn to recognise as the mighty but beleaguered elm. Late in the night he had watched a van drive down to the intersection and the driver, swaddled in a raincoat, step out to collect a package from a covered bin; he watched the traffic lights turn green and red through the night on the deserted street, till at length a solitary car drove up, as if to mollify the pleading lights, and stood at the traffic signal, waiting for the red light to turn green.

Here, in this orderly, obedient place, where men came to collect the garbage in the rain and cars obeyed traffic signals on deserted roads in the dead of night, he would make his home. The iron weight of despondency that had settled on him after speaking to Prakash and Manohar lifted; he would ask the desk not to forward their calls anymore.

*

His advisor Bill Moreland called him for a meeting.

Well ... Bill Moreland began in his soft southern accent.

Ash—he slipped in quickly, you can call me Ash.

Bill Moreland from Mississippi had a square fleshy face, thinning brown hair and a thick red neck that disappeared into the wide shoulders of his suit. He took a class in composite materials and Ashwath sat in the front row in his class, ears tilted towards the lectern to catch what he said, eyes riveted on Bill Moreland's Adam's apple that heaved when he spoke—here was a man who could move mountains. A year later, in the Halloween week, trying to shake off the mounted campus patrol Ashwath would find himself in an unfamiliar block, lingering outside a house with a white framed porch and a swing in the yard, pretending to look at the ornaments and the flickering carved pumpkins, and Bill Moreland would appear on the porch, rescue him from the horseman, and ask him to stay for dinner, but that would be a year later.

Bill Moreland had called him to tell him that he would have to take four pre-requisite courses, including the machine shop for hands-on experience, to complete the requirements to begin a Master's.

You understand what that means Ash—

It meant an extra semester and Ashwath was thankful for the green roll of dollars that had been deposited in the bank, a steady supply of which was assured by the fertile piece of coconut yielding land that was no longer his father's. To get round the limiting and rather draconian foreign exchange rules of the Indian government, they had arrived at an arrangement whereby Suchi mama's nephew Manohar would give him the dollars he required, the equivalent of which would be given to Manohar's mother in India. It was annoying to depend on Manohar, but the money was there in the bank, and it reassured him.

The arrangement gave him six more months in this beautiful little Midwestern town where the college buildings and the houses rolled down the slopes of a hillock to a lake, formed in the crater of a glacier. He walked often on the streets for the pleasure of looking at the red and brown brick buildings, noting the symmetry of their clean straight lines, their uniform unostentatious windows, and the grace of the clapboard houses set off from the road, open, inviting, which anyone could walk up to, without restricting compound walls. He could walk forever on these wide hawker-free pavements, bevelled smoothly into the grating at the side of the road.

When he arrived, summer was still lingering and on warm days he would almost collide with a skateboarding student on the impeccable pavement and was always glad of the little distraction. Everywhere there were girls in summer dresses, healthy pink limbs open to the sun, hair like tossed cornfields, and teeth flashing. On the green knolls of grass, their books lay in small heaps while they threw frisbees around, leaping into the air with an animal energy. He tried not to stare, but they paid no attention to him anyway.

For days, he struggled with the shower, trying to fix the knob in the right position so that he would not be greeted by a blast of icy cold water, and set an alarm so that he could dash down eight floors, plastic mug and bucket in hand—for which he gave grudging thanks to Sushil Khanna—and use the 'facilities' that had a door and a latch. Boosted by his post office account, he ventured out into town in the evenings, after his paid-up dinner in his meal plan—usually salad and soup. He discovered a small place downtown, attracted by an antique lamp that glowed a quiet welcome from a gabled porch. The high stools by the bar with the array of coloured bottles and the beer taps behind the counter, minded by a bearded young man who seemed always to be polishing the already impeccable glasses, looked attractive, but he preferred the cherry red upholstered seats with tables on which he could rest his elbows. The lighting was low and there were clusters of icy green bell-shaped lamps on the ceiling, the buzz in the room coming not from fluorescent lamps but the conversation at the tables, mostly occupied by young people, students probably.

I am here, he told himself, here in America, ordering French fries and Coke in a café. I am here, one with this happy hub; I am not answerable to anybody but myself. I don't have to eat and leave immediately, I can stay as long as I like, and I can come again tomorrow to this warm room and no one, no person, not a thought to bother me. He watched the waiters pushing aginst the swing doors, their trays quivering under the weight of dishes and glasses, and savoured the thought of the large tub of fries which he would dunk into ketchup and mayonnaise through the evening, and wash down with Coke, the drink that singed his throat even as the bubbles travelled down his nose. Set to the side was a wooden platform, a stage where people sang and bands performed. He suffered the head bangers and the hard metal musicians. What he liked were the soloists, usually thin young men and women who sang love songs, of pain and heartbreak. He thought fleetingly of Thippy and his parents, but they seemed like dim memories, flickering from a distant past, reminders of things that had happened to someone else.

In early September, the fragrance of resin among the oak and maple signalled that autumn was round the corner. Soon the trees, all a uniform green, turned colour—some blazing red against the icy sky, some a tender pink like the first leaves of the mango, some turned gold, and others an unshowy yellow. Fat squirrels, their bushy tails arched into perfect pennants, rolled nuts across the grass, hurrying to bury them under garden conifers, unmindful of the human feet that trod a few feet away. Even the crows—fatly feathered—seemed well-mannered, eschewing their full-throated caw for a guttural hawk-hawk-hawk. The pigeons that cooed incessantly from the ledge outside his window had fallen silent, and just the other day he had seen fat sparrows flying down from the eaves of his building, quarrelling with each other to pick the midges splattered on the windscreens of the parked cars.

Soon the leaves turned brown and the branches stuck out, bare, exposing the large ungainly nests the birds had built in them. And then, one morning, the snow was there; when he looked out of his sliver of a window, he could not see the familiar street or the grass or the parking lot—overnight, the ground was thick with snow.

Two

Capitol with an 'o'—there it was, the centre of the city upon a hill, a rather florid monument of domes and columns, where the founding fathers of the state once met to pass historic decisions, including the decision to join the union, now a monument to history, to memory, ornate home to a cultural centre, and a museum to which he often escaped on weekends, fleeing from his eager compatriots; it still remained a grand edifice of stately power.

Often, hurrying to class on the pathways past the building, he caught the glint of gold from the central dome and thought, absently, of the appeal of gold leaf covering, whether it was a temple or a government building, of its suggestion of glory and grandeur, even of godliness. The capitol of his state back home, an imposing pastiche of styles, commissioned in the zeal and optimism of just-won independence, meant no doubt to awe the gawking citizens, had an inscription on the entrance, which he had always thought was a parody—Government's work is God's work.

On a windy overcast Monday morning in October, he saw a small gathering on the piece of green in the park that abutted the capitol. There were chairs set out in a semi circle round the staue of a cowled figure that stood under a stone arch, open to the elements and largely unattended at other times. That day there was an official in a suit making a speech, there were matrons in formal hats and elderly men in coats, and a sprinkling of students, one of whom was taking down notes as the official spoke. The American flag fluttered behind the statue and there was a banner thanking the Italian-American Association. Then he remembered seeing a notification about Columbus Day and the invitation to the memorial speech at the Christopher Columbus monument.

Among the dates he had learnt by heart from his high school history textbook, to regurgitate on his examination papers, this had been one of the primary. In 1492, Christopher Columbus, a sailor from Genoa, had discovered the sea route to America and opened up the New World. He remembered clinching a quiz with the right answer. What do Santa Maria, Nina and Pinta have in common? His hand had shot up first. The names of the ships in which Columbus sailed to America. But intrepid as he was, Columbus had lost his way. He had been seeking a way to reach India and the lands beyond to spice up the meats on the tables of Europe, stubborn in his insistence that the route to India lay in sailing west. Despite the fact that his compatriot Bartholomeo Diaz had sailed down the African coast up to the Cape of Good Hope just a few years ago. And another fellow countryman, Vasco da Gama, would complete what Diaz had begun and reach Calicut in India just six years after Columbus had discovered America. So convinced was Columbus that he had reached India that he called the native population Indians, thus confounding his mistake with a confusion of Indians.

And here he was, almost five hundred years later, listening to a distinct guttural American voice floating over the green. A few phrases wafted his way—the spirit of fearlessness ... adventure ... determination ... the quest for a better life ... the will to forge your own destiny has come to signify the spirit of America. The official was announcing plans to prepare for a grand celebration of the 500th anniversary of Christopher Columbus's historic discovery, when Ashwath stepped out of hearing range.

And then he saw them. At a distance from the main gathering, watched warily by two guards of the mounted campus patrol whose horses champed restlessly on the grass, there was a group of people, huddled together, hoods up against the wind, holding placards, standing silently.

'Rethink Columbus Day', one placard read. He spotted 'Give Back Our Land'. 'Property is Theft'. Standing a little away from this group of young men was an older woman with two long braids hanging down her sides, holding up a placard he could not read. She was still there when he returned in the evening, sitting against a tree, her placard resting against the trunk. The other demonstrators had left, the chairs had been cleared, and she was alone, sitting at a distance from the bust on the pedestal. The campus guards had left too; obviously she was not considered threatening enough to be guarded. That evening, as he sat in his room at his desk, his mind kept going back to the old woman with the grey braids, huddled in her colourful shawl, sitting under the tree with her eyes closed, holding on to an undecipherable placard. He recalled in the expressionless stoicism of her face, in its creases, the rural women back home who sat on their haunches at bus stops for hours on end, waiting for mofussil buses that would not come, a lump of betel or tobacco pressed against the insides of their cheeks, in part to ward off hunger.

The beautiful domes revealed, in room after room, a pageant of their story, the acts of nature that had over millions of years rendered the land from sea to plain, and those of man that had turned a land without horizons into territory, into the spoils of war marked off between the victor and the vanquished. The museum of history had on record the solemn officialese of the victor and the sad poetry of the vanquished who spoke of their life and the things they loved with the fatality of those who could foresee their corralling—*You will plant corn where my dead sleep ... flowers we have loved will soon be yours ...*

Alone with the buzz of the fluorescent lamp overhead, he felt more acutely the confinement of his room, the incline of the roof that cramped it, and the wooden bed a foot away from him, dark and solid with premonition. He wore his jacket and his cap and stepped out. In the lounge, just as he reached the head of the stairs, he overheard the person at the desk asking somebody to call him. It was a phone call from home he knew. They were calling to ask why he had not written, he knew. He ducked his head and hurried down the stairs, into the cold wind and the grey sky.

The trees stood out in splashes of red and yellow against the ambient dullness. He made his way past the residency halls, past the neat high-banked sorority residences with the Greek lettering on the frontage, till he could walk amidst the shingled houses, separated by bits of lawn and trees. There were gnomes and toadstools on the lawn, and at Halloween, an assortment of scary monsters tamed into outré garden ornaments. Pumpkins carved into funny faces lined the window sills. It was only here that he had learned of the versatility of the homely red pumpkin—ground into soup, baked in pies, scenting candles and flavouring coffee. There were buntings and lamps hanging in the porches, in preparation of the festive months ahead. Through the curtained windows he caught glimpses of softly lit rooms, generously upholstered sofas and tables with bowls of fruit, and one lucky evening, he saw a family sitting down to dinner. It made him feel in return that he was a fragile vessel, transparent, made of the thinnest glass, ready to shatter at the softest push.

They would have planned it for days, right down to

timing the visit to the phone booth, calculating the number of minutes they would speak. His mother would have counted out the money and given it to his father. His father would have worn his cap and coat, as befitting the gravity of the occasion—a phone call to a son in America. A recalcitrant son who would not take the call. Some time in the future, after he had graduated and found a job, he would visit them and tell his father triumphantly that he had made a mark in the world, *his* world, where none of the things his family had to offer mattered. But that was in a distant future and if he thought about it too much right then, his heart might turn bitter.

*

There was a crowd in the restaurant that evening. Feeling adventurous, he ordered crème brulee; he need make no excuses for liking it—the creaminess below the singed surface, slightly bitter to make up for the rush of sugar to follow. The tall waitress with the red hair took his order. He ran into her sometimes on campus and she usually returned his smile. He gathered she was a student.

She raised her eyebrows at the crème brulee.

More people tonight? He was emboldened to strike up a conversation.

Italian specials today. I'd recommend anything with sundried tomatoes.

When he finished, he found her fetching her things from a closet near the front desk. She was leaving early, she said, as her boyfriend was going somewhere—he couldn't catch the name of the place—and she wanted to see him off. She had a casual air about her and he liked the fact that she tried to dissuade him from the crème brulee.

They fell in step as they walked down the only road leading away from the restaurant. Her name was Amy, Amy Kruger and she was studying modern dance at the university. Ash—is that your name, she asked when he told her.

It's Ashwath, actually.

I know that, she said, it's a holy tree. The tree of mythology. The upside-down tree. She had met the ashwattha tree in her comparative traditions course and again when her group was working on the tree motif in a choreography project.

He liked the sound of her voice, its timbre a harmony of several pitches, and its trick of going up at the end of the sentence, making it feel like a question.

I don't know about upside-down but I know that the ashwattha is supposed to be the first among trees, just as gambling is the king of cheats—

What I do know Ash, is that you're first among fries, you're really fond of them—just kidding—she held up her hands.

They stopped, turned towards each other and smiled. Amy tugged at her hair and said, I noticed you the first day you came in, you move very differently. I had just started on the kinesiology course—all about human anatomy and movement.

He wasn't sure if her observation was a compliment, but he had caught her interest, and he was pleased about that.

When they reached the intersection where they had to part ways, they both hesitated, and he offered to walk her home. Usually, she drove to the restaurant, she said, or when the weather was good, she cycled.

They walked past the shops and establishments that made up the 'downtown' and then downhill past bungalows set in spacious gardens set deep off the road, again without compound walls, till they reached a cluster of apartments and condos. They stopped outside an apartment building that seemed the scruffiest of all.

Three weeks back the trees outside her house, now bare and barely visible, had been beautiful, full of colour, Amy said. When she sat on the roof with her cat, she could touch the leaves.

So, she had a cat and a boyfriend, he made note.

But he could not figure out his way back. If you go left and then uphill, you will end up smack in those large houses and they'll set their dogs on you, Amy said. So she walked him to a point from where he could find his way back. See you round, she said and he clasped her hand in his.

There was a slip under the door when he reached his room, saying that there had been a call from India for him. He usually kept such messages—anything in the nature of a communication, a pulse from the system, from America to him as he thought of it. He would look at the message carefully, especially if it was handwritten—he had all of his advisor Bill Moreland's slips as also the many from his secretary, studying the slope of the writing, the order of the words, the implications of their deceptive casualness. Bill Moreland's 'Could you drop by at 4 this evening' meant that he had to meet him at four, he was not being offered a choice in the matter, and usually something serious awaited him there; Marcia's 'Sorry, nothing yet, but something may turn up soon', meant no jobs, no assistantships, no projects and he would have to bank on the proceeds of the coconut grove to see him through another semester. A 'Call from India, Tuesday, 6.39 p.m.' caused a twinge of anger, of anxiety, of the burden of duty left undone.

But that evening he felt none of these things. He crumpled the missive from the desk and flung it aside. The moroseness that had set in earlier in the evening had lifted. He thought of Amy, of the way the tints in her hair lit up under the lamplight, the foreign sweetness of her voice still curling against his eardrum, and the lingering touch of her long smooth knuckleless fingers; her hand had felt like a soft animal in his clasp.

Three

Bill Moreland's office sent him a message to say that he had been recommended a project in the archival collections. He had been hoping to be part of the main departmental project, on the reuse of structural steel in buildings, but the office informed him that all berths in that project were taken. He was assigned the task of creating a report on the history and growth of their Engineering department—this would count in the methods of enquiry and critical analysis pre-requisite course that he had to complete. They dangled a carrot; there could be a part-time job there, after he finished with the project. He had better take it as no assistantships were available to him that semester.

The departmental archives were housed in the building of the Historical Society, for which you had to walk downhill a considerable distance from the main college. He had hoped that it would be in the small one-storeyed building with large well-lit windows which had interesting objects on display—once a well-muscled leg shod in red pumps had dangled from the window sill. But that was the Arts centre. He would be working in the sombre looking brick building next to it—he thought of it as a piece of Soviet Russia in the middle of sunny America—and the records were housed in the basement.

Over the next few weeks as the light faded in the sky and the snow hardened on the ground, and the hush in the air grew deathly silent, he descended into the bowels of the earth and spent long hours sorting out papers in cardboard boxes, marked with coloured tags.

Box after box of departmental records yielded accounts of meetings, squabbles, resolutions, panic attacks when funds ran low resulting in appeals to the Board, the Governor, the President, the Council and others. He made notes in his brown notebook tracking the history of the Engineering department, from the time it was a 'scientific course' in the 1870s till it became a department in its own right fifteen years later. He marked the differences in educational philosophy, the classical vs practical debate, the bitter fights, the veiled insults that the classicists, who thought a practical discipline like Engineering ought not to be part of the university, threw at the pragmatists.

It had taken twenty-five years for Engineering to find its legitimate place as a discipline in its own right in the university, three weeks of his time and half a brown notebook. And there were still six boxes to go. Every time he looked up for relief, there was none to be found. He was boxed in, interred in this grey room. Everything in the room seemed old and eternal—from the purplish grey wall to wall carpeting with its crisscross pattern of earthworms, the tubelights stuck like wafers on the crenellated ceiling, and the reading desks laminated in grey to match the upholstery of the chairs. One side of the wall was lined with old leatherbound volumes, prisoners in their stacks. There were large mysterious blocks of sponge, again in grey, on some of the desks, with small sandbags huddled at their base.

Even the library assistant who sat in his direct line of vision was a ghostly figure with silvery long hair and a whispering voice. She was slight, insubstantial really, dressed in light-coloured trousers and blouses which looked faded, and a cardigan of indeterminate colour which strained across her collar bones, buttoned with just the single wooden button at the neck. Behind her on the wall was a large clock, its glass discoloured round the inner edges, the numerals etched clearly, leaving nothing to chance, the sharp pointed arrows of the hour and minute hands suggesting that time was not be trifled with.

He found himself waiting keenly for the student volunteer to arrive—she usually whirled in, hair askew, and in one motion, took off her coat and scarf and hung them on the rack. And then almost immediately she grew subdued, as if the grey room had sucked the animation out of her and she padded softly among the shelves, consulting slips of paper, putting together ancient volumes with corrugated spines and marking them as 'Books for conservation pick-up' or stacking papers and books neatly into bundles, 'for Helen Vanderhoef's class' or 'Mat Vecchio's art class'.

For all of the winter break, this would be his job but even the prospect of being able to go, by right, through the door that said 'Authorised Personnel Only' did not enthuse him. There were few regulars in the archives. By the time he came in, he could see the top of a white mane with grey dreads in one of the soundproof cubicles meant for audio researchers—for the rest of the morning a furious clicking would issue from there. An elderly unkempt man, an artist, came in quite often to read and draw from a series of leatherbound volumes of crumbling yellow paper—he finally understood what the mysterious beds of foam were meant for—the old manuscripts were propped up against the beds of foam and the small bags that looked like pouches of gold coins that medieval potentates disbursed among their retainers were to sandbag the pages in place so that both the reader's hands could be free.

He waited for the phone to ring, for Miss Argentum, as he thought of the library assistant, her lightly marked face either faded from age or ageless from Nordic sleight of hand, to answer in her softly inflected voice, making routine queries sound like matters of monumental importance. Historical Collections Centre, good morning ... you're welcome, let's see now ... there is a charge for service ... we are short-staffed today, you will have to wait for some student volunteers to come in ... I am sorry, you cannot take the book out ... would you like to take a look at the index ... I'm sorry but we do not allow the use of pens. Could I give you a pencil ... we cannot risk the manuscripts being marked by mistake you know ...

He got up often, more often than necessary—to use the electric sharpener that was fixed to a desk against the wall, a plump grey creature with a little round mouth, just enough for a pencil to fit in, bearing the manufacturer's double-barrelled name. It was the first time he was seeing one and was quite taken by the way it juddered into motion and yielded every time without fail, a smooth domed head with a sharp point.

Sometimes he thought of going for a short walk to stretch his legs but was put off by the fuss it involved—bestirring himself to collect his coat and hat and gloves and then the procedures of checking out of the building and checking in again. This was it for the rest of the winter, he thought—him, Miss Argentum and Hunt Boston.

*

Meanwhile, he was settling down. He learnt to say 'Hold the ice' when he didn't want any in his Coke and 'to go' when he wanted his pizza put in a cardboard box to take back to his room. When the girl at the counter said, 'Do you want a sack', he had first thought she was offering him a gonicheela, the jute sack in which coconuts and rice were stored in the storeroom back home, but it was just a plain old plastic bag. The one thing he continued to find strange was that he had to buy water to drink and not just fill up a bottle from a tap.

In the supermarket, the cornucopia of America awaited him—acres of aisles stocked with goods. He was partial to Hostess Twinkies and Jell-O, stacking them in his cupboard; he could eat them any time of the day. Raisin-cinnamon loaf, apricot-oat, banana-walnut, chocolate-zucchini (it must be good, that zucchini—there was so much of it, in everything!), he grabbed them off the shelf each week, along with smoked cheese, imagining the liquid hickory smoke coursing through the pasteurised milk—it saved him from breakfast in the cafeteria that smelt of boiled fungus. Fruits that he had only read about were here in a burst of glory. Peaches, plums, nectarines—neck-ta-rine—the very roll and flow of the word infusing it with the life-giving ether, pears that came in different colours—green, but still soft and ripe, golden yellow and red, and apples with names like Song of September, Sweet Sixteen, and Pink Lady.

The strawberry cheesecake that he bought off the shelf, a sparkling transparent cup of layered sweetness at one dollar, he was informed, contained cheesecake mix, milk, graham crackers (whatever those were), oleo, sugar, strawberry pie filling, and half a teaspoon of sea salt—he liked the idea of sea salt, with its suggestion of purity, of a vast natural reserve being distilled for his use. He read with interest the nutritive facts on the packets—the number of calories per serving, the amount of fat, carbohydrates, fibre, protein, sodium and vitamins. Sometimes the packets also confessed that their contents were made in a facility that also processed peanuts and tree nuts. Here again, the same impressive zest for clarity, for precision, for making a clean breast of things, for faith in the scientific link between cause and effect, of treating consumers like adults, who with perfect knowledge could make the right choices. Caveat emptor—buyer beware, you have been forewarned.

Every week he withdrew from the bank the next instalment of the roll of green bills bank-rolled in the first instance by a fertile piece of land and then, to get past the feral Foreign Exchange Regulations Act, transported across multiple oceans and land masses in an understanding with his uncle Suchi's wife's nephew, Manohar of Cleveland,

Ohio, who would send him dollars which would be repaid in rupees, handed over to Manohar's mother in Mysore.

*

He fell into a pattern with Amy, walking her home on the days he ate at the restaurant, timing his fries and Coke to finish as she wrapped up her shift. It meant a considerable detour and he kept it up even when it grew cold and the snows came and the ground grew wet and slushy. He found the cold air exhilarating. When he tended to be careless with his hat, Amy said with a straight face—When your ears feel cold and frozen, just rub them hard, they'll break and come off in your hands. You can fix them back after winter is over. There were several things Amy said, when he couldn't tell whether she was serious or joking. He liked that about her. Perhaps it was an American thing.

On weekends, when the weather was good, they drove out into the countryside. It was part of their unspoken understanding that she would call him when her boyfriend, whose name he learned was Stevie, was not around, an arrangement he accepted unquestioningly and with alacrity.

Early in autumn, late summer actually, Amy called saying she was driving to a place that used to be a sea once, about 400 million years ago. She was working on an idea for costumes for her next project. Would he like to come? Intrigued, he wore his jacket and hat, grabbed a box of Hostess Twinkies, and left to meet her at the Ale House.

The site was the flood plain of a river, a tributary of the Missisippi that had changed course, exposing a vast bed of limestone with calcified remains of coral reefs and fish. The layers of rock had trapped the history of these creatures for hundreds of millions of years till a whimsy of nature had laid this 400-million-year-old secret bare. Long before the Ice Age, before the glacier had trundled down these plains, geologists speculated, they had been covered with shallow seas full of fish, which were probably destroyed by an asteroid.

They drove on miles of highway through John Deere country, cornfields of brown and copper and gold, heavy with grain waiting to be harvested at the end of the month, stretching for dizzying distances, their uniformity broken only by tall pencil-like silver silos, the Tin Man's hat from Wizard of Oz, Amy said of them, and snub-nosed structures that should rightly have been nuclear warheads but were only sheds to store corn. Amidst the corn and the placid sheep and cows, billboards reached out into the sky imploring 'Think before you act' or 'I am a child, not a choice'.

They turned off the highway, or the interstate as it was called, and came to a feeder road overlooking a vast wide expanse of weathered limestone. It stretched out choppy and uneven, more plain than river bed—bare, treeless, exposed white. On the verge of the wide, shallow gorge was a wooded outcrop, marking the bounds of the site. They walked up a ramp and entered a park, reading the explanatory plaques.

If this had been a sea it must have been fairly swimming with creatures. Amy unrolled sheets of butter paper on which she wanted rubbings of the corals. They hit a rich vein almost immediately. A wall of what looked like fossilized snakeskin, honeycombed with 'eyes'—the Hexagonaria which would shimmer in silver tulle, Amy said, as she covered the ground lovingly with butter paper and threw a pencil across to him.

They tramped across the gorge all morning, following the long segmented stem of a sea lily, broken into pieces and stretched across the rock, which they followed like clues in a treasure hunt. It blossomed into a perfect head, pressed intact in the stone. Amy rolled out sheet after sheet of butter paper, trying to capture the crystalline folds of a clam-like creature which the plaque identified as a Brachiopod, prickly Spinatrypa that looked and felt like nettles and clusters of small horns.

Further up against a cliff wall, there was the impression of a large armoured fish, the remains of which had been excavated and carted off to a museum. Much later, when the seas had dried up and the fish gone, ice caps had advanced on this plain and creatures of enormous size—mammoths, mastodons and sloths had roamed the continent. At a site a few hundred miles away the remains of a giant sloth were being excavated. It seemed unbelievable, standing on the tame rocky bed, in view of parked cars and the hum of traffic from the interstate a little distance away, that such a time could have existed and that they, he and Amy and the group that had just arrived, were merely specks on a timeline.

After walking on a bit, he and Amy rolled up their sheets of paper and retreated into the picnic tables in the visitor's gallery. Amy brought out a flask of coffee and he his box of Hostess Twinkies, which Amy fell upon, much to his surprise and gratification.

*

On their next trip, they had their first fight, of a sort, and their first making-up, if it could be called that.

They drove to another tributary of the Mississippi, a slow backwater of the river, more a lake, which showed up as a blue squiggle on the map, where a large colony of pelicans had been sighted. It was a windy day and they spread a rug on the grassy bank and stationed themselves, as had several others from the local bird watchers club. Amy had her sketch book, a pair of binoculars, a camera and a flask of coffee and he had cinnamon-and-squash bread with cream cheese.

Swan Lake—yes, anyone would want to do, but the beauty of this heavy bird, the great American white pelican, is what appeals to me. Pelican Lake—that's what I want to do, Amy said.

She herself suggested to him a bird of exotic plumage, unusually coloured, with her long supple dancer's limbs and her alabaster white throat, which he understood was not just a turn of the literary imagination. He considered her a true artist who could, from everyday things, from what she saw around her, from the evidence of the world, distil abstract concepts, and turn them into stories of her own. Her mind seemed to recognise no barriers, that no connections were impossible, no constraints could hold her back, a free spirit in every sense. A true American.

There must have been thousands of them, jostling and snapping, spread out in small colonies on the mud flats in the expanse of water. Their girth, their heaving, and the large sacs that palpitated at their throats reminded him of the motorcyclists they had seen at the gas station. Theirs had been the solitary car till half a dozen Hell's Angels prototypes came revving up their Harley Davidsons, bulky, tough-looking middle-aged men in black with a pink insignia on their shirts, their shirt sleeves cut off, their tattooed biceps standing out, their sparse hair bundled into ponytails, with equally tough-looking women riding pillion with them.

Cool, Amy had said, pulling out her notebook immediately. These guys are cool. What's the right word—hip, yeah they're hip.

As soon as they settled down on the grass, a friendly ornithologist from the rug next to theirs came across to give them some pamphlets and to share his pair of powerful field glasses. While the ornithologist taught Amy how to see the sights in the field glasses Ashwath turned the binoculars on to the lake and was rewarded by the sight of a lone bird, a great American white pelican, full worthy of its appellation, sailing past, like a dignitary on parade. In the morning sun, the icy white feathers hurt the eyes. The tight corsage, when ruffled by the wind, lifted to reveal a secondary layer of black tail feathers. Its neck and head looped in a sharp S—not as graceful as a swan, but good enough. A small black eye rested in a yellow bed and its large spatulate bill curved downwards to a blunt edge; a rather unsightly wart rose on its upper lip.

That's an active adult, ready to breed, the ornithologist said. The knob will go away once the breeding season is over.

Someone called from the ornithologist's group. A red-tagged pelican had been sighted. He left in great excitement taking his field glasses with him. Would you like to come, he asked Amy as he was leaving and held out his hand. Amy reached for it and left with him, without a backward glance.

Ashwath had the flask and the cream cheese to himself. He sat on the grass, trying to read a pamphlet.

A small group of birds swam past him, as grave as judges about to deliver a verdict, when suddenly, in a choreographed move, they thrust their heads deep into the water, bottoms up pointing to the sky, came up for air, snapped their necks back, opened their bills and worked their neck pouches furiously, perhaps to swallow a fish. The effect was comic, like a bunch of matrons quivering with rage.

He looked around for Amy but she was nowhere to be seen, nor was the friendly ornithologist.

What is it, Amy said, when they were on their way back. What is bothering you?

He looked at her and said nothing. Her hands lay poised on the steering wheel, her painted nails glinting like weapons.

The breeding habits of the great American white pelican?

He was just being helpful, that's all—

He said he didn't think you were a cream cheese kind of girl ... he gave you his number ...

Ash! It's really none of your business. Why should you get so hot and bothered about that? You are still quite red in the face and neck. Why Ash I believe you are sunburnt!

So the prickling sensation on his neck hadn't been out of anger. He looked at his bare arms and saw that they were covered with patches of small red rash.

You know, I wouldn't think—Amy began and stopped.

You wouldn't think what?

He knew what she had been about to say. She didn't

think he could get sunburnt, being dark-skinned to begin with and coming from the tropical climes where the sun beat down all day, his skin had no right to be so thin.

Nothing, Amy said. There's calamine lotion at the back in a flap behind your seat. If you can reach behind you ...

He sat still, making no move to reach for the lotion or to speak to her.

When they reached the Ale House she did not stop to let him off as she usually did but continued home with the promise of more coffee—with milk and sugar, as he liked it.

He had walked her home several times but had stopped at the door of the building. By night it had seemed sombre but by day it looked downright shabby, even a little rundown. The staircase leading into the open porch of the building was choked with leaves and the handrail was unpainted, a bare brown wood. The landing on the ground floor was crowded with bicycles. The floor carpeting was worn and stained in patches and the heating vents on the floor were full of fluff. The door to one of the houses on the ground floor opened and a middle-aged man came out. He looked unseeingly at the two of them and went out.

The staircase leading up to Amy's second floor flat smelt of cat pee. Outside her door there was a cluster of potted plants—coleus, begonia and anthurium—plants with brightly coloured leaves, which, when you came closer you realised were clever imitations in plastic which could pass off for real in the diffused light. Amy's name, the alphabets cut out in paper, was pasted on the door. She unlocked the door but it would barely open. Deftly, she slid her hand in and removed whatever object was blocking the door and flung it inside. When the door finally did open, just enough to let one person in at a time, he saw a heap of shoes behind the door—trainers tangled with flip flops and dancing shoes with scuffed toes.

The room was so cluttered with things that there was barely space to move. The shelves against the wall were stacked with books—some lying face down, their spines straining, with random objects piled on top of them. There were books on the floor, and cardboard cartons full of clothes; the frill of a pink tutu and a pair of leg warmers, their creases still intact, hung out of a box. A central wooden table, painted a fluorescent green, the paint slapped on roughly in layers, had several charcoal sketches, mostly of dance costumes, scattered across and also a garment with a darning needle sticking out of it.

There was a large window on the west-facing wall from which the light streamed in, past the ruched up Venetian blinds, making the clutter look plausible, even picturesque.

A white leather couch by the window was the only space free of things and a ginger cat sat on it, its legs stretched out, suggestive of Egyptian royalty. It wore a yellow collar with a blue bead. As soon as it saw them it let out a small miaow and jumped out of the window.

The room, the clutter, the benediction of light, and the cat mostly, had a calming effect on him. His anger, his resentment against Amy, settled down. He felt instead a warmth welling up within him for her.

All of the furniture and most of the other things, the pots and pans and even the books had been reclaimed from dumpsters, Amy said, from students who had been in a hurry to leave and move on after finishing their course. The white couch which she loved and often slept on had been rescued heroically, from the edge of a landfill.

The walls were covered with paintings—framed by hand, in rough hewn wooden brackets. He recognised the large-sized painting on the wall. It was a recreation of the fossilised creatures on the limestone bed, only these were perfect, perhaps as they had existed originally. A crinoid sea lily floated across the canvas, long-stemmed, each circular segment clearly etched, blossoming into a perfect head with arms of even length sprouting from a minutely painted calyx. Plants with large tentacle shoots and scaly branches wound round the spiky burr of Spinatrypa and Favocites. In one corner of the canvas, shards of ice were beginning to form and there was a suggestion of a woolly animal. The whole thing, the canvas itself seemed to be set in a dark gel-like substance which pulsated in the light; one could imagine that it would glow in a dark room.

This is one of Stevie's best—it's called 'Night Life', Amy said.

He wouldn't have thought that Stevie O' Sullivan—thin, bearded and distracted-looking, who had barely met his eye the one time Amy had introduced them to each other—would have had something like this in him. Her constant references to Stevie, he realised, did not bother him as much as her brief flirtation with the ornithologist.

On the opposite wall was a collage of photographs. Prominent among them was one of a middle-aged couple, who seemed to have lent some of their features, a less faded form, to Amy. They were standing close together, smiling up at the camera, a balding man in a white tee shirt and denim jacket and the woman with short bright brown hair and gold-rimmed spectacles that took up most of her face. She wore a dress with a close neck and a lace collar. The background stretched into the desolate distance with a house at the far end. They looked kindly and undistinguished. A young boy, grave, solitary, with Amy's mouth, held up a baseball glove. Amy came over and stood close to him, looking at the photographs, soft-eyed.

She was standing so close that he could see the fine down on her cheek, below her ear, the carmine curve of her reticulate mouth, the rise and dip of her clavicle under her translucent skin. He made a move towards her, and it seemed to him that she too half turned to him. And then his eye fell on another photo—of her and Stevie together, much younger, wrapped in each other's arms.

Just in time.

He fell back at the force of the photograph, the implosion almost, of vitality, and yes, of happiness. What was he thinking? Her whole life was up there, red-flagged in pictures, in symbols. His photographs were in the collage, his art all over her house. They were going trekking in the summer to Canada to view the Burgess Shale fossils.

Your parents? he asked unnecessarily.

And my brother Duke.

The coffee, as Amy promised, had milk and sugar, and it came in a hand-painted mug. They sipped their coffee in silence under the watchful eye of Stevie's Dunkleosteus.

They lived in Iowa, in a small town called Ashbury, almost on the banks of the Mississippi. That was her home. She had lived there all through her teens, the promise of Chicago and St Louis looming hours away by car, but till she was on her own, she hadn't seen either city. After she finished high school she had moved out of home, from her small prairie town and had been on the move since then.

She had been lucky with grants and scholarships—that had allowed her to be what she was—a free spirit, an eternal seeker. Her mother's family was of Irish mining stock—she touched her unruly hair—and her father's people had immigrated generations ago from Schleswig-Holstein. They were modest people. Her mother worked as a para legal and her father was a small businessman, running an auto parts shop. She and Stevie had been in the same school—high school sweethearts who had moved out together.

So she was at heart a small town girl, he thought.

Stevie was doing a graduate program in art at a college in Chicago and also working at a design studio there in Lincoln Park, which kept him very busy, and at some time she guessed she'd move there herself. Would he feed and walk her cat when she was away home on Thanksgiving weekend, she asked. Her neighbour who usually took care of her cat would be away too. He grasped at it as at a straw after his near miss.

These names, her history, meant nothing to him—to him, they were all uniformly American. When it was his turn, he hesitated. He could not imagine summing up his parentage or his background so succinctly. Instead he gave her the card he had selected from the stationery section in Walmart. It showed a little boy sitting inside a Dodge Ram truck, its blue colour the exact blue of a starling's egg, holding up the American flag. The boy's eyes looked up at the flag, uncomprehending yet of its promise, but assured of its future. The caption inside read, Make your own destiny.

That is why I came here, he said. That is what I want.

Four

Just as he was beginning to despair that he was locked into eternal servitude with the engineering archives, his project took a turn. The last set of boxes yielded a file of manila folders with the discreet advice, For Council Members Only. It was a cache of 1960s letters. In the mid-1960s there seemed to have been an upheaval in the College of Engineering. A faculty member, one Philip Clarke, questioned the endowment of a chair in the Chemical Engineering department by a chemicals company 'of dubious reputation and intent'. He also asked why the Biochemical Engineering department was accepting research projects that contributed eventually to bacteriological and herbicidal warfare. Clarke's letter appeared to have stirred a hornet's nest. There was a barrage of responses from the council members to Clarke's objections. The Dean of Engineering replied that the college would continue all research projects and sources of funding as per the state and federal laws. The Dean of Faculties reminded Dr Clarke of his need to adhere to the Code of Conduct for Faculty, that he himself had consented to when he accepted the position, more so when his period of probation was still on and he was yet to come up before the committee for tenure. He had the right to recuse himself from individual projects as a conscientious objector, but that too would come up before the committee. There was a laddish letter, an invited response from another faculty member who reminded his colleague that the mainstay of the chemical companies remained chemicals that went into an array of products that made life more healthy and hygienic, such as soap, and toothpaste and deodorant—in short, things that kept Clarke and others from looking and smelling like what the cat brought in, and if their chemicals did not go into brake fluid, Clarke would have to give up his car and would never be able to reach his classes or his protest venues on time. Another letter brought to Professor Clarke's notice that the same chemical company produced artificial limbs and had funded the artificial heart research project.

Philip Clarke's replies were filed in another folder. Did it absolve the company, he asked of his laddish colleague, and university engineering departments of responsibility for experiments with 'newer, improved' versions of napalm (B? C? D?) and Agent Orange? Were they not bound to teach their students about the responsible use of chemicals? Was the college not getting tied in with large corporations and by default, the military and the government? A provost weighed in to say that these were matters of policy, beyond the jurisdiction of the university, and best not commented upon. The laddish colleague wrote back asking Clarke to grow up and recognise the compulsions of a country at war and which was 'discharging its responsibilities as a world leader'. Now that they had entered into the arena of ethics and morality, Philip Clarke asked, was it not necessary for engineers to be connected with and take responsibility for the social consequences of their work?

Philip Clarke disappeared from the letters after that. He reappeared much later, in another brown box containing material dated to a later period, replying to a series of memos from a committee charging him of conduct unbecoming of a faculty member and specifically of participating in an anti-war demonstration and inciting students to picket a Marine Corps recruitment centre. The last letter from Philip Clarke was a letter of resignation, where he regretted his inability to comply with the directives of the college. Further, he urged the Dean of Students and the provost who also headed the Committee of Human Rights to listen to the voice of their conscience and of the students on campus right then.

Ashwath had found that last letter moving, despite his resolve to look at the letters only as evidence in the history of the Engineering department. 'Take back your world', Philip Clarke had urged the students, in his last letter, and then there were no more letters from him.

Other than the correspondence between Philip Clarke and the Council, there were several papers in the brown box, and newspaper clippings, tethered into neat little bundles, which revived his flagging interest. There was a collage of photographs from the demonstrations against the Vietnam War—students sitting on the grass with black arm bands, relaxed, chatting with each other against the backdrop of the Capitol; a sea of faces lit up with candles from the vigil on Moratorium Day; two boys on hunger strike, sprawled on mattresses in the Columbus enclosure—he recognised the cowled figure. Earnest-looking, bespectacled students, inches away from a contingent of helmeted policemen held up placards which said 'Dow Shall Not Kill' and 'Go ROTC'. On the steps of the Capitol stood a crowd, reading out, as the caption said, from a roll of paper splattered with blood, the names of soldiers killed in the war. There were photographs of chubby-cheeked dolls mounted on stakes and being set on fire—symbolic of children who had been burnt by napalm.

As he sifted through the newspaper clippings, tagging what he thought was relevant to his project, he paused at one clipping. It was a black and white photograph of a woman struggling with helmeted policemen who were hauling her into a waiting police car. She had pushed herself high against the shoulders of one of them, who had clasped her round the knees, her hand raised in a fist, the other holding a placard. The policemen were a helmeted blur but the woman, young, stood out clearly in a white shirt, the muscles of her neck straining, her long hair in a tangle, her eyes looking frenzied behind her glasses. The caption read, a university student, a member of the SDS, demonstrating against campus recruitment by Dow Chemicals.

He put his finger on the photograph to mark the page and looked across the room at the assistant's desk. The resemblance was striking; no, it had to be her, a youthful unfaded version. The long hair, the slight frame, the myopic eyes behind the glasses were the same, surely.

For the rest of the morning he found himself studying Miss Argentum surreptitiously—he still did not know her name—his eyes darting between the photograph and the desk. That afternoon, when she closed her book and left her table with an air of finality and collected her coat from the hanger, he hurriedly put away his documents in the brown box and followed her.

The noon winter sky was a grey cement wall stretching low overhead—so low that you felt you could reach out and touch it. She pulled her coat close round her and tightened the belt, and tucked her long hair into the fleecy hood. She walked slowly, careful to avoid the snowbanks, placing her foot on the clear patches of the pavement. He noticed that she walked with a limp, her left foot coming down just a fraction too late. She walked downtown, past the Ale House and turned in to a small deli that he had seen but not eaten in. She nodded to the girl at the cash counter and made for the tubs on the warmers in the middle of the room. He stood behind the tall shelves, examining the preserves on sale, and watched out of the corner of his eye as she picked up her tray, made her choice from the tubs and got it all weighed. Then she went to the counter at the other end, and searched among the bottles on display. When he paid for his small pot of apricot preserve and left, he could see her sitting at her table, by herself, with a small amount of food on the plate in front of her and a long-stemmed glass of red wine.

*

One night there was a heavy metal band playing at the Ale House. It was a local band that had made good on the circuit and come back home to play. The music was loud and jangly but rhythmic, with the gutted words in the singer's throat emerging as sharp sounds. He found the noisy performance appealing. He was getting adventurous with his food too. On a Mexican special night he had sopapillas, salsa and guacamole, and was comforted by the hot garlic after-burps on the walk back home in the cold night.

When the major attraction band took a break, there were smaller groups and soloists who played, keeping the crowd warm till the band came back. That night, after the guitarist crashed on his chords for the final time, and as the whooping died down, a singer walked on to the stage without ceremony, sat down on a chair, and started strumming her guitar. It was Miss Argentum from the library, still wearing her faded sweater with the large button at her throat, her hair falling over the sides of her face. She hummed a bit and then sang a sad song, something about a love not so true that broke her heart. She had a high-pitched nasal voice with a husky undertone, and a pleading-yearning turn that flattered the lyrics. Her next song was a Donovan original, she announced, from her student days. He was intrigued by the words and quite liked the bumpy, staccato rhythm.

... I'm just mad about Saffron, Saffron's mad about me ... she sang ... *Electrical banana is gonna be a sudden craze ...*

There were fewer heads turned towards the stage, and a low buzz of conversation broke out, like an undertone to the singer's music. A few people got up and left. She began on another song. The lyrics, she said, were made from Michael Herr's war dispatches. This was a softer song, and she crooned the words into the microphone.

The moon ... nasty and full ... a fat moist piece of decadent fruit ... soft and saffron misted ... over the sandbags ... into the jungle ...

When she finished her song and got off the stage, he could hear only the sound of his clapping.

Oh that's Paula, Amy said. She's been around forever.

Back at the archives, combing through the newspaper clippings, he found what he was looking for. Among the list of people indicted for felony and misdemeanour was a Miss Paula Petersen of Clear Waters residency hall. The charges against her, in connection with participating in an anti-war demonstration that had turned violent, included causing malicious injury to a building, assisting escape from a police officer, disorderly conduct and assault with intent to cause great bodily harm. Apparently Miss Petersen had chosen to go to jail in payment of the $100 fine imposed upon her. She was also one of the four suspected of breaking in to the university offices and placing a dead rat on the glass-topped table of the Head of Student Affairs after several conscientious objectors had been reclassified into 1A category, or made immediately available to be drafted for unrestricted military service. The paper quoted Miss Petersen's poem, which the protesters had turned into an anthem—*The lonely stone in the gutter calls out/ To me, use me, use me/ Against rot-see/ Beware the officer with the soft hat/ Who stops by for a chat/ Smell a rat, smell a rat ...*

When he followed Paula on the slush-filled pavements, the slight hooded figure through the falling snow, into the organics co-op from where she emerged with a paper bag from which the heads of leeks or the top of a bottle of wine protruded, and she drew her hood closer and stamped on her sodden feet, he felt a strong rush of feeling welling up within him for her, something he could not understand or define.

Perhaps he had willed it but it happened sooner than he expected. When she stopped at the door of Trader Joe's, instead of going in, she turned around and confronted him—Do you want to speak to me, she said.

He had been anticipating this moment all along but he was not prepared for it.

The photograph in the files, is that you ... he blubbered. I heard you singing at the Ale House the other day, on karaoke night ... songs from war times, you said ...

Oh—she looked away from him and smiled a small distracted smile. He imagined that she was flooded with memories.

I believe we are blocking the way.

They walked to the Ale House which was close by, and sat outdoors despite the cold for she wanted to smoke.

I thought you had a question about your project at the archives, she said. That photograph, yes. I didn't think it would turn up somewhere. It got me a lot of attention, a lot of hate letters ...

Close up, he noticed how smoke-stained her teeth were, how her little finger trembled in the air when her hand came up to her lips.

The songs she had sung had been a legacy of her music major days. The Electrical Banana song had set off a new trend in the residence halls—a rumour about the hallucogenic effects of banana smoke. Her then boyfriend had been one among those who had believed that the banana, when properly treated and smoked, releases serotonin, just like LSD, and was finally the legal and organic alternative to the chemical drug. For days and weeks and months they had scraped the insides of banana peels—Cabanita Golden at 10 cents a pound—collected a pile of pith, baked the dried powder and smoked it in joints. They believed they were getting a natural high and by the time the great banana hoax was discovered, that it was all wishful thinking, they had given it up anyway.

At the archival collections he now felt emboldened to go up to her table and ask her a question about the contents of a particular folder or for a suggestion on what else he could consult. Sometimes he would suggest coffee when they were leaving at the same time. She was always willing and he hoped, as winter progressed and gave way to an uncertain spring, that they would be friends.

She was a career anti-establishment person, she said, having begun in college in her home in Hartford, on the east coast. She had started her self-training, as she put it, taking things from shops. She spoke of it as a kind of discipline, a sadhana; shop-lifting and thieving were words used by the other side, the establishment. She hated the thought of money—a twist of green that rules us, and of property—land that has always belonged to someone else and was taken by force. Property is theft, she believed, like the Anarchists. Her family had been in the insurance business and empanelled lawyers to Colt for generations. It grew so bad that the very sight of the factory dome made her ill. She still remembered the first time she was caught—it was a tube of Revlon lipstick tucked into her mittens. The tube had fallen out at the door and the thrill of it had been so great that she had peed right there on the floor. They had all converged on her—the security guard, the store manager and the tearful checkout clerk, with the janitor mopping up behind them. Many of her friends were doing it, she said. It was their way of getting back at the system, at the false order of things.

The store had not pressed charges but her parents were called. The college had called them, and on their advice, since she refused to admit she had done anything wrong, she was moved out of her college. So she came here, to the anonymity of the Midwest, away from her sharp community. She was to continue her course in music, but her blood was up. On this campus she had met a similar castaway, Bill

Randall, soon to be Clyde to her Bonnie, ideologue and future leader of the Students for a Democratic Society—SDS—originally from San Francisco.

When the demonstrations were at their peak, Tom Hayden, a founder of the Students for a Democratic Society, had visited their small campus. It's all in your hands, he had told them, it's up to you to decide how you are going to use the enormous power you have. Student movements were a symptom of a society that was breaking down, and the detonation of a new order. There were about two hundred students packed into the small hall and she and Bill Randall had had to stand at the back to listen to him. Tall, thin, with short hair and a trimmed goatee, dressed in a suit and tie, and quite soft-spoken, Hayden had appeared more like an executive in a corporation, the kind that he used to decry, but he had made her see that she was participating in a movement far bigger than her individual acts of protest.

She had joined the movement to catch Bill Randall's eye and also because it suited her wild streak. But she began to sense the truth of what handsome Hayden had said. Her early acts of rebellion she now saw not as radical, but juvenile. In challenging her family, she had ignored the fact that she was still dependent on them, and in the thrill of shop-lifting, she had not considered the checkout clerk who would have had her pay docked and the janitor who had had to clean up her mess after her. The loop of big industry, the automobile manufacturers and the oil companies that had contaminated the beaches of Santa Barbara with oil and killed off so many birds and sea creatures—and also given her her Joan of Arc moment when she had posed for the newspapers cradling a blackened, dead seagull—and the phrase the military-industrial complex, began to make sense to her. Her convictions had to translate into deeds. Immediately, she returned the car her mother had gifted her and cut down on her shopping. The discounts, the coupons and the sales that she was always on the look out for were lures to get people to buy more, consume more, and eventually waste more.

She had given up going to classes for the life around her was teaching her so much more than the cocooned airtight classroom and the only music that made sense was the music of protest. For a long time, she had cultivated the cult of grunge, a deliberately shabby look, cutting her long hair short, and wearing ill-fitting clothes. She had also decided to pull out of the Miss Homecoming pageant, joining instead a sit-in to protest against it.

At that time, it seemed truly as if their student power could disrupt the political system and build a new society. Bill had moved on from the SDS to form a more radical splinter group called the Students for Action, which she joined, becoming part of the small hardcore of 'hell raisers' as their Vice President had designated them.

But within a year after it was formed, their splinter group was 'busted', their members outed one by one. The authorities seemed to be clairvoyant, they seemed to have sniffed out their mailing list of radicals, the passwords to their undercover meetings, the offices that they would target. Several core members were arrested, taken from the most unlikely places—friends' houses, even from cafes. And then it emerged that their splinter organisation had been infiltrated. 'Pitcher' Coleman, one of the most active members, older than most of them, had turned out to be an FBI informant. She had learnt of this much later, several years later, after she had left the college without taking her degree. She had hero-worshipped Pitcher Coleman, it was he who had introduced her to Norman Mailer—Hot Damn Vietnam. She recalled the Mailer quote that he had marked out for her—Bombing a country at the same time you are offering it aid is as morally repulsive as beating up a kid in an alley and stopping to ask for a kiss!

But even before that the group had been falling apart. She had begun to feel her enthusiasm, both for protest and for Bill, flagging. Even Jimi Hendrix and Janis Joplin were gone by then. The sleep-ins on winter nights on the grass and the repeated hosings had taken their toll. She had come down with pneumonia, which had left its residue in her spine—she had developed a limp which never quite went away, and which grew worse in the cold weather. She believed that President Nixon was finally done in by his own karma, as perhaps Bill Randal and their group too. She was not to meet Bill Randall again, and heard from a member of the disbanded group that Bill had gone on to become the foreman of a factory in St Louis in Missouri. She herself had tried joining the Peace Corps but it hadn't worked out.

When she was still debating on what to do next, whether to move out of college and this small town or not, a force of nature, a tornado, had decided for her. She had gone down to the basement of her building as soon as the lashing rain began, before the warning knell, and when she emerged from the basement, the apartment block next to hers was gone—taken by the funnelling glutton—and the tree outside, solid of trunk, was twisted and halved, its glorious head ripped off. She saw it as a sign that she must leave.

But you came back here, he said.

Finally, this was the only place I could stay in, the place I could call home and which would have me, where I could live my life.

The landmarks that Paula pointed out now were innocuous. It was difficult to believe that the cosy Italian pizzeria with its cheerful cherry-coloured seats and striped awning had had its frontage wrecked not once but twice by protestors against environmental pollution because it had been an automobile spare parts shop, a dealer of General Motors products.

Placid too were the lawns and pathways adjacent to the Capitol, the Christopher Columbus Square and the small enclosure for a war memorial, across which students hurried to their classes, bordered in season by tulips in a pleasing mix of colours, bearing no ill-effects of a decade old trampling by angry feet. He could not imagine that on similar cold nights, on the frost-covered grass outside the Capitol, which stood calm and unmoved on the hill, thousands of students had gathered and camped out, convinced they would storm the bastion and start a revolution.

The only groups that gathered on the lawn, as he had seen, were knots of girls planning the Homecoming event, and the one procession he had witnessed on the streets was the Homecoming parade, where colourful floats and merry makers had gone down the very same streets as the demonstrators trashing windows had, ten years ago. Even the ROTC, the Reserve Office Training Corps, had a place in the Homecoming event; he passed its sanguine office every day on his way to the Ale House.

Blameless too were the corridors of his residence hall, now full of testosterone-fuelled men filling the lounge, dressed in tee shirts bearing the college colours, putting up posters and discussing their plans for cookouts and tail gates at the big weekend football game. Teargas cannisters had once been flung in the corridor outside his room and students had come out in a panic, coughing and spluttering, their eyes on fire, to be marched out possibly into a hail of night sticks, while the rooms were searched for sticks of dynamite or Molotov cocktails.

The Guardsmen who had gone after the demonstrators like a bunch of starved pigs let loose in a field of ripe corn, in the words of one demonstrator, had been barracked in the adjoining fair grounds, a gently sloping sunny green space, which he and Amy had visited the other day for a dog show

Are you happy now, he asked Paula. Are you happy with the way things turned out?

What kind of question is that, she replied. I remember, the arresting officer at that time asked me why a girl like me, clean cut an' all, was part of the demonstration, and I told him that was who I was. It was the only kind of life I could live then, and now that time is past. I live a quiet life now, but I do what I want to do.

She volunteered at the women's healthcare clinic, because helping women make their own choices over their bodies was important. She still studied music and had enrolled for a refresher course the coming semester—and she worked on music therapy at the children's hospital. Two evenings were spent at the organic co-op. And yet, she could chuck it all up and move to a farm—an old friend had said he needed a partner to keep his farm going.

Five

Summer was hot and dry, long days with the sun shining so late that the night was all but forgotten.

Sushil Khanna turned up one Saturday with a hamper of food and said they were all going for a drive. He wanted to show his new flatmates from India a bit of the summer countryside, the green stretch of the cornfields and the river creek. Would he like to join them?

It was a long time since he had seen Sushil Khanna, so he agreed. Besides, he was curious about the new Indian flatmates. Pratap Reddy was from Vijaywada and Manoj Saini was from Delhi. Manoj seemed to know Sushil Khanna well—our families are old friends, he said.

Haven't seen you for a while, Sushil Khanna said, catching his eye in the rear view mirror. Seat belt, Manoj, seat belt. You are not in Rajinder Nagar now.

Manoj was sitting in front with Sushil, Pratap and he were at the back. Been busy, Ashwath replied, looking out of the window.

Over all of winter? Even during the holidays? I don't think you went home ...

So that was what was bugging Sushil Khanna. That he had not gone over for Diwali to Sushil Khanna's apartment to play cards or to his uncle's house near Gary, Indiana, over Thanksgiving and Christmas, as the other Indian boys with nowhere to go had done.

Manoj was fiddling with the dials on the dashboard of the car.

Play some music. The cassette right on top, Sushil Khanna told him.

The overture of the song began, a mouth organ played a few bars. Manoj started singing in anticipation of the song. The mellifluous voice of Mohammed Rafi filled the car. *Kisi na kisi se, kabhi na kabhi*, Manoj sang along with the jaunty lyrics, in a flat earnest voice, intent on the words.

Ashwath liked Mohammed Rafi's voice though he could not follow all the words of the song. He knew some Hindi, unlike Pratap who knew no Hindi at all.

What does it mean, Pratap asked.

It's from the film *Kashmir ki Kali*. Hit song. All of Rafi's songs were hits. It means sometime or the other you have to give your heart to someone, Manoj said. He sounded as if he were explaining a lesson to a student.

The next song began, an introduction of vigorous drum beats. Both Manoj and Sushil started singing as soon as the drum beats began. *Dil de ke dekho dil de ke dekho dil de ke dekhoji*—Also Rafi, Manoj said, and the same actor, Shammi Kapoor. It means try giving your heart to someone—those who take others' hearts should also learn to give theirs ... Ashwath tried to hide a smile.

It's not funny, it's a love song—Manoj turned round as well as his seat belt would allow him. He seemed offended.

Arre, you don't have to tell our friend here about giving his heart away, Sushil said.

He grew alert at once, his mind waking up from the passive lull of cornfield gazing.

He has left his behind at home, Sushil said, in a pretend-hearty manner. Don't look at me like that, Ashwath. You may not take calls from your people but we know all about it ...

Arre Ashwath, I wouldn't have thought you were

a Majnoon type, Manoj said, taking up Sushil's tone of banter. Majnoon ... Manoj sighed and closed his eyes. I'd like to be a Majnoon too, going crazy for love ...

Ashwath felt a hard flame rise from the pit of his stomach and grow, like a tree spreading its fiery branches along his shoulders and throat.

But our Majnoon seems to have found his heart again. He's got new Lailas here, he has a preference for goris. Too busy, eh? Forget friends, no time for family ... No Diwali for him ... but for the fireworks going off in his heart—Sushil Khanna guffawed, and even Pratap smiled at that.

Stop. Stop the car—Ashwath said.

The laughter of a moment ago vanished, as if burnt by the heat of his rage.

Arre, Sushil was just joking. And you took it seriously—Manoj tried.

Sushil Khanna brought the car to a halt at the side of the road. Be reasonable Ashwath ji. You must learn to take a few—

He fumbled with the catch of the door and flung it open. The heat rushed in, a hungry guest.

Where will you go, it's 80 degrees and we're miles from home, Manoj said.

Sushil's shoulders were a wall, his eyes were on the road. Pratap watched with friendly curiosity.

He stumbled into the fields, and kept going into the green. He waited till he could hear the car drive off.

All round him stretched the fields, even, uninterrupted, with the sun glinting silver off the silo set well within. He sat down on the ground and closed his eyes, waiting for the clamour in his head to die down. He listened to the sussuration of the wind through the sheaves, the background hum of the crickets and the occasional high note punctuation of a bird. Later, much later, he would see the fields and the birds and all that they had been witness to, transfigured on Jackson Pollock's canvases. But the blip of art was at a distant spot on the curve of his future. Right then, all there was, was the heat, the relentless stretch of green with no horizon in sight and his sense of being the only man on earth, to be born and to exist.

A silo would mean a farmhouse. Just as he dusted himself and started walking towards a trail by the side of the road, he heard the phut-phut of a tractor. The man driving it was so much the quintessential farmer—straw hat, denim overalls and weatherbeaten face, that he was sure it was the heat playing tricks on him.

The tractor stopped and he got in.

Lachancha, the man said. Lakambie.

Yes, he replied, submitting himself to whatever rite those magic words might imply.

They drove on a narrow road that forked off the highway, and then for a distance on a dirt track, arriving at a large, peeling barn. The 'farmer' got down and went into a relic of a shed that seemed older than the barn, while he waited. He could see right up to the tower of the barn, a squirrelling maze of ladders and wooden slats. The whole place smelt faintly of dung. The man returned with a surgeon's gear—a gown, rubber gloves, a cap and transparent eye guards.

When he saw the others in the field, working the rows of corn plants, he knew what it was. The detasselling crew was in the fields—usually school students working a summer job, making their way through earmarked rows, removing the tassel at the top, preventing the pollen from the tassel from pollinating the silk or the feathery pink female flower that was on the lower reaches of the plant. So the rows of corn plants, thus beheaded, would be impregnated by seed from other plants and not their own, producing a healthy hybrid crop of seed corn, the fat and pride of the land.

And then he understood what the farmer's mumbles, the Freemason's password to the lodge, had meant. Late aren't you? Lucky I came by.

He was lucky too that he had come in late in the morning, most of the work was over, done by the crew, and the rows were being checked for any tassels left behind. But still, when he returned, the school bus bringing him back, his hands were sore and he was itching all over, despite the protective gear, and his shoes were caked with mud. But there were compensations. He was paid quite well, double what he was paid for his job at the Archives, and all thoughts of Sushil Khanna had been driven clean out of his mind. He was an oaf, merely, he decided. Quite harmless.

*

There was a letter waiting for him when he reached his room. The desk had sent him a message two days back asking him to collect it but he had forgotten. So they had put it on his writing desk when the door was opened for the cleaning crew. It was a lightweight blue thing—a single sheet folded over with gummed flaps—the prized aerogramme, meant for letters to foreign shores, costing much more than the ordinary inland letter and available only in the main post office. Unlike the inland letter, which was stacked in the cupboard, the aerogramme was bought cautiously, only when required, to write to the rare relative abroad. Perhaps his father now stacked these as well, along with the inland letters. He knew he would find in it his father's precise pointy handwriting, crimped as much as possible so that he could write more, fill it up with questions and homilies, running right up to the edges so that he had to be careful to slice the flaps open just along the knife crease of the folds.

But this letter was not cramped, not running over to the flaps and sides—all the information was contained in a single sheet. His sister was getting married. The boy, his father said, was from a good family, though not from their immediate community. He had mentioned a name, a lineage, a family tree—son of so and so of such and such place, but it did not ring a bell. Halfway through the letter he closed it, folding it along its creases; it was too much for him to take at one go. The weariness of the day, the sheer pendulum of its offerings, claimed him and he fell back on his bed. His head ached—the vein at his temple was engorged and lumpy, like a green snake with a rat in its belly—and his body seemed swollen and taut. There were nicks on his arms, despite the long gloves, and the blood had dried up in them. His fingers were rubbery stubs. There were welts on his calves and his toes looked shrivelled and white as if they had been soaking in brine. His shoes, mud-encrusted and lying in a heap by the door, were ruined and they were fairly new.

Through the fog in his mind a man's face emerged—he could place the man his sister was going to marry. A dark-complexioned man, stringily muscular, with a rasping voice and an animated manner—the whites of his eyes glittered when he spoke. He felt a sharp tug of disappointment in his gut—his sister could have done better. The man, much older, had been part of her music fraternity, a stand-in for her music teacher when he was away. He was also a senior vocalist who performed in minor concerts.

There was the one music competition where the man had been a judge. He remembered borrowing Satish's scooter to take his sister to the competition—the star performer could not go wobbling to the venue on the carrier of a bicycle, dressed in her finery. His mother had allowed her to wear the pearl pendant necklace meant for special occasions. He had driven carefully, in silence, for Savitri had been too tense to indulge in her usual chatter. He had seen her into the green room and she had been swallowed by the happy bustle. The small room was hot and dingy but it did not seem to matter. When they arrived, the harmonium was wedged in the doorway. He helped free the instrument but in the process bumped it on the ground—the harmonium player shouted at him and the other man carrying it and immediately tested it to see if it had gone off key. In a corner, the tabalchi had tossed the blue satin covers off his tablas and was tapping the wedges on the side with a small hammer. The singers had pulled out their notebooks—a last-minute check on the kritis they were going to sing. A tea boy came round and handed out thimblefuls of hot tea. Five minutes to go, get ready, a voice called out from the stage. The mridangam player—he's not there, somebody pointed out. There was a flurry of consternation and even as his sister was beseeching him to go fetch the idiot on his scooter, the mridangam player appeared at the door—like god himself as someone called out—freshly bathed and anointed.

He sat in the second row. The first row was occupied by the judges and the vidwans, the maestros who performed, and ran music schools, with students jostling to be associated with them—they would pick the promising ones and groom them to become performers.

His sister's performance was flat and lacklustre. She looked nervous on stage and her voice sounded strained at the high notes. A girl from a rival school got the prize. His sister's school on the whole did not do well. There were tears in their corner of the green room and much gnashing of teeth. The winning team exulted at the other end of the green room, just a few feet across. His sister sobbed that the judges had been partial and then that it was her mother's fault. Her mother had insisted that she oil her hair and tie it back in a tight plait and had made her wear a thick, dun-coloured silk sari. And the other girl in her light Banarasi, with false glittering jari, her bobbed hair and horror of horrors—with lipstick on her mouth—had bedazzled everybody, the judges first. And then this man had consoled her, standing close, patting her shoulder, telling her she was a good singer and that she must learn to take such things in her stride, and that one day she would give a solo performance, a fullfledged concert on this very stage. Keshav Rao, his name was, his father had written and he was head clerk in a nationalised bank. His family owned land up north in the state. When would Ashwath be able to come? They wanted to have the wedding as soon as possible. Besides, there were enquiries for him too. Had he found a job?

They all fell away—Amy, Paula, even the cheerful boys with whom he had pinched the tops off the corn flowers and trampled into the ground. He was back in the large hall with the red oxide floor gleaming in the morning sun, his father pacing up and down, waiting for Suchi mama to arrive, his mother saying nothing but banging the pots and pans in the kitchen, and his sister in a heap on the sofa, twisting the end of her sari into a damp rag. Every anxiety, every practical concern he could understand perfectly without anyone saying a word. Was this boy's family—strangers, as they were not part of their community, one of 'our people'—up to the mark? Who knew them? Who had vetted them? (Would they ask for a dowry?) How would they raise the money for the wedding? From the kitchen the sharp clang of the pans meant that his mother was angry—first with his sister for having had an opinion in the matter, for having voiced it and not allowing them to decide for her. And then with him, for not being there, for allowing Savitri to fall back on her own resources, for having escaped from his obligations. And then would come the more practical concerns. What shall I do with the jewellery—how do I divide it? The pearl necklace for Savitri and the gold coin necklace for Ashwath's wife. Ah what was she thinking—her daughter wanted to marry an unknown man, a stranger whose ways would be peculiar, so different from theirs, and her son, well he had abandoned them, he had virtually broken off ties with the family, not written or enquired after their well-being. But a son was a son was a son—part of her own, and a daughter was to be gifted away, a treasure that she was keeping in trust for someone else, and he could imagine her pain that the someone else was not of her choosing and would never quite measure up to her daughter. He could hear them all in his head, even

Sushil Khanna, whose anger he could sense, for having turned his back on family and friends, his own kind, and preferring another.

Of Amy what could he tell? Of what she was and why she did what she did. That she was beautiful and kind he knew. But what was her mind made up of, what were her thoughts, her desires, her secrets? He could not imagine a conversation between Amy and her mother, the woman in the photograph with the eager transparent face, who looked as if she had not had a single ignoble thought about anybody in all her life—what did the mother want for her daughter? What words of advice, of warning did she give her daughter? What was their private signalling device? What would she say if her daughter came home with a brown boy, a person beyond the pale? Paula he had followed like a picture book, the series of illustrations, one leading to another, a wondrous creature out of Marvel comics or a character in a novel.

When last they met Paula said that she had felt like a woman looking for Mr Goodbar and he had felt confused. The only Mr Goodbar that he knew, he had blurted out, was the Hershey's bar of peanut chocolate with its yellow and red wrapper. She had laughed out loud at that, she who barely spoke above a whisper. She was referring to her confusion, she said, like the woman in the film, looking for thrills outside of herself, seeking affirmation from others for her acts, for her pranks, thinking that she could find herself by denying her circumstances.

What did he know of this place, this mad place, where the days were disorderly, where the blazing heat of summer was followed by deathly cold and snow, where the sky curved vast but did not shelter. So much had happened here of which he was not a part, for which he did not feel, which was only a curiosity. He felt as if he stood in an open doorway in the draught of cold air, not knowing whether to go in or leave.

He thought of the gold-domed Capitol, sitting on the hill top like a crown on a royal head, in a glacial scoop, now a manicured lawn where pet dogs gambolled, but where strange fish had swum and creatures long gone had called home. This was the place where the bones of the long dead were interred, where the laments of the vanquished echoed alongside the declamations of their conquerors. But here too the memory of a sea of candle lights still flickered in hope, hope that the future would be different from the past. These were all specks in the vastness, in the flow of time. Surely, there was a place for him in this flow, he who was as insignificant and inconspicuous as an ear of corn in the miles that stretched, limitless.

He forced himself to calm down and unfolded the letter again. There was a bit about money that he had missed. The money left over from the sale of the coconut grove and other lands would come in handy for the wedding, his father had written. He understood that statement—innocuous, an aside merely, but what it meant was that the money was no longer available to him; he had to stand on his own feet.

He studied his feet, his toes now looking less wrinkled, the nicks on his calves now purple at the edges. He could flex his fingers without feeling the tightness, the skin no longer shiny, bright. He had been called to the test and he had passed; he had been let in through the gates.

Somewhere in this vast expanse there was a place where he could tuck himself in.

Of course there was no going back, no stepping into the same waters, into the same cave from which he had emerged. His time here in the college was almost played out, he had to look for a job and see what was in store for him.

III

One

It was still raining when they left for the railway station. The sky had been overcast for the past three days and it had drizzled incessantly—a lachrymose cyclone in the Bay of Bengal.

They were to visit Keshav Rao's parents in a village in the northern part of the state, a part that none of them, not even Suchi mama had visited earlier. A tough plain-speaking millet-eating people, not like the soft, silver-tongued rice eaters here in the south, Keshav Rao had said, laughing. That was the thing she liked about him and which had first attracted her to him—so forthright and pithy, but always with a smile or a laughing reference.

Her parents were going to make a formal proposal for their daughter to marry Keshav Rao. They would offer the basket of fruits that her mother was guarding as if her life depended on it and say here, with this we offer our daughter, take her now as part of your family. This business had drained her father—who stood on the railway platform, helpless, looking around for Suchi to come with the tickets, take charge of the luggage and guide them to their seats in the right compartment. When the time was right, her father had no doubt expected that his brother Suchi would scan the community circles and produce a groom for her—a boy from a good family, a boy earning a four-figure salary, and all would be well and familiar.

But no boys were forthcoming. Here she was, a fresh graduate in Home Science, all set to make a home, but marriage had been eluding her. She did her best to hone her skills, working alongside her mother in the kitchen, taking charge of the pickle and the papad-making—top work Kaveramma had left, now that her son had a job in the US and sent money home, dollars that multiplied manifold into rupees. She enrolled for a tailoring class and an extra music class, and put away, at her mother's bidding, her 'man's' NCC uniform and the medals she had won at the Republic Day parade in Delhi, one even for rifle shooting, and kept herself busy, primed. It also helped her to miss her brother a little less and not remind herself that he hardly ever wrote.

But still, the people who responded to the feelers that were sent out were not the right kind—the boys and their families fell short on several counts. Suchi mama hinted that a whiff of Ashwath's tantrums had wafted out. Keshav Rao passed the test on two counts—he was a 'cultured' person, and he came from a respectable, land-owning family. His family supported the annual music festival organised in their part of the state—it was a grand affair, attended by several important singers and students and rasikas.

Here, in the big city, he was one of the 'room boys'—he shared a room with other working men from his region. The room was close to her house and one evening, when he had substituted for the teacher and explained to her, singing in his rather hoarse voice and sledge-hammer style but in perfect pitch, the finer points of a raga that was eluding her, she invited him home. She had never done this before, brought a 'boy' home, but he wasn't a boy, he was the (substitute) music teacher. Her father, surprisingly, took to him almost immediately. With her father, Keshav Rao did not discuss music, he talked politics. They spoke about Indira Gandhi's return to power after being voted out for having declared a state of Emergency in the free, disorderly, rumpus-loving country. That year, 1981, was also the year her brother had left for the US, after behaving in a way that belied who he was, as her mother put it. Keshav Rao was good-humoured and quick-witted, and soon the kitchen produced cups of 'chaha' along with coffee, and her father made none of his slighting comments about tea drinkers.

Her mother, who was checking now under the seat of their cramped compartment to see whether the baskets of fruits and sweets and lengths of unstitched cloth that were to be given to the boy's family were safely stowed, had not given in so easily. The people are unknown to us, we are not familiar with their ways, she said, carefully avoiding comment on the 'boy'. She held out for two years and capitulated after a visit from top work Kaveramma.

Kaveramma came one evening, dressed in a silk sari, her eyes glittering with purpose and innuendo. She slipped in through the front door before they realised, and when her mother came out from the kitchen to see who it was, there was Kaveramma sitting on the sofa, wearing the necklace that had lain in their locker for so many months, smiling from ear to ear. Prakash had been working in the US for almost four years now. She believed it was a bank, she did not know much about these things. All she knew was that by the grace of God, he was well-settled. Their own Suchi's relative Manohar had helped Prakash a lot and she was grateful for that. In expression of her gratitude, she had come to them first. She was looking for a suitable match for her Prakash, she said, her eyes sliding suggestively towards Savitri, and let the words dangle in the air. What she left unsaid was that now circumstances had changed and the playing field had been levelled, with her star being on the ascendant.

Her mother said, I will get you some coffee, and went into the kitchen. Kaveramma followed her, cast a quick authoritative look round the shelves as if to check if they came up to scratch, and said in a confiding way that she didn't want to say it in the hall in front of the menfolk, but she had heard that Ashwath was finding the going tough there—too many distractions, and well, you had to be first-rate, really. He had only to call her Prakash, she added, who would be only too glad to help.

After Kaveramma left, her mother brought in the cups and plates of snacks—Kaveramma had not touched them. She threw the snacks out and spent a long time at the kitchen sink, scrubbing the dishes. She did not say a word to Savitri or to her husband. Savitri noticed that her parents and Suchi mama did not discuss the visit as they did most things. It was as if Kaveramma had not visited them at all. A few days later Savitri's mother said to her father, within Savitri's hearing, if she is set on him, we might as well visit them and settle things formally.

*

The train gathered speed into the night. Her mother started unpacking their dinner and the smell of sambar-rice filled the air. It was hot inside the compartment, despite the fan—a caged thing on the roof with four stubby blades—

and the smell made her gag. But her mother insisted that she eat. Her father looked out of the window, out of the cloudy plate glass pane at the darkness outside, and when her mother asked if he wanted pickle he clicked his tongue impatiently and said whatever, whatever, as if he could not bear to take his eyes off the darkness outside. Suchi mama had a seat in the compartment next to theirs and was dozing off sitting shoulder to shoulder with strangers. He came to with a start when she called him to give him his banana-leaf package of sambar-rice. She knew that her father had taken her brother's desertion hard. He should have been there by right, taking charge of things, the son of the family.

Some time in the early hours of the morning, before it was light, her father left the compartment and came back wearing his Mysore peta. She herself had washed and ironed the length of unbleached cloth, cream-coloured, edged with gold thread, but then it had been remote from what it was now—a turban for a man ready to perform a solemn, daunting duty. She felt a nervous tug in her stomach when he came in and sat down, the turban shining on his forehead, as compelling as fate itself, but her father would not meet her eye. She and her mother took turns changing in the cramped wet train toilet into their silk saris—Keshav Rao had laughed when she asked if they could check in to a hotel to freshen up, and when the train stopped they got down, as if emerging from a cave, blinking in the harsh sunlight.

Keshav Rao had come to meet them at the station. He bent down and touched her father's feet, and that was all. He looked sober, his suggestive eyes stilled, his mouth in repose. Perhaps it was also the way he was dressed—in a white shirt and dhoti. The dark column of his throat and his face emerged from the depths of his white collar, and she thought he had never looked so attractive as he did then.

An autorickshaw was waiting for them outside the station, a large ten-seater, one of the two available in the place. We have it all to ourselves, Keshav Rao said in a satisfied way, we will not share it with anyone. It will be our private taxi. He seemed proud of the garish contraption, painted in all the colours of the palette.

The land was flat—flat, hot and rocky. On either side of the road there were hunkering red outcrops of rock, striated with darker bands of red like gashes in their sides. At one point the overhang of the rocks was so low and the passage between them so narrow that they felt they were being ejected from an angry womb onto the narrow grey road. The soil was sandy, a mass of little pebbles, as if it were the residue of the rocks eroded after years of hard work. The only vegetation they could see was thorny bushes, their branches spreading wild like tentacles, what they called the Bellary Jali back home, and a spiky grass with roots like webbed feet, clinging to the ground. This was a place for survivors—tough species who could make do with little and whose vitals had to be wrenched out of the earth.

They turned off the main road on to a path between the fields, rutted with stones. The auto jostled wildly and her mother signalled to her to hold on to their basket of offerings.

The crop stood green in the fields, speckled with tiny pearls of grain, months away from harvest. The soil, turned over in the fields, was black and clayey. The fields seemed to stretch forever, unencumbered, right up to the red craggy hills in the distance, soaking in every bit of the sun.

The road turned into a small cluster of houses. The auto spluttered to a stop and then they heard the silence, the silence of a day dried to a crisp, unrelieved by the breeze, punctuated by a stray bark from a dog in the distance. The house was small and set deep in the compound. It was flat-roofed and rectangular, with small windows, and running all along the front was a covered porch supported by pillars.

They made their way to the front door, looking to see if there was anyone waiting at the doorway, but Keshav Rao headed them off to the side. Before they went in, before they greeted anybody, they were to wash their feet, which they did by the washing stone, with water stored in a tin pail, scooping it out with an old can. A dry crust of moss adhered to the ground next to the washing stone.

They sat inside a large room, flagged with slabs of black weathered stone, filled with the hushed light of the morning sun. The light played tricks on their eyes and cast shadows in parts of the room, making it seem full of people.

Keshav Rao's mother looked much like him, tall, with a plump face and a knobby nose, calm-eyed and still of bearing. His father, smaller of build, was similarly composed. Her father's Mysore peta shone like the moon in the dark room—it now looked a little excessive and did not quite go with his trousers and spare coat. Keshav Rao's father, dressed in a dhoti and kurta, and a silk roomal wrapped causally round his head looked at ease, a man comfortable in his skin. Can I have a tray, her mother asked, breaking the silence, using the English word 'tray'.

There was a low-voiced consultation between Keshav Rao and a young woman, who she presumed was his sister Vinutha—Keshav Rao's mother had not made a move nor involved herself in the conversation—and a little girl was dispatched. She returned from the kitchen bearing a large, heavy brass plate. Her mother fussed with the packages. They were crushed from the train journey and the fruits had begun to smell.

Her mother-in-law-to-be turned to her and said something. She, in turn, looked pleadingly at Keshav Rao—she could not follow the northern dialect, nor the broad accent.

My mother says, will you sing for us, Keshav Rao said.

She had not prepared for this. She looked round the room, hoping for reprieve—the men's feet came into view at once for only they were given chairs to sit on. Her father's toenails, tough and yellowing, heels seamed with cracks, Suchi mama's feet tucked right behind, Keshav Rao's father's, uniformly brown with clean pink soles and Keshav Rao's, long, strong and sinewy, the feet of a master, a thing of beauty. Down on the straw mat where the women sat, her mother said nothing, made no sign to her—her face looked lustreless, as if she had given up long back.

She cleared her throat, ready to get it done with. Keshav Rao's sister came back with the shruti box and set the scale. The scale was set too high—she realised it as soon as she started singing. She had set off on an invocation to Lord Ganesha in Hamsadhwani that played among the higher notes. Her voice rose to a shriek, and an alien note, not meant to be in the raga at all, crept in the lower octaves. She finished in a hurry and the hall remained silent.

Next, it was Keshav Rao's sister's turn. She sang in a high sweet voice, a bhajan extolling the virtues of the Devi. She closed her eyes and was lost in her own song. She sang of the beauty of the goddess, her clear brow, her fish-shaped eyes, her eyebrows like scimitars, and her gaze—gentle, somnolent and all-seeing. She sang of the fruits and flowers the goddess held in her many hands, the jewels that adorned her breasts and hair and the fragrance of her presence. She sang of the many virtues of the goddess—she who granted the bliss of knowledge and removed ignorance, she who provided for all creatures, the ocean of compassion who drew all her children to her bosom, she who dispelled darkness and fear, she who rode on the waves of the ocean, the sun, the moon and the fire, the Devi who destroyed evil and upheld righteousness.

When she finished there was silence—a silence of reverence, of overflowing hearts. Her father folded his hands in gratitude. You have invoked the Devi herself, he said, you made her stand here in front of us.

They moved to the dining space and sat on the floor, which was cool and pleasantly rough against the skin, surrounded by a constellation of perfectly scrubbed brass vessels. The jowar rotis came hot off the griddle, still puffed up on their plates—granular, dry and fragrant. The fumes of the red chilli paste hit their sinuses before it was served; it lay in a small heap, coarsely ground, speckled with white seeds and glistening with oil—she was afraid to eat it. The small brinjals in the yengai were perfectly cooked and had a liberal helping of gravy. On a sideplate there were long green chillies, fried transparent and crystallised with salt.

Except for the buttermilk which they all drank in thirsty

gulps, much of the food went back untasted. We are rice eaters, her mother mumbled apologetically. No stomach for spice.

The family land holdings extended deep behind the road on which they had driven, Sadanand, who she gathered was Keshav Rao's uncle, said. They would have seen some of their millet fields on the way to the house. They were getting two crops a year, the new hybrid high-yielding variety was resistant to pests and mould. They had successfully controlled the sorghum midge and the stem borer. Sadanand had graduated from the Agricultural College and supervised the fields himself. She hoped that her father would not come out with his standard reply of how the land reforms under the land to the tiller scheme in the 1970s had evicted his family from much of their land—prime paddy growing land—and what was left was being decimated bit by bit to pay for his son's education and his daughter's marriage.

A visit to the temple and the rock cut caves nearby was proposed. The women would go to the temple, and after that the youngsters could continue to the caves.

They went out of the house, into the compound; the whitewashed walls deflected the sunlight with the zeal of an army repelling an attack. The grass on the ground looked scorched. All round them were the millet fields, parched in the sun. A bus stopped on the road a little way off, and started reversing, readying itself for the return trip. The driver got off and came running up to their wall and poured himself a drink from the large pitcher on the platform outside the house. There was a jug of water, a pitcher of buttermilk and lumps of jaggery on a stainless steel plate arranged on the platform outside, like offerings at a shrine, for thirsty passersby.

These are good people, she told herself. They will do right by you. You will be happy here.

*

First, the temple visit. The women got into the autorickshaw. Red in the distance, the Kaladgi Hills beckoned. The shrine was at the base of the hills, set in an open courtyard. It was an unostentatious temple. There was just the main cell, small and plain, built of large blocks of stone, hewn no doubt from the rocks amidst which the temple stood. The spire, a rudimentary pyramid, rose in three steps, curving at the top, no frets along the base or sculptures in relief, a little bigger than the square of the cell, giving the whole structure a top-heavy look.

The eyes of the goddess gleamed silver from the depths of the dark sanctum. She was swathed in a red garment of rough cotton. In this avatar, she was the guarantor of womanly virtues, of health and progeny, the protector of children. Women worshipped her for she granted the wish closest to a woman's heart, Keshav Rao's mother said, the wish for a good husband and healthy children.

They made their offerings and stood before her with folded hands.

Savitri made a fervent prayer but her devotion was half-hearted. The heat had begun to affect her—she could feel the sweat on her face and the dampness spreading from her armpits. The stiff silk and the gold thread in her sari scratched against her waist every time she moved and the pleats were wrapping themselves against her ankles, threatening to trip her up.

She finished her perfunctory prayer, opened her eyes and turned to go but one of the women pulled her by the elbow, smiling. Not yet. There was another avatar of the goddess that she had to worship. There she was in a shallow cell, next to the main shrine, so innocuously positioned that she could be easily overlooked. The goddess of modesty, Lajja Gauri, etched in minute relief against the stone wall. A tall woman, she lay on her back, her legs drawn up to the sides of her belly, in the act of giving birth. Each part of her was clearly etched—her breasts, her rounded stomach, and the cleft from which the small head of her child would emerge. And since she was the goddess of modesty, she had been spared a face; there was, in place of her head, a lotus, in full bloom, each petal etched in stone. And she was bejewelled as a goddess should be, her necklace lying heavy between her breasts, arm bands with heads of serpents, anklets and bangles—thick, substantial, weighty. The tracery of her garments was delicate; in her hands she held lotus buds.

Savitri stood transfixed by the figurine, staring at the curve of her thighs and calves, the lines at the base of her stomach, so much so that she forgot to to bow her head and neglected the tray of flowers and vermilion and to take the blessing from the flame. She felt the first flutter of panic rise in her, a butterfly flexing its wings, making its way to her throat.

A group of women came in—a young girl, still in her bridal finery, with two older women—and they made way for the newcomers.

They started ascending the hill—up steep steps cut into the sides, and a wave of heat swamped them. The others seemed unaffected by it though. They bounded ahead, the men first—Keshav Rao and his young uncle Sadanand, who looked after the fields, and a cousin who lived with them and studied at the local college, followed by the women—the cousin's sister who was visiting, and Vinutha. They all were agog to see the caves—it was the first time the cousin and his sister were coming here. They climbed the massive steps with ease. She tucked her pallu in at the waist and hefted up her pleats, determined not to be found wanting.

Around them the hills rose, red and brown, striated with black right through. The town nestled in the valley between the houses were modest and painted uniformly white and built close to each other. Many had aluminium sheet roofs held down with large stones, in case a rough wind should carry them off. In the distance, when the haze cleared, was a thin wedge of green—the Malaprabha river.

Early in the morning, before the haze forms, you can see the river clearly, Vinutha said. The Malaprabha river was where the chaste Renuka, wife of the fiery rishi Jamadagni, was supposed to have bathed. So chaste was she that she made pots of the sand on the banks of the river to fetch water for her husband's rituals. One morning a group of handsome Gandharvas, heavenly beings known for their beauty, stopped by the river and Renuka raised her eyes from her pots and looked at one of the frolicking Gandharvas. After that, her pots no longer held water, condemning her in the eyes of her husband.

The cave temples were cut deep into the hill—an interjection into the craggy face, the flags of rock, layer upon layer, forming a continuous pattern.

... the ingenuity of our forefathers ... to sculpt such images ... cut the rock to build pillars and temples ...

rocks that you see here formed 2500 million years ago by sedimentation from shallow seas ...

They heard the voice before the speaker came into sight. It was a college group, led by their teacher, whose floppy hat obscured his face, except for his thick glasses.

Look at the small cells at the back of the cave ...

The group surged into the cave. She sat at the entrance, in the light. She would not go in. Even in the open air she could smell the bats. Lord Shiva at the entrance was magnificent enough. A little thick of limb, legs bent sideways at the knees, one of his many arms thrown right across his chest in a classic dance mudra—he was dancing the tandava, the dance of destruction, in his avatar as the Lord of Dance, Nataraja, even as his son Ganesha and his mount, the bull Nandi, watched in wonder. The ganas in the frieze, Shiva's attendants, comported themselves with glee. The coarse grains of the stone lent a rock-hard strength to Shiva's legs, and the angry red colour of the stone, if she had followed the good teacher correctly, came from the iron impurities in the stone.

The college group emerged from the cave. The teacher was now explaining the composition of the rocks. She caught the words gneiss, quartz and feldspar. The students shifted on their feet.

Watch out for the monkeys, one of the students said, as the group swept past her to the next level of the caves.

She must have climbed at least a hundred steps to reach the next level, she thought. The small of her back was soaked and her thighs wobbled. She yanked her pallu out of her waist and wiped her neck—she felt the sting of the gold thread cutting into her skin, and the welt beginning to form. She saw Vinutha first, making for the steps.

Water, she called out. Could I have some water?

Water? Vinutha sounded perplexed. It's just a little way down now. We'll go over the side and soon be home.

She fell back, feeling rebuked, like a child. To her left, in an alcove, sat Vishnu, looking relaxed, on the coils of a serpent, each scale etched clearly, one hand on his thigh, the leg folded in lotus pose, foot resting with its sole pointing upwards. His eyes were closed and he smiled companionably at her. It's very well for you, she said to him, you have a serpent's hood for an umbrella. She fanned herself with the pallu of her sari and her gaze turned upwards to the carved ceiling. Directly above her, on a bracket supporting the pillar against the ceiling, an amorous couple clasped each other. The young man, a god perhaps, was holding the woman up to his chest. She thought of Keshav Rao. When she was struggling to catch up with them on the steep steps, Keshav Rao had turned and given her his hand—a warm full-blooded clasp, throb against throb—and almost immediately had let go of her.

She felt a pang of sadness course through her. Would it always be like this ... would she always feel bereft of love ...

She heard a now familiar voice coming up, and fled, up the steps and over to the side where she had last seen a flash of Vinutha's green sari. Here, the steps had fallen and she steadied herself over the rubble, reaching out for the wall. She seemed to have entered another cave, a shallow dark cave, perhaps off the regular circuit of visitors for it had an abandoned feel to it. When her eyes got used to the dark interior she found herself staring at a large nude male. Instinctively, she averted her eyes.

They are saints, madam, a voice at her elbow said,

severely, as if chiding her for her unwonted prudishness. Virtuous men who lived as god made them. To them, the body means nothing ...

The whole cave, she saw, was full of nude male figures, row upon row, a chain pattern.

Look, see how the creepers are entwined round their legs, he commanded his flock, moving away from her. See how snakes worship at their feet, and even the gods. Look at their eyes, closed in perfect equanimity, look at the posture, the wide rounded shoulders, the strong trunk and the long arms, mark the upright stance with the body weight equally distributed on both feet—the perfect meditative posture, signifying the abandonment of the body. And yet the body is beautiful, bilaterally symmetrical—the two sides mirror each other in perfection, as saints often are depicted, to indicate that the life force flows with uniform rhythm and there is perfect control over body and mind. What you see is a specimen of physical beauty, but of one who is unaware of it, to whom it matters little. His life flow is in harmony with nature. The same life energy, free-flowing, liquid, with no obstructions flows through them all—man, animal and plant ...

Mark the iconic symbols of the saint—the exaggerated shoulders, the long hanging arms, the three-layered umbrella above the head and the sun behind.

The teacher nodded, smiling. So, what is the standard of measurement here, he quizzed.

The head, came the answer.

And twelve angulis make the human head ... An anguli being?

Three-fourths of an inch.

The teacher was overjoyed. The group moved further on, to exclaim at more specimens. She got up and stumbled down the path. One more step and her head would burst. A ledge, a tree, and the protection of a rock. She hunkered down next to it, out of sight of the path and felt about for the drawstring of her underskirt. How easy the teacher had made it sound, to abandon the body. Even the chaste Renuka had found it difficult. For a moment she wondered how she would fare on the sculptor's scale of perfection, how many angulis would her thigh measure against her head, considering that all limbs had to be proportionate to the head. She tugged the sodden knot of the drawstring free and breathed deep. Her hand moved over the mound of her stomach and her fingers curled over her hipbone, downwards.

She came to herself quickly and got up, straightening her clothes, wiping her hand on her underskirt. Down below she could see the autorickshaw waiting for them. She spotted Vinutha's green sari on the steps, almost at the exit. The town was covered with a white haze—she could only see the tips of other hills. Above her, the sky was a bleached blue, without a cloud. There was not a bird flying in it.

*

They caught the train back in the evening. The four of them travelled back to the station by themselves in the ten-seater autorickshaw. She was relieved that they said their goodbyes at the door. Keshav Rao said he would come to the station, but her father said it was all right, they would manage. His brother Suchi was there.

When they settled down in their compartment, her

father got up and went out. When he came back, he was bareheaded, his Mysore peta collapsed into a length of cloth once again. He had changed out of his suit into a dhoti. She and her mother continued to be resplendent in their silk saris, which were now quite crushed. Before leaving, her mother-in-law-to-be had slipped a gold chain round her neck. She had bent down and touched her feet.

It was now her mother's turn to look out of the discoloured glass window pane, into the speeding dark landscape. Her father looked relaxed, now that the chore was over. Suchi mama spread out his bedding and took himself off to the top berth, saying he did not want anything to eat. She waited for her father to nod off and then crawled into her mother's seat, laying her head on her lap. I cannot live here, in this place, she said.

Her mother stroked her hair back from her forehead as she used to do when Savitri was a child. You don't have to, she said. We've told them that already. You will stay with us, both of you. Keshav Rao agreed at once. Your father is not getting any younger, and neither is Suchi. We need a young man about the house—

A young man to replace the son who had deserted them, Savitri thought, for her mother had choked off, mid-sentence.

Two

For his final semester, he decided to move into an apartment. It was less expensive than staying in the residency hall. The last bit of information, casually thrown in his father's letter, was not lost on him. Money from home would not be coming forth any more. It was needed for his sister's wedding. He brooded. He debated whether to make a point of it, and then decided against it. He did not want to write home or even speak to his father. But he knew what he was entitled to.

There was Sushil Khanna's apartment. Sushil Khanna himself no longer lived there, but the others, Manoj Saini and Pratap Reddy and the latest contingent of Indians whom he had not yet met, were there, and there would be room for him for a few months. But he moved instead into the spare room in Amy's apartment—a small cupboard-like place, where the bed folded up against the wall in the morning, and a table and chair appeared in its place, free of the clutter of the rest of the small apartment.

Amy travelled a lot with the dance repertory, and kept odd training hours. In return for his lodging, he had to walk her cat and take out the garbage. Her kitchen was open to him but he would not cook. He drew the line at that. He did not mind washing up though and kept the kitchen sink clean—there was always a small pile of dishes drying on the drainboard next to the sink. When she was in town, they went out together, slipping into an easy companionship. When Steve was there, which was rare, he became the lodger and went out by himself. He grew quite fond of Mr Tibs, the cat, who turned out to be female, and who, quite surprisingly, allowed herself to be walked on a leash when he took her out. Pottering round the empty apartment, he spoke aloud to the cat, who would listen enquiringly for a while, her dark eyes unblinking, and then turn over and go to sleep.

He sent out applications far and wide. He followed up every tip from Bill Moreland's office.

Ash—Marcia would roll her eyes and say softly, as if she had a secret just for him—take a look at this week's Job Bulletin, Santa may have something for you this week. He was keeping his options open. He was ready to go anywhere—a manufacturer of heating and cooling systems (heating and cooling were big business here), electrical and power equipment—he was ready to innovate with their R&D team, go beyond their second generation equipment, push the barriers of technology, density and speed, as he told the placement representative. The offers sounded ideally suited to him—they offered a competitive salary, a comprehensive benefits package that covered medical and dental insurance, a credit union and an educational assistance programme. Also, an equal opportunity, affirmative action employer, which encouraged women, members of minority groups and the differently abled to apply. Retail banking, insurance, the media, the farming industry, entertainment—he was still trying to crack Johnny Carson though—he was open to all. Even the CIA was recruiting; he had the 20/20 bilateral vision without glasses, and no history of sinusitis or hay fever since his twelfth birthday, so he could apply for jobs in the Air Force ROTC and join the US Air Force. His not being a citizen would come in the way of that but that would soon be remedied, it was just a matter of time; he had already applied to be a permanent resident alien. He could join IBM or Coca Cola—two companies that had been shunted out of his home country unceremoniously.

He imagined a conversation with Manohar or Prakash—

Yes, Rockwell International the defence contractors, have made me an offer ... the largest I believe ... yes, R&D ...

Bill Moreland's office, together with the Career Services and Placement office, sent out a notice that the job market was tight. The early 1980s had seen a continuous downturn. Things were supposed to get better that year, from 1983 onwards, but they were yet to see signs of it. Last year, they had had a 75 per cent rate of placement success, but the job situation had not been so rough. According to 'accredited sources' the unemployment rate was at a record five-year high. There were a reported 100,000 people looking for work, not counting the several thousands who had given up looking for work. The state had rolled out a public works programme but the unions were unhappy with the 'trickle down' approach—we cannot wait to be trickled down upon, they said. The state was trying to get over its squeamishness and was considering legal gambling—lottery or parimutuel betting, as a way to create jobs. The university declared itself 'financially strapped'. Funding from the state and federal sources was growing uncertain. The Board of Regents had not been able to get the boost to the Vitality Fund from the state legislature, for faculty and staff salaries.

We are doing our darndest to help find students jobs, but we are the placement office, not a recruitment agency, Bill Moreland said.

Sushil Khanna offered him a job at his uncle's factory. They had been getting notices from the Environment Protection Agency. Production was falling. They needed a report to be written immediately; after that they'd see where he could fit in, they'd look for something in quality control maybe. His uncle would file the petition for a non-immigration worker or the Form I–129 required for his change of status. They also had a good immigration lawyer on hand to handle whatever was necessary.

So far, that was the only job offer he had received, a job offer that came even before the interview. He ground his teeth, and accepted Sushil Khanna's offer.

When he left, Amy was away. He fed the cat, wiped down the kitchen sink and watered the plants. Then he went down to the ground floor to hand over the key to the concierge. From the street, he looked up at the shabby apartment block, at the window where Mr Tibs was sitting, nose pressed against the glass, and felt a pang of regret, which he had not felt at vacating his room in his residency hall, a sense of leaving home, of things left undone, of heading into the unkown. When Sushil Khanna's blue Chevy drove up, he got in with a heavy heart.

*

It was unusually warm for end November. They had had no snow as yet that year. They left on a wet morning—it was the sixth continuous day of rain. They drove past sodden fields abandoned by rake and hoe, past harvested stumps of corn huddled from the rain, and bare black trees that reached their arms up to the heavens, as if in a mute prayer. Through the foggy window, the tossed browns and yellows of the landscape stood out in in thick slick Impressionist strokes. The notice on the side of the road read, Please do not pick up hitchhikers.

They drove eastwards, across the heart of the Midwest, through three states that followed the southern curve of

Lake Michigan. They should have done the 350 miles in about five hours but Sushil Khanna, who was driving, took the longer route to avoid the tolls. The landscape was now changing. Straddling the brown fields and the ochre woods there stood transmission towers, like giant scarecrows guarding an empty field. An industrial shed flashed by, sending a thick twist of white smoke into the sky, and treatment tanks lay on the ground like fat white chips. At one point, for a length of time, they rode shoulder to shoulder with a train that followed them into a town, the tracks intersecting the road, with houses lined up on either side.

That's the South Shore line, headed for Chicago, Sushil Khanna said. This place is quaint isn't it? Michigan City, we are in Indiana now.

From time to time there was an interruption of tract housing, a strip mall, a colony of billboards and a parking lot. They stopped briefly on the outskirts of town in Gary, at what looked like a scrapyard attached to an industrial plant.

This will only take a minute, Sushil Khanna said. When he came back, he looked very pleased with himself. Steel America. We supply to them. His voice was hushed, as if he could not believe it himself.

It was dark when they drove into the small township off the main road, and stopped at an apartment block in a cluster of modest buildings. Ashwath had expected something bigger, at least an independent house. Mr Khanna's 'industry' it turned out was a smallscale foundry producing industrial and agricultural castings.

Once he entered the apartment, he understood why he

had given Sushil Khanna and his family the larger than life dimensions. It was because of the way Sushil Khanna spoke about his uncle and aunt, as if their place was the hub of the world where every excess flow could be directed. The small flat was crowded with furniture and with people. It was a duplex on the ground floor of the building, with a basement. Sushil Khanna's aunt was in the kitchen, which they could see beyond the small stuffed room, stirring something on the fire and talking loudly to someone who was beyond their line of vision. There was a distinct smell of aniseed and mustard oil in the air. Two men were attending to a light fixture, step ladder in place, their box of tools open on the floor and a third was sitting at the dining table copying figures from a file.

Mr Khanna came home late and made straight for a room on the first floor of the duplex. He was dressed in a suit and tie, but his foreshortened arms and pugilistic stance made him seem a rough and ready man, the kind who would roll up his sleeves in a trice and get down to the shop floor. Sushil Khanna introduced him. Mr Khanna gave him a wan smile, patted him on his arm and said the foundry manager had everything set. Then he poured himself a large drink from a decanter on the sideboard, sat down heavily on the upholstered sofa, and started switching channels on the wall to wall TV. It was a signal for the two of them to leave the room. That, Ashwath surmised, was his interview, and it was over.

He had a bed in the basement, along with the others, recently come from Mr Khanna's ancestral village in Punjab who would work in the plastics factory that Sushil Khanna's brother owned in the next town. In the morning, Mrs

Khanna made them thick chapatis stuffed with potato, and served them with curd and pickle—it was not so much that he didn't like the chapatis and curd as that he was unused to it. This seemed to be the arrangement. There was no talk of his moving out or finding his own place. Sushil Khanna sounded impatient when he asked. Later, later, he said. The report first.

Mrs Khanna—Auntyji—had a tight knot of a face with eyes like jamun fruit, and her hands moved restlessly in her lap when she wasn't working. She said little to the men she housed in her basement and fed every morning. She wore what his sister used to call Punjabi dress and spoke only Punjabi. The only time she came alive was when Nimmiji, Sushil Khanna's brother's wife dropped in, and they drove a hundred miles to visit a temple. Sunoh—he thought that was her name, for every morning Mr Khanna would stand at the top of the stairs and call it out in an intimate growl, till he discovered it was the equivalent of D'you hear. A mere clearing of the throat—that was the sum total of their conversation. Mr Khanna, it turned out, had a heart for the foundry business. He was a metallurgist from Banaras Hindu University and was reputed to be a master metal caster. He had bought the foundry off the previous owners who had closed it down after an explosion in the casting furnace had let fly molten metal and caused a fire. (This was a sore point with his wife, that he had benefitted from someone else's distress, and it was the substance of her prayers, her prayaschitta or repentance at the temple. He had called it a 'business opportunity' and decided to strike when the iron was hot.) Mr Khanna had called his new foundry Butterfly, after the butterfly valve, a device that combined simplicity of operation and aesthetics of design. He had taken the business on a high-flying arc. He had subcontracted other casting materials to other foundries and eventually acquired two of them, as well as a metal shredding unit. He had ticked all the boxes, added a machining unit and a pattern shop, painting and heat treating units; holding up the castings end against fabrication had brought him several new customers. Along the way, he was joined by Jose Hernandez, the plant manager, a man after Mr Khanna's own heart, a man with large hands and a lugubrious moustache who said little but came to life on the shop floor.

For ten years, the arrow of the graph had pointed steadily upwards, and after plateauing over the last few years, it had started dipping at vertiginal speed. Their customer orders were falling off. Their foundry returns—the overflow of metal and the scrap—were high as was the reject rate. As Mr Hernandez had said to him, the very few words that he had allowed to escape—We have to vamp up. He could only agree with Mr Hernandez. If they had to retain their customers, a 'vamp up' was sorely needed. Ashwath had had a faint premonition of what he would find when they had stopped briefly at the steel plant yard on the way and Sushil Khanna had been flushed with pride that he was a supplier for a supplier to Steel America. The sense of dereliction in the large yard was unmistakable. The first thing he had noticed were the burnt pools of water with rainbow slick and the faintly sulphurous smell that hung in the air. No smoke came from the chimneys of the central shed and pieces of machinery and trucks stood askew in the yard as if the drivers had stopped suddenly and fled from a calamity.

A row of tank cars, of open pouring vats, stood on a section of railroad next to a large heap of scrap shavings. A fork lift stood poised in the sky—few objects looked as desolate as a metal hook dangling high in the sky with nothing to lift. The rust, one could sense, had begun to set in. And yet Sushil Khanna had emerged from the small shed at the side of the yard looking pleased with himself. The Khannas, perhaps, were yet to see the writing on the wall.

His mornings were spent studying the compliance and enforcement reports filed or neglected by Butterfly, and the notices they had started receiving from the EPA. But first, he had to unravel the snarled ball of acronyms. There was the TRI—the Toxic Releases Inventory, the GGRT—green house gas emissions and the EIS—air emissions inventory The SIC data report—he struggled to get at the most obvious Standard Industrial Code—did not seem to be encouraging. The air emissions seemed excessive; he looked at their surface water discharges, releases to land, underground injection and transfer to offsite locations, and pored over the figures and reports. The facility had not released any chemicals into streams or bodies of water, or transferred chemicals to any offsite locations other than publicly owned treatment works. That was all on record. There was no way of telling what had happened off the record.

A few months ago Mr Khanna had received a report from a newly created EPA monitoring wing for tracking toxic chemicals. The Butterfly Foundry was high on their list of industrial pollutants. The plastics factory, owned by Sushil Khanna's brother, was also culpable. This was all the more urgent as there were schools in the area and the air samples showed high levels of manganese and nickel, and one of the emissions, a toxic chemical, diisocyanates, was traced to the smokestacks of Butterfly. According to the computer simulation, the region around Butterfly was a toxic hotspot. The levels of carcinogens indicated by the reading posed a health risk in the long run. The funds required to modernise the plant, which would lapse into the state that Mr Khanna had found it if not 'vamped up', were huge.

Mr Khanna's office room had large windows commanding a view of the entire plant. The setting was picturesque enough—the low long sheds had a pleasant peach cladding and the modest-sized industrial tanks gleaming white at the back, all set amidst pathways in the greenery. In summer, Mr Khanna's office would sit amidst a purple efflorescence, though the trees were bare and bedraggled now. The plant looked blameless in the morning quiet; nothing it did, it would appear, could connect it with carcinogens.

Mr Khanna sat at a table on which samples of brass and steel castings glittered like jewels on display.

What do they mean we pollute the environment? Mr Khanna demanded of him, as if he were responsible for the reports on the table. How can we make omelettes without cracking eggs?

Do you see that—he pointed to the wall behind him, at the two framed photographs, the only ornamentation on the wall. One was the picture of a circular brass casting—the eponymous butterfly valve, and the other a crude iron pot, exemplifying the potbelly, standing on four legs with two ears and a thick handle attached to the ears with prominently curving hooks. It looked like a fat woman standing with her hands on her hips—there had been several versions of it at home, to cook, or lift water out of the cement tank.

That, Mr Khanna said, pointing to the metal disc, is the butterfly valve, my first, after which I named this foundry. And that—he pointed to the photo of the pot, is the Sagus Pot, the first ever pot to be cast in this country.

Ten years ago, there was nothing here, this was a shamshan, a burning ghat ... the debris was still smouldering. I built it up with my sweat and blood. Twenty years in this bloody country, I rescue it, and now I'm to be treated like a bloody criminal ...

Mr Khanna, Uncleji, you have to have a talk with your lawyer if you want to save Butterfly.

He wanted to leave immediately. His six-month window for the project was not yet up. Not that he had been asked to go. He knew that he could stay as long as he liked or his legal status would allow him, in Auntyji's basement, assured of a meal of thick chapatis and pickle and the comfort of a kind of home, but his work here was done. He could see no future here, for himself or for Butterfly.

The thought of going back home, back to India, filled him with dread. But he would have to, soon, unless he found a job. And there wasn't a single lead from the placement office, or from the various advertisements he had answered, or the cold calls he had made.

Standing in Mrs Khanna's living room, which bustled like a railway platform, there was only one thing he could do, only one person he could reach out to, with whom he had had a sort of home.

He rang up Amy.

Ash, oh Ash, come right back. I'm missing you. Steve, oh well—he's not there, but that's not new is it ... Mr Tibs is gone too—she just ran off. Please, come home.

He took the bus back. Back to the university town to which he thought he had bid goodbye. He made his way past familiar streets, past the residency hall where he had lived for two years, past the downtown shops and upmarket homes with sprawling gardens, past the old stone cottage which housed the used books shop, where the proprietor never got up from his beaten leather couch, into the narrow street and the still shabby apartment where Amy lived. He took the stairs two at a time, noting that they no longer smelled of cat pee.

Amy was at the open door; she seemed plumper than he remembered, her face looked a little puffy, her nose wider and her eyes red-rimmed, as if she had been crying. Instinctively they reached out for each other. He moved his face up, for she was taller, always, and sought her mouth and felt his whole self dissolve into her at that moment.

She led him to her room, to her crumpled bed and they sat on the edge. He stroked her hair, all along its length—it felt coarse to his touch, the plumes of his exotic bird. He heard her catch her breath, a small stifled sound, and her face came to rest on his shoulder. He ran his hands on her face, across the open pores on her spongy cheeks, the ridged edges of her soft lips, and tasted the salt at the corners of her mouth.

Her limbs were a luminous blue in the ghostly darkness. He could see her belly, plump, rounded, like a Sagus pot and below, the curled cowrie shell of her sex.

He hesitated. It's okay, she said. I'm in my second trimester now.

How was she to know that the hesitation had been on his own account.

Her spine curved long, in vertebral correctness, like notches on a musical instrument; her skin was soft and supple. Her hair lay heavy at the nape of her neck; it smelt of spring flowers and sweat. He lingered, feeling the stirring in his loins. Her cool hands on his back were impatient, guiding him, her fingers stopping momentarily on his sacred thread before she moved it aside and drew him into herself.

Three

He might well have to leave. Not just this house and this town but this country. The writing was on the wall. He did not want to face the thought but Amy had been quite open.

She made no bones about it. As he lingered in her apartment after returning from Sushil Khanna's uncle's ill-fated project, his three weeks turning to six weeks and then eight, she told him he should think of going back home. Their brief intimacy, begun on a note of needy despair in Amy's crumpled bed, had petered out. Like tired travellers arriving together at a water hole, they had drunk their fill; the afterglow had produced a familiarity, a thing akin to love. Soon they became just housemates. She fretted to hear from Steve, and he from Marcia at Bill Moreland's office at the university. Marcia dangled a plum at him—a job offer in the productions and materials management department of a food processing company—but the offer was still to be firmed up. It was a matter of placement, Marcia said. They were deciding on whether to place him at their corporate office in Chicago, or their factory in a town close by.

Meanwhile, he did chores round the house, all the heavy lifting and carrying, and applied for more jobs in the dwindling market. In the evenings he walked Amy back from her rehearsals with a theatre group from Chicago which was conducting a workshop as part of a course in the university. On their walk back home, Amy was unusually silent and she would lock herself in her room as soon as they returned. He sensed that her collaboration with the group was not going well. She had also grown larger and her discomfort was becoming more obvious. Steve's silence on the question of their future was bothering her, though her mother had asked her to come home for the baby.

One evening, when he dropped in to pick Amy up after rehearsals, there was a crowd of people round Terry, the director of the group, and Alan, another member of the group motioned to him to come over. Terry said that they had decided to abandon the play they had on hand. Instead, he had picked up a play written by a Jewish writer from Massachussetts, Israel Horovitz, and it was called *The Indian Wants the Bronx*. This play had an Indian, an East Indian in it, just like you, he said, and Indian words.

Can you read out the Indian words, Terry asked. We want to hear them the way they are pronounced.

The language is Hindi, Ashwath said. I'm not very familiar with it but I'll do my best.

The play was about an elderly Indian man, Mr Gupta, who had just arrived in New York and got lost and was trying to get home to his son in the Bronx. Mr Gupta, who knew not a word of English and could not understand it either, was waiting at a bus stop for someone to help him when he was set upon by two white youths, delinquents who picked on him first and then grew progressively violent, working their personal frustrations out on him. He was an easy target for he could not make conversation with them, repeating in Hindi that he could not understand them.

The lines Ashwath had to read out were easy enough. He read them out slowly, and Terry repeated after him. Terry was to play Mr Gupta.

It doesn't make sense to stage this play, Amy said. It's been done in New York with a famous cast—Al Pacino and John Cazale.

It can be staged again with Terry Antinori and Alan Moffat in it, Ashwath said, earning himself a small smile of gratitude from Alan, who had already started grooming a young student for the part of the second tough.

Ash, when you read out in Indian, I am new to your city, I just came yesterday, I feel it could be you speaking, that it could be a play about you, Amy said.

True, when he read out 'Main tumhari bhasha nahin samajhta, Main tumhare shahar mein naya hoon', despite the dislocation he felt with Terry repeating the lines in his accented Hindi, it had given him pause. Of course, he was at a distant remove from Mr Gupta. But, he had also seen that the two American boys had a past, a history, a trajectory just like Mr Gupta, which had made them turn on him, on his passivity, the helpless tumbled down heap—an elephant as the boys called him.

And then Amy had said—I think you should go back home. It's best for you. Now, Ash, before it is too late.

Would you Amy, he asked, would you go back?

For me Ash, whatever I do, there is only going forward, she replied. Kind Amy, always so tactful.

At that juncture, with oiled-wheels American smoothness, casually, as if by sleight of hand, things fell into place in a matter of days.

Steve drove up in a pick-up truck, Amy packed in a trice, and they were gone. Steve had finally popped the question and had hewn the ring himself in his sculptor's studio. No Tiffany's diamond for Amy, but she looked happy enough with the awkward bit of metal on her ring finger. They were going on to Esalen, to spend some time with a visiting artist who was also a Gestalt therapist. Just before leaving, Amy held his face, and with something like regret, said, Goodbye, and he knew right then that that would be the last time they would see each other. Much later, much much later, when he thought of Amy, of the brief moment of their parting, with the snow piled on the bare steps of her apartment block and hanging heavy from the branches of the leafless sugar maple, and Amy, large, red-nosed and teary-eyed, stamping her feet against the cold while an impatient Steve waited at the wheel, he wondered if he had let things drift too far, if he should have seized the day, done the white knight thing and rescued her from her shabby apartment and from shifty Steve, when there was still time.

But right then, Ashwath was in a hurry to bid her goodbye. He had in his pocket the letter from Golden directing him to report immediately to their corporate office. He was to move into the apartment that Terry shared with Alan. They had a spare third room which would cost him 300 dollars a month, with extra charges for parking, when he got himself a car. He did a quick calculation. He was starting work the very next week, Terry's offer was fair—in fact it was a generous offer; for 300 dollars he would get to live in the near North, and drive to work in well under thirty minutes. And Ash, Terry had said, I hope you have no pets. I already have Buddy, and Alan has a cat, Jacintha. The building has a rule about two pets per apartment.

He had driven in one morning into Chicago, city of his destiny, into a welter of railroad tracks and the rumble of the L, and tall magisterial buildings standing across a quiet green river that flowed placidly amidst them. There was a certain gravitas to the city, and also the suggestion of a powder keg. Anything was possible here, he felt, in a city that had changed the course of a river and made it flow backwards, uphill.

IV

One

When she first holds it in her hand, she is unsuspecting. Then she drops it as if it is red hot and picks it off the floor, reluctant to open it. The sight of the familiar handwriting with its misleading curlicues and whorls fills her with dread. And hope. Dread that it will make true her fears, and hope that it will too.

Her brother has written to her saying that he is coming home. Finally, after twenty-five years—she thinks of a pie with a quarter neatly cut out—twenty-five years, a quarter of a circle, a quarter of a hundred years. His letter, unexpectedly, is in Kannada, not English, and the phrase he has used is literary, exaggerated, larger than life, the writer imagining his life in the third person. It has the ring of the prodigal son—I am returning to the earth of my home.

Your brother has outdone Sri Rama himself. *His* exile lasted just fourteen years, her husband said, in the rare show of the wit that had attracted her to him first, so many years ago. But now it was the spark of a dying ember, for what she could see was the flash of a gold tooth—that her father had paid for—in a mouth brown from tobacco and drink.

Keshav Rao now stayed mostly in his 'den', an annexe, more a small shed-like structure next to the main house, with a pathway to the gate and an independent entrance and exit. He entertained his friends there—his drinking buddies, and conducted his real estate and share broking 'business' that he had taken up after his premature retirement from the bank, or expulsion, if Manohar, Suchi mama's nephew, who once gave her a complicated explanation, was to be believed. Sometimes she heard her husband roaring in there, like a lion with a splinter in its paw, and she knew that he had not given up practising his music altogether. It was from this shed, home of his shenanigans, that he had negotiated his absences, in the beginning for a few days—travelling on business or going home, he said—and then longer, at one point for months without a word to her of where he was going, a disappearance more than an absence, and there had been official-looking men at the front door, looking for him. She had coughed up the money then, on Suchi mama's advice, for her father was gone. So was her mother—no more homely counsel whispered into her ear, no more tangential pieces of advice which seemed to add up unexpectedly. There was a day when she was so troubled that she had thought of ending it all at the bottom of the garden—Woman, 36, jumps into own well with children—boy, 10 and girl, 6. But something surreal had happened. She had been rescued by a peacock. Woman, 36, contemplates jumping into well—saved by magical peacock.

*

The first few months of her marriage, she had been in a state of bliss; she had understood what it meant for her feet not to touch the ground at all. Those were scented evenings, a whirl of music concerts, where they were led to the front seats for he knew everyone, and she wore silks and jasmine and he sat next to her, so close that she could inhale his tobacco-scented fragrance. As they walked back home, he would sing to her, or recite poetry extolling her beauty—of her eyes like startled deer, her feet like clustered blooms and her waist as slim and smooth as the pliant bamboo.

On one of those nights, with his arms still around her, he had suggested that they have a little portion of the house to themselves, for 'privacy'—he used the English word, as if to suggest a foreign concept. I don't like to sneak into the house at night, like a thief, he said. She kept quiet, saying nothing to her father about it, thinking it was a passing thought. And then the inevitable had happened—the first of many scenes, the beginning of the unravelling. He had come late, unsteady on his feet, his eyes bloodshot, reeking of what smelt like paint thinner, and thrashed about the hall, waking her parents up.

Son-in-law, her father said, before he could check himself, we do not have such habits in this house.

In this house? Did you say this house? He had towered over her father, rocking on his heels. Then it's simple. We will have another house.

She had hoped then that they would move into their own house, even if it was a single room. She was prepared for a scene, even a showdown with her father, half hoping that her husband would storm out dragging her behind him. She would have gone anywhere with him then. For she had been weakened by her attraction for this bull of a man—none of the Mysooru Mallige delicacy and restraint about him, he had always been vigorous of appetite and direct of approach.

But he had wanted a portion of that house, her parents'

home. And her father had tacked on the annexe—a large shed and a verandah, with a roof of Mangalore tiles. She and Keshav Rao had moved into the shed. In that shed, after she had shifted, she realised she was pregnant. She was filled with joy then, despite the uncertainty and the unpleasantness; despite herself, a sweetness had entered intravenously and she found the gloom lifting, her step growing lighter. Her mother had made her come right back to the main house, so that she could take care of her, and Keshav Rao had chosen to remain in the shed.

One evening, a little after Keshav Rao's 'feeling out of sorts' as her mother put it, they were wiping the lamps to be set out on the parapet wall of the terrace for her first Diwali as a sumangali, as one who had entered the auspicious state of marriage, when her mother said, You know, when you were born, your father wanted to name you Sita, but I said no, Sita is an unlucky name for a girl. Savitri—now, there was a woman who outwitted the God of Death himself to save her husband. Savitri was her husband's saviour, a woman in command—Remember that.

That was all her mother said, nothing more. It was a hint to her, and a warning; a piece of advice and a reminder of her obligations, the obligations of a lifetime.

*

Where is the son of the house, Keshav Rao would declaim, aloud and ostensibly to himself, in the shed. I ask you, pitashri, where is the son of the house?

On Sunday mornings, a strange camaraderie would prevail in the house as they watched the *Mahabharata* on television. Her husband and her parents watched in worshipful awe, and she, between feeding her baby daughter and bathing her, caught snatches of it. That was the one time she knew her son would stay out of mischief, for he would sit on his father's knee and watch the TV screen, as long as his father sat still. The men, the epic characters in golden coronets and chunky breastplates reminded her of her husband, especially the character of Duryodhana, who epitomised the appeal of the bad man. The women, she found hysterical and shrill. Draupadi wept with her long hair all over her face. She caused in Savitri an inexplicable restlessness. Savitri timed her daughter's bath and feeds for whenever Draupadi appeared on screen.

She watched her parents watching the screen with unblinking attention—they did not stir even during the advertisements. And this, considering they barely knew Hindi, the language of the serial. But they knew the epic and the declamatory style of the actors was self-explanatory. Her mother had bought herself a *Learn Hindi in 26 Days* and applied herself to it every morning. After the show, her father withdrew into a ruminant silence, to be broken only when his brother appeared later in the morning. They discussed the morning's episode tremulously, feeling the tragedy of the tale, as if it were real, hesitant that if they exceeded the precious limits they had set themselves, it may overflow into their own lives, as if naming a thing may set it free and make it come true.

One Sunday morning, as Yudhishtira was getting embroiled in the fatal game of dice, top work Kaveramma arrived, with her son Prakash. Savitri spotted them from the terrace, so she had time to go downstairs and forewarn her parents, and also to switch off the television. But her parents were all in a daze, still staring at the disappearing point of light on the dark screen when their visitors came in.

I come home and everybody is lost in this show, Prakash said in a loud voice, ringing withAmerican confidence. Top work Kaveramma watched her son adoringly. The only show he watched like this back there, he announced, was something called *The Price is Right*, where people had to guess the price of things, household goods you could stock your whole house with if your luck was good. He had got tickets once, to be part of the audience some years back. It was in its sixteenth season now and he never missed it if he could help it.

Kaveramma spread herself out on the sofa, glittering in gold and silk. Prakash sat next to her, barrel-chested, hair gelled back from his smooth forehead, his hands with their thick knuckled fingers resting on his knees, a diamond glinting off his ring finger to show that he was taken. They looked handsome—the prince, heir to the throne, and his mother regent. This, Kaveramma was telling her, as clear as if she spoke it out loud, could have been hers, instead of that sad creature there, yawning in his crumpled dhoti-kurta.

Kaveramma would not come into the kitchen for an exchange of confidences, a between-the-women moment. She would do nothing to evoke a memory, even a whisker, of her association with this house—so the kitchen was out of bounds. She left her empty cup right on the table in front of her, not volunteering to take it into the kitchen.

This place looks quite run down since I was last here—that was to invite you for Prakash's wedding—her eyes flicked round the room and on to the unkempt garden beyond.

Prakash had married the only daughter of a land owner from Mandya—they had rice and sugarcane fields and had sought Prakash out, Kaveramma had told them. No one from the house had gone for Prakash's wedding.

She saw Prakash looking over the room with a cold speculative eye. She watched his eye wander over the high ceiling with its perfect knife-edge moulding, marred by large spreading splotches of damp, turning green—they had not been able to get a maistri to fix it—the wooden rafters near the staircase thick with cobwebs, the silver painted window grill over laid with a coat of grime, and the red floor, cracked and scratched, which gleamed, throwing out a glossy red hue, almost despite itself. And then his eyes came to rest on the people in the room—her father, looking shrunken and dazed—he had started avoiding visitors of late, her mother—composed but uncertain on how to deal with this incursion, and her husband—louche, legs splayed in an unbecoming posture. She felt it surge through her, a shaft of anger and love, yes love, and she opened her mouth to speak but Prakash spoke first. It's a shame the garden is overgrown like this ... too dark, too many trees, he said. Where he lived, in a township called Naperville on the outskirts of Chicago, he had people come in to remove branches from trees so that the sun could come in to the lawn. In fact, he had a whole tree, a grown tree transplanted into his garden when he moved—they had brought a hydraulic tree spade mounted on a truck to remove and replant the tree. He and his wife were such nature lovers.

Then Prakash got up and went over to where her father was sitting. You know that things are changing, right. So many people are developing their properties, converting their old houses into flats. This is my brother-in-law's card, he said. He is a real estate developer. Just in case ...

Her father dropped the card on to the side table without looking at it. My son will take care of all this when he comes, he said.

At which Prakash and his mother exchanged glances. She smiled at him, a small triumphant smile, and nodded.

That's the thing, Prakash said. It may take some time for him to come back. Ashwath, Prakash seemed to imply, was having problems with his status, getting his Green Card and it was not advisable to leave the US without a Green Card if you wanted to come back in. And what complicated matters was that he did not seem to have a steady job. No fixed address either.

Prakash, of course, Kaveramma smiled, is a citizen of the US.

Remember the show you used to watch before this one, the last time I was here, Prakash gestured to his mother and to the dark TV screen.

The *Ramayana*, yes ...

There was a creature there, a golden deer, a maya mriga, an illusion. Well, the American dream is like that creature. Not everyone can grab it. And the things that we bank on here, our foundations—he waved his hands around vaguely as if to include the house and the people and everything beyond—mean nothing there. One has to start from scratch. Be open-minded. Reinvent the wheel.

He writes to us regularly, her mother cut in. Sends us

cards. And so he did. Beautiful cards for Father's Day and Mother's Day, a singing card for his sister when his nephew and niece were born.

Cards, of course. We are big on cards there. One for every occasion. Prakash looked amused.

Kaveramma stood up and shook her pleats out audibly. She made a show of collecting her things. Son, ask the driver to get the taxi round to the front gate, she said. It's up to you. Prakash has given you the card, it's up to you to make up your mind.

By the way, she said, and sat down again. Do you recall the family that used to live in your outhouse? They have prospered—they have developed a small patch of land they owned near an old temple on the outskirts and all thanks to their daughter who is now someone quite important. A soothsayer or a faith healer. I believe she has powers. I knew it all along, Kaveramma said. There was a tejas in her face, even when she was here walking in and out of the yard. You could tell that she wasn't an ordinary person, like the rest of them. She, Kaveramma, was going to pay the place a visit—their herbal medicine for joint pain was supposed to be really effective. The sons of the family had pushed up their sister—they had always been resourceful, clever at seizing their opportunities ...

It's the yoga of this house, her mother said, stony-faced. People who have been part of this house have always prospered.

Kaveramma and Prakash left. They crowded round the door to see them off. Suchi mama walked them up to the gate. Her father looked longingly at the TV screen and then settled heavily in his armchair. They wanted to know more about Sanjeeva's family—which of his daughters? Thippy surely ... Suchi mama had brought them news of this sometime back, that there were posters at the temple about a Sundari Amma—a saintly woman who answered questions and gave directions on healing the sick. They had set up a trust, the local temple was actively involved, and the head priest himself seemed to have faith in her powers. Her mother had cut Suchi mama short. Eternally optimistic, equally euphemistic, a good mother, she had said—let bygones be bygones. We have never entertained talk of sadhus and mediums in this house. We believe there is a God, nothing else.

Two

Savitri is now in a permanent state of distraction. She is always mildly anxious, preparing herself constantly for the unanticipated, for the anything that can happen. She is no longer aiming for the eye of the bird, the next simple pleasurable thing, an elusive snatch of a song, something nice to eat on the roadside, the satin blouse she has coveted for so long—now her vision is crowded by the feathers of the bird, the leaves, the branches, the tree, and the sky.

When she sleeps, she is waiting to wake up, and when she wakes up in the morning, she waits. She waits for the day to be over. She has waited twenty-five years for her brother whose thoughts she could once sense even as he was thinking them.

But wait. It is bright sunshine. The overgrown garden has retracted its mindless greenery like a cat its claws. The paved path to the gate is clean and white with no cracks, no moss in its ridges. She is sitting at the top of the steps. She gets up to open the gate. Her brother wheels his bicycle out. Both of them grimace at the sound the gate makes. One foot on the pedal he turns round to look at her, his curly hair tossed by the breeze, and nods briefly. That look, that brief nod is a promise, an assurance; come evening it will be the same again, the absence in the day but a minor tangent, the gap between systole and diastole, the pause in the heart beat.

It is evening. She is waiting on the steps to hear the click of the gate. She runs to open it. He is looking tired today. His unruly hair is flattened with sweat. He parks the bicycle at the foot of the stairs for they have to go out again.

By the time he washes up and comes to the kitchen she has laid out his tiffin and coffee. On rainy days their mother has something extra for them. Ridge gourd bajjis that he likes very much.

That Satish, he says, frowning, his eyebrows in a straight line.

I know, she says.

They both laugh.

She hums the notes under her breath. He corrects her. Why don't *you* go to class, she says, peeved. I would, if they'd let me, he says, teasing her. But you'd still sing the same.

On the way back from music class, they are stopped by a policeman. Dynamo not working and you are taking dubs?

He only has a rupee for the policeman, two eight anna coins. The policeman grumbles but takes them anyway.

She springs back on the carrier. They are back to doubles

or dubs and the dynamo lights up miraculously. They stop off on the way for corn-on-the-cob, with mint chutney and red chilli powder. More, she tells the corn cob man, who obligingly passes the blackened rind of a halved lemon over the roasted cob one more time. So what if her brother has given away the last of his coins, she has a whole five rupees tied up in the pallu edge of her sari.

It starts raining. They come home in the drizzle, powdered with rain drops. The lights are on in the house. Their mother is waiting at the door. Their father is inside. They can hear Suchi mama's voice, and they know that their father too is at his happiest.

*

She remembers the night she waited for him to return. Pacing inside the house, pacing on the terrace, pacing in the garden till her father ordered her to go inside. He had left the previous evening, hitching a ride with Sanjeeva's family who were out to attend a jatre, one of their innumerable festivals, where Thippy would undoubtedly be the star, the performing monkey. They had left in their hired tempo truck, and Ashwath had taken a ride with them to check on a piece of land. Her mother was angry with Suchi mama for having sent him and her father was irritated with her mother for being angry. He has to take an interest in the property that he is going to inherit, he had shouted. You can't make a milksop out of him.

Late at night they got word that he hadn't reached the village where he was supposed to inspect the piece of land. The tenants were still waiting for him.

They have spirited him away, her mother said.

Vishalakshi, her father was constrained to call his wife's name out loud in public, in front of everybody, in front of the sundry relatives they were housing. Please, control yourself.

She lit a lamp to the gods and prayed. God, bring him back safe and sound. Never mind if he has ...

There have been no reports of any accident on the highway. By tomorrow if we get no news of him, we must file a complaint. That had been Suchi mama's final ominous word before he left.

Her brother had returned in the early hours of the morning, dishevelled, smelly, and wild-eyed. She thought at first that he had been robbed or roughed up till he started babbling about her. She then knew her mother was right; it must be the work of spirits. But her mother, ever practical, had immediately set to work to make a herbal decoction to soothe the overwrought, feverish mind.

He had jabbered on about beauty, goodness and kindness. About the two of them being parts of a whole, like Ardhanarishwara. Her mother asked Suchi mama to have his horoscope examined minutely by the astrologer.

Her father said, Vishalakshi, your son is in no mortal danger. He is just a fool.

God puts everyone to the test, her mother replied. Young or old. We must be prepared.

Her father consulted Suchi mama, who came with a couple of labourers with pickaxes. By the end of the day, the outhouse had been flattened, the rubble carted away, and Sanjeeva's belongings sent to the temple, where they lay in the yard. In case they made any trouble, a lawyer was at hand and the local police station had been alerted. But they made no trouble at all. In fact, they never heard from them after that.

Her father held out till her brother left—he seemed almost to know, to expect that he would not see him again—and then the toll that the events had taken began to show. With no known ways, no hand of custom, experience or counsel, or norms of behaviour to guide him, having run out of poojas and rituals, her father seemed to have given up. She had not suspected her father would capitulate so easily, as if the ramparts of their fort were made of cardboard. Her mother, armoured with housework, of having been the grumbling influencer and never the decision-maker all her life, fared better. She was not expected to be the all-seeing, all-knowing one. That was her husband's responsibility, and in her eyes, he had faltered as the master of the house.

Savitri's music, more, her music master, then gave her solace. Keshav Rao was the only promise, however tentative, of safe harbour and good cheer, her bridge across glum waters. More than anything else, she was a girl who needed to feel happy and high-spirited.

*

It began as a small regular flutter at the base of her stomach—a stomach as large and heavy as a cannon ball. She could not wait for it to be over. The flutter grew quickly into a spasm and she burst into the hall where her mother sat, the stain spreading over her thighs. Amma!

She remembers the stillness on the streets, the eerie silence. There was little traffic, even on the main roads, few autorickshaws and buses. They managed to reach the hospital quickly, because of the empty roads.

She is led to a small room with a white metal bed onto which she hoists herself. The coir mattress is firm beneath her. She can feel the coldness of the rubber sheet through the coarse layer of the cotton bedsheet. Her mother sits next to her on a chair, holding her hand when the spasms begin, speaking to her as if she were a child.

She stumbles into the toilet, her head dizzy with pain and confusion. The nurse undresses her and makes her wear the hospital gown that comes up to her knees and is tied only with a string at the back. She notices that it is made of the same material as the bedsheet. The nurse slips a suppository in place and orders her to hold it in. Then she says sternly, as if Savitri were in some way responsible—Did you know, the prime minister has been shot. Indira Gandhi is dead. That's what they say.

Over the next three days, the nurse brings news of the killings in Delhi, of people being burnt alive. Amidst her agitation and the tense ambience of those days she holds her child, a tiny wrinkled creature, who is so restless, cries so much that she has to nurse him all the time. She cannot help but think that her son is marked by the taint of violence, which is why he is so contrary, so beyond her control. Aprameya—the name is her mother's choice—after Lord Krishna—the boy turns out to be as mysterious and as unknowable as the Lord himself.

*

If someone had told her then that seven years later Indira Gandhi's son, Rajiv Gandhi, cherubic, pink-complexioned and calm of demeanour, who became prime minister after her, would also die a violent death, blown to pieces in a suicide bomber's embrace, she would not have believed it. He had seemed so god-like, so much larger than life, a man of destiny. And it had happened not in distant Delhi but closer home, in the neighbouring state, about 300 kilometres away, in the heat of summer in the year 1991.

When it happened, she was in the hospital again, waiting, this time, by her mother's bedside. Her mother, euphemistic as always, had had a silent heart attack. The hospital had grown shabbier but more expensive in the intervening years. A lot more had happened in those intervening years, births and deaths that had not just changed the future of her family, but the destiny of the nation, even the world. Indira Gandhi's son had found a life and lost it. Her daughter was born. Her father had had a stroke. Her brother had not visited or written. A dazzling new economy had burst upon them. It had given her husband a new job, or perhaps the illusion of one, and taken it away. The world had been on the brink of war, a conflagration that threatened to consume them all. The war in the Gulf was televised and beamed into their drawing rooms, and they watched as they ate their dinner, as if it were all a soap opera.

The young, handsome Rajiv Gandhi, for whom she had voted but who had lost the elections nonetheless, had been on the campaign trail to be re-elected, when he was killed right on their television screens, and his assassins, those who had plotted his death by suicide bomb, were discovered close to her house, so close that she had walked there sometimes to gather lotuses from the shallow rainwater ponds that formed during the monsoons.

The act of retribution for Rajiv Gandhi's assassination is

played out next door to her, quite literally. In three months, the architects of the plot to kill the former prime minister are traced to her city, four kilometres from where she lives. The assassins were injured when they set off the human bomb that killed him, and have retreated to a house in an upcoming suburban layout to lie low and bide their time.

This is a house that was on our rental list, her husband says, in a state of excitement. For Keshav Rao is now a silent partner in an investment company which also deals with real estate. Subramanyam, who runs Mani and Associates, and whose motto is, We are open to negotiations, says, Do you recall that house? 60x40 site, MS steel windows, no wood—do you remember, we had it on our list. I knew it, I knew it. There was something in the air on Sunday, there were so few policemen on the streets, and a sub-inspector I know was so distracted, so secretive.

And there they had been living, the family of assassins, in a suburb still full of coconut palms and empty plots filled with parthenium weed, buying groceries and milk, like regular people, making small talk with their milkman and maid, like anybody else.

Two days after that Sunday, on the birthday of the man they killed, as Mani said, the police stormed the house to find all the occupants dead—all by their own hand, and most dramatically. Before it reached the newspapers, every tale, every rumour found its way into Savitri's house through the milkman, who claimed to be related to the woman who had led the police to the assassins' hideout.

Mani's milkman had edged the tale with tragedy and romance. Seven of them, assassins on the run, biding their time in a remote safe house, nursing their wounds, priming their guns, waiting for the coast to be clear before returning to their country, posing as members of a wedding party. The bodies were found on the floor of the main room, six of them having bitten into cyanide pills they were reputed to wear as an ornament round their necks. The two women in the group had been found together in the hall, in a blaze of purple. They had all chosen the time and manner of their own death. The seventh, their leader, a young man, short, square of build, blind in one eye—having lost it to a bomb that went off prematurely—was found with a single 9 mm pistol shot to his right temple. How clean and heroic that sounded, Savitri thought; the man had been a poet too.

There was a flurry of letters to the local newspapers, debating on whether the assassins who had died by their own hand had been cowardly or courageous. Subramanyam and Keshav Rao spoke late into the night, glasses clinking, while she stayed up with her mother. The young prime minister had been the harbinger of good times, their new found prosperity. He had set in motion changes that had relaxed controls, invited the private sector into government strongholds, made banks more investor-friendly, retrieved the stock market from the ivory tower, made funds available for speculation, and the term 'broker' respectable. Where once there had been queues, shortages, rationing, hankering and inhibition, there seemed to be a promise of plenty. For the first time, a whiff of adventure had been injected into their circumscribed lives. He had been responsible for the new red Maruti 800 that Subramanyam parked outside their house every morning and which would be handed down to Keshav Rao soon.

Courageous or cowardly—depends on the point of view, Subramanyam said.

She had not known to what extent her son, seven years old, had been following these conversations. One Sunday morning, she watched him in the garden from the terrace and then hurried down to where he was sitting, on the cement ledge round the pipal tree. He was walking round the tree in short stumpy steps, the chamber of the index and middle finger of his right hand poised against his temple, the other two fingers curled into his palm, his thumb working the trigger.

She remembers taking his still chubby hand in hers and stroking his palm and straightening his fingers. Don't, he said, his serious face breaking into a smile. It tickles. Later in the night, when everyone was asleep, she removed the pellets from the air gun, the 'monkey rifle' kept in readiness to scare away the monkeys, and put it away in the attic. She thought of what Mani had said, a random remark. Nothing would be the same again. Nothing had been the same for her in a long time. She had long given up trying to control things.

*

In fairness to her husband, things had improved. He had made good, as he had promised, and her parents' last years had been comfortable, though their unhappiness had grown. Keshav Rao had got the house painted. He had an 'attached' bathroom built next to the hall so that her parents no longer needed to go out into the back yard to use the toilet. One morning he parked a red Maruti 800 in the driveway—it's mine, of course, he said, offended that she had asked. Bought it second-hand from Mani. The car created a minor sensation in their household, accustomed as they were to a bicycle or at best a scooter being parked in the yard. They took the bus when they all went out together, which was rare, and on special occasions—usually only a wedding merited such consideration—their father called a taxi.

It was a winter of warm Sundays. Her parents bestirred themselves, they all crowded into the Maruti 800 and Keshav Rao took them on long drives to the fields on the outskirts of the city. They stopped by a lake, spread straw mats on the grass and laid out a picnic lunch.

One morning Keshav Rao took them out for breakfast to MTR and on the way, pointed through the palings of a nearby park to a grand house with a gleaming brass nameplate and said—That is the house of our Chairman.

Seems—her father burst out, and then reined himself in. Good, he said. Seems good.

She knew what her father wanted to say. Seems too good to be true. Or seems too flashy for the Chairman of a nationalised bank, and such a small one at that.

I heard he takes too many risks, her father said, feeling the waters cautiously.

Someone has to take the risks, for others to be safe—Keshav Rao's remark was laden with sly meaning.

But for the first time since she had known him, her husband seemed happy to go to work, and spoke proprietorially about the bank. His small bank was a subsidiary of a larger national bank, and the new chairman, a young Turk, just like the prime minister, full of new ideas, had drawn the subsidiary into his fold right at the beginning. As soon as the Chairman took over, instead of the standard official intra office memo which was usually marked 'to files' and never read, he had visited the office personally. Keshav Rao came home with new notions and catchphrases. They were all going on an adventure together, the Chairman had said, and he needed the participation, the 'buy-in' as he put it, of each one of them. There would be new goals and challenging targets—for the innovative employee, the sky was the limit, irrespective of rank and designation. And then the Chairman had personally picked Keshav Rao to be in his secretariat, part of his task force.

The Chairman invited him one morning for a breakfast meeting. People think our jobs are dull, he said. But they have no idea. Times were changing. As the prime minister himself had signalled, there was no point living in a time warp. Acting strictly according to the letter of the law would neither profit their organisation nor the nation. What was required now was the spirit of innovation, of adventurism even—of course they would keep to the spirit of the law. What the Chairman was rumoured to have asked Keshav Rao was whether he was ready to fetch milk from a tiger.

It was no secret that the country was facing an economic crisis. The war in the Gulf was having a domino effect. Public policy was changing. Government control was being rolled back. The public sector was being pruned and 'privatisation' was the new mantra. The companies owned by the state, behemoths that they were, were selling their stocks and needed to park their money somewhere. Banks had to compete with each other to attract the money that these companies were making. Their bank had done well in meeting its statutory requirements, he explained. But the route to real profits lay elsewhere. Places that they were not explicitly forbidden from, they would venture into—the grey areas as they were miscalled. Keshav Rao was to be part of a small financial services team, the Portfolio Management Services group, that would offer a range of specialised services to attract such idle funds.

Sceptical though she was, Savitri was relieved that her husband was now more the man she first knew.

Even her parents noticed. Has your husband been given a promotion, her father asked.

She was doubtful. Not that I know. But he seems to be the right hand of his Chairman.

What Savitri saw was the frenzy of activity that Keshav Rao plunged into. The phone rang at odd hours, and he had low-voiced conversations with people. As soon as she heard his voice dip reverentially she knew that the Chairman had called. A man with a polished accent called often, but Keshav Rao was quite short with him—I'll see what I can do. Chairman has no time to breathe even. I tell him Sir, put a bed in the office. Cars drove up to their gate with the darkened windows pulled up. Sometimes Keshav Rao walked up and down in the garden, smoking, chatting with those visitors. She heard his excited laugh ring out in the night.

He, who had never travelled on a plane before, was flying constantly to Delhi and Bombay with the Chairman. He had a long stint in Hong Kong on a training programme. On his return from Hong Kong he had extended the shed her father had put up into a pukka annexe, putting in chic furnishing and air conditioning. His colleague Subramanyam who had been with him in Hong Kong and who had resigned from the bank on returning, had started Mani and Associates, Investment Advisors, in the shed.

Soon Mani had hired a receptionist and an office assistant and there was a steady stream of visitors to the office. Mani also fixed the gate so that it no longer squealed like a stuck pig, which also meant that they could no longer tell when it was opened or closed.

From that lull, a ceasefire of hostilities, had resulted a brief intimacy, a rekindling of sorts, and she found that she was pregnant again. But their period of rapprochement was over even before her daughter was born. For one, Keshav Rao constantly needed money for his various schemes, money that he thought she should 'lend' him, after claiming her rightful share from her father. After all, he was standing in for her brother, wasn't he?

My father will do right by me, I know. But I can never be sure what to expect from you, she had replied, sitting on her newly bought recliner, her stomach resting on her thighs.

When she demurred, Keshav Rao grew impatient. Things are changing, and we have to strike while the iron is hot. Let me put it another way—the world itself is an illusion, so we lose nothing by trying something new. Why cling to outmoded old ways? You cannot spin money out of thin air.

Where are these high returns coming from? I believe the Americans have a saying—there is no such thing as a free lunch, her father said.

Ask your father to sun himself on the deck in his recliner, Keshav Rao said rudely. The time to put your money in fixed deposits and government bonds is over. Even your Kaveramma knows better. Where do you think she got the money to send her son abroad. From the shares she bought.

Of the very same Coca Cola and IBM whose shares were sold when they were driven out. Equity—that Kaveramma understands, that's the new buzz word.

But Savitri, what are these meetings that son-in-law keeps having of late—her father asked.

People should know when to roll up their mats and retire, Keshav Rao said to his wife. Do you know who was on the phone just now? A VIP. A high net worth individual. Do you even know what that is? The Chairman of one of the largest public sector corporations was asking me, no, begging me, for a meeting. And do you know what I said? I said no. Impossible.

After resisting him for long, she gave in, as she always did. Keshav Rao had finally succeeded in pressurising her into 'borrowing' money from her father to buy shares in the stock market. And sure enough the shares had risen in value. The shares had paid for her father's new bathroom and custom-built recliner in which he sunned himself on the terrace. But there was no talk from Keshav Rao of returning the money he had borrowed.

The anointed deity of Mani and Associates was the Big Bull, Harshad Mehta, a Bombay stockbroker, reputedly a financial wizard, investment expert, punter of stocks, whose trading cues Mani followed closely. With luck and God's grace, our next car could be a Lexus, like his, Subramanyam said with a gleam in his eye and a hush in his voice.

*

And in barely two years, it was over, things turned topsy-turvy.

If she had to list her many griefs, the first would be the death of her parents.

Her father was the first to go. It had been painful to watch him in his last few years. His stroke had slowed him down considerably and encumbered his movements. He spent most of his days sitting in his recliner, watching the newly installed cable television, and waiting for his brother to visit. For only Suchi mama could understand his agitated concerns and make sense of his slurred speech. Or he would go through the cards that her brother had sent. Every year, on Father's Day, there was a card. The fragrance of print, the rich creamy texture of the card, the words of good cheer, the sense of America enveloped them in a little cloud every time a card arrived—on Father's Day, Mother's Day and then on her children's birthdays. There was one card which had the picture of a boy and a man—both dressed in denims and checked shirts, the man wearing a large hat and chewing on a pipe—sitting by the side of a river, fishing. In these quiet moments Dad, I knew what it was to be a man. Thank you. That was what the card said. The cards distressed her father. Her mother would look at the card, flip it over and say, nice. Then she would put them away to show the next visiting relative—proof that her son was doing well in the eyes of the world.

The television brought little cheer. Most of his time in what would be his last days was spent in watching the war in the Gulf, Operation Desert Storm, the war that had not just affected the fortunes of the country but her family as well—the root of her husband's newfound spirit of enterprise. For the first time a war was being telecast live, like a cricket match or a football game, the explicit horror of it brought into his drawing room, eight feet across from him, orange clouds of flame billowing from targets that were bombarded and blown up, tanks pacing the desert at night.

Her son had thought it was a game, especially the fuzzy night vision pictures crackling across the screen. Manohar, Suchi mama's wife's nephew, had brought him a set of Desert Storm trading cards which had pictures of men in uniform, heroes of the war, and an assortment of weapons, and introduced him to video games, gifting him with a home video game console, which his son had grown tired of. While her father watched the war on TV, her son guided a figure in fatigues through mazes, blowing up things on a screen and fending off attacks by tanks and lasers—enduring death by video game. She could do little to prevent either of them from their pursuits.

Her father had watched the international news broadcasts avidly, trying to reconcile his one-dimensional knowledge of the world, which had come to him through the newspapers, with the more tactile presentation. What he had had to imagine at one time, he could actually see now, and what he could see started crumbling before his very eyes, every evening. When the Berlin Wall came down, he said, I did not think it would ever happen, at least not in my lifetime, as they watched on television, the haphazard crowds, people hacking at the wall and making off with chunks of concrete. To him, the wall had seemed as solid as a natural physical feature, a mountain or a stream, and the Soviet Union, a political entity that would last forever.

He watched the news with disbelief, as every single state of the Eastern Bloc overthrew its Communist government, and like new lamps for old, new countries were created across the world. At that time there was a news report, less than a minute long, about an orphanage in one of the former Eastern Bloc countries, where little children, fair-haired and pink-complexioned, mere toddlers, played on the floor, while the older ones stood around, ghostly pale, and hollow-eyed. The oldest of them, perhaps ten or twelve years old, turned his back on the camera while the others offered their faces to it. These were children abandoned by their parents who had fled West as soon as the walls had fallen and barriers had lifted. Before the news spot was over, her father walked across and switched off the television.

God has shown mercy, her mother said, when her father died in the summer of 1992. A few months later, when the new year had barely begun, her mother followed him.

There was no one to wait with her once both her parents were gone—she had come to depend upon the dispassionate calm of her mother's eyes, her steadiness of manner and approach to all turns of destiny. She had had, as considerate as always—a silent heart attack, and after a short stay in the hospital, had come home and simply not woken up one morning, troubling no one, not even herself. Savitri had woken up that morning wondering why she could not smell the aroma of freshly filtered coffee, and found her mother in her bed, still sleeping, she thought. Unknown to them, the veins leading to her mother's heart were narrowing, squeezing the supply of blood, but not her spirit or her energy. If her complexion had seemed a little grey at times, they put it down to the poor lighting in the house.

Promise me, her mother had said to Savitri a few days after she came home from hospital. Promise me you will not let this house fall into Kaveramma's hands. No, don't protest. I saw the look that passed between them when they were here, between Prakash and your husband. This is your brother's house, remember that. You are keeping it in trust for him.

So distracted was Savitri by her parents' illness and their passing that she had not paid attention to her other griefs. To Keshav Rao's cagey behaviour.

In what seemed a continuation of the bizarre wash of events, there were men in safari suits swarming her garden, the shed office was sealed and the board Mani and Associates, Investment Advisors, taken away. Her husband called her, ostensibly from Bombay where he was away on business, that his work could take him longer than he had anticipated. How much longer, she asked. Days, weeks, maybe months, he said. He would be in touch.

She was glad both her parents were gone by then. They had had a lifetime to get used to a son who had disappeared and then to be confronted suddenly by a vanishing son-in-law would be too much for them. Suchi mama came in the evenings, in loco parentis, with a gleam in his eye and a question on his lips.

Where is your husband?

In Bombay, on work, she maintained. And that was all she ever got to know even after he returned. What her husband had done in the intervening months was a question that she had not asked.

It is the scam that everyone is talking about, which is all in the newspapers, Suchi mama said. Was that what Keshav Rao was involved in?

I don't know, she said quite truthfully, I know very little about his work. But he seemed to be working hard, doing well. There, on the wall is a certificate of merit, signed by his Chairman.

The Chairman, she learnt from Suchi mama, had suffered a heart attack and was in hospital. The Big Bull was in jail. Mani and Associates, Suchi mama pointed an accusing finger in the direction of the shed office—was a front, an eyewash, to enable deals between the bank and the brokers in Bombay. During one of those 'meetings' in Bombay, when they were being questioned by the authorities, apparently Mani had tried to jump out of the window of the fourteen-storey building, had been restrained, and sent to jail.

I don't know any of these things, she said stonily. My husband says his work in Bombay is taking longer and he will let me know when he will return.

One of those evenings, Suchi mama was accompanied by his wife's nephew Manohar who was on his annual visit from the US. Manohar held forth on the scam. Your Prime Minister Indira Gandhi, she fixed the banks. Savitri noticed he said your prime minister, and he had said it with relish. Twenty or was it twenty-five years ago she grabbed your banks and nationalised them. The nationalised banks, big and bloated, just started giving away loans, without trying to recover the money. But it's not possible to go on like that, the economy cannot take it forever.

What the mother had begun, the son had undone. But the system was simply not geared to handle the fall out of the changes the new prime minister had ushered in, Manohar said.

The market was flush with funds since the government enterprises had sold their stocks, and it was the banks' business to attract those funds, but it wasn't such a straightforward matter and there were no precedents for them to follow. Banks were like urchins peering into a cake shop, Manohar said, plenty to see but all out of reach. At best they could smear the glass walls of the display shelf with their hot hands. Eventually, it developed into a three-cornered game between the banks, the government enterprises and a new entrant, the infamous 'broker'. The Chairman of Keshav Rao's bank had been one of the most aggressive in pursuing these funds and had bent the rules to suit his purpose; only, nobody was clear on what the rules were till it was too late, and the long arm of the law had seized him. The banks had played into the hands of the brokers, who had made merry, shooting from the shoulders of the unwary bankers, who if anything at all had lost their heads.

Look at it like this—Manohar upturned the bag of sweet limes he had just brought her, and stacked the fruits in a pyramid. Imagine these are fruits made of gold, and you are a bank and this is the money you have. He divided the limes into three piles with a deft movement of his plump hands. These two piles, you cannot eat—they are a compulsory reserve. Only the third pile is yours to use but it isn't enough to feed your family. Every fortnight you have to take stock of your pile of sweet limes. During those two weeks you can play around with the limes in the three piles, eat them or give them away, but at the end of the fortnight when it's stock taking time, the pile has to measure up, the reserve has to be intact. It's just like lending or borrowing a cup of sugar from your neighbour when you need it—at the end of the month though, your stocks should add up, you shouldn't be short of sugar.

All around you, you see mountains of sweet limes in the market and every household is trying its best to increase its stock of limes. Imagine that you employ a person, a 'broker' to manage your limes, to scout round the market, to nose out the best prices and deals. It's strictly not above-board but you wink at it as long as your limes are growing in number and the broker is efficient. There is a glut of fruit in the market, the air is fragrant with the scent of limes, the householder can see them being moved in and out of his store room and is happy that he does not have to bother with the transactions. But finally, at stock taking time, the households find that they are left with bogus receipts for having sold and bought limes and the fruits themselves are nowhere in evidence or they are told that the limes they had were not theirs after all. The broker, who was being paid a commission, has been cutting deals with different households, with both sides—the buyer and the seller, even promising the same limes to different parties. Not satisfied with a commission for his services, he has begun dealing with the limes himself, parking them in his own house and helping himself to them. Instead of transacting with each other with the broker as the intermediary, the go-between, an instrument of convenience, the households were in effect, transacting with the broker, not knowing what went on behind the scenes. This is what happened between the banks and their brokers over the government funds. Imagine that your servant, whom you sent across to the neighbour to deliver a cup of sugar, has started carrying out a side business in the neighbourhood with your store of sugar and you ignore all signs of it—you choose not to see the line of ants making off steadily with grains of sugar from your store.

If Keshav Rao was the representative of the household or the bank, Mani and Asssociates was the broker. While setting Mani up as a broker was a bright idea, it was not quite above-board for a broker to be on the premises of a bank employee when he was dealing with the securities of that very bank. A banker cannot get into bed with his broker, metaphorically speaking of course, Manohar said, catching her eye. Everyone in the Chairman's inner circle was tainted. No wonder Mani had tried to escape from the board of inquisitors by jumping out from the fourteenth floor when the scheme was finally outed.

As Ponzi schemes go, it was the best, Manohar said. But too good to last. He brought his hand crashing down on the piles of sweet limes and they scattered, the golden fruit rolling all over the kitchen floor. Sorry, Manohar said, sorry, as Savitri started picking the fruit off the floor and from the corners into which they had rolled.

He just needed a little time, Keshav Rao said of his friend Mani, when he eventually returned, slinking back in the dead of night, one day, several months after he had left. Mani, who was reputed to have transacted with a fake bank receipt, offering the same security document to different banks at different prices, she never saw again. Of the Chairman, they learnt that he died in hospital, of a second heart attack. He just needed a little time, Keshav Rao repeated. Mani had done nothing wrong; his hand was forced by a government which was as quick to apply the brakes as it had been lax earlier. Keshav Rao seemed to think that it was the government, waxing and waning, that was at fault, that cut down all the kites it had encouraged to fly high, and given ply to.

Three

She had a waiting routine now. In the morning, after her prayers and meditation in her parents' room, with them smiling benignly from their photo frames, happy now as they had not been in their lives, she paced the terrace, her eyes watching the main road. It was only the milkman. She went through her husband's shed office, the bombed out shell of Mani and Associates, going through the papers that the men in suits had left behind, to see if she could make sense of his absence. The papers, most of them unused forms and vouchers, yielded no clue. She made sure the office was clean, out of habit, and a little out of hope.

In the afternoon, she kept vigil for the postman, but he brought no letters from him; then for her children to return from school, even for the monkeys which now had a free run of the overgrown garden. Her mindful state was that of fatigue from waiting.

He placed me near him that he might me keep/ In sight. He looked at me with longing eyes/ As though he feasted on me. So I felt/ My bones quite soften like melting wax ...

In their courting days he used to sing love songs to her and read poems, tinged with the sorrow of parting. She imagined herself to be that woman, waiting, keeping a lonely vigil on the hill side, waiting for her man to return, alive to every sound and sign of the forest. Her hair is uncombed, her clothes are plain and she is unadorned. The creepers wilt in sympathy, the breeze is soft on her feverish skin, the mountain stream takes care not to sound joyful.

She had always been struck by the imagery of the poems, rather than the emotions—a woman whose bangles are loosened over her wrists for she has become gaunt from pining, a woman who sighs so deeply that she quivers like a peahen struck with arrows; she is envious of the star Rohini, beloved wife of the moon, whose husband is constantly by her side. She remembers the description of a beautiful musician that he constantly read out to her ... skin the tint of mango shoots, speckled with beauty spots, thighs close set and hips broad ... She remembers his singing voice, his baritone, his eyes full of meaning, teeth flashing, she recalls his clean-cut face. In those days she had been thin, all clavicle and pelvic bone, and had longed for rounded hips and close-set thighs.

Another favourite was his song of the heroic warrior. The warrior, fettered by the enemy, escapes like a tusker from a pit in which he is trapped, unsheathes his sword and lays waste the lands and forts of his foe. He returns home triumphant, and the crimson paste of victory smeared on his chest is rubbed off by his children playing on his lap and the embrace of his bejewelled wives.

She caught herself just in time. In her loneliness, she had even imagined herself to be in love with him, all over again.

*

In the evenings she has started drifting in the direction of the temple. In the beginning she pledges simple things. I will light a hundred lamps every Friday in the temple courtyard. And then she progresses to more difficult things, to pledges that involve self-mortification. Long fasts, apart from the regular fasts she keeps on ekadasi. When she was a girl she did these things. If her brother was late she would tie a band round her eyes and wait on the terrace. I will take if off only after he comes home. When he had had a raging fever she had foresworn the payasa in the next three festive meals. Please god, keep him safe. Bring him back to me.

One Friday she found that she couldn't light her lamps in the temple courtyard. It was full of people. There was quite a crowd and they seemed to be waiting for something. One of the women waiting in the crowd explained to her. They were waiting for a healer, a sadhvi who was known to heal the sick, who took on impossible medical cases. She pointed to a few people resting against the culvert, crutches by their side. There was one young man in a wheelchair. She picked people at random and gave them advice. Sometimes she prescribed lehyas and decoctions she had made in her herbarium or she asked them to chant a mantra. At other times, there was no healing as such. They all sang or chanted together or sat cross-legged and did some deep breathing exercises. It depended on Amma's mood.

Actually, the woman said, Amma had grown up in this very temple. The old head priest had spotted her when she came to help out with the temple chores and had realised that she was no ordinary girl. He had told her father, your daughter is destined for greatness, she has a devamsha, a bit of the divine in her. And he was the one who had trained her. So it must be the old runa, the debt that draws her back here.

The next Friday when Amma was expected, the courtyard was crowded again. Savitri fell into conversation with a group of students. They were from the local Ayurveda college, they said and they had been assigned a project in Amma's dispensary. Oh yes, her herbarium was famous and Ayurvedic physicians from all over the country visited the ashram. The head of her clinic was a respected physician from Kerala who had written books on the subject. She must visit the ashram, they said. It was a sprawling place on the outskirts with rooms for visitors. Apart from the dispensary, there was an animal hospital, a school for the local village children, and of course the prayer halls where the bhajans were held.

Intrigued, Savitri visited the temple several times, to see if the mysterious Amma indeed was Thippy, but she could not get to see her. The heightened excitement in the temple premises when Amma was expected was undeniable. One Friday, in anticipation of Amma's visit the gathering broke into a spontaneous chant, begun by the first few rows and taken up soon by all those present. It was a simple, melodic, continuous 'aum' and despite her resistance, Savitri was drawn into it, singing with the crowd, tingling with the reverberations, as if her whole body had turned into a musical instrument. By the end of the evening Amma had still not made her promised appearance but they all got her prasada, a bit of root and bark that they were to go home and burn with incense in an earthen dish. That evening when she went home and ground the root with the stone pestle she recognised the smell as the odour of her girlhood—it had hung around the alcove that housed the gods for her mother used to burn it. Apart from pleasing the gods it was supposed to dispel the dampness and cure the chills. It had been a gift from the outhouse.

One evening the old head priest sought her out. It was your grandfather who took the family in at my request and gave them a place to live in your compound, the priest said. Sharane, was the word the priest used. You gave them refuge. So each of us has played the part destined for us in the greater good, and moved on, allowing the natural momentum to take over. He, the head priest, had seen her by chance at a village festival, rapt in devotion, a medium for the goddess and had recognised her as a vessel for seva, one who would use her powers in the service of humanity. There are different ways of being true to the faith. Not everyone is meant to follow the path of Shastraic knowledge, of shlokas and hymns and rituals. To dissolve oneself in the divine, even if it is for a moment, can there be greater bliss than that? Savitri bowed her head and made no answer.

She chatted with other visitors and picked up the threads of Sundari Amma's story. She ran into lawyer Rajagopal, son of her father's friend, who had been following the rise of the ashram and was only too happy to talk. At some stage in their lives the family had moved to a piece of marshy land at the outskirts of the city and there Sundari Amma's fame had grown. The temple where she 'performed' regularly had become a minor centre of pilgrimage. Through dint of effort the family had turned the marshy land into fertile ground—the brothers had been quite resourceful. They had bought the land adjacent to the marshy plot, and developed it. They had also cultivated the local authorities. Amma had started growing medicinal plants and herbs, and given her green fingers, her garden had grown.

If some people came to the place to have their futures told, their fears soothed, or simply to behold a 'superior being', others came for more down-to-earth reasons—for the cures that Amma dispensed, that worked wonders.Yet others came for the music, the simple breathing routines, the practical instruction free from dogma. A grateful devotee turned out to be a highly placed government official. An NRI specialist doctor had been cured of a debilitating disease which his 'Western' medicine had declared uncurable. There was a groundswell of interest, of gratitude. A local pharmaceutical lab was willing to collaborate on the herbarium, and the Forest Department leased them some land to extend the grove of medicinal plants. An international yoga school wanted to learn Amma's pranayama techniques. A trust was formed with several influential individuals covering a spectrum of educational, medical and even religious organisations, all under the watchful eyes of Thippy's brothers who occupied the key executive positions.

In fact, on the days she holds her durbar in the courtyard, she almost eclipses the deity in the temple, lawyer Rajagopal laughed. Who knows, we may need her blessings one of these days—He could be speaking of the deity or of Sundari Amma.

And sure enough, in a few days, she was called to the test. Her son was ill—the doctor said it was jaundice, and had recommended sugarcane juice and little else. They had to wait it out, follow a strict diet, but the boy was making a fuss about his food. And Savitri was worried about the colour of his eyes. In desperation Savitri had approached the temple priest and he had passed on advice from Amma. Amma had sent her a handful of herbs to be boiled in water. And a small clay bird, painted yellow, and a charm made of the root of the wild fig tree. She had asked for the clay bird to be placed at the child's head and the charm to be tied around his upper arm. With apologies to her mother that she was resorting to charms and spells, that she was departing from the all important paddhathi, the known ways, Savitri had done as she was bid.

As the old priest had said, each of us has to act as we should. We have to live out our prarabdhas, our accumulations from the past which played out in this life. She tried to keep this in mind over the nine days of Navratri, when she went every evening to the temple to light a fervent lamp for the safety of her absconding husband, the well-being of her absent brother and the future of her children.

*

One morning she saw a peacock in the garden. First, she heard its harsh cry and hurried out just in time to see it stepping in from the overgrown shrubbery—the tangle that had covered the section of the wall that had collapsed. A trail of colourful feathers swept the ground, its throat gleamed like a jewel in the sunlight. A diadem of four short feathers bobbed on its head. As if on order, it came to with a click, there was a whirr of russet and grey as it shook out its tail feathers, and then, after a moment's pause, as if to heighten the suspense, it unfurled its tail in an arc of a thousand blue-green eyes, centred in gold, its royal head proportioned perfectly against the gold prabhavali. The fan dipped at her, in benediction. How could it have known, she wondered, that she was so much in need of grace, of a sign of hope, an indication.

The gate squealed, high-pitched, as if in pain. The peacock gathered its train and dived into the shrubbery.

There was a knot of women at the head of the drive.

One of them, the one in white, who was right in front, started walking towards her. She recognised her then; the yards of cloth in which she was wrapped could not quell her quick step. She came up to Savitri and stood in front of her, her steady gaze seeking her out. Her skin, always healthy, glowed now, a lush coppery hue. A chaste smear of sandalwood paste stood out on her forehead. Her sari, of coarse white cotton, was edged with a line of embroidery in dark ochre. Her hair was pulled away from her face, highlighting her monkish bones and the tendons of her neck. The sari blouse, also white, was close-necked and covered her collar bones, and the sleeves came down over her wrist on top of her palm. She was, as always, barefoot.

Then she smiled at Savitri, a smile of such familiarity, of such fellow feeling and yet so full of compassion, that Savitri stood rooted to her spot at the foot of the steps leading into the house. Instinctively, she moved forward and linked her arm with the woman's and rested her head on her shoulder, like she would with her mother, had she been alive, or her sister, if she had had one. She felt a weight lifting from her shoulders, she sensed a shimmer of blue-green pass before her eyes. In less than a moment they were standing apart.

Come, walk with me, Thippy said, and they walked arm in arm to the bottom of the garden where the plinth of the house that Thippy had once lived in still remained. The flat square outlines of the two small rooms were visible, with the grass growing between the plinths. Many years later she would tell her brother—I felt sorry for her. I recognised in her a kindred soul, a woman who had had more than her fair share of burdens, of sorrow, of weight thrust upon her. We were sisters of a kind.

The only other time she could remember a feeling akin to this, this rush of return compassion was on her first visit to her husband's home town, before they were married, and as a bride-to-be she had been taken to the temple to seek the blessings of the goddess and had stood before the image of Lajja Gowri in bas-relief, the Goddess of Modesty at her most vulnerable and most full of grace. When Thippy had appeared so suddenly, without notice, she felt as if her favourite deity, her ichcha devata, had appeared before her and revealed her true form, just for one second, to a trusting believer.

On the ground, next to the plinth of the outhouse, now overgrown with grass, a pipal tree had sprung up. It now stood in front of them, a young tree, its leaves alive and vigorous, shimmering in the late evening sun. The branches were edged with new spring shoot, just-born leaves, newly red and perfectly reticulate.

She picked up a drying leaf from the ground, a skeleton, its flesh gone, held together by the tracery of its veins, the outline still intact, from its broad heart-shaped chest to its small uvulate tail.

It's the perfect tree, she said. You are lucky to have such a beautiful ashwattha tree in your garden—come unbidden and taken root, and grown to such beauty. You needn't worship any other gods if you tend to this tree—all gods live in this tree.

You must take better care of it, she chided gently, settling down on her haunches, clearing the leaves round the roots, looking round for a stone to dig a channel with. Savitri brought her a pail of water, which she poured carefully into the moat she had just built, round the base of the plant. She stood up and looked at Savitri. Then she held her hands out for them to be washed. Savitri poured the rest of the water from the pail on to her hands.

They started walking towards the gate, where the women of Thippy's group stood.

Can I have a glass of water, Thippy said.

Savitri had no other option but to invite her into the house.

You are limping, Thippy said, as they walked up the short flight of stairs to the door.

Savitri sighed. The moment they entered the house, it was as if she was restored to her life, her actual self; the few moments of happiness she had just experienced in the garden were over, forgotten.

In those days she felt the world had lapsed into its primeval self, and she the intuitive survivor in the forest, spear in hand, senses alert to the crackling of twigs and the rustle of disturbed leaves, dangers that were constant and might come from anywhere. And it was to be a lonely journey, for she had only her own resources to depend upon to defend her brood.

My mother and father are no more, she said, you must know that. My brother is abroad and my husband lives in another city, on work. I am alone here, with my children. I am in constant pain.

Lie down, Thippy said, and close your eyes. Come.

She obeyed without a second thought.

Thippy placed her right palm cupped over her closed eyes. Relax, she said. Breathe deep and roll your eye balls in to rest on your cheeks.

As Thippy moved her palm over her face, she felt her

cheeks pull downwards, her mouth slacken, then her neck and her shoulders and she let out a deep breath, as if she were expelling tissue-deep contaminations of exhaustion.

Have I been asleep, she asked.

How do you feel?

Much better. Brand new in fact, Savitri said.

Come to the ashram. You'll like it, it'll do you good. And for me it's nice to see old familiar faces. I will send a herbal mixture for you tomorrow.

The women at the gate had grown restless and had started sliding in along the cement apron towards the front door. One of the women came up to them. It's time to go, she said in a low voice, not looking in Savitri's direction. The evening session starts in an hour. We have to drive all the way back. She spoke in a variation of the local dialect, with a familiarity that only a family member would assume.

Lingi, Savitri said, recognising Thippy's sister.

Lingi folded her hands together in a formal gesture.

The other women at the gate looked like devotees. They were dressed not in white or in cottons but in silks and flowers, as if they were dressed for a celebration or a festive occasion. There was a woman with blonde hair in the group, also wearing a sari.

They stood on either side of the driveway, in a welcoming parade as Thippy walked in and then they closed round her and bore her off to their car. Thippy left without a backward glance, without waving goodbye. When Savitri went back inside, she saw that the glass of water that Thippy had wanted was untouched. Perhaps she had not wanted a drink of water at all.

*

The next morning, she had visitors from Thippy's ashram—the Nivarana Ashram, which removed all obstacles and whose guiding light was Sundari Amma. There were three people, all dressed in white. She recognised Lingi, who looked remote and showed no sign of knowing her but then Lingi had still been a child when they all had left. Of the other two, one was the ashram manager, an engineer who said he had given in to his spiritual calling, and the other was a sage-like elderly man with a flowing beard.

Is this from your sister, she asked Lingi.

We are no longer bound by our past relationships, and those of blood. Sundari Amma has many sisters now and brothers. The whole world is hers, the sage-like man said.

Amma has sent you her blessings, the sage-like man continued. He was the resident Ayurvedic physician in the ashram, he volunteered, who oversaw all the preparations after discussing them with Amma.

She opened the package which had the Nivarana Ashram's symbol embossed on it, like a royal crest.

This is a preparation meant for the restless mind, like water agitated by the wind. Amma has sent it for you, the sage-like man said. We have preparations for the nivarana of different kinds of agitation—for the mind full of regret and sadness, for that full of doubt which muddies the clear water, for the jealous mind that is like boiling water, the lazy mind that is like water overgrown with moss and weeds, and the mind that strays, which acquires all the colours of the rainbow.

And which one is mine, she asked the sage. The muddy mind or the rainbow?

He smiled. It is not the preparation alone, he said. There is of course Amma's penance; together they take away the pain of the bhaktas.

She unscrewed the lid of the bottle that Thippy had sent. It was a white curdy mix with glints of gold. A stong smell of camphor filled the air. This is to settle the stomach. Amma says to take it twice a day, Lingi said. She has also sent you a mantra. Along with the bottle there was a note. She unfolded the sheet of paper to find detailed instructions on tending to the pipal tree. She smiled to herself. Ever-practical Thippy, even when she had become a realised soul. A mantra that dictated the mix of manure for the roots and a squirt to keep the aphids out of the leaves. This was to be her daily ritual.

The ashram manager, the ex-software engineer, was taking a turn in the garden. I believe Amma used to live here ...

She pointed to the ashwattha tree. Right there, where the tree stands. In a small house.

And that one? He pointed to the main house.

My brother's. He lives abroad.

The sage-like man cut in—Amma has asked to meet you. She has invited you to the ashram. She will send word—the day and the time.

I will wait for her summons, Savitri said.

Her husband returned, a little after that, looking haggard and hollowed out, the streaks of white standing out in his hair as if they had been painted on. I have resigned from my job was all he would say. He made straight for the shed and shut himself in. She wondered how she could ever have entertained a tender thought for the man.

After that came the call from the Nivarana Ashram. Sundari Amma had sent for her.

*

She flips her brother's card impatiently against her fingers. She looks up at the terrace from the garden below. She will have to give her brother his old room on the terrace. As newly-weds she and Keshav Rao had occupied that room till they had shifted to the annexe. It is a narrow room with a high turretted roof which can barely accommodate a bed and a table. It is now a store room of sorts for nobody wants it. Perhaps it is the way it is structured, narrow with a high roof and small windows, like a prison cell.

For as long as she can remember, the sleeping arrangements in the house had been very simple. They all pulled mattresses on to the floor in the hall at night and slept on them. In the morning, the mattresses were rolled up and stacked in a small room that also served as a store room and a study. It was a large house but most of it was occupied by the hall. The one bedroom—nobody liked to call it that, it was just called the room—was given to her parents with their beds pushed to the two opposite ends of the room. Now, it was the meditation room and her study. She and her daughter continued to pull mattresses into the hall when they slept at night.

When he turned thirteen her son said he would no longer sleep in the communal hall and study in the mattress room. He wanted a room of his own, and not that room on top which used to be his uncle's and was now a store room. She had been taken aback with the vehemence of his demand. I am grown up now. I need space of my own. So she had had a room built at the other end of the terrace, a makeshift space with an asbestos sheet roof, for that was all she could afford.

Sometimes she feels she has failed her son, this boy of hers, secretive, brooding, who now communicates in short sarcastic bursts and who, like his father, has strange friends on the terrace with whom he talks loudly, late into the night. He has grown up in a dappled house, the sunshine of his childhood obscured by the shadows of her uneasy relationship with her husband and her parents' quiet sadness.

Her brother's absence was an undertone in the orchestra of their lives—an off note, low key but persistent. It had affected her parents. (Depression was a new-fangled word for which she had no use.) It had shaken their confidence in themselves, more so her father. He could only stagger up to the podium and make weak noises. In his bearing and his actions he had always declared that he was so and so, son of so and so, sole inheritor of Neel Kamal in which three generations of his family had lived and which his son would in turn inherit, solid citizen, pillar of his community, performer of prescribed rituals, giver of alms, holder of government office, progenitor of a daughter who made him proud and whom he would settle well, and a son on whose lapel the family badge shone, fed by his youthful sinews. But he had begun to doubt the faith he had lived by. Every norm, every certainty had turned hollow; he had died a disappointed man. Her mother had taken her brother's absence more in her stride. No son of hers, she declared, would fail in his duties. There must be a reason for his long absence. He would make good one day. Even when Keshav

Rao had performed her father's last rites, and her brother's occasion-appropriate card stood framed in the showcase, her mother's faith had not wavered. But it had made Keshav Rao bitter—the welcome extended to him, from son-in-law to son, had been expedient, cautious at best, grudging over time, and jealously watched by the end. And he believed he had discharged all the duties of a son conscientiously. It had sparked off fights between them, his sharpest taunts and most vitriolic comments. That was his argument every time he demanded she ask her father for money.

That kite has cut loose its string, and floated away into the sky. Here I am wobbling a little, all I need is a little push, a little leeway—why can't he show me a bit, just a bit of the indulgence he shows his son!

Her daughter was more like her, easygoing, living in the moment, wanting only to be liked. There she was, walking up and down on the terrace, her hand pressed to her ear, holding the phone.

The mattresses, Savitri called out from the garden. Put the mattresses out in the sun ...

Her daughter looked at her and waved, engrossed in her conversation.

A burst of green in the sky and she looked up. A flock of parrots, her visitors from Lalbagh, had alighted on the tall African tulip in the garden. The tree had large red flowers and broad hard seed pods. The flowers came with a cluster of sacs at the base which you could press to squirt water—it was also called, quite vulgarly, the piss pod tree or the uchekai tree—and it had never failed to engage them as children.

Monkeys—her son called out from the terrace—I can see them in the mango tree. Shall I ...

Get the crackers and light them—she shouted before he could bring out the air gun. She was afraid he might actually hit one of the monkeys, though she had taught him to fire carefully.

For the first time since she got her brother's letter, she felt her anxiety pass. She looked round the garden. The parakeets hidden in the African tulip were screeching, perhaps because of the monkeys. A cracker went off, then another. The monkeys ambled away, used to the routine. The parakeets took off in a protesting whirl of green into the cloudless sky. The house, in the evening sun, looked gaunt and sinewy, like a world-weary traveller—one who had endured much but worn well. It was a good house to come back to. But it might soon no longer be hers.

V

One

He had returned, like a thief in the night, to a sleeping city; to empty streets and the distant barking of stray dogs. That was a sound he recognised at once, from his student days, a sign of curfew that the day had ended, that the time for men was over, and yet that life still stirred in the shadows of the yellow streets.

The airport had transmogrified into an icy dome of glass, unyielding, its carousels humming, its cold hands pointing to Domestic Arrivals, International Transfers and Exit; even the rest room signs had stick figures, one in a tunic and one in nothing at all, rather than the man with the moustache and the woman in a sari and a large dot on her forehead.

He was disposed of in a matter of minutes—out in the cool winter night, beneath a purple star-studded sky, and exit bays trimmed with pink oleander.

He took a taxi, pre-paid. Hoardings high in the sky lit up the night in neon. The chief minister was inaugurating an investor's meet, welcoming them to invest in the state, this the land of the future. Which was the party in power, and who was the chief minister? Had they moved beyond the Congress Party?

Advertisements for highrises—2 BHK—what could that be? They approached a flying saucer with lighted windows—it alarmed him; the taxi driver laughed. And why not—every city in the world was entitled to a strip mall on the interstate. A road sign in yellow and black went by, a milestone from the past, announcing Byatarayanapura—he had read the Kannada script instinctively, before the English letters; he found it soothing. It was courageous of this old hamlet, no doubt as old as the founder of the city Kempe Gowda himself, to have persisted against all odds ...

Twenty-five years. That is a long time, the taxi driver said. Time enough to grow a family.

A little more than that, if one were to be exact. He had left in the autumn of 1981 and here he was, back, just as 2007 had begun.

He was expecting the taxi to be an Ambassador. From Hindustan Motors.

Ambassador? The man laughed again. He named a Japanese-sounding make. That's what his car was. Even government officials had given up the Ambassador.

He sat back, dizzy from a twenty-five-year-old vertigo. The driver was still talking when they turned off the main road an hour later. He caught a glimpse of thick low compound walls, the comfort of coconut palms and then he was in front of the wrought iron lotus that divided into two when the gate was opened. Later, when he was alone in his room, he realised the gate had not squealed, its high-pitched sound more efficient than a calling bell.

A bulb with a tin-can shade shone in the porch. The front door yielded to his touch. He bolted the door behind him. The stairway alone was lit up, the netherworld of the house lay in darkness. He went up to his old room. There it was, his old rosewood cot, his table and chair, a copper jug with a tumbler inverted over its mouth. He poured himself a glass of water—was it boiled and cooled—but it was too late, he had already started drinking it. The checked handloom bedspread was a little dusty and the pillow hard but he slept through what remained of the night. In the morning, he made his way to the kitchen out of habit. A young girl, a version of his sister, was sitting in the dining room. He had expected her to be much younger, he had lost count of the years, just making sure he sent a card on her birthday. Her brother was supposed to have stayed up for him, to settle him in, make sure he was all right, she said. But he seemed to have slept off. There was no sign of his sister or his brother-in-law.

He smiled and nodded. My old bed is there, the table and chair. Even my old gooseneck lamp is the same. It was as if I never left.

Her mother was at the ashram, his niece told him. There was a big meet of devotees, he must have seen the hoardings on his way from the airport. It usually coincided with the chief minister's investors' meet. Her mother had been staying at the ashram for the past few days. She would be returning later in the day. Of her father, she made no mention.

She poured him a bowl of cereal and doused it in milk.

He tapped the cardboard box containing the cereal. It's an American company, he said. I used to work for it once.

The irony was not lost on him. No coffee, no cooked breakfast, no curiosity, no one to meet him at the airport. He was prepared to be greeted with recriminations, for an all-night conversation, but not this.

In the front room, in an alcove, there were black and white photographs of his mother and father—they looked old, careworn, their skin papery. Their eyes gazed into a space beyond, as if they were already celestial beings. The lamp in the alcove threw a radiant light over them.

It came upon him in a wave, his grief, and he felt its weight. He sat down on the floor, the cracked grey slate floor with veins running through it still defiant in its shine. He found little comfort in its cool, equalising touch; it was exhausting—the instinctive pulse of recognition, of memory so clear that he felt he lived in the moment—the light, the physical space, his own disposition, so clearly the same—followed immediately by a sense of the present, turning memory into mirage.

His niece was pointing to a photograph in another alcove, a photograph with a garland of paper flowers. This is Sundari Amma, whose ashram my mother has gone to. He recognised her immediately, older, severe-looking, eyes focussed in the distance, dressed not in a man's bush shirt but a white sari, drawn over her shoulders. Her face looked pale, pared down to the bones.

I think I'll go up to my room, he told his niece. The jet lag seems to be catching up. Thank you for breakfast, he said formally.

Goodbye, his niece said. I have an exam today. I'll see you in the evening.

Two

He liked walking barefoot, feeling the sharp stones underfoot, even the prickly white thorns that grew in clumps on the grass at the far ends of the garden, and which clung to his heels. At the edges of the garden too, the touch-me-not trailed on the ground, and he indulged in his boyhood thrill of passing his hand over the trail to watch the leaves shrink, the leaflets closing one by one. The shy leaves and the soft pink flowers were deceptive for the stem had small thorns that pricked his thumb and drew blood.

Just a few weeks back the rain tree outside the house had been bare, with large green pods hanging from its branches; now it had a full canopy of silky pink flowers and the pods had turned black and hollow, rattling with seeds. They made work for the women who swept the streets in the morning, the fallen flowers gathered in brown mossy heaps on the pavement.

Even as the rain tree was bare, the first leaves had appeared on the honge trees, the Indian beech, a soothing mild green against the harsh sun. Overnight, their untidy tendrils had strengthened into branches, borne buds and had broken into flower—clusters of lilac-pink pea flowers, filling the air with their fresh, faintly-bitter fragrance. They formed an inviting mulch carpet on the ground where they fell. Bliss, apparently—his father used to repeat an old saying—consisted in sitting in the cool shade of a honge tree and having a meal of curd-rice. He was tempted to eat the flowers, to stuff the pea-flower clusters in his mouth; he was sure they would leave his teeth clean and floss-free and the roof of his mouth and tongue would be pleasantly furry with umami.

When he had left Chicago in January, the lake was frozen over, polar-bear frolicking frozen—the Arctic air blowing over the great waters had quelled the mass into a pale green tundra. The lick of the Navy Pier shot out into the expanse of water, a frozen curl, the snow-covered palings of the pier so many stubby exclamation marks. Large boulders of ice, round frozen rocks, had rolled up on the beach from the depths of the lake. When he had first seen the lake, he was sure it was a sea, for no lake could have a beach stretching all across its coast line, or even have a coastline for that matter. The only beach he had seen till then was the Marina Beach in Madras which he had visited when he had gone there for his visa interview, before coming to the United States; he had dipped his toes into the brown waters of the Bay of Bengal, along with the thousands who had thronged the beach.

There was an interloper in the garden, an invasive species.

I don't recall seeing that tree before, he said to his sister. It wasn't there in the garden earlier.

It's a pipal tree, ficus religiosa. It grew out of a crack between two stones on the ground—surely, you should be able to recognise it. She sounded disapproving and also a little circumspect, but that might have been the quirk of tone she seemed to have developed, a tone that could deal with any uncertainty. Savitri had changed in many, baffling ways. For one, she had acquired the proportions of a cube, her arms hanging from her sides like bottle gourds in the sleeves of her tight sari blouse. The mole above her upper lip had grown to the size of a small button and now sprouted three hairs. The animation, the quick step that had characterised her was replaced by an immobility, a heaviness that seemed deliberate.

He recognised the handsome interloper all right—the pipal, the ashwattha, after which he was named, flushed a tender March red, the branches spreading from a strong torso into an even umbrella, bearing perfectly shaped leaves. The tree shimmered in the morning sun, a red beacon, a call to the faithful, as beautiful as a peacock on display. It seemed to cover the space the outhouse had occupied. What he really wanted to ask Savitri was about Thippy's photograph—how had it come to merit an alcove and a lamp to itself, as well as a garland of flowers, in the prayer room? He could not decide which he found more intriguing—Thippy's transformation into Tripura Sundari Amma, guiding light of the Nivarana Ashram, or his sister's allegiance to it.

Savitri had forestalled him as soon as they met, when she returned from the ashram, the day after he arrived. We've been busy with the anniversary celebrations. It's been fifteen years since the ashram was formally established. The celebrations were beautiful—three days of chanting, music and meditation, and many workshops on traditional medicine. There were people from all over the world ...

Her voice had acquired a formal inflection, somewhat like a tour guide's, explaining the sights. She seemed distracted, her eyes unfocussed, but her face was transfigured by a beatific smile.

And then came the warning.

We've been getting all the news from Manohar—he drops in whenever he visits. Yes, you're not in touch with him or Prakash, but they know ... and of course, your cards ...

So the line had been drawn, the lakshman rekha beyond which he could not venture. There would be no confrontations, no confidences. In return for her silence on the state of his fortunes abroad, he would ask her no questions about her connections to the ashram, the turns and twists of her life. They took care not to be in the meditation room at the same time, not to stand in front of their parents together.

*

He fell in line with her routine, with the household. The kitchen no longer smelt of fresh coffee first thing in the morning. Savitri had replaced it with a herbal extract, a green oleageneous squid-juice like thing that she tossed off in a shot, as part of her morning ablutions. The brass coffee filter, a large gleaming piece of industrial equipment, scrubbed every morning by his mother with tamarind pulp, its golden glow lighting up a dark corner of the kitchen, which had produced, on tap, coffee for their household and its endless stream of guests, now stood in the attic, dull with dust.

Woe that coffee has been banished from this home, Savitri, he was half-serious. The gods meant us to drink it, it was blessed by a saint himself ...

A medieval Sufi mystic, Baba Budan, was reputed to have smuggled in the first coffee beans to their part of the country when he returned from a pilgrimage, past the watchful eyes of the Yemenis who guarded their brew jealously, and planted them on the hills. The British had schooled the first plantations, and now it was a state habit.

He brought down the filter from the attic and washed the dust off in the kitchen sink. The coffee filter was reinstated, and without his realising it, he had won the hearts of his nephew and niece. His brother-in-law was not a coffee drinker. He came into the kitchen late in the morning and made himself a cup of tea. Ashwath met him two days after he arrived, almost by accident, in the act of withdrawing from the kitchen, with trembling cup and saucer. He seemed startled to see Ashwath, blinking like an animal in the first light of the morning, as it emerges from its burrough. Ashwath remembered his brother-in-law as a laughing, fresh-faced man, quick-witted, a little insolent, tending to be familiar with people. He had taught Savitri music. He had also organised soirees where people sang film songs, recited poetry or that thing called the ghazal. Ashwath had not particularly liked him, but he was not a bad sort—a boy from a good family, as his father had described him, and quite dazzling in his own way—far from this cagey man with smoker's lips. And what was that on his head that passed for hair—a psychedelic thatch? a wig? a wound? To all appearances, he kept to his section of the house, a shed that seemed to have been put together in haste, which served as his office and his living quarters, coming in to the main house only for his meals.

*

The house was falling apart, he could see that. Stately as it must have been when his grandfather first built it, Neel Kamal seemed to shadow the fortunes of its owners. But Ashwath could not forgive the extensions to the house, hastily tacked on, distorting its proportions. There was his brother-in-law's shed, distending the north face, its prefabricated roof glinting in the sun, contrasting with the red-tiled roof of the main house. Another room had been added on the southern wall of the terrace, facing the road, unlike his own small room that was tucked discreetly at the back, and a bathroom that stuck out like a tumour from the side of the house. A window with monkey tops had been taken out, blinding the house in one eye.

From one end of the terrace, the end now destroyed by his nephew's room, you had a direct view of the outhouse. Only, there was no outhouse now, but a handsome ashwattha tree that had appeared in its place.

The toilets at the back of the house had long been abandoned—they were now a ruin of fallen walls and weeds where no one ventured. It had been a ritual as a boy to 'go to the backyard' first thing in the morning. At some point in these twenty-five years, his father seemed to have bowed to modern ways and advancing age and shifted the toilets inside the house.

You must come home to claim your house. It is your property that you have rightfully inherited. The summons had come from time to time from his uncle Suchi. And dutifully, he had gone to see his uncle Suchi as soon as he could. Suchi mama was sitting in the portico of his house, gnarled knees, crumpled mouth—he got up and went in to wear his dentures as soon as he saw Ashwath—they're not really comfortable, but they help, he said.

Ashwath was surprised to see how grand Suchi mama's house looked. The size of the site had been modest and the house had been old and moss-ridden, with cracked red-oxide flooring. But now in its place stood a spanking new house of generous proportions, clad in polished granite, with floors of marble and windows and doors of teak wood. A new car, not an Ambassador certainly, was parked in the portico, and Suchi mama's chair was squeezed next to it. His son Badri was an engineer, a software professional, and was supposed to have benefited from the IT boom in the city. Badri's wife was a yoga teacher. She had converted the terrace of the building into a covered shed and held her yoga and meditation sessions there. By all accounts she was an intrepid sort. She had also managed to resuscitate a piece of kharab family land and build a resort there which was booked regularly for school and family picnics and from which she ran a wellness clinic.

Yes, Suchi mama is doing very well, thanks to all the help he and his family received from us. The land on which he's built that vulgar resort was actually supposed to come to us. And that house of his violates every single building law. Badri has thrown money about right and left. All that notwithstanding, they are what they are—you can't take the curl out of a dog's tail—his sister had said. In her 'worldly' moments, when Savitri was more herself, she could be quite the wicked gossip, but more and more, to his regret, she saw these moments as lapses of character.

I know you've had your troubles, Suchi mama said, not meeting his eye, it is difficult in a land that is not your own—'para desha' Suchi had said, calling to his mind an expression he had forgotten. And troubles—kashta—were the stuff of life.

I am a citizen of that country now, Ashwath said.

Yes, yes, Manohar too is a citizen, he tells me how difficult it is, even when things are going well. He caught Ashwath's eye and there was a challenge in it.

The house—it's yours. You must decide what to do with it. You must honour your legacy, you know, it's the punya of your ancestors that has passed on to you. You dishonour them by being careless with their gifts. Where would we be without them? It is not enough to perform their annual ceremonies—I know you do that honourably, and without fail.

But—Suchi mama came to the nub of things, like he always did. The house now is a prime piece of real estate—in this city, given its location. People would kill for it. Your sister wants the ashram to have it—after getting her cut—at least, that's what I hear, and your brother-in-law, well, for all I know, he must have already sold it. Your nephew, the good misguided soul, wants to start a school or a theatre in it. Ashwath, it is your property; property that you have rightfully inherited. It is what my brother, your father wanted. Your father never trusted him, your brother-in-law. Savitri has been compensated elsewhere—all the lands in X—he named a place that Ashwath did not remember—were made over to her. She had to sell it to bail him out. That's an old story—ask Manohar. But never mind that. Your father's will clearly says the house is yours. But you can never tell. She could stake her claim—she could have a case. I don't want to say anything else. She is your sister after all ... Go meet the lawyer ... You could live comfortably here for the rest of your life if you act wisely ...

The old exasperation in Suchi mama's voice was back, as well as the old signs of disapproval—the narrowed eyes, the pursed lips. He was a boy again, trying to slip off, while Suchi tried to get him to tend to a chore, something unpleasant to do with the lands or the house.

I plan to stay for some time, he said. I will set things right before I go back.

Tomorrow, you must go to the lawyer, and then the bank. You'll need the khata papers, the proof of ownership if you have to apply for a bank loan. They'll keep the papers as collateral. The lawyer Rajagopal, Shyam Sunder's son, do you remember Shyam Sunder, our old lawyer? Rajagopal will see to all that. Badri has a man now, to attend to these things, he'll take you. I've been in touch with the manager, I've been writing to the bank regularly.

They walked to the gate slowly—Suchi mama insisted on seeing him off. When he turned back, he could see Suchi mama still fumbling with the latch, his bent legs visible below his folded dhoti.

He would have to shake off Suchi mama's heavy hand and Badri's man, whoever he was, and attend to the bank and the lawyer himself.

*

The sun dappled the walls of his narrow room as it had always done, glinting through the trees, choreographing the leaves on his wall, filling the room with shifting flashes of light. They were faces of animals, creatures of no name that greeted him in the morning, companions of his still mind, before his thoughts took over and they became shadows on the wall. Outside, the sky was already a deep, ink-stained blue. He sat on the front steps and opened the newspaper—the terrace would have been better but it bore the signs of his nephew's late night carousing. The morning air was cool. The steps had just been washed and the rangoli was in place. His mother's rangolis had been elaborate—geometric patterns coming to life out of a symmetry of dots and lines and curves, but this one was painted in white and brown, to save the bother of having to draw a new one every morning. The dots and lines at the bottom had worn out, making the design look incomplete. His sister had not noticed, or not bothered with it.

A cycle bell rang at the gate. He went up and fetched the milk. He put the damp notes that the milkman had given him to dry on the kitchen counter. They smelt strongly of camphor—he recalled the popular balm of his childhood, a gelatinous yellow plug, antidote to the summer cold, brought on by a change in the weather. He watched his sister snip the corner of the milk sachet—a thing she had always done expertly, without spilling a drop.

The milk was on the gas, the pressure cooker was already hissing on the other burner. His mother might well have been in charge. He would wait upstairs, studying in his room, or on the terrace, waiting for his sister's voice to sail up from the landing—Coffee!

As he told his niece, it was almost as if he had never left.

After her shot of green squid-juice, his sister retreated into the front room and shut the door. He could hear the low hum and repetitive tune of a chant that was played on a recorder. When she emerged from the prayer room he could see there were fresh flowers and incense at the altar. An oil lamp burned steadily in the alcove with the photographs of his parents, the wick trimmed of its burnt edge of the previous day, the cup brimming with oil. In the other alcove Thippy's face was obscured by a thick rope of jasmine buds, which looked real but were actually crafted from light green plastic wire.

While his sister retreated into her prayer room, his niece would emerge from the mattress room, which she shared with her mother, all set to leave for college.

He found that he had miscalculated her age by several

years. But she had pounced on Marilou, the copper-haired, chubby-limbed American Girl doll he had bought for her from Water Tower Place where he had worked briefly. He had pulled out his gift sheepishly from his suitcase but she had thought it perfect. I have never had a doll to play with, she said. I remember begging my mother for a doll which closed its eyes when it lay down and opened them when it got up, a doll with blue eyes and spiky eyelashes, but she said no, it cost too much. What's her name?

Actually, it says Marilou on the box. But I named her Natoma—it means 'daughter' according to the American Indians.

That's a nice name, she said. And the friendship bands you gave me—can I give one to my friend? She's my best friend. Her name is Chandan Bala.

Ah! Sandalwood Maiden?

She was tickled by that; he heard her laughing all the way up to the terrace. She would pull out her phone immediately, no doubt, and talk at length to her friend about it, walking up and down on the terrace.

Shweta—easy to please, ever-smiling, good-natured, who downed her cereal, wiped her milk moustache, swung her hair over her shoulder and left for college calling out—Bye Ash mama!

*

Aprameya was not as easy as his sister.

Ash, that's what people call me there. Ashwath is a tongue-twister, it's unfamiliar to them.

I'm going to call you Ashwath.

And I'll call you Goyathlay. Goyathlay! Hail Chief! It

means 'one who yawns', also the name of the great Apache chief Geronimo—he was very difficult to catch—just like you. He managed to get his nephew's attention. The boy smiled, a quicksilver motion that changed his face, taking away the sullen droop of his mouth and animating his face with a boyish sweetness. How old was he? Must be twenty or twenty-one, he guessed.

By the time his nephew came down from his room, still half asleep, hair rampaging about his head, it was almost noon. He had fingered the Threadless tee shirt Ashwath had brought him, studying the punning motif on the front with concentration. I like it, he said, pulling it over his head immediately.

He looks like you, Savitri said, the same curly hair and rocking gait, and knitted brows over nothing, the same ... what shall I say ... unpredictability.

He let it pass.

He could hear his nephew till late on the terrace, listening to music or talking on his cell phone. Sometimes, he had friends over and they read things out, rehearsing for a play or a performance of some sort. They are my students, Aprameya said, and the note of satisfaction escaped him, despite his trying to be as casual as he could. He knew that Aprameya was part of a rehabilitation programme being run by an NGO. But he did not speak about what he did because of the disapproval with which it was met in the family. Some of my students, my mentees are ... well ... different. They—he gestured to the house—don't like it when I call them here, but what's the harm in meeting them on this terrace? There is so much space here that no one uses, and we aren't in anybody's way. They don't get it, he shrugged.

If Savitri and Keshav Rao were united, it was in their disapproval of Aprameya's owl-like habits and his 'friends'. We don't mind you teaching them in your spare time. But why don't you finish at the centre, why bring them home? Savitri asked.

The centre is crowded—we have to leave after our allotted hour, Aprameya said. If the outhouse had still been there we could have met there ...

According to Suchi mama, Aprameya wanted the house for a school of sorts or an arts centre that he wanted to set up—all this under the influence of his so-called friends. He had threatened to drop out of engineering college and do whatever else it is that he does, so Suchi mama had heard. After Savitri had paid a massive capitation fee to get him a seat, the useless fellow. He says his work changes lives, helps people. The good lord himself finds it difficult to change lives and this boy thinks he can do it so easily.

Suchi mama, there is nothing wrong in following a career in the arts. I roomed with actors from a theatre group when I first started working, he said to Suchi mama. Some of them did very well. They made a professional career out of acting.

We are talking property here, not art, Suchi mama said, his expression conveying that he should have expected his nephew to catch the wrong end of the stick.

He wanted to tell Suchi mama of the old Native American saying, of the famous Chief Black Hawk who had countered the American government's devouring of his homeland with the bewildered and eventually powerless argument—Nothing can be sold but such things that can be carried away. He was sure that it would not impress

Suchi mama, as it had not the Americans. But it would appeal to Aprameya and his friends.

Did you tell your sister you are coming here to visit me, Suchi mama had asked him, chin jutting forward. No? Good. I don't see much of Savitri's children, in fact, I don't see Savitri or her husband too. See, you came to see me first thing as soon as you arrived. To pay your respects to the elders in the family. But Savitri has forgotten our ways, it seems. She is not the same anymore. Things are not like in your father's days. At the same time he seemed to have a grudging respect for her. Your sister, she has suffered a lot. Tumba kashta pattidale, he said, as a badge of approval.

We don't visit Suchi mama much, Savitri had said, we keep it to formal occasions. He has been spreading lies about our family. He and that nephew of his, Manohar.

I know all about your husband's misadventures, he wanted to tell her. Manohar came all the way downtown to tell me about them. But that would make him vulnerable to a similar thrust from her. So he kept quiet.

Savitri's piety was a refuge. She emerged every morning from her meditation exercise, calm, a little more distanced from the fray. Other than that, she put food on the table.

His brother-in-law he saw only at meal times. He was sure Keshav Rao timed his visits to the kitchen when Savitri was not there. He made his own tea in the morning, when she was in the meditation room. His food was kept on the table—rice, drying over the sides of the pan, a pale rasam, a cooked vegetable and a carelessly cut salad. Keshav Rao ate quickly, gulping his food down, trying to make the ladles clink as little as possible. The he shot off to his shed like a bullet. One afternoon, a little after he had arrived, it was getting late and Savitri said, Go call your brother-in-law. He had found Keshav Rao sleeping at his desk.

The table was piled high with forms for a variety of schemes—tax saving bonds, mutual funds, insurance, an IPO, forms for national savings certificates. The dust lay thick on the forms, suggesting they hadn't been moved for some time. There were empty tea cups with a slush of cigarette stubs at the dregs. But other than that, Keshav Rao's quarters were quite spartan. There was a bed against the wall, a TV set, a small refrigerator and a personal computer. There was also an ante room with a sofa set where he entertained his friends and met his clients. Keshav Rao still ran Mani and Associates from the shed, keeping the name of the company intact, though the board announcing the name was modest and discreetly positioned. According to Suchi mama, he was a crook, a thief and a conman, and worse, he had shirked his family responsibilities—he had driven his father-in-law to the grave and caused such tribulations to visit upon his wife that she was forced to court strange types of people, 'people who are not like us'. Ashwath said nothing; he was sure part of Suchi mama's description of his brother-in-law was meant to apply to him as well.

Keshav Rao seemed to have little to say to his children either. He had seen Shweta giving her father a ride on her two-wheeler on her way to college. Once in a way Keshav Rao would take out his purse and hand over a couple of notes to his daughter. Aprameya and he went out of their way to avoid each other.

One morning, Aprameya had an examination to write, but he would not wake up, no matter what. Shweta had banged on his door several times, but to no avail. Then Keshav Rao had gone up to his son's room, knocked on the door and said something in a soft voice into the hinges at the side of the door. Aprameya had opened the door immediately.

Where, where are they? he asked wild-eyed.

Who?

The policemen you said were enquiring about my motorbike?

Shweta clapped. Hundred on hundred to Appa, she said. Even Savitri smiled. For a moment, Keshav Rao had become the man of the house again.

*

It had taken less than a week for them to fall into step, to rediscover the tacit understanding that exists between siblings. After getting the milk, he helped fill the large brass cauldrons with water—drinking water which was to be fetched from the tap outside. He was surprised that this old practice still continued. Their mother had been particular that the water for cooking and drinking be fetched in a state of madi or ritual purity, and stored, out of the way of contamination, in brass cauldrons.

It's the plumbing, Savitri said, as if he had spoken out loud. It is too complicated to draw the line from the yard into the kitchen. There was little point in investing in an old house that would have to go soon, she seemed to imply, and one whose future was uncertain. We just boil the water we need for drinking each morning, she shrugged. In Suchi mama's house he had noticed a new gadget—a wall-mounted water purifier, a jumble of alphabets proclaiming its magical properties—RO+UV+UF—that could, like the gods who had churned the ocean to separate nectar from poison, convert the gush supplied by the municipality into potable water. He recalled his father's dictum—follow the Kaveri; if you have to buy a house make sure it is supplied by water from the Kaveri. His father also had a sealed brass pot, a small one with water from the Ganga, holy water, which he had worshipped every day, and had wished to be poured into his mouth when it was time for him to go. He wondered whether his father's wish had been carried out, for the pot stood, still unopened, on the altar.

He chopped the vegetables and handed them over to her.

Your hand moves smoothly with the knife across the board, his sister commented, like a ...

He waited for her to say it.

Like a—housewife.

For a few moments they stood together without speaking. They watched the branches outside the window reflected on the surface of the water in the cauldrons. In a few hours, the moon would be out in the sky, and also on the granite counter of the kitchen, framed against the window panes, as it had always done.

Do you cook for yourself, over there, she asked.

Yes, he replied briefly.

Except when I was too poor to cook, he wanted to add but held his tongue.

By the time he fetched the water, the pressure cooker was hissing, the vegetables done. It was again the old warhorse, the pressure cooker, a friend from the old days, thick aluminium body, dripping gasket, and a small weight with a sharp tongue angled to fit tight into the vent on top, with the words Patent Still Pending carved on its underside.

*

Savitri had asked him to buy greens and a gourd, nothing else, no 'English' vegetables. Watch out for the greens—his sister had instructed him. The large healthy-looking leafy ones are suspect—grown in drains and manured with human excreta. Get the local nati variety—more modest looking, even a little bedraggled.

The market was bursting at the seams. There were mounds and mounds of fruits and vegetables piled on the pavements, the baskets jutting on to the streets. The women minding them strung flowers calmly as cars and buses travelled inches past their elbows. From time to time the vendors were 'evicted' but they came right back.

Beans, carrot, cauliflower—the prices were astronomical, Savitri was right. If he remembered correctly, these were winter vegetables, but now they were there in heaps in the hot season, bright in the blazing heat. Mushrooms—the poisonous nayi kodai of his boyhood, fungal growths that appeared on the stumps of fallen trees after the rains—were now buttonholed in sterile plastic packets priced sixteen rupees a pouch. There were apples too, varieties of them, in neat pyramids.

Best-selling—the fruit vendor pointed to a pile of Red Delicious, ruby red with a wax polish sheen, and a small sticker vouching for its soundness. The Ruby Red had travelled a long distance from the farm in the Midwest where it had originated, close to the college he had attended. Best-selling all over the world—

He smiled at the vendor and shook his head. Next to the Ruby Red were piles of Washington apples, Honey Crisp, and the water-filled pink-striped Fuji—imported from China.

He pointed to the bananas instead. A dozen, he said. I am a poor man—he tried to explain but the man held out his hand for the money and turned to talk to someone else.

He moved on to the flower vendors. He was expecting to find fat buds of jasmine—flowers that announced themselves first with their fragrance—woven with davana leaves and the orange off splash of kanakambra. But there were very few strings of jasmine left. You must come early in the morning or much later in the evening. That is the time for jasmine, the woman said. You can take these instead. People have started using them for worship. You can even stand them in vases, for decoration. She pointed to the roses and carnations and another flower—was it the gerbera—tightly rolled in corrugated cardboard with just the tip of its head peeping out.

He walked home just as the petromax lamps were being lit, carrying his modest purchases in a wire basket. The birds, Savitri, he told his sister. The sound of the birds coming home to their nests in the evening. There used to be such a cawing at dusk when we cycled back from your music classes. I didn't hear them in the market. The trees are there but the birds have gone missing. Or they've grown quiet. This place has changed so much.

Three

The year turned new in the heat of April. The honge was now a dark undistinguished green. The copper pod had flowered in clusters of soft-petalled yellow flowers—you could catch their mild fragrance if you could recognise it. The rain tree outside had shed its pods, which were embedded in the melting tar, the seeds showing up in relief, like teeth in a skull. A young man's skull, a Native American Assiniboin chief would add, with the perfect teeth announcing to the world that he had died in war, defending his land, and not waiting at home, allowing his teeth to rot or wear out eating dried meat.

Aprameya was to climb the neem tree in the garden and bring down the flowers.

Stay on the trunk, don't climb on to the branches, Savitri instructed him.

Watch out for the monkeys, his sister said. They might recognise you and carry you off ...

I'll kill you, just wait!

Shh ... not on Ugadi day—Savitri admonished.

He climbed down with a fistful of leaves and white flowers. I'm not having any of that bevu-bella stuff, I'm warning you right now.

His mother started sorting out the untidy heap, making no answer to his show of bravado. She would separate the small bitter-tasting white flowers and mix them with pounded jaggery, and spoon out small quantities of the mix to them all—the new year began with a symbolic exhortation that the sweet and the bitter went hand in hand, and must be accepted with equanimity.

His niece carefully separated the jaggery from the neem flowers and put only the jaggery in her mouth, and pulled a face. You can never really get the bitter taste out, she said.

Savitri spooned out the mix on to his palm—fifty-fifty, she said—in equal measure.

No, he wanted to say, I have lived the bitter every day. What I wish for is just a taint of sweet.

Manohar says he invites you over for Ugadi every year but you haven't gone, even once.

He looked up in anger, unprepared for Savitri's attack. It was tacitly agreed, he thought, that they would not tread on each other's toes.

Manohar? I want to have nothing to do with him. Prakash either. What are they to me?

They are the only people from home, the only family you have there—

Family! Don't *you* talk to me of family ... people from home—better to stay as far away from them as possible.

Immediately, he regretted that he had allowed himself to be provoked. But Savitri had turned on her heel and left. She was in a hurry to get going.

Keshav Rao was nowhere to be seen. Shweta and Aprameya were going out with friends. Savitri had a programme at the ashram, the Ugadi Special. There was to be no festive meal at home—no obbattu, ambode, payasa—she wasn't going to cook.

*

There was to be a special prayer at the ashram to mark the new year. They were expecting a lot of guests, many devotees. Apparently, it was Savitri's big day. She had dressed with care, in a pale green silk sari, and emeralds in her ears, with a matching pendant at the throat. He recognised the expression of old—determined, a little anxious, eyes watchful, ready to do battle, when she was set for a music competition; always feeling that she would not come up to scratch but ready to challenge anyone who said that. Her natural love of bright colours she seemed to have held in check out of deference for her Sundari Amma. Savitri was to lead the bhajans and the chanting.

In the early mornings, the ashram had a slot on the FM radio, where they played devotional songs and dispensed advice on a host of problems that listeners called in with. It was Savitri who spoke on behalf of Sundari Amma.

I have been to so many doctors. Is there no cure for my stomach ache? a woman asked.

In the grave voice that Savitri had assumed for the radio, and a formal turn of phrase, she gave advice. She spelt out a decoction of tulasi leaves, cumin and several herbs, and a poultice of betel leaf and castor oil.

My limbs tremble, as if in fear. I wake up in a sweat. I think someone has cast an evil eye on me. I'm involved in a property dispute with my brothers.

Feed the poor, Savitri advised, on Friday, Saturday and Sunday. Take the herbal prescription recommended by the ashram three times a day.

I've received a frog made of metal as a wedding gift. Is it a good omen? Can I keep it?

The frog is an evolved creature. Also a sign of luck. It has a long tongue that cleaves to its palate in the front of its mouth and not at the back, at the throat, so it's quick on the uptake. The frog is a keeper of deep secrets. Accept your metal frog gratefully and treat it well.

Savitri, what is this you are doing, he asked, afraid to say more.

Helping people.

Savitri, these are paid-for slots on the radio. They are advertisements for the ashram ... Maybe, but the problems are real. The people are real, her eyes flashed. He braced himself for the outburst.

There were men in my garden, Savitri said. Strange men, stomping all over the house, looking me over, saying they were officials from the bank. I was alone in the house with the children. Suchi mama gave me moral lectures, and Manohar, complicated explanations for financial fraud. Kaveramma too came sniffing around trying to see if she could get the house for cheap—that was the worst. Where were you then? And my husband? It was she, Sundari Amma, who rowed me ashore. I remember the first time I heard her speak to a girl. It was more informal then, fewer people, and she would meet people personally and speak to them. The girl had written to her. She seemed genuinely distressed. She and her family were beset with debts. She had a month's time to solve her problems. But the time was not enough. She said suicide was her only way out. I still remember her advice to the girl. She spoke to her several times. You have to go through many lives to merit the human form. Your life, your form itself, is a blessing. It hasn't been attained so easily, so you cannot toss it aside as casually as you would the peel of a fruit you've eaten. When you're in trouble the waters seem murky, your vision is blurred. Wait till the waters settle; they will become clear and you will find a way out. It seemed as if she was speaking to me, to me alone.

Savitri, he said, she couldn't have read the girl's letter. She cannot read or write.

It's getting late, Savitri replied. I must leave.

At the gate she turned round and said—I'd still say no to the marriage.

I want to meet Thippy, he shouted after her. Tell her that.

She's Sundari Amma now, show some respect—And it's not up to you to decide that you can meet her.

The jasmine that grows in your own backyard has no fragrance, he called out. Remember that.

*

There was a hush on the streets, a holiday hush. A lone autorickshaw, rickety, black-and-yellow, was making its way up the street. It stopped and a man got off. Ashwath hailed the auto. He climbed in, in to the warm vaporous clutch of the body that had just occupied it.

It was too hot in the yard, so Suchi mama was sitting in the small covered verandah, his grandchildren playing about his feet, several pairs of footwear scattered around the front door. Both his sons were there, the second one visiting, and there were other relatives too, from Suchi mama's wife's side as well as theirs. The Ugadi celebration at Suchi mama's place was a big affair, just as it had been in his parents' time. The mantle had now passed on to Suchi mama. There were few visitors to Neel Kamal, he realised. And Savitri held no celebrations, no feasts.

Look who's here—Suchi mama said to everyone who came. Our boy from America is visiting. After twenty-five years ...

He recognised Malati, a cousin from his father's side, who used to visit often as a girl. She came up to him and said something bright, something innocuous, her manner arch, even flirtatious.

So you remembered us at last, after all these years—She looked about him expectantly.

Malati was wearing a Mysore crepe sari; a pearl necklace of several strands hung on her bosom. Her face was moist and pink—almost edible—the snow-powder look in place, her eyebrows drawn uncompromisingly with pencil. He was grateful to her for the effort. At one time his mother had been half contemplating her as a match for him, he remembered. By now she must be a grandmother.

Ah Malati, you haven't changed at all. You still look like the girl you were, he said.

He walked into the hall where the men were sitting and allowed himself to be drawn into the small talk. They spoke of the muddle of politics. When he left, the Congress party, the GOP which the textbooks had identified as the party that won the country freedom from the British, the party of Gandhi and Nehru, was at the helm. Indira Gandhi had won the national elections. On the state stage, several wily old Congress hands were coming to power-sharing deals. The seasoned Devaraj Urs was making way for Gundu Rao. But that was twenty-five years ago; it could count as history.

Little had changed in twenty-five years, it seemed. The horse-trading and the power-sharing combos, muddled, quarrelsome, downright dishonest, were still going on. The billboards and newspapers were awash with acronyms and alphabets. Kumaraswamy of the JD (S), son of the old-timer Deve Gowda had just wrested the chief ministership from a Congressman whose name he did not recognise, on the understanding that he would relinquish it at the appointed time to a third person of yet another political party. At the centre, the Congress party was in the saddle. A man with a turban, calm of demeanour, was prime minister.

Ashwath!

There was a cluster of chairs in the balcony abutting one of the rooms. Someone thrust a glass of lime juice into his hands. He made his way towards the chairs, trying to place the person who had hailed him. It was the cousin who was in Canada, his band box look shouting out his discomfort. He was wearing chinos and a tee shirt with a collar and his bare feet were curled under the chair. He smelt as if he had just been released from shrink wrap. His father, Ashwath remembered vaguely, had been something of a dandy. They exchanged greetings, new year wishes. Ashwath tried to recall his name.

You must have found this place much changed. Come, sit down—He wiped the plastic chair next to him with a paper napkin. How can people wear silk in this heat! I like it that you are still grounded ...

He had assumed that they were both on the same side. He had also assumed that Ashwath had done well for himself. People often did that here. Anyone who was visiting from the US had to be a tech entrepreneur or an investment banker at the very least. Ashwath had found ways of deflecting their questions when they started probing. It was a synonym for eyes, this man's name. Nayan, no. He searched again.

And you are in ...

Was, Ashwath said. Was in industrial foods ... logistics.

But not any longer. As you said, I like keeping things simple and uncomplicated.

Ah! The man sighed. This country has become unrecognisable. Greed—it has been overtaken by greed ...

He looked quite desolate, a large, trim man with a big head and clean white toenails.

The floor inside is Italian marble, as also the modular kitchen—that was the first thing Badri told me. He rolled his eyes.

The steel funnel of the exhaust fan caught their eye; it looked like an art object.

At one time you had to go abroad, to America to become prosperous. But not any longer. Who would have imagined that cousin Badri—I wish him well, of course.

Lochan, that was his name, he remembered now. He also knew that Lochan had recently tried to buy a flat in the city, converting his Canadian dollars into rupees, but had found that the prices had gone too high. Purchasing power parity, that was the phrase he was looking for; the dollar had failed the rupee when it came to real estate in Bangalore. Lochan had sent Suchi mama feelers for a flat, a small one, even two bedrooms would do, if Ashwath wanted to pull down Neel Kamal and build flats in its place. It's only a matter of time, Suchi mama had added. Make up your mind and you'll have builders lining up at your door. Of course, I'll guide you to the right one.

They could see Badri's wife walking towards the balcony with a group of women. She was taking them up to her yoga hall. The yoga and wellness retreat that she had planned at the resort, the one built on the kharab land that should rightfully have come to him, according to Savitri, was booked up full. Badri's wife was regretfully telling someone she would reserve a place for her in the next session.

Have you seen the room where they house the gods? Cousin Lochan lowered his voice. See the silver mandapa—we were the first to order one like that and take it back with us—of course without the coloured stones. Now everyone has it. It's not a question of devotion, it's just a fad. People have become more fearful, clutching of their good fortune. They need constant reassurance. If not from god, from godmen or even godwomen ...

Ashwath stood up. Come over and visit us, Lochan. He held out his hand. I'm here for some time now. Have to settle a few things before I leave.

He walked away quickly, before the other man could say anything else. He would rather sit with the older men, where all he had to do was listen, and no one pressed him for his reactions. The festive mess in Suchi mama's house was reassuring. The aroma of food, the bustle of women, the sound of children playing and a flow of platitudes from the men. This was what he had been used to—he could return to it very easily.

*

The bank had sent for him. His signature, apparently, did not tally.

Twenty-five years is a long time. I've grown up, he told the bank official, a young woman probationary officer, dressed not in a sari but trousers and a long-sleeved business shirt. You could place her anywhere—La Salle Street, Wall Street, Nariman Point, Mahatma Gandhi Road—and she would be fish in water.

You've changed your logo too. You have a geometric figure, instead of the dog you once had.

She smiled. We have to keep up with the times, keep in step with people's needs. We are the tech capital of the country, remember? There has been a complete overhaul of processes, computerisation of accounts, net banking. And a new vision. The interlinked circles meant the bank and its customers were equal partners. The bank was no longer a watchdog, keeping an eye on people's money. They had paid the designer close to a crore of rupees, that's ten million, she added for his benefit, and the whole re-envisioning exercise had taken two years.

Nayi bank, Thippy used to refer to as, for it had as its logo an eager-to-please dog, alert, head tilted, ears cocked. The first time he had run into her in the bank, she had been staring at a pay-in slip, looking to deposit a cheque made out to the temple fund. He had filled out the slip for her, and then held his pen out. The clerk at the counter had quietly produced an ink pad. Thippy had waved his pen aside, inked her thumb on the stamp pad and pressed it down where it said depositor's signature. He had found the gesture natural and unselfconscious. (But Savitri had burst into furious tears when he told her how charming Thippy had been.) It had brought to his mind the couple from his non-detail English text, Krishna and Sushila from R K Narayan's *The English Teacher*. He felt he recognised himself in Krishna, the English teacher of the title—a simple straightforward manliness despite the small ambit of his life. And Thippy, like Sushila, was instinctive, spontaneous, and self-willed. Of course, Krishna was completely in love with Sushila.

Much later, many years later, a long-distance finger

had uncoiled in his memory and touched him, when on a bitterly cold January evening, he had stepped into a poetry reading in North Clark Street more to get out of the cold and kill time before his next hourly wage job was to begin and where with some luck he could chase the waiters and get at the finger food. A young black girl had read out something, more as a filler between the star performers of the evening.

To be in love, she had announced, in a harsh, not unmusical voice, *is to touch with a lighter hand ... You look at things through his eyes. A cardinal is red. A sky is blue. When he shuts a door—is not there—your arms are water ... you are the beautiful half of a golden hurt.*

The words had flowed, a melancholy ripple, and had startled him into a sense of what he had lost. Later, he discovered that the poem was not written by the girl who had read it out but by a famous poet named Gwendolyn Brooks who was raised in Chicago.

I am thinking of developing my property here. I may need to apply for a loan, he said on impulse.

Of course, Sir.

Immediately, she straightened up. Gone was the casual, chatty air—he was a Person of Consequence. I will get you the forms. We can start the paperwork right away. She picked up the phone on her desk and dialled a number.

She smiled an engineer-turned-hedge-fund-manager welcome at him. He looked away from her, out of the window.

Done, Sir. She handed him a printout of the documents he needed to have. As soon as you get these, we will start processing the loan. It's all very simple now. You'll be surprised.

He got up to leave, refusing the bright Neha Singh's offer of tea, putting her Customer Relationship card in his pocket. Banks made him uneasy; he could not trust them. Too big to fail, Neha Singh's transoceanic counterpart had assured him, several years ago in a savings and loan bank on North Clark Street, but it had failed anyway. Crashed with a bang. Taking his savings with it. The biggest bank in the city.

*

Thippy sent him an invitation to visit the ashram.

Don't look so happy, Savitri said. The ashram management has invited you, it isn't a personal invitation. You must understand she is no longer the Thippy you knew. She is Sundari Amma now, of the Nivarana Ashram.

I knew she would ask to meet me, he said.

As he stood waiting in the shadow of his room on the terrace, she walked from the outhouse—its door seemed always open—in the only clothes she seemed to possess, a long skirt that hung till her ankles and a man's shirt, with a towel slung on her right shoulder. The hibiscus bush obscured her from sight. He could only see her hands, a red glass bangle on an angular bony wrist. She emerged, with his mother's copper plate full of red flowers, and again disappeared from sight as she walked to the back of the house to leave the flowers on the ledge outside the kitchen. When he heard the gate squeal, he knew she had left for the temple, and he too could go in and get on with his day. Sometimes his sister would appear at his elbow, silently, and stand with him.

Coffee, Savitri would say. You haven't come down for your coffee.

Of course she knew, she always did.

*

The Nivarana Ashram was located in a distant suburb of the city, in the midst of casuarina groves. He remembered cycling to reach there long back, past kuchcha roads, open fields, and a few houses, more like huts with concrete walls. It was a small piece of land located in a place that seemed to be of little use to anybody—either the farmer or the authorities. It had been, as if stamped with the ultimate badge of disapproval—outside BDA limits—the City did not care to turn the place into sites and layouts, and the municipality made no promises of water or electricity.

But the land-hungry city had devoured this suburb in stealthy swipes, leaving its teeth marks everywhere. The main road, a narrow tarred strip, only recently turned into a pukka road, was choked with traffic. The large double tyres of a moffussil bus, like conjoined doughnuts, stood at eye level, dangerously close. He could see the grooves in the rubber, worn out patches with stones embedded in its crevices; from its exhaust pipe there came a steady stream of black smoke. There were cars, cycles and motorized two-wheelers in front of them, set in aspic as they were, and from a non-existent elbow at the right, a scooter was trying to squeeze in. Each vehicle was free with bell and horn, as if it could blast its way out of the jam on waves of sound. From time to time, the fog horn of the bus resounded above the noise of the lesser vehicles.

The auto driver sat unfazed. He had been driving

autos for the past fifty years, he told Ashwath. When he first started the minimum auto fare was eight annas, and four annas per additional kilometer. Now, nobody could recognise those coins unless you said fifty paise and twenty-five paise. And soon those coins would no longer be legal tender; the government was talking of phasing them out. It was Indira Gandhi, he said, who had raised the minimum auto fares. She made it one rupee minimum and fifty paise per additional kilometre. Now of course the minimum was fourteen rupees. But it still wasn't enough. Which is why he was forced to charge a flat rate and not according to the metre.

For this auto, this rickety old thing? You want to charge extra? What about a discount on my jarred bones? Ashwath said.

The old man shrugged. He had to make a living after all. It cost him a hundred rupees a day to hire the auto and he ran it every day between five in the morning and eleven in the night. Why didn't he go for a new model? It cost a hundred and fifty thousand rupees. He seemed affronted that Ashwath had even suggested it. I've agreed to come on this road because I have a return pick-up. I have to bring back some deliveries from a farm off this road. If not I wouldn't have agreed to your hire.

The road seemed endless. They continued, in fits and starts, jostling and rattling.

The vehicle ahead of them, a tempo truck, stopped abruptly and several women who had been waiting by the side of the road hoisted themselves in, hanging on to a rope that dangled from the roof of the truck, clambering over the low hatch. The frame of the truck was covered with tarpaulin and other than the low hatch, it was open at the back. Once they had heaved themselves in the women had settled down on the floor and almost immediately, opened their bags, taken out steel dabbas and started to eat. As the tempo truck picked up more passengers, the women who got in later had to stand, holding on to the rope for support or they sat on the hatch. Every time the truck went over a pothole the women swayed, fell against each other and giggled. If the driver jammed the brakes suddenly the ones sitting on the hatch could go flying out but they did not seem to care. It seemed like a happy truck; the saris were colourful and the women wore flowers in their hair. Their bare midriffs gleamed like freshly kneaded dough.

Garment factory workers—the auto rickshaw driver motioned to them—there are two factories down the road. All our export garments, these are the women who make them.

At one point a path forked off the main road. The auto stopped and set him down. You have to go down a kilometre on this path, the driver said. And take the other road when you return.

The other road?

There's a ring road on the other side. Lots of buildings coming up here, so they got together and got the government to give them a road.

Buildings? Here? I remember there was a lake here. Full of lotuses.

Lake? Lotuses? The man turned, impatient to go. This is an IT city now—they are growing software factories here. This whole place, all these houses, will go. There is a tech park coming up on either side of the ring road.

*

The auto left. On one side was the crowded road and on the other a forking path leading into what seemed to be a deserted wilderness. He suddenly felt like a traveller abandoned at the edge of a new city whose towers beckon but whose lore of lawlessness precedes its fame.

He smelt the drain before he could see it, and when he caught sight of it, it stood as wide as an irrigation canal full of black water; further up it was surmounted by a massive metal tube with a valve on top. Then he remembered. There must be a bridge close by, across the drain, a sturdy bridge, made of bamboo. He had been here with Thippy, riding with her on his carrier, rattling on the dirt roads. There must be a small cluster of houses too, at the edge of the fields, through which the dirt road zigzagged.

The dirt road remained, now flinty with stones, and with deep channels on either side, thick with sludge. Each house had constructed a small bridge to cross the drain and reach the street. The houses too remained but surrounded by larger construction projects, whose skeletons loomed in the background, and over which tall forklifts hovered like predatory cranes.

The houses were small and self-contained. Through the open doorway a room was visible; perhaps that was all there was to the house. The door would remain open all day, but a smaller slat of wood, a quarter door, was pulled across the bottom of the doorway, no doubt to prevent the toddler of the house from crawling out and falling into the sludge-filled drain. The wooden frame of the doorway was marked with turmeric and vermilion; in the foot-wide space between the door and the drain, along the wall, stood a garden. The tulasi in an anointed tin can, bearing signs of fresh worship. Out of another can a vine climbed up, the glossy leaves and glutinous stem of the basale, the Indian spinach, soon to yield a good sambar. A money plant grew on the other side of the door anchored in a plastic bottle. On a lintel above the door, red chillies dried in the sun in one corner, and at the other end stood a pair of canvas shoes, newly dripping with white polish. There was a festoon of mango leaves across the top of the front door. Every sign of good health, auspicious and domestic, was there to be seen; a life lived to the full in the space handed out to them. It seemed pitifully little to combat the skeletons of buildings that loomed in the near distance; small shrines on the lip of a greedy maw.

When he peeped into the open doorways he could see that some of the houses were still arranged the old-fashioned way—several rooms built round a common courtyard, each room housing a family. There were empty plastic buckets lined up in the courtyard, waiting no doubt for the brief hour when there would be water in the taps—it was a frenzied ritual; he had witnessed several cat fights over water.

He remembered this stretch as a cluster of huts amidst open, indeterminate land. But now several plots of land had been fenced off, some with concrete walls topped with barbed wire and jagged shards of glass. The plots were overgrown with shrubs and castor plants, the owners biding their time, no doubt till the 'IT factories' offered them a good price for their land, once deemed worthless. Some plots were just full of garbage, heaped up in mounds—bags of garbage had snagged on the barbed wire fence, spilling their guts out. The paths leading off the dirt tracks were lined with discarded plastic bags, which glinted in the sunlight, like silver bells and cockle shells, as in the old nursery rhyme. In the thick of these houses, he caught a fragment of old brickwork, the delicate trellis of a balcony, but it was lost in a mess of newly slapped-on cement.

There were small shops set up in housefronts, selling vegetables—somewhat shrivelled; a hardware store—displaying trowels and spades, tools for masons, a bakery, a butcher promising chicken that was Younger, Tender, Better—it sounded lofty, like the Olympic motto—Faster, Higher, Stronger.

He walked on. There had been attempts to clean the drain. Small mounds of grey solid matter were heaped up at regular intervals on the dirt road. There should be a tent theatre here somewhere—ah there it was! A movie hall where the more expensive tickets afforded a metal chair and the janata class sat on the coir matting in front of the flickering makeshift screen, with the soundtrack blasting in your head. There was a poster on the wall of the theatre—a pink-cheeked cowboy in a stetson riding a plump horse. It was a Tamil film, he could not read the letters.

Outside the tent theatre, at a cart standing on a slab across the drain, two men dipped their hands into vats and their hands emerged encrusted in what looked like blood. The legend on the cart said Gobi Manjoori, Fried Rice, Fish Fry. A small heap of red lacquered fish lay on one side of the cart. The men were preparing the cauliflower flowerlets for the Gobi Manjoori—the local version of Manchurian, dipping them into the sauce. A conch shell, a lemon and a few dry red chillies dangled in a mobile over the fish in the cart, to ward off the evil eye. At one time, he remembered, one of Thippy's brothers, the eldest, had a food cart like this selling food outside the high court; he had been doing very well.

He walked further. Some of the large tracts of land were under litigation, with half constructed buildings which seemed to have been abandoned suddenly—a bone of contention between strangers or even between brothers. He was reminded of the time he would go with Suchi mama, grumpy and footsore, to visit a godforsaken piece of land somewhere—all those trips had come to nothing; they had not been able to retain any of those lands.

A fence of high aluminium sheets was being erected round an empty plot being readied for construction—it had carefully skirted an anthill which bore signs of worship—there were fresh flowers and incense sticks with the ash stacked in a small smoking column. On the lone tree in the middle of the plot there slung a hammock; a dog slept near by in the remains of a bonfire. A large construction crane rested on its side, entwined with a creeper, in temporary harmony with the child in the hammock and the dog amidst the ashes, like a giant held down with string. A business centre was promised here.

Closer to the main road, on the other side that the auto driver had spoken of, the buildings were complete, already occupied, and doing business. Here was West Chester (West Chester?) Service Apartments, a row of identical narrow balconies jutting on to the road, a wary security guard at the gate. Another building under construction was to have a paying guest accommodation with high speed broadband connectivity. He could not tell where the workers on these sites came from—small-made, light-complexioned—from a north Indian state perhaps. He had passed by a mess, the sort that served local food, and had not been able to recognise the script on the signboard—it had not been in Kannada, Tamil or Telugu, any one of the south Indian languages he was familiar with.

Six months later, he was to pass this way again. By then there were dramatic changes. The cranes had woken up and done their job. A spanking new business centre, fronted with icy green glass, was up and about. A fleet of vans stood in its yard, ready to transport its workers. The paying guest accommodation was announced, Vicky's Punjabi fast food had come up, the abandoned buildings, apparently still under litigation, had been invaded by a forest of creepers. The Sun Light Facilities Management and Security Services—security was big business here on the outskirts—which advertised itself as an ISO 9001 company, occupied the first floor of the Paying Guest building. There was an appearance of order, a smartening up that was in evidence. There were fewer garbage bags, the silver bells and cockle shells had been cleared, and there was something else—it took him some time to put his finger on it—the open drain had been covered with perforated cement slabs. The Gobi Manjoori food cart stood at ease outside the tent theatre—he had added Chinese Chop Suey to his menu. On one of the plots where a makeshift sari-hammock had slung down from a tree, weighted by a small sleeping form, child of a woman who worked on the site no doubt, the building stood completed, and in an exactitude of ironic symmetry, it was now the My Baby Store, the glass front bearing the picture of a young mother in a lacy dress with spaghetti straps, holding up a baby with limbs like sausages.

*

The Nivarana Ashram was fenced off from the rest of the open land. Joseph Gliddens's invention to mark territory in the treeless prairies had travelled well—a bristling barbed wire fence marked the acres of perimeter of the ashram. He was frisked by the guard at the entrance, who spoke into a walkie-talkie, in Hindi. The guard, the whole posse of them, looked smart in their berets and uniforms. They were not local people, he could tell, they looked as if they were from the northeast. It was a thumb rule, his brother-in-law had told him, to get your workforce from outside the state. The local people were expensive, lazy and they had political heft.

He walked down the path in the middle of the casuarina grove. The trees lent an air of solemnity to the place, as befitting an ashram, hooded, straitlaced. There should be bushes around, red with bandhuka flowers, in full blossom, as beautiful as the god of love himself, but the path was clear, clear of all undergrowth.

There were two picturesque hut-like buildings by the banyan tree—one said Reception and the other, Store. Across the huts, on the other side of the banyan, was a large golden-domed building—the prayer hall. The dome was scalloped into many spires, each one resembling the roof of a different place of worship—the multi-stepped vimana of a temple, the steeple of a church, the dome of a mosque and the terraced roof of a Buddhist pagoda. There were several young men and women manning the Reception, all dressed in white and calm of demeanour. They spoke softly to each other and to the visitors who queued up at the desk. Many of those who had congregated in the waiting room seemed like first-time visitors. They were looking around, a little awe-struck, with humbled curiosity, and most of them carried large bags. There was a girl at the desk which said May I Help You, to answer any questions.

Would he wait in the lounge for his turn? There was a buggy to take all visitors to the main offices. He could have a tour of the ashram if the estate manager sanctioned it. A volunteer would take him around.

He got into the buggy with three others—a middle-aged couple from somewhere up north, visiting for the first time, who said nothing but smiled benignly all through the ride, and a striking-looking young man, who made a full confession of his life in the few minutes that it took them to reach. He worked in a BPO in Gurgaon on the outskirts of Delhi, but was originally from a small village in Orissa, by the coast. He was sick and tired of everything. He was thirty years old. He had been working at his job for ten years. He had heard about the ashram from a friend. He hoped to work in the garden here, the herbarium that was so famous, to rediscover his green thumb.

They drove on the bund of the lake, full of pink lotus flowers. The leaves—large, leathery and somewhat bedraggled, lay flat on the water and the flowers arched themselves up, as if to catch the rays of the setting sun. The couple in the buggy turned to each other. Ah, the woman said to the man. Look at them. Burning pink, like jewels. Hewn from ruby.

They got down at a cluster of buildings with tiled roofs. His companions from the buggy were led into the main office while he was directed to a path on the side. It led to a small garden enclosed by a hedge of golden duranta, which true to its name glowed in the gathering dusk. The hedge enclosed a stretch of lumpy lawn and at the far end, the twisted branches of a tabebuia in full yellow flower. To his surprise, he saw a peacock on the lawn, pecking at the ground, its tail at rest, slivers of luminous blue-green flashing as it moved.

Again an ante room leading to offices whose doors were firmly shut. An attendant appeared almost as soon as he sat down on the sofa.

Fruit juice or herbal tea?

He waved her away.

If you change your mind, the pantry is right there, she said. You may have to wait a while.

Unlike the Reception, this room was crowded with things. He got up and walked around to take a closer look at the display. There were glass-fronted cabinets all along the walls, full of what looked like gifts from devotees—glittering crystal, brass and silver lamps, figurines of gods and goddesses. On top of the cabinets there were plaques and shields from colleges and private clubs, and other institutions, even one that sounded like an affiliate of the United Nations, in appreciation of Amma's and the ashram's contribution. There was one from the Meeting of Peace Harmony and Health granting her the status of Citizen of the World. On the central wall there hung a photograph of Thippy, framed in LED lights. It was a replica of the photograph that Savitri had in the prayer room at home. Thippy's eyes and small even features were lit up by the lights framing the photograph. Her eyebrows, thick, meeting in the middle of her forehead, and her steady expression gave her a look of gravity; she looked wise, as befitting a guru, a leader of people.

He waited in the ante room by himself. There were no other visitors. The doors of the offices remained closed, and he could hear the low murmur of conversation behind the closed doors. The door to one of the rooms opened and a young man came out, carrying a sheaf of papers, speaking on his cell phone. After ten minutes he went back into the room, still speaking into the phone and the door shut before Ashwath could get a glimpse of the inside of the room.

There was no sign of the attendant either. An invisible audio system piped music at a low volume—the chants of the ashram, meant to soothe the nerves and put the mind in a meditative state. He could recognise the timbre of his sister's singing voice in the chants.

He sat on the stuffed sofa and leafed through the flyers and magazines on the glass-topped table. There was a coffee table book about the ashram and he started turning its pages. The Nivarana Ashram described itself as a spiritual enterprise, holistic in its approach to life. He flipped through the pages till he came to the section devoted to Sundari Amma—the photograph on the wall was the standard issue—it was replicated everywhere. There were smaller photos of Amma—in the ashram garden, tending to the plants, Amma with the animals on the ashram farm, feeding the cows, scrubbing them with her own hands.

'Born in a village nestling in the foothills of the verdant Western Ghats,' he read, 'Tripura Sundari Amma was considered to be special. The hamlet where Amma was born is said to have attracted sages and rishis who chose it for their abode. It has long been considered a punya kshetra—a blessed land ...'

'Descended from a clan of landlords, her group of the family dedicated itself to the service of God and branched o ıt early to become the spiritual mainstay of the village and their local temple.'

'The origins of Amma's calling and her family temple lie in a beautiful story. A local farmer, who owned a small piece of land in the hamlet, had noticed a certain radiance of light in a grove of trees on his land. It happened after darkness fell, over a number of days, as if the earth herself was glowing amidst the trees. One night he had a dream that the goddess was asking him for a house on his land in that grove. When he woke up in the morning he found that his wife had had the same dream. Though he could ill-afford it, he built a temple for the goddess, a modest shrine, and made it over to the village. After that, he grew prosperous, his lands multiplied, and the temple attracted several devotees. It was the custom of Amma's people to dedicate the firstborn son to a religious life, free from the demands of the land or any trade. but in the case of her family, it was the daughter on whom the mantle fell.'

He flipped a few more pages and read at random.

'She was named Tripura Sundari, after the beautiful goddess to whom the temple was dedicated. One of Amma's girlhood tasks was to take flowers to the temple every morning. She had an inborn love of plants and animals which showed itself in time as a gift of healing.

'The family and the local people first noticed her special powers at the festival dedicated to the goddess at the temple in the village. The young girl would go into a deep trance, almost turning lifeless for a short duration. When she emerged from the trance, she had simple remedies for those who had gathered at the temple seeking succour for their many ailments, physical and emotional.

'When Amma was a young girl, the family moved to the city, called to the service of another temple, and here Tripura Sundari Amma's gifts were noticed by the head priest of the temple. He took her under his wing and initiated her formal spiritual training ...'

'On a piece of waste land that the family was given on the outskirts of the city, a marsh at best, they built a small structure. From such humble beginnings has the Nivarana Ashram grown to be the centre of spiritual power and healing. People from all over the world come to seek Tripura Sundari Amma's blessings, and to be rejuvenated by the alternate healing methods practised at the ashram.

'Amma's remedies are very simple—a leaf, a herb, a root, a natural rhythm of breathing, and simple chants that soothe the nerves, invigorate the body and fill it with a positive energy.'

'Q: Why do so many people visit the Nivarana Ashram?

Ans: To lead a good life.

Q: Why do people from all over the world follow Amma?

Ans: Because her advice is simple, practical and effective. It comes from the heart.'

There were testimonials from various devotees on what the ashram and Amma meant to them.

A childless couple blessed with a child, a doctor with a persistent stomach ache, which her own medicine had been unable to cure, but which had disappeared after a session at Amma's prayer meeting and a few doses of her tulasi extract, a girl who met the man she later married, through

Amma's guidance, a grateful student whose concentration had improved after drinking a decoction of Brahmi leaves as Amma had advised. Some were love letters to Amma—a woman who said she knew Amma was always with her because of the fragrance that followed her everywhere—Amma is there in my senses; she fills every pore of my being.

In time, the Nivarana Ashram had branched out, responding to the demands that were made on it. He flipped through another section of the book. There were lists of the other activities of the ashram—schools, an orphanage, a nursing school, a hospital.

The organisation chart of the ashram, the details of its various activities and the people in charge was laid out in the end. Savitri was there smiling widely, in charge of Communications, described as a vidwan in Carnatic music and Amma's childhood friend. Thippy's brothers were there—Srinivasa—he recognised Gunda of old—in charge of the Ashram Estates and Marketing, Venkatesha was in charge of the Ashram Canteen, the oldest brother was the Treasurer. There was a statement of accounts at the end—details of income and expenditure—everything, it seemed to say, was transparent, all was above board.

The door to an office room opened and the dark ante room was filled with light. The young man he had seen earlier, the one in the khadi waistcoat, ushered him in. Srinivasa Dasa will see you now, he said. Gunda was sitting behind a wide table, its green baize cloth covered with a sheet of glass. There were several papers under the glass top, the standard issue photograph of Thippy took up half the table. Gunda was dressed in a white kurta-pyjama and an angavastra edged in gold thread.

Amma does not give private darshans, he said. She usually restricted her public appearances to the chanting sessions. Of course, her devotees were constantly in touch with her through her aides. Why Amma had sent for him, Gunda said, was to talk about Neel Kamal. They understood that he was the rightful owner of the house now. What were his plans for the house? Would he consider selling it to the ashram? They needed a place in the city for their office. Besides, there was the ashwattha tree on the property which Amma had blessed and which was exciting a lot of interest in the devotees.

He stared at Gunda, who stared back, impassively, his hands folded on the table top. They sat in silence for several seconds.

I have no intention to sell, he said at last.

He got up to leave.

It's time for our evening meal, the young aide said. Please join us at our dining room.

All our food is steam-cooked, untouched by hand, Gunda said, catching his eye. And it is all vegetarian.

That was the only sign, a tangential acknowledgement of their past association. If not, they could well have been strangers.

A swift dart of anger set his limbs on fire, clogged his throat. The old impulse revived, to wrestle Gunda to the ground for his insolence. He wanted to say something scorching, something incinerating about the tinsel paradise over which she was queen and they, her brothers, glittering knaves. But there was the question of hygiene in public places, so he swallowed the hot gob of phlegm instead of spitting it out.

He turned at the door on impulse. Tell her, he said, she will have to meet me first. Tell her to come home.

He had had the sense all along, as he waited in the ante room, sipping on his khus juice, amidst the bric a brac of her new life, that she would not meet him. Riding back to the front gate in the buggy, on the darkened road, with the wind rushing into his face, carrying the over-sweet fragrance of the night queen, he had felt for a moment that he was on an infinite journey, on an unknown road, and he could well travel like this forever. Of course the ride lasted only a few minutes. He was at the gate, being frisked by the guards, collecting his bag and his mobile phone, on his way out. He put down his light-headed moment to a sense of relief. He was quite glad not to have met her.

Four

He decided to take a bus to the lawyer's office. The autorickshaw was working out to be too expensive and his sister had said no to the bicycle. The traffic was insane, she said. There was no comparison to what it had been when he was a student here; it had been a bullock cart city. When he went for his morning walk now, he carried a stout stick with him to ward off the stray dogs. It was his niece's gift to him. She had come running up to the gate on the first day he had set off on his walk and given it to him. Just hold it in your hand. They won't come near you. Here, Amma wants me to give you this. His nephew had dug into the crotch of his tight jeans and pulled out a plum—a cell phone. It's an old one, I don't use it anymore.

I don't want it, Ashwath had said. I hate these things. They make me anxious.

For a moment, his nephew looked genuinely bewildered, then he caught his sister's eye and they went into splits.

He was the cause of much amusement to both of them, he realised. Ash mama, there are no ten paise coins anymore, and don't expect the auto driver to return, what's that you call, four annas to you, his niece would call out from one end of the terrace within her brother's hearing.

They could not believe that he read all the exhortations painted on the frames of the autorickshaws and buses. Ash mama, his nephew would say, I am sure you'd actually report an auto driver to nearest police station if the driver demands excess fare.

He protested. I'm not that bad, he said.

And no, policemen don't demand bribes if the dynamo on your cycle is not working. Nobody notices cyclists any more. Where did you get that word—dynamo? Dynamo ... dynamo ... Shweta chanted as if it were a mantra.

He was the subject of much giggling conversation that Shweta had with her best friend, as she walked up and down on the terrace, her cell phone stuck to her ear like a clam. When the best friend finally visited, she brought him out—my Ash mama—as if he were a prized pet or a strange object, which she had been saving for the moment.

He knew that he was expected to rise to the occasion. Ah Chandan Bala, the Sandalwood Maiden! Pleased to meet you at last, he said.

It delighted the girls. Chandan Bala gave him an arch look, suggesting a familiarity with awkward truths. He wondered what his niece had been saying about him.

She is from Jharkhand, his niece said—another cue.

Jharkhand?

Ash mama doesn't know, Shweta explained to the Sandalwood Maiden. When he went abroad, India was very different. He left in the olden days, before we were even born. When was it, Ash mama? Yes, you told me. 1980, I think.

Jharkhand is a new state, Ash mama—and Uttarakhand, the Sandalwood Maiden was emboldened enough to add. And Chattisgarh.

We'll get a map of India with all the new states for Ash mama's birthday—

We are going to the bakery, Ash mama. Want to come with us, Shweta would ask.

He scrambled to his feet, glad to be included.

That girl is perpetually hungry, Savitri would grumble. It looks like they don't feed her at her PG place. Here at all times, no one to keep an eye on her, does what she pleases ... And don't allow them to twist you round their little finger Ashwath. They should show respect to elders.

Shweta, the fair-complexioned one, so Savitri had misnamed her for she had turned out to be dark-skinned. Perhaps it had been wishful thinking on his sister's part. The cabinet in the upstairs bathroom, which he had to share with his niece, was stocked with sachets of New and Beautiful—a skin cream that did not believe in mincing words. It had on its cover a young woman whose expression changed from gloomy to ecstatic over several frames as her skin tone changed from brown to pink.

Your mother used to apply turmeric and sandalwood paste, he told her.

She shook her head decisively. Too messy, too much work, she said. This one moisturizes and reduces dark spots. It has shea butter and aloe vera, she said, in confiding tones.

Some evenings were special. Chandan Bala arrived with an air of suppressed excitement, her cheeks inexpertly rouged and her mouth red, as if she had drunk a cup of blood. After his niece had finished her preparations, he would find in the bathroom, next to the sink, tissue paper streaked with colour, looking in the fading light like butterflies with their wings half open. She would leave, with a look of intense concentration on her face as if she had accomplished a difficult task, trailing a fruity fragrance on the terrace.

Goodbye Ash mama, she would wave—a child's gesture, her hand still plump, the curve of her cheek still rounded.

Have a nice evening, he would call out from the terrace, not having the heart to point out her scabby elbows.

*

Children these days are not what we used to be. Docile, obedient, listening to their parents. Things have changed now, Savitri said.

That's a good thing, he thought to himself, even as he nodded in agreement with his sister.

Shweta had finally decided he was on her side. You're my friend Ash mama, she told him, generously. Twice he was called to intercede with his sister on behalf of his niece on matters of life-or-death.

Ash mama, you tell her. She won't let me ...

Shweta wanted to get a tattoo.

Nothing doing, Savitri said. Like some village woman.

He recalled the tattoos on Thippy's face—three dots, like an inverted triangle, on the promontory of her chin. He used to fix his eyes on her chin, too unsure to meet the steady, guileless gaze of her eyes. You want to marry a girl with brands on her face and arms, his sister had thrown at him, like marks on cattle? For shame.

Every one has a tattoo. All the girls in college. Some boys even. Chandan Bala has a snake on her arm—Shweta pleaded but Savitri would not budge.

There was a play Shweta wanted to see. Savitri could not bring herself to utter the title aloud.

The Vagina Monologues—Shweta said, in heckling tones.

That's the Eve Enschler play.

See, even Ash mama has seen it.

It was a long time back ...

But you've seen it, haven't you?

Her brother was allowed to do all kinds of things, Shweta said, and nobody stopped him. He was rehearsing a violent play with guns and knives, and his mother said nothing to him.

He's a boy, Savitri said. Besides, he's older. You aren't eighteen yet.

I'll be eighteen soon.

The play was traded for the tattoo. An inflamed patch appeared on Shweta's wrist. Soon it quietened into a black butterfly.

It looks like a lump of grime. I feel like asking you to wash it off ...

I wish I too lived in a hostel, like Chandan Bala, with no one to bother me. I could be free like her, like a bird. With Shweta, the tears disappeared quickly. She could still be distracted, like a child. In lieu of the play, that very evening, they had gone shopping together. He had bought her her first sari—for her graduation—a soft pink silk, patterned with white. She had laid it out on the bed, put her cheek against it, and stroked it, crooning, as if it were a pet animal.

Thanks Ash mama. Love you ...

Love you too.

He still found it embarrassing to speak the word out loud, or even to name it. The American way was to end every conversation with an assertion of it, and this need for constant affirmation or perhaps it was just a conversational quirk, had travelled easily across the oceans, and had been appropriated. The word was now a door stopper, a punctuation mark, a full stop substitute in a sentence.

From his room he could hear the strains of her guitar exercises when she practised on the terrace. He recognised the strangled chords of 'Take Me Out to the Ball Game'. It reminded him of his early attempts to understand baseball, to make sense of it in his cricket-loving mind, sitting in the bleachers at Wrigley field at the Cubs' game and watching Harry Caray on the screen, mouthing along with him, root root root for the home team.

What's a crackerjack, Shweta asked, when she paused between bouts of tortured playing.

It's a kind of sweet popcorn and peanut snack.

He asked her if she knew what a ball game was, or where the Blue Ridge mountains were.

They are just songs for guitar practice. I don't need to know their history and geography. Chill, Ash mama—she would say in mock exasperation.

Do you know Britney Spears? She's American—Chandan Bala challenged him one evening, with a direct boldness. This was some kind of test, he gathered, one he knew he would fail immediately.

I've never heard of her, he confessed. But I once roomed with an actor who had a part in an Altman film. The actor had a pet frog, which was a live prop.

Oldman? Old man?

No. A-L-T-M-A-N.

Never heard of him.

Shweta allowed him to watch CDs of her favourite films with her sometimes, the evenings that Chandan Bala was not around. He had learned to recognise her favourite hero and the latest songs. He watched the television screen one evening, as a song played and Shweta's preferred hero danced to his latest hit. She was watching the actor with an expression that he could only describe as adoration, mouthing the words along with him. The song was catchy, with African drum beats in the chorus. A group of young men danced, facing the camera up front, with the hero occupying centre stage. Their moves were athletic and synchronised, all of them moving in unison, while the young woman who was being wooed sashayed past them in one corner of the frame. That was all she had to do.

I want something something, crooned the hero, something something ... He sang to his lady love, promising not to annoy her with letters or phone calls or waylay her; he wouldn't roam the streets like a madman either, if he didn't win her. As she sashayed past him down the side of the frame, he tried again. He would not touch her (inappropriately) when they were in the cinema together, he promised, nor kidnap her, nor burn her with acid, and rowdysim, he swore, was unknown to him—here he charged out of an alley and laid down a 'long', a curving machete, penitently at her feet. She wouldn't find a Majnoon like him if she searched the earth, so make up your mind, he urged.

His niece had been watching the screen with rapt attention, her mouth slightly open, and she caught his eye. Her expression altered immediately.

Don't, okay—I like him very much. And it's only a song ...

But I didn't ... She held up her hand to stop him mid-sentence. I know exactly what you were going to say, she said severely. Just don't say it. Besides, he's the son of your favourite, Raj Kumar. You liked the father, I like the son.

*

I'm going to give you a surprise on your birthday, Shweta had announced to him. He had gone to the temple in the morning with Savitri, where she had a puja performed in his name—for a long and prosperous life.

Ash mama—Shweta had hailed him from the courtyard as soon as she came home from college. Get ready.

After a hair-raising ride on the pillion of her scooter, where she had consistently overtaken cars and even buses on the wrong side, and started off at traffic signals before the light turned green—You have to take calculated risks, Ash mama, if not you'll be stuck in traffic forever—she stopped in front of an elegant bungalow.

Temple over in the morning, Ash mama. Now time for shemple.

She was gifting him a haircut in an upmarket hair salon. It's a unisex parlour—that's the fashion now. Chandan Bala's friend works here.

They entered a large hall of mirrors with bays and cubicles and complicated-looking chairs with control levers and graded headrests. A fat white pipe ran along the breadth of the hall ending in a mouth shaped like an old-fashioned telephone receiver. The front desk had a smiling young man and woman, identically dressed.

And is this, he asked, more out of embarrassment, the Starship Enterprise? And that—he pointed to the white chute—your resident python?

No, it's the A1 Unisex Salon, the girl replied.

Of course, the Starship Enterprise would mean nothing to her. It was way before her time.

And that—it was the young man's turn—is the air conditioning vent.

Tsangte!

A diminutive girl, with northeastern features and a smooth helmet of curving hair, appeared and greeted Shweta like an old friend.

This is my uncle Ash, Shweta said. It's his birthday today. I want you to fix his hair. It's a birthday present. He lives in the US and cuts his own hair.

That was it, his horoscope in two sentences. Everything to be known about him could be jotted down on the back of a postage stamp.

There was no time to be awkward or to remind himself that no one had touched his head in near memory in a gesture of such intimacy, let alone a strange young woman. He took heart in that the chair to his left was occupied by a large woman of uncertain age and to his right by a very young man, and leaned back in his chair, closing his eyes to whatever was to come. He allowed the warm water to wash over his head and felt himself relaxing. He felt his scalp being massaged briskly with a sweet-smelling oil and then a visor of some sort, an inter-galactic transponder at the very least he made note to tell his niece, was fitted over his head. He was sure, he told her later, the electrodes would destroy his memory. But all it did was wrap his head in a warm cloud and he was led, bemused, to his chair. In a few snips of the scissors Tsangte was done. She took off the cape covering his shoulders and held up a mirror to the bald patch at the back of his head.

His niece was waiting for him in the lobby. She looked at him with the disinterest of a scientist examining a specimen.

Ash mama, what do you think?

Great, he said. He didn't think it had made the slightest difference. Thank you. It's the best birthday present I have ever received, he said quite truthfully.

At home, the Sandalwood Maiden was waiting. They had plans for the evening. From the terrace he could see them at the gate, stepping on to the street. The evening was flush with the ambient light of the setting sun, as if it were reluctant to let go of the memory of the day. He saw his niece and her friend walking out on the road. Chandan Bala was wearing a white shirt which glowed in the gathering dusk, a pink creamy pearl. Their faces, as they turned to each other, looked innocent, sweet.

He had felt a pang of regret, almost a physical sensation, a sharp tug beneath his breastbone, for the vast barren stretch behind him, for the love that had passed him by. Too late to seize the day.

*

The bus came round the corner, red and white, the 6E he was waiting for.

Go right in, the bus is empty, lots of space, the bus driver bellowed. Why do you want to hang around the door? If you have a death wish, let it not be from falling off my bus—he ground the floor gears, and the metal hood of the gearbox next to him throbbed. This was where the women dumped their heavy bags as they climbed in and which would steadily heat up as the bus progressed.

So, bus drivers were as irate and irritable as they had been.

The conductor tore off his ticket and scribbled the amount of change owing at the back. He had to collect it before getting off. Up on the head board, next to the rear view driving mirror, were the injunctions of old. He was immediately comforted by them. Kannada Kamadhenu. Karnataka Kalpavriksha. Their state was the wish-fulfilling tree and their language, the cow of plenty. Ticketless travel is an invitation to punishment. (That was politely put, he thought.) The country first, always. Smoking is prohibited. For complaints and suggestions call xxxxx.

The seats were new—the ergonomic bucket type with built-in cushions, the universal bus seat; he could well be on the CTA. The older soft stuffed seats had been more comfortable, though they were often shredded, with the sponge spilling out.

The bus started filling up. Three young women, girls yet,

boarded, dressed in black trousers and red shirt, the uniform of a well-known retail store. They chattered, unmindful of the other passengers. Their faces, scrubbed clean, had an open rustic look. He could imagine that they had only just stepped out of their long skirt and blouse. They reminded him of Thippy when he had first seen her. From their accents he could tell that they had newly come to the city. They looked confident—perhaps it was the trousers. Two of them got off and the third girl, fallen silent, clung to the hand rail, with a faraway look in her eyes.

The city sped past, shops, more shops. A board leapt out—Quick Marriages Pvt Ltd—they were making no bones about it anymore, no point being coy or slipping horoscopes in vermilion and turmeric edged envelopes to matchmakers. The bus went past close packed lanes, past a large yard stacked with clay idols of Ganesha—they were getting their last coat of paint. Some were shrouded in plastic sheets, to protect them from the rain. They stood row upon row, gleaming pink and gold, in different sizes. So it was time for Ganesh Chaturthi already. He realised that he had been here six months and nothing had been decided. If anything, he was more undecided than ever.

He wrestled his way out of the bus, just managing to jump off before it started again. He stood rooted to the spot, unable to move as another bus came to a halt next to him, so close that the exhaust fanned his shirt tails up and blew his hair into disarray. He could not recognise this place. There was a mall right there on the main road where a modest row of shops had once stood. Cars sped past and were swallowed into the basement of the mall. The lawyer's office had been on the first floor of the only multi-storeyed building on this side of the road. He stumbled on the footpath. Nobody had heard of the building or the lawyer. Some people turned away even before he could ask them.

Yelneer ...

He had come to rest in front of a pile of tender coconuts. He held his hand out for one, never mind that it was ten rupees. He fell on the straw, sucking thirstily.

It's over Sir, the vendor said. That's just the straw drinking air.

He cracked open the empty shell and scooped the pulp out, soft and trembling, like egg whites, but sweet to taste.

Paper ganji, he recollected the term with a kind of relief.

He walked in the direction the vendor had pointed him. All the shops and offices on the main road had moved to parallel streets, off the main road. He walked past the high compound wall of some sort of institution—a school perhaps or a college, with pleas painted at regular intervals, not to urinate on the walls. Illi mootra visarjane maada bedi—he was struck by the needless poetry of the plea—please do not inundate us with your waters—visarjane or immersion was a term he had always associated with idols in a pond, to be sent home every year after the festivities and welcomed back the next.

The yelneer had been a bit much. He could not help himself. He joined a fellow man in inundating the wall, glad that no tiles with pictures of gods had been affixed to it, and immediately felt better. That was cheating, he thought, just as he did when people put out statues of angels as dibs in the snow to mark their parking spaces, to seek divine intervention in trivial pursuits, much like swatting a fly with a hammer.

*

He climbed up a narrow staircase and entered the office. Rajagopal's business seemed to have expanded. The large hall was a sea of metal file cabinets with heads bobbing in between like buoys in the water. Rajagopal sat in a glass-fronted cabin, its door smeared with fingerprints. He had inherited the business from his father who was Suchi mama's friend.

The papers are clear. You can sell.

Rajagopal sounded triumphant as if he had clinched a deal. The house was his. His father's will had made it clear. His sister could not claim a share, Rajagopal said, despite the changes to the Hindu Succession Act, the house did not quite qualify as ancestral property. She has no locus standi, Rajagopal lowered his voice, inviting a confidence.

He could also recommend a builder who would develop the plot and build the flats for him. If he began the processes now, the flats would be ready the next time he visited.

I'll think about it, give me some time.

Of course, you can put the proceeds of the sale into a capital gains account. Or even transfer it abroad. I can advise you on the procedures.

He shuffled the papers in his file, got up and shook hands with Rajagopal, aware that he had disappointed him.

Wait—Rajagopal said. Here is the will you wanted me to draft. Once you finalise it, we can put it on stamp paper. I have put down your—

He grabbed the papers and left, avoiding Rajagopal's eye.

He had fled, or he thought he had, from the snare of family, and here he was, back in its coils, in the well of its theatre, back in the mesh of samsara.

*

He recalled the scene he had witnessed when he had just arrived. Aprameya had been up with his friends till late in the night and in the morning the terrace had been strewn with plates of leftovers, cigarette butts and empty bottles. The boy had not emerged from his room until noon. Savitri had remonstrated with him, and then, in a rare gesture of conjugal solidarity, appealed to Keshav Rao.

Why don't you build me a den like you did for yourself, the boy taunted. I can keep it under lock and key when I become a guest of the government.

Get out of the house, Keshav Rao shouted.

It's not yours, so you can't ask me to get out.

Ashwath had stepped in to prevent Keshav Rao from striking his son.

Does he want me to follow in his footsteps? He thinks nobody knows what he did? Or become a religious nut like my mother?

Aprameya, he is your father. You can't talk to him like that—Ashwath had said weakly.

And you Ash mama—Aprameya returned. My mother, your sister, says that it took you twenty-five years to get over the argument you had with your father ... I admired your guts, walking out like that. And I will too, if they badger me about what I do, the people I mix with ...

Aprameya's group had an assortment of people, all part of the adult learning project. But there were two people whom Ashwath had seen often on the terrace, the two who need me the most, Aprameya said. They were among those who had signed up for the English class that he taught and the play that he was directing. Chotu, small-built, wide-eyed, always with a baseball cap worn back to front on his head, even when there was no sun in the sky. He worked at sorting plastic in a waste segregation unit on the outskirts of the city but had begun with ambitions of being a security guard in an office building—he longed to wear a blue uniform. But he didn't make the grade. They said I was too small-built, didn't have the right physique, he grinned.

Where are you from, Ashwath asked, in the Hindi that he could manage.

Delhi, Chotu said. No, Calcutta. And then he shrugged. Oh what does it matter, Before that, the Sunderbans, Khulna ... We had lands, he said, we were farmers. Before we lost it to the river. We had to leave.

Ever since he could remember, he wanted to be in films, and this was the closest he had got. Only, the NGO through which he had come into contact with Aprameya, whom he called Appu Sir, wanted the play to be about his life. What kind of life is mine? My life is not the stuff of dreams, of films, he smiled, the gap in his teeth standing out. I'm not famous, I'm not Shah Rukh Khan ...

The sibling duo of Shankar-Shankari intrigued Ashwath. Shankar was a stocky young man with a smooth face and well-marked eyebrows—the kind of looks that would fetch him women's roles in a Yakshagana performance, where men played all the women's parts. Sometimes Shankar's sister visited—he caught sight of her hair and the glitter of her sari on the terrace, and heard Shankar's guttural voice above everyone else's.

Ash mama, Aprameya mocked. You're really naïve aren't you. They are both the same person! You couldn't tell? Really?

Aprameya had first met Shankar at the traffic lights

where he had worked out a fine line between begging and coercion. He usually targeted young men on two-wheelers and autorickshaw drivers, hoping to overwhelm them into parting with money.

I'm sorry, I'm just a p-o-o-o-o-r boy—Aprameya had said to the arresting-looking creature in the purple spangled sari and long hair, and a seven o' clock shadow that the foundation had been unable to conceal.

It's not p-o-o-o-o-r, but poor. I know that much English—Shankar-Shankari had said, looking hurt in theatrical exaggeration. Don't make fun of me, I'm an artist, a dancer and a singer. I am respectable, just like you.

Aprameya had had the presence of mind to pull out the Theatre for Rehabilitation card from his pocket before the lights turned green. Call, okay? he said before driving off.

Both Chotu and Shankar had called at the office and the NGO had assigned them to Aprameya's group. All Shankar wanted was to be recognised as an artist, a performer. He came from a village in the north of the state, where the cult of the goddess Renuka-Yellamma was predominant, and he had known, since he had been a child, a boy-child, that he wanted to be a devotee of the goddess and join the community that worshipped her and had dedicated itself to her worship. But his father would have none of it. He was a respectable man, a land owner with a government job and daughters to marry off. How could he tell people that his eldest son wanted to leave home and live like a vagrant, to join a community dedicated to worshipping a goddess, however much he might revere her? Instead, he had managed to get his son a job, as a clerk in the animal husbandry department where he worked, and sent him far away from home, to the state capital, to cure him of his 'ailment'.

As his father so delicately put it, he did not want his son to end up as a prostitute of indeterminate sex. So here he was—Shankar from 9 to 5, six days a week.

Like me he has to decide what he wants, how to deal with his father. These people, your precious sister and brother-in-law, Aprameya jerked his head towards the house, they have no idea of the lives of others.

Aprameya, he wanted to caution him. Each of us carries our own burdens. You don't know how they have lived either ...

The last time they had spoken, his nephew had favoured him with a confidence.

I've decided to drop out of college, Aprameya said.

Unlike Shweta, Aprameya was not asking for his intercession, he was doing him the courtesy of informing him.

I didn't want to join an engineering course to begin with. They insisted. It's amazing, the only time they agree with each other is when they have to coerce me into doing things I don't want to do, when they want to give me an ultimatum.

Aprameya—he began

It's done, he said. He had already enrolled in a course run by a very prestigious repertory to study theatre. It's very tough to get in. I tried last year, but didn't make it. This year, they were impressed with my work at the centre, Aprameya said. And a Dutch group had responded to his proposal to workshop and possibly fund his play, the one he was working on with Shankar and Chotu.

I have yet to tell them. But I will, soon. They'll kick up a ruckus. Will you—he hesitated, his eyes shadowed with uncertainty. Will you be there when I tell them ...

Before Ashwath could say anything, he continued in a rush—When I used to write to you, as a boy, I always imagined you as a conqueror of sorts. The cards you sent me, the lines you wrote in them, they made me restless, they helped me imagine a life for myself, outside this—he stretched his arms out to cover the house and the terrace. I want to be like you. I want to get off the beaten track.

It had left him speechless, this unexpected admission from his nephew, this chink in his armour. But of course, he was still a boy. The last thing Ashwath had ever imagined was that his life would be seen as heroic, the stuff of myth, that he could be a conquering hero returning to his motherland. He could imagine Savitri's mirthless laugh if she got to know. Yes, he had thrown caution to the winds and stepped out on the road but milestone after misleading milestone had gone by, leading nowhere; every inkling, every intuition had dissipated in a cloud of smoke. He had made the journey in good faith, he had landed even if shakily and he could still measure the ground with his feet. That much he could say.

All he was granted was a moment. Yes, I will be there when you tell them, he said. I will be with you. He would tell his sister, a man cannot be defined by his family all his life. He has to step out of its shadow and do things, hamhanded it may be, but in his own way. And then his nephew was gone, and he was left alone to untangle his thoughts in the calm of the evening with its fading light and the comforting clamour of crows returning to their nests in the trees in his garden.

*

On the way back from the lawyer's, he decided to take an auto. He didn't quite feel up to the bus. Besides, he was canny now, to select a new green-and-yellow one, with a rear engine. It didn't jolt as much over the potholes. The autorickshaw was brand new—the knotted rope of buffalo hair across the front was black and dust free and the lemon-and-green chilli mobile was still fresh. The auto was 'hypothecated' to a bank, and dedicated to Kabbalamma, who seemed to be the patron goddess of auto drivers.

The autorickshaw had an information card on the bar on the passenger side, with the driver's name, address and photograph. The studio photo showed a smart young man in a coat and tie; the man at the wheel was in standard khaki, unshaven and unkempt. He drove slowly and seemed preoccupied.

That's a good photo you have in the information card, Ashwath said.

Yes, the man replied absently. They paint on the tie and suit in the studio, at no extra cost. Taking Ashwath's comment as an invitation to talk, he kept up a steady stream of conversation, His given name, not the one on the information chart, was Nagesha, first among serpents. He was married, no children yet. His horoscope had no flaws. But business wasn't good. He had the loan to pay off on the auto ...

Ashwath got off at the market, not taking the auto all the way home, not wanting to listen to the man's chatter any more, and paid him extra. He stopped at the hardware store—he wanted to put up some shelves in his room. More and more, it occurred to him, he was nailing himself in, and he had intended to make a flying visit to his home, his city, with no plan in mind, and no obligations. Across the road, in the chaat shop that had spread its tables across the pavement, he spotted his niece. She was with the Sandalwood Maiden and a tall young man whose cultivated biceps were set off to advantage in his short-sleeved tee shirt. He was showing them something on his mobile phone and they were peering over his shoulders. Happy youth, he thought to himself, happy with a few pieces of potato and tamarind sauce, and a square foot of pavement.

He left the main bazar and stepped into the bylanes of its hinterland, a locality he was familiar with. The lanes were narrow, the houses modest, built in the old Trust Board single-storeyed model. Some houses had added another floor. A game of street cricket was being played, with bricks for wickets. The bowler stopped in mid throw to let him pass. Further down, a shuttlecock tossed steadily in the air. A small boy wobbled on a cycle, his lips pressed in concentration, while a weary looking woman walked behind him, her hand poised behind the seat.

Dusk fell. The children went indoors. A music class was in progress in one of the houses. He could hear the small piping voices practising the scales, making heavy weather of the beginner's janti varase. A young mother, infant on hip, called across a neighbour's wall to come home now. A door opened—Gate! Gate! she called as a small figure ran past.

He stopped at the corner shop to see if the dapper Shetty shopkeeper was still there, and he was. He had gone bald and his frame had shrunk a little, but he was as neat as he used to be.

Ashwath anna! His voice chimed with pleasure. Heard you were visiting.

So word still got round quickly.

I have a big shop on the main road, a supermarket. My son sits there. It's one of those things where people help themselves. I much prefer to stand behind a counter, and keep my old shop. And you?

A customer stepped up to the counter—a woman clad in a black burkha, with a veil covering her head. Two eggs Shetty, she said. Her voice was musical, and her manner familiar. She must have been an old customer.

Why two eggs ma, the whole basket is yours, Shetty said, roguishly gallant.

She giggled at that, bringing her hand up to cover her mouth, the henna on her palm stark against her skin. This was the goranti as he knew it, not the intricate patterns that his niece and the Sandalwood Maiden had acquired, but a red circle in the middle of her palm, and the first digit of every finger, including the nail, stained red.

Shetty handed her the eggs in a paper bag, she threw him a prancing smile, and left.

Their exchange had been easy, the language a mix of the local Kannada and Urdu. He had forgotten the cadences of that patois, a smooth mix, where language had lent itself to necessity, to the music of communication.

Under the lamp post, at the corner of the street, two elderly men in tennis shoes were taking leave of each other. When he grew closer, one of them hailed him. He recognised him as an acquaintance of his father's, who used to come home sometimes.

I hear you have come back, he said. It's so rare these days. We are all so scattered ... so few coming back home ... boys from good families.

He was reminded of the auto driver who had dropped him off at the market. He had prefaced his chatter with—Do you know our language, our ways? Do you belong here, do you understand my concerns, he meant. Are you a true son of the land of plenty and of the wish-fulfilling cow?

On an island in the marketplace, where four streets met, there was a flagpost painted red and yellow, the colours of the state, the colours of the cup-shaped flowers of the Thunbergia Mysorensis that had made a home for itself on the grill of his bedroom window. The altar of the flag post carried the bust of a man who was a true son of the soil, a mannina maga, the hero of countless films, handsome, dashing, romantic, now decked in gold paint except for the whites of his eyes and the pupils, and the black pencil-line moustache. This was the father, the hero of Ashwath's generation, while his niece favoured the son.

Ashwath used to bunk college regularly to catch his films, first day, first show, at Majestic. Last he remembered, he had fobbed off an errand to see *Operation Diamond Racket*, a gangster film. After seeing it once, he had gone again several times, till he knew each frame, each song by heart. Even before the credits came on the film had him hooked with its sense of intrigue—the headlights of a speeding car and a man's white-gloved hand on the steering wheel. The camera followed his shoes as he opened a door stealthily and applied the right combination to the safe in the room. But an eye watched through the window and sure enough a hooded figure crashed into the room and a fight ensued. Not a single thrill had been missed. The glitter of diamonds as they poured in a stream into the palm of a hand, two halves of a torn note that had to be matched, the clinching password 'Diamond Queen', and the suave CID inspector on top of the game, ahead of every move, handsome in a sharkskin suit and a bow tie, perfectly self-possessed whether he was riding a horse on the beach, in the middle of a car chase, in a swimming pool surrounded by beautiful women, or in a nest of snakes in a glass well. The fight sequences were straightforward, the dialogue unambiguous but the plot was labyrinthine, which he liked.

On the other hand, it was the sense of melancholy that had marked the film *Kasturi Nivasa*, the story of a doomed man in a doomed house, a man who is hunted down by his destiny even as he upholds his duty, his dharma, with honour, a man marked for tragedy, who sought it out even, willing fate to rob him of everything he had. What he had not lost, he had given away. The tragic hero, so handsome—and how well tragedy became the handsome man; surrounded by goodwill, he had been bereft of love, destined to die a lonely death.

His mother and his sister had wept at the end of the film and he had teased them for that, more to conceal the fact that the brooding, stylised narrative of the film had got under his skin.

*

It was dark by the time he got home. His niece was waiting for him.

Buns from the bakery, she hailed him. That's all for

dinner tonight. And curd rice. Your sister is staying late at the ashram. Her eyes were bright with suggestion.

Yes? He wondered what she had up her sleeve.

Shall we go to McDonald's?

That was it. That was all.

When he had first arrived, he noticed that the house at the end of their street, where the Shafiuddins used to live, and who had lived there as long as he could remember, had been torn down, and a new building was coming up. It was a large plot, with fullgrown fruit trees. His niece and nephew had laid bets on the new building—it would be a shopping centre, no, a bank or a business centre. He had recognised the golden arches from the distance, even as they were being erected.

Our very first McDonald's, right down our road, his niece had been excited beyond measure. There's a clown sitting on the seat in front of the shop—I thought he was real, the first day I saw him. I'm sure you go to McDonald's there ever so often, you're lucky. You must tell us if the burgers taste the same. They are supposed to, anywhere in the world ...

He told her quite truthfully that he had gone to McDonald's every day for three months. The job in the kitchen washing dishes—disguised as 'hygiene assistant'—had come handy and fitted neatly just before his last stint of the day at the bookshop. He had even participated in a demonstration for higher wages, carrying a placard in Pioneer Court along with the other workers.

I'll take you there as soon as it opens, he had promised her. I recommend their milkshakes and their coffee.

So McDonald's it was—the décor and the menu looking the same as everywhere else.

I saw you in the market today, he began.

Mmmm ... I'm loving it—she closed her eyes and bit into the McAloo and heaved at the straw of her milkshake. A small mountain of soft dessert sat in a tub next to her milkshake. He, was drinking coffee.

That was Jimmy, she said, her eyes still closed to negotiate the size of the burger. Chandan Bala's BF ...

Chandan Bala's BF?

Boyfriend, Ash mama.

Chandan Bala, he had gathered, went to college in the daytime and worked in a BPO, taking calls from customers across the world, at night.

He recalled the single rose that Shweta had been holding on Valentine's Day and her intense, long-lasting phone conversation on the terrace that evening. And you, he wanted to ask her. Do you have a BF?

Ash mama, I'll ask you a riddle. Let's see if you know the answer.

Chandan Bala and her BF were forgotten, tossed out of her mind.

Two boys go to a temple. One sees the other light a cigarette with the temple lamp. He is so shocked that he ...

Faints?

No.

Slaps his friend?

No—last guess.

Bursts into tears?

No—drops his beer bottle!

You should see your face, Ash mama—she was laughing so hard that she spluttered bubbles of milkshake.

Leaf Lotus Pearl Umbrella—he challenged her.

Of course, Ash mama, it's such an old one.

It was an old one—a multilingual pun, facile, a school boy's joke. It was a literal translation of Hey Kamala give me a kiss.

She was eating the dessert now, shaking her head at him, and smiling, a smile almost maternal in its tenderness. Oh, Ash mama, she said, you really don't know anything, do you?

*

Upstairs in his room there was a note waiting for him on the table, slipped under the gooseneck lamp. His old scratched teak table and his indestructible gooseneck lamp. And a yellowed piece of paper, as stiff as parchment clamped tantalisingly under the heavy metal lamp. But his eyes went first to his desk calendar attracted by the date circled in red. Twenty-sixth of August. Two days from then. She has agreed to see you, his sister had scribbled in the margin of the calendar face. She will come to Neel Kamal. He could hear the cold disapproval in Savitri's tone and sense her reluctance in the grudging slope of her letters. Twenty-sixth of August. Twenty-six years to the day you left. Do you remember, Savitri had written. It must be destined, after all.

He pulled out the piece of paper from under his gooseneck lamp. It snagged at the edge and tore but he put the two pieces together. He recognised the handwriting as his own. The date at the top right hand corner read 26th August, 1981. It was the note he had left for Savitri before leaving for the airport, flinging the front gate open and hearing it squeal one last time as he stepped into the waiting taxi, glorying in the fact that he was riding alone in it, his arms stretched out on the back of the seat which would have been crammed with his family members had he let them. I will return after I have made good, he had said. And then you will see me for what I am. I will show you.

VI

One

He had come of age in Reagan's America. If the claim on a country and its first citizen was too grandiose, he would say in more famous words, he had been a contender. For ten years he had been given brownie points by Reagan's America and he had faithfully cashed all of them at the bank. He had played the game by the rules, pursued the American Dream and acquired the three Cs of success—a credit card, a condo and a car, and a fourth—a corporate job. The three great comforts had been his—money in the bank, honey in the jar and a car in the garage. He had even gone one further. He had found a favourite bar and a diner.

He had been cautious. He had emerged, like a field mouse, watching at the edge of the field, the sheaves still about his ears, waiting, listening to the footfalls, to the thrum of the cars on the highway. He had made his sombre way in the city, free-style, teaching himself, trying to disavow both 'character' and 'fate', for these were old burdens, burdens he had come here to shed. Another writer had said that the city had two faces, one for the good boy and one for the bad boy. What about the in-betweens, he wanted to know, or the thwarted, the meek and the clueless, of whom the detective novels said sooner or later, '... And then his luck ran out.'

He had started out well. He had probationed and had

then been confirmed in a growing food and beverage processing company, appropriately named Golden, with an ear of corn as its symbol. With food, he knew he couldn't go wrong because people had to eat. Since he had taken to heart the Socratic dictum that the unexamined life was not worth living, he had also enrolled for weekend art classes. Gently urged by a Polish girl, an artist who lived in a loft in Wicker Park, who had introduced him to potato pierogi when he felt homesick for steamed kolkotte, he had made the weekend drive in his brand new, statement-making red Caprice on grey winter weekends, the cold wind by the lake almost freezing him to immobility, to evoke the sun in Turner's paintings or the great expanse of the Midwest in Pollock's abstract expressionist canvases. He had bought a checked sports coat from Sears and gone clay pigeon shooting with his boss, an admirer of Lee Iacocca and Jack Welch, at his country club. He had shared an apartment with an actor in a highrise in a gated community, which had a uniformed doorman, a swimming pool, tennis courts and a 'tot lot', with signs saying Keep dogs off the grass, and where the term 'common elements' did not mean the list beginning with aluminium, gold and argon. He had sat in on the rehearsals of a theatre group, opined on the script and the dialogue, and made roasted corn with mint chutney for after-rehearsals on winter evenings. He had gone to the library on Michigan Avenue, trailing it as it changed homes, and begun reading greedily. It was here in the library that he had come across *Breakfast at Tiffany's*, the film vivid in his mind, for it had whetted his appetite for America in his far off home, setting off in him a strong urge to experience the place. It had, in a way, made him aware of an individual destiny, far away from all known moorings, and he had felt the excitement of adventure. Above all, it had suggested to him the possibilities of love, just when he was feeling its first stirrings, when the dense matter of his heart was being quickened by an unknown feeling; he could recognise the thing, its sweetness, its capricious play, its surrender. So, in this library guarded by the green lions and the tall columns, he was saddened by the trick the film had played by giving the story a false happy ending, feeling as if all that he had held true so far was negated, that he had been shored up by false pretences all along.

Just as he was beginning to feel he was sure of his footing, he was thrown off. The system had malfunctioned. Art was not to be trusted. It had given him the wrong prompts. There were, for instance, the two films he had seen, just weeks apart. *Ferris Bueller* he could understand, he had enjoyed the film with the confidence that comes from identifying with the protagonist. Ferris was playing 'hookey' from school, like Tom Sawyer. A person should not believe in 'isms' Ferris had said, he should believe in himself, and he had agreed. He had quoted Ferris Bueller at the clay pigeon shoot and struck a chord immediately with the others. He knew all the landmarks featured in the film, found the pranks fun, and approved of the mild, pretty heroine and of the idea of wrecking your father's Ferrari. This, to him, was America. And what was more, on TV, his favourite critic Roger Ebert had liked the film too.

A few weeks later, he had seen another film playing at the Music Box, a theatre housed in a lovely old-fashioned building with a green wrought iron marquee and fairy lights above the box office. He was distressed by *Blue*

Velvet—he could not understand its contrary messages; thankfully Roger Ebert had hated it too, but his partner on the TV show, Gene Siskel, had liked it. Here were clean-cut American teenagers behaving completely out of character. There are opportunities in life for gaining knowledge and experience. Sometimes, you've got to take a risk, the young man had told his sweet-looking girlfriend, little prepared or preparing the audience even for the kind of experience he would gain or the risks their morbid curiosity would lead them to take.

*

When the morning was good, he would drive along the lake, *the spray-flung curve of shore*, though it was a much longer way to his office in the west Loop, for the joy of seeing the lake first thing in the morning, to be calmed and uplifted simultaneously. *I came sudden, at the city's edge/ On a blue burst of lake*—he thought of Sandburg's poem. Blue burst of lake—he liked that phrase. It summed up his spirits, the vistas that had opened up before him.

His boss, Ray Bertrand the manager of the Production Planning and Materials Management division where he was a trainee executive, had said to him in their one-on-ones—You're doing good, Ash.

You are in the heart of the food business, so remember that you feed America, Ray Bertrand had declared on their first day at the brand new corporate office. At their orientation session they were shown a short film on how the company's flagship brand, its breakfast cereal, was produced. Despite himself, despite the smart aleck comments from the rest of his team, he felt himself being pulled into the romance of the venture. Sheaves of corn, acre upon acre, glinted in the light of the setting sun. The corn fields seemed endless and endlessly fertile and prosperous. An ear of corn, artistically tossed, detached itself and made its way into the ringed logo of the company. The corn from the fields was harvested, loaded into trucks and was soon on the highway, a heroic convoy travelling to a far horizon. At the factory, every step of the way, it was handled by machines—large, efficient, motorised—the men appearing peripherally to drive the machines or not at all. The corn was cooked in a huge steaming chamber, tossed in a turbine, crushed between gigantic rollers, tumbled into a dryer and then sent out, exhausted, on a clean white conveyor belt to be packaged and boxed. In another run, the flakes were mixed with nuts and chocolate chips, crushed, slathered with caramel and chocolate, and then guillotined into small bars. Along the way, the uneven flakes, those that did not come up to scratch, were sieved out, the rest passed through a chamber where they were sprayed with a hot syrup—like me dog pissin'—McMurtry, the raffish probationer with a front tooth missing, said, and there was a low rumble of laughter, at which Bertrand raised his eyebrows.

Things could not have begun on a better note. The food industry was growing. America, the world, was hungrier than ever and was waiting for Golden's cereal. Bertrand projected maps, graphs and charts on the screen in the conference hall. The food industry accounted for a good chunk of the GDP, and employed the largest number of people, second only to the US government, so there was plenty of room there. He could not, Ashwath felt, have been in a safer place.

His team was set a project; they plunged into reports, into data and graphs to find ways to become more efficient, make do with less, push up the profit margin and delight the customer. Their job should have been easy considering that more and more people were not cooking at home—they were eating out, or heating up frozen dinners—hamburgers, pizzas and sandwiches, in order of popularity. The research team, Bertrand said, had come up with a unique data point—peas, the universal favourite, did not go well in the frozen TV dinner, because they scattered all over the family room when they thawed.

Bertrand drove them with a whip hand. They were to look at inventory, estimate demand, decide decide decide—he counted off on his fingers—how much to stock, how much to order, when to push and when to pull, how much to standardise and how much to differentiate. He drew a circle with a marker, jabbed two dots, an arrow head and a crescent moon one below the other, and a fool's cap on the top of the circle. This is the customer, Bertrand said, and he is king! The customer is the one that pays you, the only one. Forecast, forecast, forecast, Bertrand dug his spurs in—forecast supplies, forecast demand, anticipate the information you require, foresee the competition, get clairvoyant about what the customer would want tomorrow. There was simply no getting away from it—derive, speculate, forecast—like a bunch of frickin' magicians, as McMurtry said.

At the end of the sessions, Bertrand asked each of the team members for his takeaway. It was to be framed in a single sentence, like a slogan. No risk, no gain, McMurtry, who had fixed the gap in his teeth—got to look pretty now—said. Get the right algorithm, this from Jesse Reoff, the tech geek. Streamlining is as important as replenishment, Ashwath offered, feeling doubtful. Kyle from Operations had made an animated presentation centering round a worker he named Mr Corny about the day-to-day challenges in the plant—the chute getting choked (an air lock in the vent), fork lifts going on a joy ride down the aisles, the alarm bells going off like an air raid, and a mountain of corn flakes tumbling down the conveyor belt at the hapless Mr Corny. It faded out with the moon shining outside the window and MrCorny still sweeping up the mess on the floor. It was a funny little film and Kyle's takeaway line was 'Expect the unexpected'.

He thought he had not impressed Bertrand, but still, when the training was over, and they were returned to their mother departments, Bertrand had picked him to be part of the 'lean mean team', the agile team that was meant to get cracking and get results. There were rumours that the lean mean team would get stock options. By the end of the year they had a new CEO with a new daring vision. The food manufacturing industry was no longer as steady as it had been and Golden was slipping in its position as leading food manufacturer. The company would venture into places it had not gone before. The new mantra was 'diversify through acquisitions'. The company had gone on an aggressive buying spree. They were going into specialty retail—clothing, sports accessories and chain restaurants and sales were expected to double at the very least.

The lean mean team worked like never before, assisting the company's strategic management team with the pre-acquisition diligence, in collecting the data and compiling the reports. The team expanded, no longer so lean but meaner still. For the first time they were to have a woman on their team—a consultant from the buying section, Intimate Apparels—McMurtry reported, conjuring up visions of a slim figure in lingerie, as also someone from Industrial Foods, a man, who they imagined to be a toughie with tattooed forearms.

After the deals were inked, the lean mean team was invited to a special event at the CEO's country club. The new CEO—a large loping man with a square head and a slick of ash blonde hair—was known to be an outdoors person. They were to spend the morning shooting clay pigeons, walking around and ending the afternoon with a beer. It was a large team that rode out in two SUVs. There were people from all the divisions as far as he could tell—Purchasing was covered, also Packaging, Sales and Marketing, and Supply Chain. McMurtry, Kyle and Jesse were the only ones he knew. The girl from Intimate Apparels turned out to be a tough no-nonsense type and proved a dab hand at shooting flying objects.

The CEO was there in person to greet them, and a few other people, managers from different divisions, difficult to recognise out of their suits. Ashwath had prepared for the event by buying a sports coat—a checked pattern from Sears, and walking shoes. Each member of the lean mean team was introduced by Bertrand to Chris Sonnemaker, the CEO, and got his two minutes of personal time with him, before it was the next person's turn to lay a permanent impress on the man's mind. Sonnemaker was reputed to have the memory of an elephant and a sharp recall of names and faces.

Ash from Production—that's a great coat you have on. Have you handled any of these before?

Only an air gun to scare the monkeys off the trees at home ...

And home would be?

Right now it's at Golden, Sir, and an apartment near the Gold Coast.

And then his personal moment with the CEO was over. He hoped he had made a good impression.

Watch the target, follow the bird with your eyes as it flies across, Sonnemaker urged encouragingly, as each of them took turns and the others watched. He felt the heft of the .22 against his shoulder and looked down the long smooth double barrel of the gun. He followed the target with his eye, took aim and fired. He missed; the bird flew unharmed. He gave up after a few tries and retired to the lounge.

The managers had congregated by the bar stools and some junior executives had joined them. As they downed their beers, the talk turned to television and the shows on it. Bertrand confessed to watching *Family Ties*. That's the one thing my family does together, he said. The marketing division head joined in saying his son now styled his hair in a mullet, like Michael J Fox. Apparently the show about liberal parents and conservative children had the highest audience. Somebody mentioned *The Cosby Show*—the show that went best with TV dinners. Ashwath said he liked to watch Johnny Carson and Jay Leno, though it had taken him a while to 'get' the humour. He had found Johnny Carson's jokes difficult to understand, his asides about people, his familiar manner with the president of the country, his wisecracks about the president's dog, it had worried him in the beginning, but now he was getting used to American humour.

In the barbecue pit, a small area enclosed by a hedge, a pig was being roasted in a box. What they could see was the top of the box, covered with glowing lumps of charcoal. The two men standing guard spaded the ash off the top of the box and opened the lid. They caught a glimpse of the pig, stretched out on all fours on a rack, before the men turned the rack and took their knives to it, scoring the skin with crosses. They shut the box and fed the top with more charcoal.

The girl from Intimate Apparels, who had shot all her flying pigeons with her shot gun held in one hand, said she had grown up on a farm. She told them a funny story about killing chickens on the farm. She had to garrot them with wire and was not good at her job, so she had to endure the headless chickens flapping around, sprouting blood, screeching like deflated balloons. Enough, she decided. She was going to get out. She flapped her hands and rolled her eyes—she could tell a story really well.

The pig was done. It emerged, its skin a crisp pinkish brown, stretched on all fours and was turned on its stomach. It had a face too, teeth showing in a grin, ears turned inwards. One of the men started dismembering it, and handed out chunks of the sepia-coloured meat on paper plates, his clean apron stained down the front by the time the seconds and the thirds were over. The group ate in silence. Ashwath sipped on his Coke and ate some nuts.

The afternoon stretched on. Sonnemaker told them a story about his hard-working immigrant parents, who had moved to Indiana from the south and the many jobs he had taken up to save to go to college. Almost everyone had a story, Ashwath saw, about putting a distance between themselves and the familiar, before it turned deadening and oppressive, for them to get the right perspective. Better a path where one had to clear the undergrowth before the road became visible, than the smooth highway laid out for you, impeccably tarred but leading only straight ahead. The girl from Intimate Apparels he could see had felt as stifled as he had been, and could understand her strong urge to leave. She had dealt with the difficulty of her circumstances by turning them into funny stories.

This was still the country where hard work, determination and a streak of imagination, of the ability to take a calculated risk could pay off, Sonnemaker said in his winding down speech. He himself was inspired by strong leaders. He had Lee Iacocca's autobiography on his table; he liked a leader who could talk straight like Lee. Jack Welch had proved that you had to think out of the box to succeed. The epitome of achievement, for him, was Magic Johnson, who would be the face of the sports accessories company that they would soon acquire.

Sonnemaker drove them back in his SUV. Ashwath was impressed with that—that the boss would drive his employees himself. Ashwath sat at the back with McMurtry and Jesse and Wendy, the girl from Intimate Apparels whose name he finally learnt. They ribbed him about his coat. Chris loved it, Ash, Wendy said.

On all counts, he thought, the day had gone well. He felt he had acquitted himself satisfactorily; he had also enjoyed himself. He could smell the musk of team spirit in the air. The lean mean team could claim to know the pulse of the company. They were on the cusp of a major turn, a change that would shake up the organisation and change the face of business, and he was part of the task force entrusted with the job.

*

His days at work were long but his weekends—sacrosanct, American—were his own.

In his mind, these years would settle into a carnivalesque blur; he would think of them as his Ferris Bueller time out, to prepare him for the real thing.

He liked the idea of staying on the twenty-fourth floor, of being conveyed up in a lift large enough for a small family to live in, of having an indoor pool, spa, sauna and steam room at his command—though he had no intention of using any of them, they were too intimate for use—and a heated garage for his brand new Caprice Sedan, that grinning monster at whose sight his heart lifted each morning. The building was situated almost on the lake, and on a clear day you could see the expanse of unrestricted blue from their twenty-fourth floor balcony. Mr Morris, the agent whom Terry consulted on a variety of matters, from investment advice to restaurant locations, had got Ashwath a good deal on the car. He had also introduced him to the manager of a savings and loan bank on North Clark who would give him the loan for his condo and his car, and also take his savings.

There was an electric buzz in the apartment when a play was being cast and rehearsed. People kept streaming in to meet Terry and Alan—actors, artists and musicians. For the actual rehearsals, the group shifted to the basement of a building which housed many businesses including an art gallery, that Terry's businessman father owned. Ashwath sat through readings and was invited to rehearsals. The group was staging *Of Mice and Men*—he had finished reading the script in one sitting. It is, Terry said, a modern classic. Ashwath had been witness to the arguments that Terry and Alan had had about the script. Alan wanted to refashion it as a love story between the two men and Terry kept saying he couldn't see it that way. But there were other things in the script that had struck Ashwath first. It had made him see things a little differently, as if his vision had been refocused, his glasses upgraded. He had found the depiction of the life of the poor in this land of plenty arresting. Not just the countryside, in the city too and even now, there were people like that, who went from one small job to the other to make ends meet, returning to a bunk somewhere, a lice-ridden mattress like the two men in the play. And yet they had hope, their dreams could well be realised in this land where everyone had the opportunity at some time.

Of all the people who streamed in and out of Terry's rehearsals and the apartment, there were a few regulars. Agnieszka, whom Terry called Agnes, struck up a friendship with him. She was a tiny blonde Polish girl from Pilsen, who wore pleated frocks which made her look like a doll, and a bandana to hold her thick hair off her forehead; one would expect a girl like her to use a fruity perfume or a flowery one but she smelt faintly chemical all the time. Agnieszka lived in a loft in Wicker Park, in a building converted from a storehouse, where the bricks were still exposed on one of the walls. On winter evenings, she would come in, paler than usual, her face tinged blue because of the cold in the high-roofed loft. Her small angular face was pared down to the bone—a sharp nose, mouth cut as if with a knife and high cheekbones—she reminded him of an icon of a saint. Much later, he would see a likeness to her in an illustration in a book that was laid out on the coffee table in a house where he would go, not as a guest, but as a waiter in a house party, and would peer over somebody's shoulder to get a good look. Alexej von Jawlensky, 'Portrait of a Girl', the kind guest moved and made space for him. I knew a girl like that, he would say, holding the tray forward. Didn't we all, the guest would say, smiling.

Agnieszka had an old beat-up coupe and when she drove, she sang. *Sweet dreams are made of these*, or she danced behind the steering wheel doing a nasal imitation of Kraftwerk and House music and he would know that her day had gone well. She had got work done in her attic studio. Her loft in Wicker Park was a large unstructured space, sectioned off into a kitchenette, into which the light poured in from the large windows and skylight, lighting up her hair, setting it on fire. At one end of the room stood an old-fashioned easel with the canvas covered from prying eyes and an assortment of kettles on the table for the still life in progress. She had moved out of Pilsen where her family lived, to be here, amidst writers and artists. Next door was a guitarist whom she had never seen but whom she sometimes heard. Agnes, Pierogi Princess, Terry sometimes called her. It was only much later that Ashwath learnt that this was not prompted from her love of the Polish staple but because her family owned a string of bakeries which had made them a small fortune.

Sometimes, during rehearsals, Terry would put the group through vigorous dance moves, all part of the prepping, and the actors would collapse on the floor like a heap of puppies. Terry would move to the side of the room, on to a mattress, and pull out a small box of papers and when he said Ash, do you have a pen, Ashwath understood that it was not to write with but to push the edges of the paper in. He would watch them warily and also with longing, passing the glowing stub on to the next person when it was handed to him, inhaling only passively, the smell of grass and the cinnamon scented rolling paper that Terry favoured. Sometimes Agnieszka would summon him over to join the heap but he would shake his head, not without regret.

He had often thought that she and Terry were lovers, but was not sure, perhaps they had been at one time. Everybody seemed friendly with everyone else and you could not quite tell the tenor of relationships, at least, he couldn't. Terry seemed at times partial to the actress who was playing Curley's wife and the lead in *Educating Rita*, and Alan, to one of the young apprentices, but he too seemed to keep changing his mind. Agnieszka was given to mood swings and would sometimes not turn up for days, and then appear suddenly as if nothing had happened, without a word of explanation. I thought you had fallen ill, he said the first time she reappeared after a sudden vanishing. You are sweet, she said, looking at him gravely for a moment. But don't worry about me.

On weekends he and Agnieszka scrambled about cooking for the reading groups; it was such fun, and they were so easy to please. Ashwath grilled corn cobs on the electric grill, brushed them with butter, and slapped on a mix of sea salt, green chillies and mint chutney. Everyone loved the grilled corn the way he made it. The actress playing Curley's wife taught him the Mexican variation of grilled corn—elotes—with a sauce of sour cream, feta cheese and mayonnaise. Sometimes Chandra, an Indian student of journalism at Medill, dropped in and together they made gulab jamuns out of Bisquick and powdered milk.

Soon, he was fixing rum coco for the cast—neat, just like Burton in *The Night of the Iguana*—Elbert, one of the actors said, as Ashwath sliced off the top of a green coconut, scooped the soft crust in a neat circle and handed it over with both hands, in a ceremonial gesture.

Elbert was playing Crooks, the stable hand in the play. He was also the father in *Raisin in the Sun*. Ashwath found the tone of his voice attractive—soft, with the hint of a growl. Elbert was much older than the rest, the only black person in the cast, and the only one with a true claim to fame—he had had a part, small as it was, in the 70s TV sitcom *Good Times*. Sometimes he scored music for Terry's plays, and Ashwath waited for the evenings when Elbert put the saxophone to his lips and closed his eyes, for the sweet rich liquid stream of sound that would soon follow. Much later, Ashwath would chance upon a show by a black artist, Archibald Motley, and would spot in a canvas filled with musicians and dancers, a saxophonist in the foreground with a striking resemblance to Elbert Davis. But by then, this life would be behind him.

Hey Ash ... Elbert was still waiting for him to say something, as were the others who had gathered round the counter.

Back home, in winter, on the roadside, you have a man who roasts corn on hot coals set up on a bicycle cart, Ashwath said. After getting it nice and done, he paints it with red chilli paste using the tuft of a coconut for a brush, and then a quick rub of lemon rind. And you eat it with your mouth and your eyes watering.

The coconut, yes—the trick is to pick the right coconut. You have to knock it on the head and sound it out to tell that it is still halfway to becoming a fullgrown coconut, that it has plenty of water and the meat inside is still egg-white soft and sweet—he stroked the coconut on the counter and waggled his fingers, as if he were playing the tabla.

Then you give it to the man with a machete who chops off the top of the coconut, leaving a black greasy stain on the white neck. After you have drunk the water, no rum in that but, the man with the machete will hold the empty shell between his knees, exposed under his tucked-up dhoti—that's sarong to you, and crack the shell open, slice off a bit of the green shell and offer it to you as a scoop to eat the meat. And that is a meal in itself ...

Terry, you must get this man to work on a script, Elbert shouted across the room.

It seemed only right that he should be playing a part himself. He lived among actors now, after all.

Shucked corn and tender coconut water—he had least expected to see them together, so far from home, across so many oceans and continents, amidst ceramic plates and frosted glasses. As he was unveiling the cob on the prefab kitchen counter, redone in teal blue because that was Terry's colour, pulling away the silken tassels that hid the corn, he paused involuntarily, the memory of riding with his sister to her music class on the road laden with the fragrance of roses coming back to him, the corn burning on the winter coals, and the squat forearm of the corn seller framed before his eyes with startling clarity. It stayed only for a moment, like a tooth twinge, a sharp painful spasm, and it was gone. He would send them a card, he decided, or write over the weekend.

Get the ice, Ash, Elbert was saying, in his offhand sing-song way, pronouncing his name like a caress.

Sure thing, he said, sure thing.

Agnieszka was mystified to hear he was vegetarian. One weekend, a Sunday, a frog that Terry had given him to mind went missing. It was an important prop in a film in which Terry had a small part and Ashwath had volunteered to take care of it. He could have sworn it was in the perforated box.

Terry was frantic. Ash, I am sure you've eaten Mr Frog ...

It was Agnieszka's moment of triumph. No he couldn't have—he's vegetarian. He can't eat anything with legs, and eyes and a tongue, or which hatches—or which has a mommy and a daddy.

She commiserated with him—no red meat, no chicken, no fish ever! To be condemned to Lent food, and out of choice!

She would take him out sometimes to the intriguingly named Earwax Café near her house, for a pretend meat sandwich, made out of seitan or wheat-meat, or to a Polish diner with red checked table cloths, the linoleum floor and lace curtains on the windows and the worn upholstery giving it a distinctly homely feel. Agnieszka ordered potato dumplings and packzi doughnuts for him and vegetarian pierogi filled with cheese and black pepper, topped with sour cream. It was the hand-pressed edges, the frill pinched between thumb and forefinger to keep the filling firmly in its sleeve, that brought on another twinge of memory. He recalled the aimless bustle of festive days, the house full of guests whom he resented, the endless chatter, and the smell of hot oil hanging round the house like a noxious vapour, and stacks and stacks of kadabu, the deep fried ones with coconut and jaggery filling almost always overdone, and the steamed ones—white, like small beached whales, with a bulging belly of pulses. He had lost all track of the calendar—the festivals had all gone unmarked—and he couldn't remember if he had sent his sister a card for Diwali that year.

His weekends were full. There were shows and galleries and new pubs to visit, a perpetual frisson in the air; there were always people around, and Agnieszka. As they walked around her neighbourhood, she pointed out the church she went to, the beautiful, imposing, red brick St Mary of the Angels Church. It surprised him that she was observant, and he said so to her. I wouldn't be an artist if not, she said seriously. She also showed him the street on which Nelson Algren, her best writer ever, used to live, two blocks away from where they were, off Damen, on Evergreen Avenue.

You look a lot like him you know, that small and kind of lost look, like a little dog.

They were standing on the pavement, in the ambient light of the evening, when she said that, that bit about him and Nelson Algren. That was his moment, he sensed it instinctively. In the glow of the setting sun, Agnieszka seemed locked in a bubble of mellow light, her face upturned to him, like an offering. One lightly curled fist, finger tips smudged with paint, hovered in the air, as if in readiness to return an embrace. He hesitated, the fiasco with Amy still fresh in his mind, and the moment passed. She turned and bid him goodbye.

*

To augment his education, to become a fit member of the new world, he had decided to take art appreciation classes. For eight weekends he had driven downtown, Studs Terkel's gravelly confidences on FM radio helping him brave the cold grey air and the biting November wind, to a small gallery near Grant Park. They were a class of ten, he the only man in the group. The women—all art lovers—looked resolute, determinded to immerse themselves in their passion. He confessed he was an Etch a Sketch enthusiast. The instructor, an artist friend of Agnieszka, put up a projector and showed them pictures. They planned visits to galleries. They discussed colour, its quality, its tones, how great artists used techniques to produce effects. His head was in a constant pleasurable whirl.

Tell me what you think. What do you like about the painting, the instructor would ask.

The veil of mist across the painting, the smudgy effect ...

The roughness of the brush strokes, as if the paint has caked on the canvas ...

I like that it speaks immediately to me, that everyone can understand it, that it is not esoteric, Agnieszka, the painter of still life, said. That everyday scenes can be the stuff of art.

I like that it is mysterious, Ashwath said, that you can

never fully know what it means, that it could mean different things to different people, or at different times and we are free to think as we do.

Painting, the instructor said, at a basic level, was the creation of colour and light. On a bleak grey afternoon, they discussed the sun, the source of all light. The instructor projected several paintings by an English artist—Ashwath was hearing of him for the first time—an artist called Turner, a renowned painter of light. The gallery had a painting by the artist, on loan from a university collection, which showed the volcano Vesuvius erupting. A white light blazed from the mouth of the volcano, the heavens swirled in red raining debris on the waters, and human figures fled from it as from an apocalypse. There were other pictures by the same artist that the instructor showed them; in one of them, like the Vesuvius watercolour, a figure, an angel, stood in the vortex of a centrifugal whirl of fire. Agnieszka saw it as an indictment of man, a warning to people to repent, a fiery lament—the angel's wings were on fire and his wand appeared through the flames as an admonishment, and human figures cowered in the foreground.

That may be, Ashwath said. But in its essence it is a celebration of light ... Ashwath felt a sense of release—here he was, a novice, free to voice his opinion, his views on par with those who knew more, but not better. He looked again at the blaze at the centre of the paintings. The sun is a ball of fire—a child's textbook introduction—and here it was in truth, in front of his eyes. The sun is god—these were supposedly the artist's last words.

Exhilarated, he recited the twelve names of the sun, and then the Gayatri, the hymn in praise of the sun, the dispeller of darkness, the one who illumined, made radiant and removed ignorance.

Immediately after his recitation Agnieszka had clapped, the instructor had said Bravo and the class—all the nine women—had swivelled round in their chairs to look at him.

Please, once again ...

What does it mean?

Immediately he felt shy, and a little shamefaced at his showing off. He had made public his act of prayer, a hymn that was meant to be recited in private, as an act of communion. In truth, his prayers had grown irregular, half-hearted. There was so little time for anything.

*

He received letters from home—heavy, laden with platitudes. His father wrote in English. When are you coming home, it has been years since we saw you. How is your new job? His mother wrote theatrical versions of the same thing in her round Kannada script. My eyes are tired of shedding tears. They wonder when they will have the good fortune of seeing you again. He put the letters aside quickly. He sent them, in return, big bright beautiful cards with cheerful messages in them.

He would visit soon, as soon as he had paid off his car loan, saved up some money and got his Green Card. Not just a visit, he would make an entry.

One evening, he had a visit from Manohar.

You are looking prosperous, Manohar said. It sounded like an accusation. They were sitting in one of the small hospitality lounges on the ground floor of the building that housed his condo. From the lounge they had a view of the garden and the pool, a blue undisturbed stretch of water, and tree-fringed paths beyond.

I'm doing okay, he said carelessly. Planning a trip back soon, he said, hoping to forestall Manohar. I'm getting used to driving around in this weather. Thanks for the offer of your old car. But I'm thinking of a Chevy; K5 Blazer, or even a Lotus convertible.

The instalments will be killing!

I can manage, thanks. Sorry, busy this weekend, can't make it. I'm working on a script.

Oh, play acting?

He let that pass, impatient for Manohar to leave.

Manohar had brought news of a bereavement. Suchi mama's wife had passed away. It took some time for Ashwath to figure out who that was. He stared at the plastic packet Manohar had handed him, of dry flowers and uncooked grains of rice, wondering why Manohar was giving it to him. When he came back to the lobby after seeing Manohar off, he saw Alan and Jake, the handsome lead from *The Heart is a Lonely Hunter*, the newest addition to the group, on their way up. He looked again at the damp packet in his hand, and threw it into the trash before hurrying into the lift with them.

Two

As safe as houses, so the saying went, and what could be safer than a bank that lent money to buy homes—we cover l-o-o-o-o-ng term mortgages, as the executive at the

Home Savings Bank, a thrift bank, had sung out to him—and where one's savings were safe. The banker was a solid citizen, a trusted man, with good judgement of character, and in turn possessor of good character himself, for after all, he was a writer of loans, a granter of credit, a waver of wands. Ashwath was attracted by the word 'thrift' that seemed to speak to his blood, stoking his latent caution. A loan that could be repaid over ten years, and savings that funded such loans were as close to permanence as possible. Such a bank was truly a nayi bank, it merited a watchdog as a symbol. The other magic term was 'federally insured', the assurance of a safety net that the government extended. It made eminent sense to invest his savings in such a thrift and to take out a mortgage on a home loan, and a car loan. The warm red of the Chevrolet Caprice sedan greeted him, grinning through its fender-teeth. He pictured himself in the driver's seat, with the little blonde Polish artist who had just befriended him by his side, driving in to the twin corn cobs of Marina Towers, a building he had coveted on sight.

But the Home Savings Bank, in callous disregard of its promise, had failed. The network of savings and loans, the scheme is too big to fail, the promoters and newspapers said. Even the city's oldest bank with its regal row of columns, an emblem of solid citizenry, pointed out to tourists in passing on La Salle, had failed, both victims of speculation.

It's the way the system works, Manohar said. He had reached out to Manohar in a panic, an act he regretted almost immediately. Every time the authorities give an institution such as a bank more air, more breathing space, more opportunities to grow, people go berserk—too much oxygen to the brain can cause hallucinations. Too many unsecured loans, reckless lending, too many financial adventurers with no real knowledge, Manohar said. It's like allowing a person whom you have first starved to have a free run of a feast. He's bound to eat himself sick, and then you put him on a diet of bread and water ...

Prakash—you remember our Kaveramma's son—he's doing very well, an expert in these matters, he's the king of quants, an ace at applying mathematical models to unwieldy data and complicated financial instruments and analysing them. You must get in touch with him. He'll be able to help you out.

Across the street from the city's oldest bank, was its comrade in arms, the Chicago Board of Trade: on its façade, carved in relief, were venerable old men, hooded in shawls, guarded by the American eagle, holding sheaves of grain, the symbol of plenty, harking to a distant past, to the beginnings of the Board as the arbiter of trade in grain, much before it was replaced, in the course of time and events, as an overseer of 'futures', before it was caught in abstractions and fictions, in elusive time. The CBOT had sublimated the produce of the land into a chimera, the bank had made his money vanish into thin air.

Much later, when the panic had settled and he had come to accept that this is what destiny had in store for him, to grant him his heart's wish, that of perfect anonymity, of being every man and no man, with nothing to stand or lean on but his own feet, he had met Manohar again. He had tried to give him the slip but had not succeeded for Manohar came downtown often on work and had cornered him at the restaurant where he worked as cook's help and sometimes chief of salads.

Manohar had come all the way just to tell him that he had heard that his brother-in-law was involved in a similar Ponzi scheme—selling government securities against junk receipts—and had been cast in jail, a fall guy for higher-ups. Swindling games were the same across the world, after all.

What goes around comes around, Manohar seemed to be saying. There was no escaping the family karma, even if you thought you had escaped the family. He put it down to spite on Manohar's part, and paid no attention to him. When he sent his sister a card for her birthday he added a post script. I hope all is well with you. In reply she wrote I am getting a Satyanarayana pooja done for the well-being of the whole family. He had to be satisfied with that.

*

What he would remember was the kindness of people, if not it would be free fall all the way. Bill Moreland, his advisor in college, and his efficient secretary Marcia, had tried to tell him something again and again but he had not paid attention. On the contrary, he had been angry; he thought they weren't trying hard enough to find him a job. All the signs around him had pointed to a blip in the job market. He had caught a lucky break with his job in Golden. You have to be ready to grab the low hanging fruits when you find them and then steel yourself when the going is not good. In an economy of unlimited opportunity, the falls were sudden and there were few safety nets. For the ease of a steady life, he had to go home.

In his first year at college, it was his habit to explore the neighbourhoods, and he had spent hours walking in the quiet streets, watching the softly-lit rooms, sometimes with the silhouette of someone reading at a desk, or the flicker from a TV set. One evening, he had found himself on Bill Moreland's porch, quite by accident. It was just before Halloween and there were lighted pumpkins on the window sill, all in a row, like Diwali lights. The front door opened, Bill recognised him, and invited him in. The family was about to have dinner. The table had been laid and he found himself moved by the sight of this simple, daily act, the dining table with its plates in place, the cutlery all laid out, a low light hanging over it, a glowing orange. The scene seemed to him like an act of prayer, a private moment of contemplation into which he had been admitted.

Bill's wife opened a can of soup when he told them he was vegetarian. It was the first time he was eating soup poured out of a tin and he was not to know then that this would be a prescient act, that the red and white Campbell's tins would follow him into the future. Garbanzos? Bill's wife pointed to another tin, but he shook his head. He did not know that they were mere chickpeas. Garbanzos sounded like something large and bloody.

How do you like it here? Bill's wife asked. She was wearing a knee-length pleated skirt and a modest blouse with a jacket of the same knitted material, and was smiling at him. Her head was tilted to one side and she had a kindly expression on her face.

Everything is the same here, he replied. The houses, their porches, the lawns, even the clothes people wear ... all similar. Everyone has the same life.

Bill's wife uncrossed her knees, pressed her palms together and laughed, looking at her husband. You make us sound like a bunch of bores!

No, he was at pains to reassure her, I think it is a good thing. It frees you up to think differently, to live your own life. It had come to him even as he spoke, and he was grateful to Bill Moreland's wife. She had reminded him of why he had come there and why he was staying.

*

Ray Bertrand at Golden too had gone out of his way. He was now VP, head of the main brand of Golden's breakfast cereal, and need not have troubled himself. Ashwath could have been given the proverbial pink slip, left on his desk by the unseen hand, with the security guard accompanying him to the gate with his box of personal effects.

I have been here seven years, he said, when Ray Bertrand called him to his office. This had been his first job, right after his Master's and now, just as he was beginning to feel settled, that he had found a home, he had been asked to go.

Seven years is a long time in one place, Ash. Even the economy gives itself a shake once in ten years, as it is doing now.

He waited for Bertrand to continue.

The butterfly effect, Ash—a blip in a distant radar, a regime change in a distant country, one country invading another halfway across the world, afflicts the prices of oil and rocks prices all over the world ... sets heads rolling. The banks are also in crisis mode ... His allotted two minutes had extended into ten as Bertrand explained to him the effects of stagflation and the challenge to the company to grow and generate profits when there was a downslide in the economy. Then, on the back of a flyer which had Magic Johnson spooning breakfast cereal into his mouth as he twirled a basketball on one finger, Bertrand had drawn a curve. The marker in his hand had hovered over the base of the curve and he said the employees in that region, the stack at the bottom, whose performance had been constant, had to go. But he had delivered, hadn't he, Ashwath interjected. It is not enough to deliver, Bertrand replied. You have to excel. Those were the rules. And he, Ashwath had been found wanting. It was not just a pronouncement on his performance, Bertrand softened the blow, adding, but also on the performance of the economy and the company. The businesses they had acquired were not doing well—the growth strategy may not be the right one, it might need a mid-course correction. There were rumours that a new CEO may come in and streamline all the businesses of the company.

This was not the time, Ashwath realised, when Bertrand was being so thoughtful and taking so much trouble to explain things, to tell Bertrand about his problems—that his savings had been wiped out and his mortgage had crashed in the banking crisis—it would only be a footnote in Bertrand's story. Already Bertrand was looking impatient. The tip of his nose had turned white and he was picking objects off his desk and putting them back noisily.

Bertrand said he would see if there were openings in the Industrial Foods and Specialty Clothing businesses, drop in a word to those managers, but a bright guy like him would have other options, maybe even better offers up his sleeve. He did not want to stand in Ashwath's way.

*

His luck, he always said, followed the president's. The president's two terms and his own ascendant star ran side by side. By the end of the d cade Ashwath could no longer deny that he had become part of the ebb and flow, his fortunes linked to the rough and tumble of his adopted country. When the sunshine of the 80s ended and the economy slid into a recession, he faced the bleak 90s in sympathy with the market one could say, with a derelict bank account, without a job, a house and the comfort of old friends. Agnieszka was the first to leave and then Alan, to nurse his niggling respiratory ailments which were becoming more persistent and also, presumably, a broken heart since, Jake, the handsome lead from *The Heart is a Lonely Hunter* had left, and finally, Terry to LA to try his luck in Hollywood after doing several small parts in the movies. They had all, for a while, withdrawn into themselves, afflicted by a hundred-and-fifty-year-old ailment that a visiting French writer had diagnosed the country with, that of a 'strange melancholy among plenty'. Terry's father, it turned out, was a vice president in one of the largest retail chains in the country, and Alan's family, whose business was a remnant of the stockyards, had made their money supplying beef to the city. (Many years later Ashwath was to learn that Alan had been in the first stages of the rampaging AIDS to which he eventually succumbed.)

Morris, his trusty agent and financial planner, found him an apartment a mile north, off Fullerton and Clark, close enough to the lake as he wanted, in a beautiful midrise brownstone with bay windows and boxes bright with geraniums. In a few weeks he discovered that the building was owned by a squatting landlord. The apartment block was part of a foreclosure—the owner had defaulted on his mortgage. Ashwath found that he, along with a few bewildered South East Asian fellow tenants, had narrowly escaped being evicted in the middle of the night and charged with felony, theft and burglary. Morris still claimed that the property was clean and that the authorities had it all wrong. Morris also assured him that he would get back the money he had lost when the Home Savings bank had crashed, but he had to wait for the law to take its course and the courts their time.

For Ashwath, this was his anointment to the equal opportunity and anonymity this land had promised him, a release from the sunlit prison of the American dream, as a native son had put it, a reversal of the four Cs of success. He was proactive with the first two Cs—he sold his Caprice (through the intrepid Morris)and gave himself up to the Chicago Transit Authority and the L; he cut up his credit card into tiny pieces and flushed it down the toilet, finding this last act greatly liberating. The newspapers and flyers were a consolation—they contained stacks of discount coupons and news of sales. In a balancing act of equal and opposite force, his condo and his corporate abandoned him. He bid goodbye to the mortgage he had paid and his dreams of an apartment by the lake, close to the beach.

He also managed—an act of overkill by the fates—to slip on the ice and fracture his ankle, and was laid up in his foreclosed home for a further two weeks. Again, Morris was helpful. Ashwath was to realise the efficiency of the system as sung through the jingle to which he had paid little heed till then—*Need cash, need it now/ I have an annuity, but I need cash, get it now*. He was allowed to sell his annuity in exchange for a small lump of cash, of course at a considerable service fee.

Just as there was atonement, prayaschitta, for sin, there were ways out for acts of stupidity and the slings of fate.

Three

He wasn't quite sure about when his father died, like the man in the book he was reading who said Mother died today, or maybe yesterday, I can't be sure. But novels were confections, unreliable things. You couldn't trust their truths. The confusion was caused in part by his sister's telegram. Dear Respected Father passed away yesterday at dawn. Cremation over. Yesterday? Yesterday as compared to the day she sent the telegram or the day of the cremation or the day it reached him. He was sure only of the year. 1992. She hadn't waited to find out if he could come. Who had performed the last rites? Not her husband, surely? The telegram was wordy without being informative. It went against their respected (not dear, though) father's dictum of economy, of frugality. It wasn't necessary to say Dear and Respected, for instance. And then his resentment had transferred to his father. Couldn't he have waited? Why did he have to go in such a hurry?

This message, these ten words, had made their way from under weeping monsoon skies, over seven thousand miles, to arrive at his door on a summer's day. That summer's day, the sun lay thick like shellac on the streets, to recall a prodigal writer son of the city; it slid down the Viking hat of the Hancock as it stood watching, and poured off the flared hips of Picasso's baboon in Daley Plaza, it reflected shards of glass off the lake and obliged the careless bodies that lay face down on the beach to be sunburned. Turner's god was bountiful, and also indiscriminate, amoral; he had learnt not to take the sun personally.

In the early days, he used to be a gawker. The tall buildings, standing quietly by the river, reducing it to a stream, he saluted from a distance—their fearful symmetry was beaten out in a hellish furnace, surely. He stopped to watch the cranes on the street, one Altec limb flung out, cupping in its palm a man in a glo-vest and a hard hat, changing the bulbs on the electric poles or the credits on the marquee of the Chicago theatre on State, which he walked past everyday. The street-sweeping Pelican whose injunction, DO NOT FOLLOW, he had explicitly disobeyed, he found to be the most riveting creature. He had followed it, when he lived on Fullerton, watching its whirring retractable limbs that expertly sucked the leaf litter, as it went under a viaduct and out of sight. Those were the days when he was recovering from the accident on the ice and hobbled around on crutches, and watched the street from the bay window of his aesthetically pleasing midrise, little knowing that he was being scammed by a squatter landlord, who had let out a building marked for foreclosure. He had been lucky to stay till his ankle mended.

If the Pelican was an elegant creature, the snow plough and the snow blower were heroic, as heroic as the red firefighting trucks. On winter mornings, the salt truck was a tiger moving in the grey darkness, squirting salt on the streets.

Selling off his Caprice, he had felt a pang—he would be that deracinated creature, a man without a car in a land where the machine was king. He had found odd solace in a news item he had read in a science magazine about a scientist in his hometown who had transformed the bullock cart by replacing its wooden wheels with rubber tyres, to make the load easier on the bullock. He recalled the majestic single-humped bullock, auroch wild, that had roamed the streets in the vicinity of his house in his hometown, as if it owned them, when it was unharnessed from the cart by its owner, a kerosene oil vendor. When dusk fell the man would come calling the bullock by name, urging it to come home.

He found the animals he encountered in his working beat soothing—the strange standing beast splayed in all directions, all mandible and legs, irresolute of form but essentially beast that he saw first as he emerged from the pedway at the Thompson Centre. From there onward to the plaza to see the baboon—squat, bewildered but resolute in snow and shine, beaten into shape if his old acquaintance Sushil Khanna was to be believed, in his uncle's furnace in Indiana, where it was outsourced by US Steel. Then south on Dearborn Street to see the gracefully stooping red flamingo, its cousin the flying dragon, in a garden in the Art Institute, and the green lions themselves, majestic, mute, standing guard outside the institute, whom he saw regularly on the days entrance was free.

There the animals stood, adrift from their creators but moored in their appointed places, each with his own story, speaking only when spoken to, but always ready to have a conversation, suggestible, forgiving, full of grace. The buildings were too tall, too remote; besides, they bore evidence of human habitation—lights, lifts, windows, even people.

That beautiful summer day, the day of the telegram,

when the beaches hugging the curve of the lake were full—Seurat's Sunday Afternoon come to life a hundred years later—he went into the art gallery, not to his usual place to join the crowd in front of the Seurat—it was too placid a painting for his mood that day—but to another one. There was another painting he had come to favour of late, a Matisse figuring bathers by a river, in Cubist style, hanging in the modern art collection. It looked crude and unformed at first sight; four columnar figures, with blank oval faces. The more time he spent studying it the more he felt its answering gavel in his bones. The river was a thick band of black running from the top of the canvas to the bottom in a straight line. The four figures were placed equidistant from each other from left to right, with equal pride of place. One of them sat on the banks of the river, as if on a chair, with one stubby leg in the water. To one side of the thick black band, painted like signs on a zebra crossing, were spikes of green—the forest by the river. The four figures were preparing to bathe in the river, or so it seemed, despite the diminished will their maker had given them. They were women, you could tell, not just from the little scoops of breasts or the half-hearted triangles of their sex but the modesty of their bearing, their shame. That was what it was, he realised; shame and grief etched in their blank faces and the lines of their crude unformed limbs; it was there in the incline of the neck, the supplication of the limbs and the surrender of their breasts.

By the time he left the gallery, his appetite for self-flagellation almost filled, it was late evening and the prodigious golden light was beginning to mellow. He found a seat on the L, to his surprise, despite the crowded hour.

The telegram in his pocket crackled, a painful reminder, but there was no point looking at those ten words again. Every time he read them, they smote his heart anew. He took out the book he was reading and read afresh the first few lines of James Baldwin's essay. On the twenty-ninth of July in 1943, Baldwin wrote, my father died. On the same day, a few hours later, his father's last child was born. Baldwin had turned nineteen on the day of his father's funeral. While his father's body lay in the undertaker's chapel, a race riot had broken out in Harlem, New York.

At that point Ashwath closed the book and turned away—the contents of those few lines were far in excess of his constricted brain, his overflowing heart. But with that gesture he had made an unforgivable mistake; he had made inadvertent eye contact with the person sitting next to him, and broken the unwritten rule in public commuting, that each one be absorbed in a private space despite the physical proximity, that there be no attempt at bonding, at communication. He opened the book again.

The writing was so clear, so direct; Baldwin had cut open his heart and laid it out on these pages. His father had been a preacher, a cold man, even cruel, whose children had been afraid of him; Baldwin had had contempt for him. Baldwin described his last visit to his father, who lay shrunken and shrivelled on the hospital bed, fed entirely by tubes, where he tried to summon up the sorrow he could not truly feel. By the next day his father was gone, his mother was taken to the hospital and his new sister was born, and he himself was engaged in trying to find something appropriate to wear to his father's funeral.

The only 'real' conversation that Baldwin could

remember having had with his father, his step-father actually, was when he had asked him abruptly, whether he would rather write than preach. Baldwin had been in high school, editor of his school magazine, but also a young minister, a rival to his father. Baldwin had said to his father, Yes.

Ashwath recalled the one 'real' question his father had asked him, looking him in the eye, amidst the platitudes, the homilies, the admonition and the plain instruction that formed the bulk of their daily interactions. Pedda—idiot, fool—was the word his father usually prefixed all instructions to him.

Do you really want to go to America?

He recalled the rush of anger, of bitterness, of cold hatred that he had felt at that moment. Yes, he had replied, Yes.

And so it had been granted to him—he had chafed against his collar and broken free—to run wild, feel the wind in his hair and then find his path. No bit-and-bridle anymore, or the cloying affections.

A year before his father died, working in New Jersey, Baldwin said he had lived with a rage in his blood, often taken for madness. The last night in that town, he had been as usual refused to be served in a diner. He had walked out, and walked on the dimly-lit streets blindly, overcome by the sensation that all the people on the crowded street were moving towards him, their white faces gleaming.

That morning, that perfect morning, Ashwath himself had walked among a crowd on the beach, of blissful sunbathers, little girls in pigtails swinging a perfect hoola hoop, dogs gambolling on the sand, gulls taking a pigeon-toed stroll and young men flinging themselves about in pursuit of a ball; he had stood in the thick of an admiring crowd in a gallery and been shamed by a painting. And now trapped amidst columns of limbs and blank faces on the train, he felt for himself the indifference of the shining happy people—even the street preacher on the corner of State and Madison had not told him he would go to hell—and had vacillated between thankfulness and despair. In a way, this is what he had wanted—to be freed from the burden of his past, in this youthful country which encouraged you to seize the day, make the most of it, which did not make much of destiny; here he could experience real exhilarating isolation where it was possible for no one to know you and for you to know no one, where you could be the master of your fate, maker and mender of your mistakes.

The busker on Michigan Avenue had greeted him with a golden blast from his saxophone as he walked past. He was reminded of Elbert Davis, the actor from Terry's group who had had small parts in his plays. He had almost stopped mid-stride to check if the man was indeed Elbert, but had carried on. One evening, the evening they had heard him on the sax for the first time, Ashwath and Agnieszka had dropped him off at the edge of the housing project where he lived about a mile away from the art gallery where they had been rehearsing. Elbert had walked out into the cold air that cut through layers of clothing, towards one of the identical hunkering highrises on either side of the street. It had been an exceptionally cold night, belying the warmth of the room and the magical music they had just left behind. Amidst the snow drifts and the treeless landscape, the buildings loomed. They had driven away quickly after dropping him off. Ashwath had thought of Elbert's long fingers hovering over the stem of the instrument, the tendons on his neck straining with the blasts of the sound, the clean spitless movement with which his mouthpiece had come away from his lips and the way he had gyrated to the sounds of his music. And then, of him disappearing into the brooding buildings in the darkness.

Several years later he would see a film, alone in a theatre, where he would go more to kill time between jobs and keep out of the rain but which would bring him out of his jaded fugue, a film about two young black basketball players from the housing projects who had struggled against the system to make it to the NBA. One of the young men had been from the same housing project as Elbert—he had thought of Elbert then, and the cold evening when he had been swallowed up by the snowbanks amidst which the buildings stood. Elbert had never mentioned how fraught his walk from the street to his house was, where an ambush may lie in wait on the stairways every time one went home; he had instead made an offhand, laughing reference to his brush with celebrity, when the mayor had moved in to his building, as a gesture of solidarity with the underclasses, stayed for a few weeks and thrown a party before leaving.

One of the boys in the film who had won a place in a suburban school remarked that it was the first time he had been around so many white people, who did not talk the way he did. He had found it hard but also that he could adjust to it.

The word had come back to Ashwath, like the foods from his home. 'Adjust' was a good word, adjustment was a way of life—it gathered under its skirts a plethora of meanings—to accommodate, to tolerate, to grit your teeth and bear it and finally to get on with it. In the film, the school coach sat in a room that had on its wall the motto, He conquers who labours. Ashwath could understand the boy's predicament, his bewilderment at the strange rules in this new world, not of his making but where he had to succeed, where a single quality he had, a talent, was what was valued and wanted, but not the rest of him, of what he stood for. He could succeed only if he gave in.

His world and theirs. That there was honour in the other world was true, the thrum of night and day could not be denied. As the balding coach in the film, dressed in a shirt with stripes the colour of the American flag said in his speech to a gathering of one hundred of the best basketball players, in an impassioned rush, quoting his mother—God bless her—This is America, you can make something of your life here.

Yet there was a rip current in the seemingly calm waters, the smooth flow against which you floundered, which dragged you in. Ashwath had simply not been able to fathom the waters. As far as he knew, he had played by the rules, done his boyscout best and he still did not know how he had blundered. He had been measured against an unknown, invisible scale and found wanting. His American dream, to use another American expression, had remained a pie in the sky.

His neck had begun to ache. He closed the book and when he looked out at the flashing darkness, he realised that there was something odd about the train. He remembered looking up from his book when they had passed Fullerton.

He had seen the neat red brick building with windows at regular intervals, De Paul university, like a slab of chocolate with evenly laid out squares. As he prepared to get off at Wilson, the train went over a bridge and a stream and then a row of modest brick buildings each with its own dumpster, like a possessive suitor. He sat up and took note. There was nothing even remotely as picturesque on his regular Red Line route and then the stations passed—Paulina ... Addison ... Montrose. The stations were unfamiliar—the train seemed to have switched to the Brown Line and he hadn't even noticed. He got off at the next station and began to make his long unfamiliar way back.

It had grown dark by the time he got off the L. At first when he saw the white flakes descending slowly he thought it was a case of unseasonal snow and then when one landed softly on his shoulder he realised that these were the catkins of the cottonwood trees that grew further up the street and showered it with 'summer snow' every spring. He picked the catkins off his shoulder and walked on, making his way past the listless panhandlers, past a clutch of church volunteers who were buttonholing passersby, clinking their collection boxes at them—one of them had handed out a packet with something soft and squishy in it to him once, which he had taken to be a custard pie for he had been hungry, only to find a small soft-rubber foetus wrapped in a pro-life pamphlet, past the men already sprawled outside the honky tonk bar, to his regular retreat, where he would have a drink with his silent companions—the one blameless mug of beer or glass of house wine he had now begun to permit himself, before going back to his box-like home in an apartment hotel. It was in the pub, sitting in the four-seater at the back, far away from the Men's, when they were sipping their drinks, bound by the unwritten pact of grunts and nods, for no one was prepared to receive a sudden unburdening—only the immediate present, the quality of the beer, the weather, the Cubs game on TV or enquiries about the waiter were permitted, that he was found out. There was Sam Lee with her grave eyes, Tim who said nothing at all, and the horror-house actor who was telling them about the new act that he was part of, in the upcoming Halloween season, with the Son of Svengoolie, the king of TV horror himself. And suddenly he was there at his elbow—Suchi mama's wife's nephew Manohar, a ghost from his past. Ashwath had simply stood up and walked out with him, on to the crowded street.

He had made Manohar sit down in the lobby of his hotel, on the shabby sofa, a safe distance from the caged receptionist who said as soon as he saw him, Ah your visitor has found you ...

Shall we go up to your room, Manohar asked.

No, he said. We can talk here.

Manohar had come to offer him money, a loan so that he could go home. Prakash was willing to underwrite his ticket expenses and he, Manohar, any ceremonies that had to be performed.

There is no point, he said. The cremation is over. I got the telegram this morning.

But that was not what he wanted to say. It was the first thing to come out of his ambushed mouth. What he wanted to say was, Never come back here—how dare you out me like this.

You need not have waited for me, he said at last. You

could have left a message at the desk. Or called. They make sure I get the message.

Four

There was no question of going home. For one, he had no money; he was also fighting for the elusive Green Card, which would allow smooth egress from the maze, after letting him enter. Like his mythological cousin who knew the mantra to enter the complex battle formation but whom the gods had neglected to teach how to exit, he would be trapped at home forever if he went back. He just needed to be patient, wait just a little, his lawyer had said.

But his tryst with Reagan's America, his Ferris Bueller interregnum, was over. He had been given a glimpse of the future and could see it, like Algren's man, as clear as a wolf's head in an empty window.

*

The apartment hotel, a single room occupancy in the 46th ward, was on the edge, depending on how one looked at it. The lobby for instance could be dismissed as dark or assessed as shabby-genteel, it all lay in the eye of the beholder. The signboard with the name of the hotel glowed invitingly at night with backlit neon lights; by day, its rusty frame and rivets were visible, and the chains that held it up against the wall. The patterned linoleum floor was world war vintage, the kind that did not show the dirt. There was an old leather sofa with two chairs—no upholstery that could stain or cushions that could be removed, and a central table with newspapers and newsletters from several social and church organisations fanned across it. The TV was on all day long and they had tried to conceal the musty unaired smell, unsuccessfully, with room freshner. The man at the desk was always in a suit and at night, he pulled down a wire mesh and caged himself in, with only a small window open to hand across keys or the telephone receiver.

A single suitcase held all his worldly possessions. He was on the second floor, a floor full of identical rooms, separated by a corridor, where his suitcase kept hitting the wall as he walked to his room. At one end of the corridor was the fire escape and at the other, a common bath and toilet to which he was given a key.

It was much like starting all over again, when he had come to this country as a student. But now, all hope was replaced with certainty that this was how things would be, and that brought a sense of calm. In the room there was a bed by the wall, a dresser with his clothes neatly folded in and his suitcase pushed under, and a small table with a chair and a lamp, where he had no letters to write but which would house a brown paper bag with his next meal in it. In this room he would find himself resorting to prayer, and putting up a small shelf on the wall to house an idol to which he would light incense every morning, making sure it would not agitate the smoke detector.

His window looked out on a side alley, on the worn brick backs of buildings with tacky siding on the walls, a thicket of poles and wires and in winter, the blackened snow that lay piled between the dumpsters. There were warnings against parking in alleys and the assurance that violators would be towed away. He admired the order, the system that was in place, the city in command—it had even posted detailed instructions about handling rats. The meticulousness of the instructions struck him. No parking when snow is 2 inches deep. No Parking 7 a.m. to 9 a.m., Tuesdays. A country was made great, surely, by its parking instructions.

In the days of his artistic education, during that brief brush, he remembered going with Agnieszka to an exhibition of photographs on America. The photographer was the famous Henri Cartier Bresson and there had been a queue for tickets. He had been struck by the way Cartier Bresson had composed his photographs—like paintings with a narrative, and there was one titled *Chicago*. An apartment block reared in the background, several bricks missing from its scabby surface. The bare unpainted wooden staircase indicated that this was the back of the building. A makeshift clothesline with children's garments stretched across. The windows were closed, perhaps even boarded, the shades a patchy stained white. The wooden chute that ran along a staircase was broken, some of its slats fallen in. A low picket fence separated the building from a scrubby sandlot, with dirt pathways beaten in the sparse grass. In the foreground, against the scabby brick wall, the American eagle reared on its haunches, its wings lifted, its feet pinioned on the cement platform that said God Bless America. A little distance from the platform, a cement star lay on the ground. For a piece of public art in such a forlorn setting, the eagle was surprisingly well-proportioned, its hooded eyes and curved beak standing out, as also each scalloped detail of its wings. Three small children played at the base of the platform. A little black dog, alert, full of life, stood next to them, looking up at the eagle. The exhibition had no photos of the lake, the river or the famous skyline. And now he could see it for himself, an extension of what the photographer had captured, in the neighbourhood and in the streets that were now his.

He bought himself a sturdy jacket at the Army and Navy Surplus store and a pair of second-hand snow boots. They made him feel like a fur trapper but would last him for the rest of his life. Thus equipped, he set out on his daily forays for food and work or simply to get out of his coffin-like room, always keeping an eye out for the squad car. There were places which could bring a chill to his heart, thresholds he hoped he would not have to cross. These were not the taverns or bars, whose yellow smoke-lit, hot interiors he glimpsed, or the cubicle hotels with smaller rooms and no windows, but the day labour office where men lined up to try their luck afresh every morning, the free kitchen with its queues of 'respectable' men and women, where, but for a small slip, a twist of fate, the men could be in suits and the women in décolleté dresses standing to enter the ballroom in the vicinity—still the idle thought crossed his mind as to whether the kitchen would have a vegetarian option—and the pawn shops with their discreet signs, We buy gold. Not that he had any gold to sell but he knew that selling your gold was the ultimate sign of distress in a household. He recalled the whispered confabulations that his mother had had with top work Kaveramma, as she carelessly handled a pendant or a chain that Kaveramma was pledging against a hand loan. Kaveramma's son Prakash was here thriving somewhere in a leafy suburb, having made good on the promise of all the gold that his mother had pawned.

He learnt to keep to the kerbside, closer to the street, to stay away from the gangs of boys and the shiftless men who lurked in the doorways of shops and bars looking vacantly into the distance, to smile at the earnest evangelists who were waiting to accost passersby with their existential quizzes, and the bald, pale, robe-clad devotee of the Krishna's Consciousness cult who hung around the newsstand and pressed pamphlets into his hands.

The presence of the soul-scouts was not surprising, for this was also the place for hospices and halfway homes, as if it were holy ground, where people had retreated to say a last prayer of hope or penitence before they died. There was a park nearby which had its own story to tell, a palimpsest that was renewed morning, noon and night. In the mornings it rang with a chorus of happy voices when children from a nearby school played in its tot lot. In the afternoon, a line of bemused men and women from a nearby mental rehabilitation facility made their way to the park, to sit on the benches or to walk under the trees, to the encouraging noises or plain pushing of their minders—he had once seen a dapper-looking man challenging a dog that was being walked, matching it snarl to snarl, bark to bark. In the evenings, the drug peddlers took over, uncaring of the police cars that cruised nearby.

And yet this ward had once been an elegant place, a gracious space, a flapper's playground. It showed itself here and there, in an excess of detail, like an over-iced cake, or a glimmer of grace, like a gleam from a genuine pearl in a necklace of paste. There was the ballroom, reminiscent of corsets and coat tails and pumpkin coaches, with its high cliff frontage, patterned with diamonds of fleur de lis, and alcoves of grinning jesters, which now had to endure the excesses of teenagers and rock music fans. Close by was the largest theatre in the city, now closed, its baroque frontage open to the elements, more a monument to a glory past—to him it only served as a landmark to locate the second-hand bookshop where he was to find a part-time job. And just next to the book shop was the historic cocktail lounge, the legend flowing in a green cursive hand, where Al Capone's regular booth was pointed out to him by the friendly barman.

He had his room—that he had, spartan to suit his newfound quest for yogic simplicity. He had followed the injunction, equally by necessity as of choice, to retire to a solitary place, to live alone, his senses restrained, watching how much he ate, and how long he slept—it was a good thing they kept the heat so low, it helped him in his self-discipline. Despite the hobos and the infirm, he lived a minute from the L stop and close to the lake, two blocks from the beach. Late into the night he could hear the trains pulling in and out of the station, and sometimes his room shuddered when a train passed—he found it comforting; it reassured him that he was in transit, not a permanent resident, and that he could always get up and go. On the nights he could not sleep, when a storm or the persistent whine of an ambulance had kept him awake, he stood at his narrow window, watching the L bridge and the trains, anticipating the heady rush of sound, waiting to catch a glimpse of Algren's yellow salamanders bend all one way before they disappeared into the red-lit rain.

Rainy nights brought out the worst in the man who lived in the abandoned building off the alley his window overlooked. He could hear him cursing and the sound of glass being smashed. Ashwath was always a little fearful for him but there was nothing to it; the man, whom he had come to recognise, would turn up again, outside one of the bars or sitting on a hydrant on the pavement, his eyes closed in a stupor. Just the once he caught the man's eye when he was urinating; the man had doffed his penis at him, either as a threat or in invitation, he could not tell.

*

Of the others in the hotel, transients like himself, he had little idea; most were elderly single men, thin, racked, and sometimes women whose eyes wandered. But these were not convivial places, lasting friendships could not be made here, where no visitors were allowed between 10 p.m. and 8 a.m., and no pets ever, the rats visiting the room notwithstanding. In the corridors, when they passed by each other, or at the concierge's desk, their eyes did not dwell on the other with speculative interest or even cold calculation but darted away in panic, anxious about the demands they might make, or some ghastly human truth that the other may reveal. He did the same when he saw another brown face on the street for he could see his own story reflected in those wary eyes, that helpless gaze, the look that said this is not me, the true me, strong, shining, relaxed, witty, contented, full of things, taken leave for the moment, and put this me, an imposter, in his place. He spent such long periods speaking to no one that he could feel his breath turning fetid in his throat and on his tongue, and he feared his vocal chords would lose their elasticity for want of exercise.

So he was awkward when the woman with the long hair spoke to him as they waited for their laundry at the coin-operated machines in the basement.

It's the mattress, you just have to burn it, she said.

He was startled to be spoken to, even a little frightened, by her low flat hard voice and her blue-eyed stare. He had noticed her in the lobby a few times because of her long thick hair, streaked brown and gold, and the delicate way in which she picked her steps.

How could she have known, he wondered. Was the itching so obvious, or the weals visible, or the small flecks of blood on his bedclothes that he had just put in the wash?

That's the only way you can get rid of the bed bugs, and the blood on your clothes. The snap trap's best for rats. You don't have to worry about their coming back.

After imparting this life-saving bit of wisdom, she collected her laundry and was gone.

The next morning he saw her at the A&W, where he usually stopped for coffee, after buying his newspaper from the kiosk on the street and before he caught the train to the first of his multiple jobs downtown. He had finally learnt to like his coffee black, and not just because milk and sugar were not handy, or because he had to parse his resources carefully. Sometimes, he ordered the hash browns here, along with his coffee, but usually his breakfast was a roll he had collected on his way back from work, from a thrift bakery that laid out its misshapen, unsaleable wares at the end of the day to be picked up at half its price or for a few cents, or a pay-as-you-can deal.

From his usual corner at the restaurant, he had a view of the arches of the viaduct and the L train. It was an unexceptional sight, but it kept him in a constant state of alert, for he knew that several men, rendered homeless, slept at night under the expanse of the viaduct, and the city in its attempt to discourage them from making a home there had pinned a minatory announcement on a rusty board on the wall, that all unattended and non-portable items would be removed. When she caught his eye, she nodded slightly, and he knew that that would be all. The few tables that were occupied at this time in the morning had single occupants and there was little to disturb this ocean of solitude, not even the slight buzz of conversation when an order was placed. From the weekly cleaning lady he learnt, at the cost of an uncleaned room and the smell of cigarettes overlaid with strong perfume, that the woman who had spoken to him was Samantha Lee, one of the Lovelee Sisters—tragic accident that—and that the man with her, the short one, he's been in Korea, can't hear or think straight since he came back, went to college, had a nice house in Park Forest, and a sweetheart whom he married. But he now lives in the halfway house down the street ...

He located the newsclip in the Community College library and read up about the Lovelees. Samantha Lee was one of the three Lovelee Sisters who had a star act in a circus some years ago, which was a favourite with the audiences, who often demanded an encore. The sisters used to perform a series of synchronised moves, all the time suspended by their hair from a frame that was lodged in the ceiling. During one of their performances, the metal rung holding up the frame had given way, the Lovelee Sisters had plunged twenty-five feet to the floor with Samantha at the bottom of the heap.

Her hair was still lush and long but she seemed not to have recovered from her injuries. There was an air about her, of fragility, suggestive of a person on the mend. And then he knew who she reminded him of—Paula at the library in his college, who had had the same tentative air about her, of a person who had plunged into battle, unafraid to heft anything that came in the way, but found when she was in the thick of battle, that the ground had shifted beneath her feet, that raw courage could only take you that far, and hence had learnt to step gingerly on what had once been her stomping grounds.

He met Sam Lee again, outside the Buddhist temple on the corner of Leland and Racine, where he went sometimes to look—meditate was too presumptuous a word—at the calm face of the Buddha. A figure standing in a lotus with one palm raised upwards and the other downwards, poised in a mudra of benediction, made sense to him. He bowed his head to the radiating sun on the wall.

He had settled down here, he realised, in this corner, to a solitary life in which he viewed himself as a participant and not as an observer. He had a routine, a route on the Red Line, a bus stop at the end of the street; he had a place for coffee, an end-of-the-day bar and he had finally persuaded the Korean place on Argyle to skip the fish paste and the beef in the bibim bop, and the crowning fried egg. He liked the royal spread of the dish. It reminded him of the festive meals served on banana leaves at weddings; always a reluctant wedding guest, he used to consider those meals a chore, but he missed them—the sampling of salads and curries and pickles on the edges, salt, sweet and savoury at its appointed place on the leaf, and the rice in the middle.

In Sue's Kitchen the bibim bop was served ceremonially—a deep bowl of the main dish with a constellation of small side dishes. In the bowl, a smooth eggshell blue, nested a bed of purple rice topped with a variety of vegetables. He could recognise the swirls of carrot and radish, cucumber, sprouts and a little clot of seaweed. Among the side dishes was the cabbage kimchi stained red, which he would make for himself when he had a kitchen of his own, slices of yellow translucent sweet radish, squares of glistening tofu and a nest of green glazed cold cooked seaweed. He liked to taste each thing individually, after noting its texture, colour and smell, and then, as if he had pushed decency far enough, he would mix it all up with the rice and the red pepper paste and fall on it, bending his head over the bowl. Sometimes the waiter would bring him pickled sesame leaves—thin delicately veined leaves stacked one on top of the other—steeped in sesame oil and chilli paste. He had become adept at peeling the leaves off, wrapping one round a bullet of rice and conveying the thing to his mouth with his chop sticks, all in one motion. The waiters had started looking on him more kindly, he was sure, after he had stopped asking for a fork for his bibim bop. In some time, when he would move to an apartment hotel where he would have a small kitchen to himself and learn to cook all his meals, he would be partial to napa cabbage, with its white fleshy heart like a giant chrysanthemum, and the black sesame oil and melon seeds, which he had first tasted at Sue's.

He found a quiet bar with a Wurlitzer that played old songs, where he could sit for a while before going back to his room at the end of the day. It was an old bar, so old that the tables, etched with graffiti, and chairs, their seats tight and shiny, looked like antiques. There was a cluster of bottles behind the counter, of thick opaque glass and a framed cutlass above it which gave the bar its name. The old jukebox, solid, with a colourful arc of lights, played country music from time to time. The drinks were a round more expensive than the other bars which were regular dives, so it was quieter and you could find a place even on a weekend evening. He had discovered it, very simply, by following Sam Lee into it and she had beckoned him, this time with two nods, that he could join her and her companion and thus had begun his journey at a new table, with new friends, if he could lay a stake to friendship there.

Sam Lee's companion was a middle-aged man with a gristle of short white hair evenly cropped round his head. Apart from the introductory grunt, he said little. This then was the cleaner's Korean war vet. Ashwath noticed the shell-like ornament behind his ear, a hearing aid. After the first meeting at the bar, Ashwath saw him around here and there, once in the lobby of the hotel. He seemed to be an odd jobs man, but he gave no sign of recognition when they ran into each other in the lobby, not even a nod, like Sam Lee. Sometimes there was a fourth at their table, an actor, who had aspired to become a stand up comedian, and was now a ghost in a house of horrors. His job was to jump out at willing victims, who had paid $20 for the horror package, and scare them as best as he could. He had given their table discounted tickets to a murder-themed dinner, popular with corporate executives, where over a salad of choice and tomato vodka cream sauce they had participated in a simulated murder. Ashwath had been an important player, the doctor, the one to find the body and estimate the time of death—when he had been stabbed through the heart with a kitchen knife.

*

Thrice a week in the evenings, Ashwath worked at the used books and records store next to the grand theatre, his last job of the day, before going back to his room. One evening, the store had arranged for a reading by war veterans. A small space had been cleared at the entrance, a few chairs assembled and a mic put up. There were a few students from the nearby Community College, otherwise it was largely a gathering of men in assorted jackets and trainers, no suits or smart dresses in evidence. But there were more people than expected. All the seats were taken and there were several people standing in the aisles.

For the first time Sam Lee's friend, the Korean war vet, met his eye and nodded in recognition. That evening, Tim—Timothy Burke—read out his poem, 'Chip-Yong-ni'. It was a surprising poem, describing not the battle but a building with red scalloped edges, the only structure standing in the wasted icy landscape. He read out another one called 'Ode to Lima Beans' that went—*I dream of meat and potatoes/ Chicken—spaghetti—tomatoes/ But all I get/ Is lima beans, lima beans. I wear you close to my heart/ Love of my life/ lima beans, lima beans.* The third piece that he read out, in the five minutes allotted to him, was a story which he called 'Walk Down the Aisle in White'.

The soldier leaves his small town, his parents' farm, for the first time when he flies out to war. When he returns he goes back to college, thanks to the GI Bill, gets a job, meets a girl and they have a beautiful wedding. They move into a Levittown-type settlement, among other young families. He sells agricultural equipment, his wife does up her house, bakes in the brand new kitchen and they watch *I Love Lucy* and *The Adventures of Rin Tin Tin* on TV. There is a parallel story in the soldier's head, which runs all the time and which grows bigger and bigger. He thinks of the makeshift hospital ward in which he was laid up, his foot shot through with shrapnel and a piece embedded in his head, which the doctors cannot extricate. He is surrounded by injured soldiers. The nurses are angels, and there is one young nurse in particular, always impeccably dressed in a white uniform, who walks through the aisles, and has promised to go with him to the movies once he can walk again. The camp is hit. The nurse is horribly injured. She turns her pleading eyes on the soldier. He takes pity on her and puts her out of her misery.

During the reading, Tim stopped in between to clear his throat or for water, which he drank in long thirsty gulps out of a bottle, while the audience waited for him to resume reading. The story was written in a simple, straightforward style and was quite affecting; it was also evident that the soldier in the story was Tim himself.

After the reading, Sam Lee nodded to him twice, which meant he was invited to go to their regular bar for an after-drink. That evening their table was loquacious as never before. Sam Lee told Tim that Ashwath was from Bangalore, and for the first time Tim looked him full in the face.

To your reading—Ashwath raised his blameless glass in a toast. I have a story about the Bangalore torpedo, Tim replied. Did he know the Bangalore torpedo?

No, Ashwath admitted. He did not.

It was apparently a simple device, a linked pipe of metal tubes, filled with explosive TNT, to break through barbed wire and metal fencing, and nifty when it came to breaching enemy lines. Tim had been the Bangalore torpedo man of his unit, an expert at setting it up, and blowing up walls and enemy fencing, with artillery machine guns on standby.

Ashwath, Sam Lee said encouragingly, goes to the Buddhist temple off Broadway, you know the one that you ...

Ashwath said he was named after the holy tree, the ficus religiosa or the Bo tree under which the Buddha was supposed to have meditated. Tim nodded, acknowledging the tangential reference to his reading.

Other than the pink shell behind his ear, there was another ornament that Tim wore on a chain round his neck. Ashwath had thought at first that it was a silver cross but on closer look it turned out to be something else, an object that Ashwath could not recognise. It was his most prized possession in Korea, Tim said. His P38 can opener to open his can of C rations, yes—the love of his life, key to his lima beans.

For the first time, their sombre table had smiled and talked. Sam Lee had looked radiant with her hair back lit by the low lights. That evening, when he walked back to his room, there was music in the parking lot off the corner. Just that morning he had seen a squad car parked close to the kerb and a couple of uniforms frisking two young men in hoodies in the parking lot, and now there was a band tuning its instruments for an impromptu gig. The nights were sometimes kinder here, less implacable than the day, more ready to compromise, to let things be; they could still surprise you with the promise of pleasure.

*

There had been one job interview he was hopeful about, and for one last time he had his business suit cleaned. He had answered an advertisement from the production facility of a foods company, for the post of a maintenance supervisor—he was to go to the factory in a small town in the heart of the Midwest, located deeper than his college, an eight-hour journey by bus. He read over the advertisement, lingering over the job requirements and the acronyms he had become unfamiliar with. He would have to implement CPFR, which unlike the first aid respiratory procedure that it suggested at first sight, actually stood for Collaborative Planning, Forecasting and Replenishment. He would also be expected to show initiative in SIOP—Sales, Inventory and Operations Planning. He had, in a leather portfolio—a parting gift from his teammates in Golden—all his certificates and a letter of commendation from Bertrand, whom he hadn't seen for several years, and from the Community College where he had been a grading assistant.

As the bus pulled away from the kerb at the Union Station stop, he felt for the first time since he answered the advertisement, a flutter of nervousness at the pit of his stomach. It was a little after five in the evening, the close of a fine October day, but windy as always. The setting sun, spreading its shellac patina on everything, reflected blindingly off the tall buildings, and he shut his eyes against the excess. They wove past a posse of Fed Ex vans, he caught a glimpse of the green lions guarding the Institute of Art, they were next on Taylor Street, and then the bus was clipping its way across several bridges. At Comiskey Park, the sun dipped below the horizon, showing through the bare branches of trees on the roadside—an undistinguished row with neither leaf nor flower, only bare trunk and branches.

He wondered why the company had responded to him at all. It had been so long since his job at Golden, the letter from Bertrand, quite glowing in its recommendation, was six years old. The testimony from the Community College about his excellence as a grading instructor seemed quite irrelevant—how did it matter.

As the bus ploughed into the darkness, he found the billboards flanking the interstate cheering. For a second, a Culver's burger loomed—larger than life, the ubiquitous signboard for America. A fat slice of yellow cheese, sliding out between thick slices of bread, the patties well done and textured, droplets of fat flecking the slices of tomato and onion, a green flag of lettuce in between, and the whole squished on a bed of creamy white sauce. It made him realise how hungry he was, and the pit stop was an hour away at least. Side by side with the burger, the billboard featured a thick churn of chocolate in a glass, the texture of a concrete mix, with chunky pieces of chocolate caught in a swirl on top. He had eaten nothing all day, but for his first cup of coffee at his usual A&W.

Hi mom, you okay? You okay? Yes mom. Yes mom ...

The seats had high backs and he couldn't see who was speaking.

I'm speaking from my new phone, the Japanese thing ...

He listened to the conversation in the darkness, the voice deep and gurgling at the end of a sentence.

Mom, I've got to let you know that I'm missing you already. I'm missing my dog. I'll call you later. Yes, when we stop.

There's an article in *The Tribune* today, I'm carrying it for you. I told you about the tax exemptions for senior citizens ... Aww, why are you going to bed earlier. You used to stay up till eleven. What? You have to feed her dumb cats? Why?

He pictured the speaker—a young man, overweight and bespectacled, with anxiety issues, no girlfriend, still dependent on his mother, the type who was quick to feel sorry for himself.

Another voice came from the darkness, this time from behind. A woman's voice—clear, hard, sharp, salty, not unattractive.

Hi! No, no. Awake now ...

I've heard this so many times before, maybe thirty or forty times. You're having trust issues with him, you're second-guessing him ... I'd just leave if I were in your shoes.

A middle-aged woman, not a girl, tensile of mind and body.

He's had long experience of buying and selling businesses ...

So she wasn't hectoring her friend about a man in a romantic relationship—it was a business partnership.

The young man with anxiety issues called his mom again.

Hey mom, we are running late. Do you think maybe Al can meet me at the bus stop. No, if I take a cab it'll cost me as much as a ticket ... no, I'm not, I'm reading *Time* magazine now. There's a light by the side of my seat. Yes ... no ... I'm okay.

Here they were, speaking aloud their intimate thoughts, private in a public place, in their own bubbles, uncaring of what the others thought. Perhaps they were so open because it was completely dark in the bus—they might not have been so bold in broad light, when they could see each other's faces. He did not know how many people there were on the bus—he did not care to count the heads that showed just over the top of the seats. Whom would he call, if he could? He thought about it awhile, running his sparse list in his mind. If he called his mother, like the anxious, cash-strapped young man, it was likely that he would have had a similar conversation; only, food would be thrown in.

Have you eaten, son?

Yes mom. A cheeseburger with a chocolate shake. Off a billboard in Muscatine.

But of course he could not call her even if he wanted to. His father had died some years back and his mother had followed him faithfully. If he called his sister, she might not take his call.

It was late when he arrived at the modest hotel where he had booked to stay overnight. Would you like your suit and shoes refreshed, Sir, the night clerk asked. We could have it ready by the morning.

Refreshed. That was a good word, he thought. And he knew immediately that his journey, like those of so many others who had got their clothes and shoes refreshed before him, had been futile.

He had not got the job. And that was the last attempt he made to get a regular job—Bertrand's letter would be returned to its envelope till it would yellow and crumble in time.

Five

Everything he did, was in the spirit of an offering to Him.

Every morning, he encased himself in the protective armour of prayer, placing his right hand on his heart to invoke Shiva, Vishnu in his feet, Hara in his hands, the Sun and the Moon in his eyes, Rudra on his forehead, and Agni surrounding him in a fiery but gentle embrace ... Finally, he would close his eyes and see, reflected in himself the divine form, the embodiment of knowledge, splendour and light, blessed with every virtue, especially the one he craved most—that of equanimity.

Everything he did, was in the spirit of an offering to Him. He would go about his work with efficient detachment, being as a lotus leaf upon the waters, resting serenely in his body—the nine-gated city.

*

Eventually it came down to the use of his hands; his ability to turn his wrist quickly enough to keep the roux from burning, to hold the handle of the knife down and move it across the cutting board in a single motion, and to keep his finger tips from being sliced off on the mandoline.

And what do you do, Mr Ashwath?

I am a food processor.

He would be, without irony, if that was his destiny, the scrub in the valley, if not the pine on the top of the hill. Be a bush if you can't be a tree, the voice, unmistakable, had surged through the cackle of static—Martin Luther King, little knowing of the fate that would soon befall him. If you can't be a highway, he had urged, just be a trail;

if you can't be the sun, be a star ... be the best of whatever you are.

Much later, he would impress a temperamental chef who was out scouting for vegetables at the farmer's market, say that the trinity of women he swore by were his mother, Mrs Irma Rombauer and Mrs Beth V. His mother, for being able to look at a thing and know its texture, flavour, proportions and taste. Mrs Rombaeur, for her *Joy of Cooking* which was at his bedside, and Mrs Beth V for bechamel, espagnol, tomato, hollandaise and veloute—the basic sauces that would confirm him as a food processing professional for he was sure nothing lay beyond their frontier.

But that turn in the tide of his fortune still lay in the future. When he finally got his Green Card thirteen years after he had applied for it, fifteen years after he had set foot in this country, it seemed a formality for he had few skills to offer.

He took an early Red Line to the Loop and emerged to a tangle of railway lines on Randolph Street, from where he proceeded to a succession of part-time jobs. He had explored the slippery slope of the term 'Assistant' in a series of restaurants in the morning, and in the late evening, at a private art gallery in the near North. Some jobs he had lost to the vagaries of finance, and some to those of nature.

He had begun to like his job as Assistant Supervisor at the self-professed leading gallery for local artists in the River North district, a job he had landed through Terry's good offices; there was just one catch though—there was no Supervisor for him to assist. Along with a security guard he managed the place, opening it three evenings a week, seeing to the office and the visitors. It came down to answering calls and recording the number of visitors, handing out flyers and checking the lighting. He had been given strict instructions not to explain the works of art or even read out the flyer. Visitors had to contact the artists directly. Sometimes, the artists hung around, offering themselves as guides to the few visitors.

The gallery was housed in a Louis Sullivan building, turn of the century, beautiful, with timber joints projecting out of walls. Early one Saturday morning, the building had burned down. The gallery owner called to say his services would no longer be needed and he did not visit the place, not wanting to see the burnt ruins of what had been a work of art in itself.

Almost to the day, three years later, the restaurant on Jackson Boulevard, where he worked in the salad station, closed down. A tunnel under the Chicago river had leaked, flooding several downtown buildings, including his restaurant, as also the subway. It was the longest part-time job he had had but this time it was he who had decided not to return, though he had liked the elegant café with prints on its walls, of food and drink.

On one wall, between the bar and the small seating area was a Norman Rockwell print of the Thanksgiving turkey; a perfectly browned bird was being lowered at the family dinner table by a matriarch. Displayed diagonally across from it was Roy Lichtenstein's pixelated, plump, yellow, no-frills turkey, sitting in a pie dish.

At some time, the owner must have given thought to the décor, it could even have been the arena of his self-expression—or her, maybe it was a woman, the more he thought of it the more he was convinced that there was a feminine sensibility behind the choice. In the lobby, in the glare of a spotlight, so that it would not be missed, hung a print that he found intriguing, even a little repulsive. He was surprised at the choice of this painting in an eatery. It was called, predictably, *The Snack Bar* and was by an English painter, Edward Burra.

It showed two people, a woman and a man, at a counter in a diner. The woman, in a fur coat, and a large pearl in her ear, was eating something, perhaps a sandwich. She was looking sideways, distracted, her eyelids a bright blue and her red mouth stretched in a perfect rubberband arch. While one hand held the sandwich, her other hand, bejewelled, rested against a coffee cup. Across the counter, in the foreground, so closer to the viewer, was a man with perfectly groomed hair and a straight nose, giving her a sly look, while his hands were occupied in slicing a large bolt of ham. Two slices, curled, pink, as delicate as wisps of cambric, lay on the cutting board, while his hands plied the block with a knife, carving another slice off. The human figures were arresting but it was the block of ham that stood out. He loved the clinical lines in the painting, and the suggestive corporeality of the meat.

At this restaurant, before it was flooded out, and along with it, his job, he arrived early at the a.m. shift, in the pitch dark in winter and when dawn was breaking in the summer, in time for the breakfast rush. Here he had moved from breakdown person cum dishwasher to kitchen help in the salads and cold foods, the no-stove section, but he was the Man Friday, and it was implicit that he had to pitch in as decided by the chef. He began the day by cleaning all the surfaces in his part of the kitchen beginning with the copper pipes below the sink, which he scrubbed getting down on his knees. And then he started ticking items off the prep list that the chef had left out on the counter, as he dealt with them one by one, which usually began with chopping a mound of assorted vegetables.

Late one morning just after the breakfast rush, when he was taking a breather before the preparations for lunch began—he was, in fact, examining his parboiled toes on which he had spilt hot water and had carried on nevertheless, since there had been no time to attend to his foot immediately, regretting that he had not followed the advice to wear hard shoes in the kitchen and not tennis shoes which were easier on the feet but helpless against hot liquids—when the chef came to the ante room where he was sitting. The chef had looked at his bare feet with disbelief, told him this wasn't the ruddy shoe shop and then asked him to get back to his station to fabricate the protein that the purveyor had just delivered. Fabricate the protein, was exactly what he said. The man in the grill station had not turned up.

There was a chunk of marbled meat on the counter at his workstation. He could only stare at it in amazement.

Get to it, come on, the chef said. Your hands, your hands, no gloves—slide the knife backwards. Gently, gently, as if it were a baby. Push the tip of the knife beneath the silver skin and pull it away—don't hack at it ...

He cut open the chunk of meat, the knife sliding easily through—he was surprised at how easily the knife slid through—leaving a hinge at one end, like an open book with a spine.

Wash, wash!

He washed his hands, patted them dry.

Then, with his bare hands he rubbed the coarse grains of kosher salt into the chunk to drain it of blood from the surface. He could smell the garlic paste as he rubbed into the meat, massaging it well—a mix of cayenne and black pepper, oregano and thyme, that he had made in the morning—smearing the whole with olive oil and topping it off with sea salt, the kind his mother had used in her cooking, digging it out from a sack that stood in their dark store room. He had tied up the dressed 'book' of meat with a string, as instructed, and put the thing into the fridge. After an hour or two, closer to lunch, the chef would roast it in a skillet. But he was done with it.

After he had washed his hands, he contemplated his fingers that still remained faintly pink—stained, and thought of the texture of the meat—tender, soft and yielding. He felt victorious in some sense, filled with a sense of achievement, as if a long-standing hurdle had been crossed. He could say he was the last heroic link in the disassembly line; his reading of Upton Sinclair was now complete. For a moment he felt a sense of kinship with the well-fed woman with the scarlet lips whom Rudyard Kipling had encountered in the stockyards a hundred years ago, which he had visited out of a similar curiosity, only Kipling had thought fit to condemn her for her 'hard, bold eyes', for not being ashamed of enjoying the spectacle of slaughter.

Shame he did not feel at his transgression, but a feeling of relief, like one does at the loosening of the bowels, an act over which one has no control, and yet one that is driven by volition. Still, a time would come when he would assist a chef in a Michelin-starred fine dining restaurant, a chef who was a television personality, one who would handpick him on a whim. He would come to learn that sweetbreads were not breads that were sweet and think nothing of a recipe that involved simmering pig blood, corn starch and mustard together and then topping it with chocolate and huckleberries, or to make the lobster rest in the freezer before putting it in the pot, since a thrashing lobster would make its flesh anxious and spoil the dish.

But that was still to come. Still to come was the turn in his fortunes, a lumpsum settlement salvaged from his savings and loan loss which would allow him to rent an apartment closer to the lake, quite literally at the edge of the water, with a kitchen and a bathroom to himself and also a tiny balcony—he could cook for himself and not live on take-out. Still to come was the final badge of approval—citizenship of the United States of America.

All that was still in the future. Right then, in his small room, where he had a key to the common bathroom at the end of the corridor and an allotted hour at the washing machine in the basement, he had no space for knowing metaphors or exquisite images of solitary people. He had on one wall a print of Georgia O'Keeffe's apples, rounded, like the curve of a baby's cheeks, in glowing tints of red and yellow, and next to it, a picture called Wrapped Oranges. There were six oranges in the picture, rolling on a polished table, four still wrapped in white tissue paper, every line of the crumpled folds visible. One of those was in the process of being unwrapped, the white tissue unfolding, in preparation for the fruit to be eaten, but before that to be held, cradled and inhaled. The dimpled texture of the peel so vivid that he could feel the fruit in his hands, its smell flooding his box-like room, and taste its tang on his lips. He had picked these pictures because they seemed wholesome and healthy; there was a careless suggestion of plenty in fruits stacked tight or rolling about on a polished table. They also suggested an inviting hearth, hospitality, chatter, a gathering, an expression of generosity in a life that was in reality frugal, cautious and above all, solitary. Something like Warhol's *Soupcans* or his *Car Crash*, specially ordered prints of which his theatre friend Terry had displayed on his walls and which he had admired and understood, he could not have. He could no longer have anything to do with things academic, from which he was detached or which he could admire at a remove.

In the mornings, before he left, he packed his lunch—a sandwich with peppers and Monterey Jack, a monkish white cheese that was soft and mildly tart—and sat on a park bench; a man alone eating out of a brown paper bag.

Most days he cycled from his eatery on Randolph Street to his next job further north in the loop in the gallery district, making a detour onto Kinzie Street, past a large red brick building, where a chocolate factory was located, and the air was redolent with the smell of malted chocolate. Sometimes he stopped off at the factory store for their chocolate covered raisins if he felt he could give himself a treat. But that was rare; he made do with the sight of fruits and the smell of chocolate.

Six

As soon as he picked up his ticket from the travel agent on Belmont Avenue, he put it away. By some miracle he hoped, under the weight of his clothes and papers, the date on his ticket would change and he would discover he had arrived too late to board the plane, or the pages would fuse and the woman at the counter—there would always be, wherever you went, a counter, even in the afterworld, with someone behind it to bar your way to something essential—would declare that she could not let him through. He had imagined several scenarios of his return, secure in the knowledge that he would never be called upon to make that journey.

His father's death—and soon after his mother was gone too—had slowed him down, the world appeared to be wrapped in a glaze, with him observing it from afar. He had felt free of the hand on his back, a loosening of the bonds of the flesh, which was the ultimate goal of a man's life, according to the prayers that he recited. And yet, he had been quick to get the card that said he was a Person of Indian Origin, and that he could extend his stay as long as he liked should he ever visit.

In the new millennium his fortunes had made a modest upswing. For one, he had recovered part of his losses from his savings bank failure and was able to move from his single room occupancy to a tiny studio apartment, where he had a kitchen and a balcony with a view of the lake. And he had a steady job.

It was a stroke of luck, his landing a job with a TV star chef, just when he had resigned himself to working a series of part-time jobs in the Loop for the rest of his life. He had stopped off at the autumn farmer's market to pick up something for his night's meal, and was rifling around in the baskets of zucchini and pumpkins when he had caught the eye of a tall man with a high complexion. The man was cradling a gourd, his long artistic fingers wrapped round it as if it were something precious.

Not that one, Ashwath had said instinctively.

And why not? The accent was Italian.

There had followed a conversation on how to pick the right gourd. Unlike a pumpkin, a gourd should be soft, pliable. Not taut. It should be heavy and dark. When you hold it to your ear, the seeds should not rattle. A pumpkin, on the other hand, should be hard, not too ripe or dark in colour—takes more time to cook.

How do you know this? The man seemed astonished.

I used to buy vegetables for my mother.

What do you do?

He had made no reply to that.

Would you like to work in a kitchen, assisting the chef?

The man had scribbled a number on a piece of packing paper, without a name or an address. Ashwath had not recognised him without his chef's hat and the white smock that he wore on TV.

He saw them as signs pointing him in the direction of home. The very first sign was sighting the betel leaf. Wandering in the conservatory at Lincoln Park, whose curved roof and boulevard had reminded him that day of a boyhood haunt, the Glass House in Lalbagh, he had strayed into the room that housed exotic plants and found there a vine of the betel, of the Piperaceae family, a struggling thing with small glossy leaves. It had brought on a sympathetic rush of betel-and-arecanut saliva in his mouth, and put him of mind on that rainy April afternoon of festive meals in distant sun-filled courtyards, which ended in the guests crowding round for the betel leaf-lime-arecanut beeda, occasions he hadn't really enjoyed.

Again, the claw clutch of the Water Tower, Algren's comical old humpty-dumpty, which he walked past every day without a pause in his thoughts or his stride, had conjured up the battlements and turrets of the incongruous Tudor-style palace, which had been built by an Englishman for the Mysore royal family and now stood empty in its vast dusty grounds in his home town; he had had no particular attachment to the building and the visits had not generated any special excitement in him as a boy.

Hurrying down Michigan Avenue, he had come to a dead stop opposite the All Saints shop, staring like a tourist, noticing for the first time a window full of old Singer sewing machines. It was a neat gimmick, very eye-catching. There it was, the black leg· operated model with its round steel sideways head, at which his mother and top work Kaveramma had sat, every afternoon, the whirr of the machine, a quick stop followed by the snip of the scissors punctuating his afternoons. So many hems had been let out, collars turned, old shirts converted into swabs, bits of silk fashioned into blouses and skirts.

The arc of memory seemed to be complete when he had come to rest outside a sparkling storefront to find that it was Tiffany's and at that very spot, though in another city, Holly Golightly, his first love or maybe his second, had stood chewing on her pearls and her muffin, peering at the trays on display. He had tracked down the book to the public library and had been devastated to find that the film had not been faithful to the book. But that was another story, the story of his growing up and coming of age, even if it was a little late.

*

Going to the art gallery for an exhibition by an Indian artist was a death wish. He was sure to run into someone he knew. And unlike on the street where the tacit rule for possibly-Indian brown faces was to look away quickly if they caught the other's eye, that would not be possible when you were cornered.

At first he could not spot any evidence of any art work and then he noticed. The grand staircase was decked up, lit up in festive coloured lights. Each riser of every single step had a colourful festoon of words, a luminous garland rising up to the top, till the landing. And then it continued beyond, on the flights leading to the egress points.

He started reading the words. Sisters and brothers of America ... Something stirred in his mind, a schoolboy memory. He recognised the first words from his middle school textbook. He asked at the desk for a hand out on the work.

Sisters and brothers of America—a salutation that had included strangers in their embrace and was supposed to have been greeted with rapturous applause by the packed hall, the packed hall here, in this very place where he was standing, by an audience curious to hear the monk from India speak.

That had been more than a hundred years ago, on

the 11th day of September in the year 1893, at an event the textbook had called, somewhat grandiosely as it had occurred even to his callow unformed mind, the World Parliament of Religions. It had been one of the side events at the World's Fair, a grand celebration of Columbus's discovery of America, hosted by the city. (Every event, every meeting, seemed to be prefixed with 'world' for nothing short of that would do for these shores.) The representatives of the world's religions had gathered at this parliament; he could imagine the stir caused by the saffron-clad monk with the arresting face, the deep-set, large eyes set off by a turban.

He walked up the stairs, reading off the risers, checking the flyer in his hand—Sisters and brothers of America, I am proud to belong—he read, each word framed in a different colour—yellow, red, blue, orange, green—To a religion which has taught the world both tolerance and universal acceptance. We accept all religions as true.

It was a clever piece of work, very simple, and yet it had in the full resuscitated a memory and encoded it in a new history, rendered what could have been an exercise in nostalgia to a reminder that the new world was still an unfinished project. Neither the date nor the colours were innocent; they had acquired a new meaning, overlaid on the old. The colours were specifically chosen, the flyer explained, these being the colours designated by Homeland Security to signify different levels of threat—red, as befitted its stature, signified a severe risk of terrorist attack, fading to orange, yellow, blue and green as the levels of risk declined.

He climbed up several more steps, past the landing, towards the exit and continued to read. Whosoever comes to Me, through whatsoever form, I reach him ... However men approach Me, even so do I welcome them, for the path men take from every side is Mine.

These words he knew well, for he recited them in the morning. He had become quite regular also in his sandhya prayers, recalling the rituals, the gestures and the words quite easily, despite having given them up for many years. He had simplified the ritual for himself for He was supposed to accept the simplest of offerings—fruit or water, a leaf or a flower, if made as a gift of love, as an act of devotion. It was to help him be stable of mind, to be as steady as a lamp in a windless place, or the ocean that remained tranquil, never overflowing despite the many rivers emptying into it, with all their debris. That ideal state was to be the goal of man. Balanced between all poles of opposites—pain and pleasure, heat and cold, equanimous in good luck and bad, neither shaken by adversity nor hankering after happiness, to whom a lump of earth, a rock and gold were the same, exciting no different feelings.

Part of the prescription he already followed. He lived alone, in a solitary place, in a room as close to a monk's cell as he could get, eating but little—all that could fit into half a coconut shell which was the prescribed monk's portion, not fussy about his food, comfortable in his body—that thing defined so precisely as the dwelling with nine gates.

The book also said that the human mind was impetuous by nature and difficult to control, flapping like a cloud that had been rent by the wind. But stability did not mean inaction, a shirking of duty, that too he knew. He could not get away by 'lighting no fire/ At the ritual offering ... by mere restraining'. He was named, was he not, after the ashwattha, first among trees, His embodiment no less, restless, hardy, springing from crevices in walls, with leaves of unparalleled beauty, and shade so generous that platforms of gods dwelt in its canopy. The roots of the ashwattha were supposedly in heaven and its branches bent earthwards—so it was the mysterious tree, the tree that could be eternally contemplated upon and meditated beneath, but whose secrets lay locked within, the answers to be found in the minds of the believer.

*

He had left the exhibition at the art gallery in a hurry, a little unsettled. No more high art and uncomfortable equations. All he wanted was to get home, pick up a falafel wrap from the Turkish eatery on the way, and watch the Simpsons on TV.

Another Indian artist, at least his name sounded Indian and Punjabi at that, was erecting a sculpture off Michigan Avenue, where the tangle of railway lines and parking lots had been. It lay shrouded under an elaborate tent-like structure for a long time, and when unveiled, turned out to be a strange shiny object, a huge steel egg-like thing, causing a havoc of dazzling light till it was scrubbed down to reflect the skyline more sedately.

More Indians. He had passed by the signpost at the intersection of Michigan Avenue and Monroe, saying Swami Vivekananda Way and there he had run into Prakash, top work Kaveramma's son.

Hul-lo, said a familiar-unfamiliar voice and he knew, even before he recognised the face behind the voice, that he himself had willed this encounter. It was the moment he had been dreading and anticipating in equal measure, all these years. He was surprised it had taken so long for them to cross paths. They had met once so many years ago, at Manohar's house, where, thankfully, there had been too many people for them to have a conversation; he had waved across the crowded room at Prakash, and that had lasted them all these years. But there had been no getting away from him. He always sent word through Manohar, made offers of money and goodwill. Manohar himself seemed to look up to him; his was, after all, the unmitigated success story. His widowed mother had worked herself to the bone, pawned all her jewellery to send her son to America and here he was, an analyst at one of the Big Four financial auditors—come through in flying colours; he had also made the required move to the suburbs several years ago.

Prakash had grown sideways, chunky, square, full of the well-being of prosperity. His shirt and trousers were branded and his shoes looked top end. The steel grey jacket slung casually across his shoulders looked like it had come off the window at Neiman Marcus, round the corner. Ashwath could smell his aftershave.

He had to come home, Prakash insisted, there was to be a party at his house. Besides, Prakash said, you haven't met my wife and daughters. His younger daughter was home now for a few days. She was studying at the business school at Northwestern. Sushil Khanna would be there. Did Ashwath remember him?

There was no getting away from it. He could not think of an excuse quickly enough. Better to get it over.

They arranged to meet at Union Station from where Prakash often picked up his daughter when they rode home together. Prakash had it all set up. They would take the Amtrack train to Naperville—the Illinois Zephyr—and Ashwath would return the next day on the Carl Sandburg. His daughter insisted they take these trains for their names. His girls were grand, he said, the younger one had him twisted round her little finger.

Prakash spoke incessantly, stopping only when the ticket collector came to check their tickets.

Hey, the ticket collector said to them. Pow wow, pow wow.

It was on the tip of Ashwath's tongue to say—We aren't that kind of Indians, but Prakash spoke first.

Hey bud, how're you doin', Prakash smiled at him.

The man smiled back good-naturedly, and moved off.

Ashwath closed his eyes and pretended to be asleep for the rest of the hour's journey. From the station they got into his car and Prakash resumed his monologue. He was planning to change his car soon. He was torn between a Honda Accord and a Toyota Camry, and finally the Camry won out—its engine, 136 horsepower, 2.2 litre four, excellent. As smooth as butter.

They drove into wide streets, trees beginning to show the colours of fall. They stopped at a White Hen pantry. Prakash made a call to his wife, and for once he said little but acknowledge her instructions with grunts. Half a mile later they were in a quiet row of houses set well off the street. They drove into the garage and the sliding shutter slid into place with a click. Prakash had his head cocked to his side, waiting for the sound. It's supposed to be noiseless, I fixed it myself, he said.

The garage, large and roomy, looked like the power tools

and hardware section of the Home Depot where Ashwath had once had a job, just for a few months. There was a variety of hand tools, hammers, hacksaws and drills stacked on the handmade shelves along the walls. Step-ladders, he counted two at least, slept on the wall. Rakes, large and small, spades, paint brushes, mops and brooms were propped up against the tallest wall. The open cupboard had several jars and bottles. In one corner was a mass of looped wire and rubber tubing. All the shelves were numbered, the containers in the cupboards organised according to height. A battalion of gardening machines stood on the floor. He spotted a large lawn-mowing scooter with the snout of a suction pipe at its side and two large bags at the back, a leaf blower with a long trunk which looked brand new, and a snow thrower. This garage, obviously, was Prakash's temple. He could see where his weekends went. He realised that Prakash was waiting for him to say something.

Wow, he said. Wow.

I keep it all ship-shape myself, Prakash nodded, satisfied.

They stepped out into the garden and not into the house, as he had expected. The grounds stretched out across houses; with no compound walls to demarcate the yards, the grounds had the feel of a forest. Prakash's yard had several oak trees and a ginkgo at its edge, its leaves fluted and golden. He remarked on the tree to Prakash.

Yes, Prakash nodded again. But you had to be careful of the seeds. If crushed underfoot, they could set up a stink. They had suffered a whole season before they had traced the source of the smell and spent a fortune on pest control.

Prakash clapped his phone to his ear. Al?

Al, it turned out, was the leaf collecting man and not

one of the guests expected in the evening. Prakash went back into the garage and emerged with his walk-behind leaf blower. He walked down the length of his garden blowing the fallen leaves to the side and there was a pile just in time when the old rusty van with the leaf collecting trailer drove up.

How're you doing Al, Prakash shouted.

Al smiled behind his beard, took off his cap and wiped his head. Ashwath recognised that blank look of incomprehension of the slightly hard of hearing; he had seen it any number of times on his friend Tim.

They watched the truck setting off, a little wobbly and uncertain.

They went in and put their coats away in the closet under the stairs.

Take off your shoes, Bhagya is very particular, Prakash said.

The drawing room was furnished in white—white stuffed leather sofas, cream lace curtains, fluted golden lights and a ceramic bowl with white flowers on the central table. A Kalamkari print elephant was framed on one wall. On the opposite wall was a Thanjavur-style Krishna and Rukmini on a swing, rich with gold foil and glass beads. It sent out a glow into the dark room.

Bhagya used to take classes in Mysore before she got married—Prakash waved his hands. It was clearly a thing of the past. Then Ashwath remembered. Prakash had been pursued and netted by a rich land owner, whose daughter wanted a groom settled in America. She worked now in a bank and was due home any minute.

The kitchen opened out into a dining space, the TV

room, and an outdoor patio, where tables and chairs were arranged for the afternoon.

In one corner of the white drawing room, in two brass pot holders, there stood curry leaf saplings, their leaves glossy and green. They looked exotic here in this foreign setting, objects of beauty.

They are a nuisance, Prakash said. I've fixed special lights to simulate sunlight in winter. But Bhagya loves them. She empties her coffee grounds into the pots—keeps them healthy.

The door leading from the garage to the house opened and Prakash's wife came in. Like Prakash she was square of build and was dressed in trousers of a heavy synthetic material and a lilac coloured shirt with long drooping collars. Her hair, ramrod straight, hung in a curtain till her jawbone. There were deep trenches below her eyes.

Bhagya, this is Ashwath—Prakash hesitated.

I am an old friend from Bangalore, Ashwath said. We ran into each other on Michigan Avenue and he invited me home.

He wondered whether to fold his hands in a namaste or to shake hands.

Nice to meet you, Bhagya said. Her voice sounded neutral. He couldn't tell if Prakash had given her the back story.

Cash, get your friend some coffee. I'll change before the others arrive.

Cash, so that was what his wife and probably his friends called him. He was sure Prakash was happy with his shortened name. He wondered if Bhagya had been shortened to Bag.

Bhagya returned from her room upstairs quite quickly. She was wearing a sari and had on long earrings. The trenches under her eyes had disappeared and she looked quite nice.

Ananya, their daughter had taken up an internship in a consulting firm, Bhagya said, if not she would have been here. She was glad her daughter was not very far from home. They were staying put here because of Ananya, who was getting a degree in business from the Kellogg School. If not she'd rather move to California. She had a brother in San Diego. And not to mention the cold.

Ashwath handed over the box of Indian sweets he had bought from the No shirt No shoes No service shop on Devon Avenue. Apart from the best sweets, the shop also had terse injunctions painted on its door. No pets allowed. No soliciting. This too he liked, the finger-wagging, the euphemism for begging. It made him think fondly of what he had left behind. A few doors away he had spotted yet another comforting sign, a handwritten note saying that the shop had a Sumeet Mixie on sale—the Sumeet Mixie was the very first gadget his mother had allowed herself after many misgivings and lamentations that she was failing in her duty by replacing the grindstone with a mixie.

As an 'assistant' in an Indian restaurant, a place with velvet curtains and thick sauces, where the smart Mexican waiters passed off for Indian, one of his many responsibilities was labelled 'inventory and purchase', which meant accompanying the owner's son on shopping trips. That year, the owner's son wanted to put up a stall at the city's food festival and experiment with his cuisine. It was on these trips that he learnt to distinguish a vegetable by its colour, texture, its weight and heft, to tell the freshness of a spice by its smell and whether it looked spry in its sack or wilted; he learnt to estimate quantity, volume, weight and size. He could look at a spice tray, an assortment of herbs, and pick a combination that would work, that could be classic or piquant or downright adventurous. He had become, as Prakash described him, a food professional. When he would make his eventual trip back home, he would find the market that he visited often as a boy much changed, replaced by a mall and sleek glass-fronted windows, and that the market as he remembered it—the array of shops and the spangler-clad mannequins, the untidy kirana shops with their wares spilling out of sacks—still lived in far away Devon Avenue. And the realisation would leave him completely confused.

That's nice of you, Bhagya said, you shouldn't have bothered. She put the sweets away on the kitchen counter, close to the sink.

And then they started arriving, all the couples. The closet and the sofa that had been set out in the landing overflowed with jackets, scarves and bags.

There were loud greetings. He was introduced as the childhood friend from Bangalore whom Cash accidentally ran into on Michigan Avenue after almost twenty-five years, fancy that. For a few moments he was a person of interest and then their eyes swept past, as if there was nothing really to hold them there, on to their friends and acquaintances.

Shanti and Mukul, doctors from Aurora—their son had just got into Duke University—in the heart of the Midwest, Meena and Suhas, Tarun and Sarah, Vijaya and her husband whose name he couldn't catch. They came with gifts, flowers, and casseroles of food. The dining room filled up, it was too windy on the patio. He helped bring the chairs in.

He found himself sitting on a two-seater with Vijaya, so close that he grew cross-eyed with the effort of looking into her face.

I run a non-profit focussed on healthcare, mentoring entrepreneurs, Vijaya sipped her drink slowly, not affected by the seating arrangements. What she loved and what had brought her success was her gift for people, she said.

And what, Vijaya asked, did he do.

He was saved from answering by the new arrivals.

Sudha, at last, someone said. Sudha threw her hands out at the door theatrically and handed her bag to her husband to put on the table. She was dressed in Western clothes, the only woman in the room to be dressed so, in a moss green raw silk skirt and jacket. After hailing all her friends, Sudha went to work, arranging her bags on the kitchen counter.

She pulled out a cake from a cake box and set it on the table. There were murmurs of appreciation from the guests who had begun gathering in the kitchen as soon as they saw Sudha, waiting for her to pull out a rabbit from her Treasure Island bag.

It's plain vanilla, she said, waving her hands dismissively. Wait, wait, be paaay ... shent, it's coming. She pulled it out with a dramatic flourish and a crinkle of wrapping tissue—Bhagya and Cash!

She put them on the cake and tapped them on the head and they bobbed, obligingly.

Oh look! Personalised bobble head dolls! That's so sweet of you, Sudha!

Cash, come in, oh do! Look what Sudha has for us! Just for a minute, baba, not more. You can get back to your guy talk after that.

Bhagya posed in front of the cake with the dolls bobbing on it, with Prakash, and with Sudha, and commanded her friends to photograph them.

But Sudha wasn't done yet. She emptied another bag—a colourful spillage of peppers—on the counter and looked for the right knife from the rack. She was going to make a tapas like no one had ever tasted, straight from a Spanish chef.

Let's not hurry, Sudha sing-songed. She had to have the right wine for it. The bottles clinked musically as she pulled them out and set them on the counter—a rose wine, a blend of shiraz and cabernet sauvignon, just right for the tapas she was going to make, and the cottage cheese thingy. The sommelier had recommended it personally. It had been commended at the International Wine Challenge in London.

Screwcaps? Somebody teased.

She smiled triumphantly. Refusing all offers of help she unscrewed the top of the bottle and produced a pipette-like device—an aereator—which she proceeded to plug into the mouth of the bottle. This would introduce bubbles of air into the wine, aereate it to soften the tannins.

Why did the bottle have the dimple in its bottom, Sudha asked, looking around like a child who had said a naughty word and was waiting to see what would happen.

Ash may be able to tell us. He's in the food service business, Bhagya said from across the room.

This depression here, the punt as it is called, he put his

thumb into the hollow at the base of the bottle and held it, feeling self-conscious. His action seemed to him faintly vulgar. It is to prevent the sediment from rising, especially when you pour out the last glass. It also makes it easier to hold the bottle and pour with one hand. He poured some of the rose wine into Sudha's glass.

She drew him aside to the love seat. She was learning about wines, taking a course with a sommelier. She also wrote poetry, she said, and had enrolled for a creative writing course online. Ever since she read Poe's *Cask of Amontillado* as part of her course, she had been wanting to try it. She was hoping to fall in love with it, she said, but she didn't care much for sherry. Could he recommend ...

Someone hailed her from the other end of the room and he made good his escape. Soon, the men and women had made their own separate groups. Prakash said he was looking to buy another car. He would give his Camry to his wife. Tarun said he was waiting for the auto show at McCormick's Place, where there would be hundreds of models on display, literally hundreds—a grand buffet for them to choose from. He already had his discounted tickets on hand.

And you, Tarun turned to him without warning. Ash, what wheels do you favour?

The wheels of public transport, Ashwath said quickly, a little too quickly.

That's wise, someone said.

No sweat, no bother about parking dibs or white-out ...

You must live in the city ...

Yes, in the heart of it. In an apartment. No hassles of raking the leaves or mowing the lawn for me.

Of course, of course, Tarun said heartily, picking up his drink and moving away.

Would you—Bhagya's gentle voice said at his elbow, passing him the tray of hors-d'oeuvres. He stepped around the room, as people interrupted their conversations to toothpick things off the tray or shake their heads, smiling at him politely. Back in the pantry the portable toilets man, who was introduced to him as the Sanitation Sultan of the Midwest, gave him his visiting card but Ashwath shook him off.

He stood alone on one side of the room, suppressing the urge to throw the heavy nondescript brass object that stood on the mantelpiece at the large glass window, for the pleasure of hearing the sound of breaking glass. They all reminded him of characters out of *The Truman Show*—the men with their cars and golf and professional ease, their razor sharp superwives, the couples who wanted to do South America one country at a time, their children's success and their unbearable energy. He could have told those men a thing or two not just as a food service professional but also from his experience in luxury retail at a high end departmental store, something that none of these marketing men would know. He would have told them that he recognised a cheap, off the rack suit in a minute. He would have told Tarun to take off his chalk-striped trousers which made him look like a Chicago gangster and that a green shirt, even for an evening, was a strict no-no; and also to use an ear hair trimmer. He would have told Srikant that deodorant was a must. He would have advised his good friend Cash to remove his pencil line moustache and leave his gold chain in his cupboard.

He left the gathering and made his way up to the guest room. He hadn't much of an appetite for the assortment of foods that had been laid out, to be eaten out of paper plates, each with a serviette stacked beneath. On the stairs he ran into Sushil Khanna, the one person he had been bent on avoiding when he was in college, whom he now recognised immediately. But Sushil Khanna could not recognise him. Ashwath asked after his uncle and the foundry, and Sushil Khanna still did not remember. The foundry had closed down long back, and his uncle had passed away some years ago. His aunt now lived with her sister in Portland, Oregon. They ran a home service eatery there, for Indian food.

There were flowers in the bathroom and soft towels. The handwash next to the sink said sweet mandarin and lavender enriched with vitamin A & D. The label sounded fancy. He thought of the narrow shelf next to the sink in his room with its meagre contents—a tube of toothpaste, a can of soap suds and a bottle of mouthwash. He examined his teeth in the handsome mirror. He had good teeth—all his own. He flossed and rinsed regularly. His nails were clean and clipped straight. His hands were well cared for—they had to be, it was a job requirement. His hair was neatly trimmed and his gaze was steady. If he could not look youthful, he had to look ageless, always ready, still in the game.

The cars had driven away; the noises had stilled. He wondered if Prakash had told his wife that his mother had once done top work in Ashwath's mother's kitchen and that he had regularly worn Ashwath's hand-me-downs. But that seemed incongruous now, a fabrication, even as a story.

He wanted to leave immediately, to unlock the door

and walk out into the night. He fell, instead, into a restless sleep.

He was woken up by the sound of the rain and he lay awake listening to it pattering on the roof. The clock on his bedside showed that it was six in the morning. It was still dark outside. The garden lights and the street lights were on. They lit up the small puddles in the dip of the pavement and the garbage bins that stood like the sentinels of the night. For a minute he thought he saw someone crawling on the grass and then realised it was the ghoul on the moors, a ghastly, life-like Halloween garden ornament. He stood at the window till the sky cleared up and filled with light. There were low clouds on the horizon, like hills in the distance, and a very thin sliver of moon in the sky. Squirrels chased each other on the branches of the oak trees and darted across the grass. The impeccably raked lawn of the day before was covered with leaves as were the eaves outside his window. There was a pile of neatly chopped logs in one corner of the garden—probably from the oak tree that had fallen. Prakash said he had paid 500 dollars to have the tree brought down and chopped up. That would be most of my savings, he remembered thinking, almost all of it. Well, Cash would have his work cut out for the morning.

Bhagya dropped him to the station, looking sleepy-eyed. Cash was yet to wake up, she said. He had barely gone to bed.

Do come over, she said, Cash has so few old friends. She stifled a yawn and apologised. Sorry, it's been a long night.

Thank you, he said. It was a lovely party. And a pleasure meeting you.

*

The coffee maker had stopped burbling and his room was filled with the rich aroma, so intense that he could almost taste it. He poured himself a mug—black and strong. He switched on the television hoping to catch an NBA rerun with Magic Johnson or a Cubs game, or even Siskel and Ebert reviewing a film, any film. There were forest fires raging in Texas and floods on the east coast. A woman in Kentucky had kept some people drugged and chained up in her basement for their social security payments and her neighbours had not had a clue. Their children had been playing with hers, above the basement all along. He flipped channels. He paused at the public service ad, the one that was being telecast regularly in the last month. People, full face, of different colour, age, looks, girth and occupation, came up one by one on the screen, each saying 'I am an American' and then the phrase, E Pluribus Unum—Out of many, One—before the screen went blank and faded to a point of oblivion. He flipped some more. There was a film that caught his attention, a film about contagion. A young man was being interviewed, a man in a white coat who worked in a lab. His job was to inject bacteria into the guts of rats to test their immune system. An army officer, a grey-haired woman spoke of the dangers of contagion, on viral and bacterial infections and the importance of washing hands. A doctor then spoke of respiratory disorders, pulmonary disease. He stopped, and took his finger off the TV remote. A New York doctor was analysing the dust collected from the plume that hung over lower Manhattan. The camera cut to a man with a protective mask lying in a hospital bed, a paramedic who had rushed into the whirl of dust. A year later his hacking cough had progressed and he was finding it difficult to breathe. The young man was worried about his family.

He was surprised at how often the word family came up in this land of loners. Outside, on the street, on buses and trains, even in parks, they were there, all by themselves, at best in twos—couples. The camera panned more grey dust. The New York doctor had analysed it as a combination of several things—concrete in gas form, jet fuel, asbestos, glass, building material, fabric and human bodies. A woman said she had called her brother in the building to say, Thank god you're safe. But of course he wasn't. He had just not had the heart to tell her. There was a ticker running at the bottom of the screen, running fast, with the names of the dead. He caught an Agarwal, Patel, Singh ... It was supposed to be the best life, the woman was saying, working in the best building in the world, with the best view, a view of the ocean, a view of the torch of freedom, living the American dream.

His pocket crackled. He pulled out the visiting cards he had collected in Prakash-Cash's house. Was it just the previous evening? He picked up a card that had fallen to the ground—from Rishi K Kumar, Septic Services and Sanitation Engineers—the Sultan of the Midwest. Get in touch if you need a job, he had said ...

He had forgotten Suchi mama's letter that Prakash's wife had handed over to him when she had dropped him at the station in Naperville. The letter has been sent care of Manohar and he in turn had entrusted it to Prakash. It was written in Suchi mama's habitual blunt manner with no time or patience for niceties while observing all the conventions. He was sending the letter through Manohar because he wasn't sure his letters were reaching—he got no replies from the other end. After the salutations he said, you have to come home to put your house in order. It was different when your father was there. But the house, Neel Kamal, is yours and it has to be set to rights. You have to shoulder your responsibilities. He could not get away, Suchi mama was reminding him, by lighting no fire at the ritual offering, by mere restraining. Ever since his father passed away, Suchi mama had been beseeching him to come home, and take charge of the house, and he in turn had made the usual excuses. But of late there had been a tone of urgency in his letters, and in this letter, the imperative could not be ignored. Land values were shooting up, Suchi mama had said. If he came back, he could be a rich man. He was still young enough for the future to hold possibilities.

It wasn't quite the return he had planned, but he couldn't put it off anymore. He should really think of packing, of buying a new suitcase. He had better use that ticket before it lapsed.

VII

One

How long must a man wait for his destiny to catch up with him? When he had left the frozen waters of Lake Michigan in January, there was a splinter of ice embedded in his heart. He had been watchful not to pull it out because then he would have to deal with the haemorrhaging. A quick trip to settle the house, he had told himself, to claim what was rightfully his.

From the terrace he looked at the ashwattha tree that stood in the place of the outhouse. Every morning, when he looked at it, it gave him a start, a slight shift of deferred recognition in his brain somewhere. He marvelled at its tenacity, that it could sprout in a small crack in a wall and split the wall open if left unchecked. And this vagrant was the first among trees, sheltering alike the truth seeker, the weary peddlar, and women who brought their children to watch the restless sun in the leaves or play amidst its deep lobed roots. So hardy a tree would last forever, it was not surprising, and could even accomplish the task of being upside-down, its roots firmly in heaven, and its branches reaching down to earth, each pulsating leaf a song. Its branches and buds were supposed to signify human foibles and weaknesses, which one had to overcome, and reach for the sky, for the roots that grew there. Hardy, lush and bountiful as it was, it was the symbol of impermanence, a call to freedom from worldly ties, from samsara. It sounded fanciful, but not surprising, and strangely uplifting—the grandeur of the lore and the beauty of the tree went well together. And in his yard, stubborn, persistent, it had grown out of the cracks of the foundation of a building that had been destroyed, taken root and turned into this handsome creature.

He had not been true to the call of the ashwattha, to himself. Far from being free, he had allowed himself to get enmeshed in worldly ties. He had allowed the splinter of ice to melt and now there would be gore. His nephew and niece had started the process. Shweta—sweetness itself, his sister reincarnated, and Aprameya—so much like him, only better, courageous, more deserving. Savitri—his own pulse, and Keshav Rao—he had begun to look kindly upon his brother-in-law, even as he recognised his low cunning. And now Thippy had sent word to say she would visit Neel Kamal. The circle of samsara was complete.

He thought of his nephew and niece, and the letters they used to write to him with the auspicious symbol Sri at the top of the page. We are well. How are you? I am now in the third standard. My final exams are next month. Amma got me a pink silk long skirt for Deepawali. When I jumped down from the gate it caught on the spokes and tore. Amma gave me a tight slap. That bit had got past his sister's vigilant eye. In a previous letter he could make out the words, imperfectly erased, Ajji wants to know if you are coming home for Ugadi this year at least. I am on the cricket team, his nephew was less effusive, more distant, matter of fact. From next year I will start cycling to school. And then the letters had stopped. His nephew first, as soon as he entered middle school. His niece's letters petered out gradually. All well here. How are you? Affly, Shweta. He liked the dimunitive 'affly'—it looked neat on the page, efficient conveyer of arm's length intimacy.

He had not been prepared for the surge of feeling of what he would call love. There was Aprameya standing on the terrace, trying to hide his cigarette behind his back, pulling a hand through his curly hair, saying, You have had a life Ash mama. You have done what you wanted, lived by your rules. You are nobody's pooch, I like that. I'd like to live a nomad's life. I want to do what I please. Stop where I want. Change my name to Salman Khan—that was a joke, okay, don't look so alarmed—he is a film star ... Not have to ask for permission all the time, to leave yourself open to the option of No!

As he watched the boy silhouetted against the balustrade and then the sky, with a devil-may-care tilt to his head, and a touch of uncertainty in his eyes, he wished he could reach into the cavity of his chest and grab his heart, and hold the squamous thing tight in his fist to stop it from beating so hard, just for a second, so that he could calm down and think of what to say.

Aprameya, he said, you are truly a free spirit, not burdened by the past. Sieze the day. Follow your heart.

At that, the boy put his hand out and smiled at him, for a moment, and then he was off.

He was back in college again, standing on the terrace, his steel tumbler of coffee growing cold on the parapet wall, waiting to catch a glimpse of her. He remembered the sunlight on her flat-boned forearms, the fine bronze hair glinting in the first rays of the eastern sun. She seemed to be bathed in a golden aura, even as she went about her mundane chores in the garden. Her toes in the grass were knobby, like small white pebbles, and her bare feet, wet with dew, left a trail of footprints on the cement paving. Nothing could be more becoming on a woman, he thought, than an ankle length skirt, the seams at the hem coming undone, worn with a man's bush shirt and a towel slung over one shoulder. It kept him going all day, a moment's glimpse, his vitamin supplement, inuring him against his mother's tight-lipped disapproval, his sister's barbs, the sniggers from the kitchen.

If she asked him for the house, what would he say? He had started feeling quite tender towards it, like one would towards an old love who had lost her looks. A battle-scarred behemoth, pockmarked, blind in one eye, missing several teeth. It was so much more than a house, it was a spirit, a live thing, which woke up with the sun each morning, and they who lived in it were anointed by its grace.

*

The pink jasmine trailing on the arch over the gate was in flower as was the champak; their fragrance filled the morning air. The mango had flowered late this year and there were fruits in the tree, far too many and too high to reach. He heard the monkeys chattering in the trees. They had been among the mango and jackfruit all morning.The gardener had set off a round of crackers already to frighten them, but they had returned after a while.

He paced the garden, impatient to see her. But this would not do. He would sit still and wait for her by the ashwattha tree.

Savitri watched him from a distance. Their silences in the kitchen had grown fraught but neither of them said a word. His brother-in-law was clumsy. His attempts at faux bonhomie wearied Ashwath. I can get things done, he said, buttonholing Ashwath in the garden, out of Savitri's hearing. I know some important people who can make the loan easy and a builder who can get round the regulations, even dodgy khata papers, he said, meeting Ashwath's eye for the first time.

Thank you for the offer. But I haven't decided to sell. They must have come to know of his visits to the bank and the lawyer. Wrap it up quickly, Suchi mama urged him, before they do you some harm.

Thippy did not give them much notice. Her secretary called to say they were coming in an hour's time.

I had better get the house ready before they come. Amma travels with her entourage. Security. Press. Savitri's voice was tense.

No—really?

She turned round and went into the house without replying. He sat down on the stone culvert round the ashwattha tree to wait for her, taking deep breaths to quieten his clamouring heart.

Shut the door, Aprameya, he heard Savitri call out from the terrace. The monkeys are about. They are here, she said. I can see them turn into our street.

Almost immediately he thought he heard a car stop outside the gate. He sat by the ashwattha tree and waited. Through the slats in the gate he could see a group of figures clad in white, the women in saris and the men in kurta pyjamas but he couldn't tell who they were. There seemed to be a van parked by the kerb. After a long wait the gate opened. Two men stepped in, followed by the women. He searched for Thippy, wondering whether he would recognise her after all. From the corner of his eye he saw a flickering flame in the front doorway; of course, Savitri would want to welcome the party ceremonially, with an arati.

The gate opened and the noise in his head was exceeded only by the chattering monkeys in the mango tree. He could feel the tendons in his neck pushing out, straining in anticipation. For a moment, he was distracted by a sound, a flat, harsh crack, and then on its heels came another, followed by a scattering of loud sharp outbursts and a capillary of pain spurted through his limbs. He looked down at his feet, astonished to find them standing in a reddening pool. He felt himself sinking, his hand clutching the ashwattha tree for support. His last, inconsequential, thought before he sank to the ground was that the sky was such a bright blue and that it looked so familiar, and so endless, that he could not quite recall where he was.

*

You are lucky, it's a flesh wound. Superficial, a puncture, Harish said.

He recognised Harish as the diffident but bright boy, a poor relative who had come from the village. He had attended medical college staying with them in their house and had now set up a flourishing practice. No damage to any nerves or the bone—no fracture or serious ruptures. I'll need to put a few stitches since the wound is in the fleshy part of the calf; a pressure bandage may not be enough.

Low velocity missile wound—that was how Harish described it. He prescribed a course of antibiotics and painkillers. And this you can keep as a souvenir—Harish dropped a small steel ball into Ashwath's palm—it was the pellet from the air gun that had been embedded in his calf.

You must ask Aprameya to be careful. He tends to get excited about the monkeys. If I recall he had burn injuries some time back, caused by those crackers, Harish said, looking carefully at Savitri.

Savitri was pale and apologetic. Thank god, she said. Thank god nothing happened. We are lucky. Harish is discreet.

*

The next morning, Savitri was summoned to the police station. She went, accompanied by Keshav Rao, and the legal advisor to the Nivarana Ashram. Ashwath lay low indoors, out of sight of the news reporters who knocked on the door. A television van was parked outside the house and Savitri ordered the gate to be locked and for the phone to be placed off the hook.

By afternoon there were reports of an attempt on the life of Sundari Amma of the Nivarana Ashram by jealous rivals. The ashram had grown by leaps and bounds in the last few years, and now had a considerable international following, especially Caucasian. It had just been awarded a large grant, for its Ayurvedic R&D lab, beating down the competition. One news channel wondered if it was an inside job, the result of a power struggle between two warring groups. A minister, a devotee of the Nivarana Ashram whom Amma had cured of a painful condition, had expressed deep concern. He urged the Director General of Police to give the matter his personal and immediate attention. By the end of the day, after Savitri was closeted with the legal advisor of the ashram and the DGP's office, the ashram issued a statement saying they had no cause to think anyone would want to attack Sundari Amma. She had no enemies. She was an emissary of peace, a healer. People came to her for succour from far and near. Amma bore no ill will towards anyone. Amma had visited her childhood home, and her devotee who lived there, also an ashram employee, had been in the process of welcoming her. The family had been a little too enthusiastic with the celebratory crackers. No one had been hurt.

An over-zealous cub reporter had spun out a romantic tale about Amma stepping out of the ashram for the first time in several months, to visit her childhood home and the local temple in which she had served as a girl. There was a timeline occupying the report.

11.00 hrs: Amma arrives at Sri Lakshmi Vishnu temple

11.20 hrs: Amma's entourage leaves the temple

11.25 hrs: Amma arrives at the gate of Neel Kamal, her childhood home

11.27 hrs: (and here there was a red splash on the page) Sounds of firecrackers or shots?

11.29 hrs: Amma's entourage leaves Neel Kamal

13.00 hrs: Amma returns to Nivarana Ashram

16.00 hrs: Amma leads prayer meeting in the ashram prayer hall as usual.

An astrologer who had read Amma's horoscope said that Amma had made a mistake in stepping out of the ashram to recall her past. Henceforward she should confine herself to the ashram and to ascetic life and prayers.

In a week's time, the Director General of Police himself issued a statement scaling the 'suspected attack' down to an 'incident', and explained that there was no evidence at all to suggest anything to the contrary. The search of the devotee's premises had yielded only an airgun which the household kept to scare off garden pests. No case had been filed by or against anyone. The ashram had also asked for police protection to be withdrawn. However, the police would continue to monitor the ashram for some time.

*

The day after the attack, before she left for a meeting with the DGP, Savitri suggested he move out of the house, into a hotel, immediately. Harish was discreet yes, but one could never tell, not with the press hounds around. They were constantly nosing around for stories about Amma. And then there was Suchi mama, who could be quite fanciful. So many beasts to be fed.

Savitri, he said. I will move out to the hotel for everyone's peace of mind.

It would give him the space to think about the house, this house, his legacy which was turning out to be both a promise and a millstone round his neck. Suchi mama was right. The house would not hold out much longer.

He settled down in the hotel with a certain familiarity, of having recovered an old footprint, ways that had lain dormant. It made him uneasy. Again, he had become the man who ekes out the day, waiting for it to end before returning to his single room. He read the newspaper in his balcony and watched TV in the lobby of the hotel. On Day 1, the life of Sundari Amma, head of the Nivarana

Ashram, was on the first page of the newspapers; on Day 2, the 'imbroglio' as one newspaper termed it, had shifted to an item on the third page. By the end of the week, after the Director General of Police had scaled the whole thing down from an 'attack' to an 'incident', it was over. The raucous debates on prime time TV on the perils of the new age guru—Is spirituality the new business opportunity? Is superstition the new religion?—were over.

By the end of the week the photograph of a missing girl, a girl who had gone out to work on the night shift of her job at a call centre, had taken over the front page. Come back home, the appeal printed below the photograph read. Mother is ill. Finders will be suitably rewarded. He felt a pang of recognition at the face. She looked so much like his niece, or her friend, in fact she could be both of them put together—the same guileless eyes, tremulous mouth, and plump cheeks, still to lose their puppy fat.

*

Savitri sent word. How long did he intend to stay? Was he thinking of returning home? She doesn't mean Neel Kamal, his brother-in-law reported blandly. Suchi mama, who had been told that he had moved out to a hotel to avoid the unnecessary excitement, rang up and said, you must decide on something. There is a time for everything. The water will flow over your head soon.

At the end of the week a body was recovered, that of a woman in her early twenties or late teens, from the scrubland on the verge of the city. But it had not been identified. They were still speculating whether it could be the missing girl. There was a photograph in the newspaper, of people lifting a shrouded body, and the hand, a small brown thing with fingers curled in, and a knotted bracelet at the wrist, had slipped out. It was the kind of thing he could imagine his niece and the Sandalwood Maiden exchanging, a symbol of undying friendship.

At the end of the week, too, his brother-in-law came to see him again.

Keshav Rao looked ill. His face was stained an uneven grey and his eyes had sunk deep into their sockets, as if he had not slept for days, which he probably hadn't. His multi-coloured hair, thick and unruly, had turned almost completely white .

Aprameya had not called for days now. They were worried. Sometimes he did that. Spent nights at a friend's place, but he always called to let them know where he was. He had left home the night of the 'incident' and hadn't called since.

Shweta, placid Shweta, had started fighting with him. Her friend was staying with them right then, having been kicked out of her PG digs. Her father was coming to take her back home. Boyfriend trouble apparently. He had started turning up at her PG place and causing trouble. The proprietor had asked her to leave. Shweta wanted Chandan Bala to move in with her—there are so many spare mattresses in the house, Shweta said, thinking a bed to sleep in would take care of all the problems.

Jimmy? That's the boyfriend, isn't it, Ashwath said. I remember. He was much older.

Jimmy? Yes. No, that isn't his name. He was a guy she met at the gym, so she called him that. She doesn't even know his real name. His brother-in-law clicked his tongue.

Guileless, you called them. You are the guileless one, brother-in-law ...

Keshav Rao sat down heavily on the plastic chair and covered his face.

We need you to make some calls, to find out where he is. Try to reach him. Tell him his mother is worried.

Why me? Why should I call him or his friends?

Ashwath—his brother-in-law's voice was sandpapered with impatience, and exhaustion. You have Aprameya's old mobile phone. All his friends' numbers are stored there.

Have you gone to the police, he asked, and bit his tongue almost immediately. His brother-in-law rolled his eyes at him and said nothing.

Please, will you call Shankar and Chotu? Their numbers are on your phone. They were with Aprameya that afternoon. The three of them left together. Besides, anything to do with publicity or the police would scare them off—could I have some water? He lifted the empty jug and poured it out. Never mind. This room smells.

He stood in the middle of the room, hands on his hips and stared at Ashwath in furious despair. They eyed each other, two men dissimilar in nature and by instinct, mistrustful of each other, uneasily bound.

How is Savitri, Ashwath said.

Your sister is at the ashram most of the time, Keshav Rao replied shortly. She has undertaken a penitent fast—not much use but she keeps doing that from time to time.

He walked out of the room and shouted down the stairwell, into the lobby for water.

Call Shankar.

There is only a Shankari listed here ...

It doesn't matter, Keshav Rao said. It's the same person. Here, give me that phone. I'll call, you talk.

The phone rang. The ring tone was a popular devotional song in praise of the Devi. A man's voice, deep and guttural, answered.

Shankari?

Who's this? How did you get this number?

Shankari was performing at a play that evening and taking the night bus out of town immediately, along with the troupe.

I don't know where he is, I haven't seen him in days, Shankar-Shankari said. It won't serve any purpose, your coming to meet me.

Ashwath persisted. His mother, my sister, is ill, he said. Please. I need to talk to you.

The phone crackled in his ear. He heard a muffled conversation at the other end. Hello, he said. Hello Shankari?

I can't stop you—Shankar-Shankari seemed to relent. We have to pack up and leave immediately after the show. So I can't really promise anything.

I'll be there before the show. I look forward to it, Ashwath said to which he received no reply.

When they were at the door, a room boy came running up with a jug of water. Don't you fill the water regularly? You need to be told? Keshav Rao pretended to cuff the boy on his head. Ashwath knew that the exaggerated play was meant for him, a person who hadn't the wit to keep his water jug filled on a hot day.

I know what my responsibilities are. I am not a bad father, Keshav Rao said, whatever you may think. I keep track of my children. I know what they are doing.

Six

The theatre space was beautiful; a new building had arisen on the grave of an old one. He was not familiar with the locality. It had taken him forty minutes by bus to reach. He had come alone; his brother-in-law would have been a handicap. Shankari might even refuse to talk to them.

From the landing rose a wide flight of stairs, mighty, majestic, as if reaching for the skies. It opened into the auditorium, a semi-circular ring of cushioned benches, looking in to the well of the stage.

There was a crowd at the foyer, of formally dressed men and women, the women in saris and the men in sober shirts. He suddenly became aware, under the lights of the foyer, of his scruffy clothes and chappals, and moved away to the shadows to wait.

He settled down in his seat and read the leaflet he had been given along with the ticket. Shankari's troupe or the one she hoped to join was well known for performing an old form of folk art. They were a group of Jogappas and Jogatis, performing through traditional song and dance, the life of the goddess Renukamba to whom they were dedicated. The gist of the play was there on the other side of the leaflet but it was too dark for him to read. He was familiar however with the myth of Renuka—a woman who was beheaded by a suspicious husband and brought back to life by a violent son.

There was an announcement asking for all mobile phones to be switched off, and then a moment of pitch darkness when all the lights were switched off. Several phone dials lit up briefly, before being extinguished. There was a rustling of saris, a clearing of throats and then a moment of silence in the darkness.

He recalled the evenings on the terrace of his sister's house, rather, his house, Neel Kamal, talking to his nephew's friends, his 'students' as Aprameya insisted, while they waited for their 'teacher' to come home. Shankari, whom he had met as Shankar, handsome, barrel-chested, a face with strongly marked features, like an image chiselled out of wood. He had enrolled in Aprameya's class to learn English. Unable to join the group of Jogappas and Jogatis back in his hometown, Aprameya said, Shankar had been packed off to this anonymous city by his father in the hope that his only son would regain his 'manliness'. Here Shankar had taken to assuming his Shankari avatar, banding with a new group and hanging around at the traffic lights, scaring young men into handing over their money, which was where Aprameya first met him.

A decorated pot bearing a bust of the goddess had appeared on the stage and it sat in solitary glory in the spotlight. The deity wore an elaborate head dress of peacock feathers, and jasmine and kanakambara flowers. She bore all the auspicious marks of marriage. Across her forehead were stripes of vermilion and turmeric powder, and a necklace of black beads with a gold and coral pendant, for she was, in the first instance, the symbol of a chaste wife.

A group of Jogatis, women pledged to the goddess, sang an invocation to Her—they were dressed much like their goddess themselves, in red-bordered saris, flowers in their hair, foreheads dressed in bands of sacred ash, vermilion and turmeric, arms laden with glass bangles. They sang in full-throated praise of the goddess, their voices ringing out.

The lead singer, the head of the troupe, took a bow. For eighteen years I lived as a man, and now you see me as Renuka, yes I took on the name of the goddess when I dedicated myself to her. I have been Renuka for thirty years now, serving at her temple and performing her story wherever I am invited. Today I am here with my fellow devotees, performing on this grand stage, amidst you respectable and rich people, tomorrow I go back to my village and sweep the courtyard of the temple, and become an insignificant devotee of the goddess again, living on the largesse of alms givers.

Their singing was rhythmic but harsh, and not particularly melodious, but as it progressed, he liked its staccato rhythms, the flat style, accompanied by a single-stringed instrument that produced the plangent note of a rubber band. An orchestra appeared on stage to support the singers—a harmonium, a small dugdugi drum which made a sharp rapping sound when struck on either side by the tassels which were attached to it, and then he recognised Shankari at the drum-shaped instrument with the single string that had produced the plangent rubber-bandy sound. With one hand she plucked at the string inside the drum while the other commanded a stick, a small pole with a cluster of bells attached to it. The sound of the rubber band was relieved by the periodic jingle of the bells. Renuka, the lead singer introduced the members of her troupe. Shankari was playing on the instrument, which she identified as the chowdike. The dancers walked up and down on stage, swinging their arms and hips, throwing their false plaits over their shoulders, and turning with little twirls and twists.

The ensemble was effective, if somewhat homely, and by the middle of the performance, he had begun to enjoy the repetitive rythms, the harsh flat delivery and the chorus of unharmonised voices.The lore of Renuka he knew well. But the Jogatis and the Jogappas had introduced their own variations to the story, challenging the happy families version, and its smooth, roughage-free conclusion. In their version, Jamadagni cursed his four disobedient sons—Go live as eunuchs! And the community of Jogappas traced their kinship to these four sons of Renuka. When Parashurama, the obedient son tried to seize his mother as his father had ordered, she fled to a village by the Malaprabha, for she was a local girl after all, and she was given shelter by the women. In his haste to do his father's bidding, Parashurama ended up beheading two women, his mother and her local protector.

I cannot restore your mother, Jamadagni said. You have killed two women. Those were not the terms of the boon.

Parashurama raised his axe against his father next. You are going back on your word. I will be forced to kill you.

Go to the Himalayas, his father commanded. Bring back the waters of the holy rivers and pour it on your mother's body.

Unerringly, the hasty Parusharama poured the magical waters all wrong, such that the two heads were transposed. He brought back to his father the woman with the villager's head and his mother's body. And the other version, with his mother's head, stayed home by the river where she belonged, becoming the patron goddess of the troubled, the traumatised and the plain muddled.

On being revived, the first thing Renuka did was scold

her son—You are a bumbling, violent boy! It would be best if we stayed away from each other! There could be no peace between mother and son, she declared, no peace in families. The performance ended with mother and son agreeing to shut out the sound of each other's voices and the sound of their music and their prayers, vowing that their voices would fall silent to the other.

In the final scene, the troupe appeared on stage, balancing pots on their head, bearing idols of goddess Renuka. They bent backwards to the floor and forwards, without supporting themselves, and the idol stayed put on their heads. It was an admirable feat, and their performance ended with a standing ovation.

Ashwath made his way out before the end, when the applause was just beginning, to wait for Shankari.

The story is very different from what I know, Ashwath said, in an attempt to break the ice, to put Shankari at ease.

It's what our guru has composed. It's our story.

They looked at each other, and Ashwath looked away immediately, not wanting to stare.

This city is not for me, Shankari said, wiping her face with the edge of her sari. I've decided to go back home and tell my father. My place is here, with this group. I've been intitiated into the group by my guru. She has given me diksha as a Jogati. I will live among them, they will be my family ... She knew nothing about Aprameya's whereabouts. She was grateful to him, it was he who had helped her see the light, helped her summon up the courage to confront her father, to tell him this was the life she had chosen, to acknowledge the truth about herself, that she could not be what she was not. It would be difficult for her father, for her mother and sisters, she was their only son after all, the man of the house.

There was a flurry backstage and sounds of heavy objects being moved. I have to go now, Shankari said.

You know what, she threw over her shoulder as she turned to leave. Try talking to Chotu. He may know where Aprameya is.

*

He was waiting for his brother-in-law at the circle, directly opposite a red neon sign that said Baron's Inn. It was close to the hotel where he was staying, in a quiet residential locality with large houses—it suggested respectability and modest old money. But some were selling out, to places like Baron's Inn, and commercial establishments were creeping in. He stood on the glistening pavement, wet with the day's rain, in the red glow of the neon sign, feeling a little unreal, a little like a mobster in a Hollywood gangster film. The smell in the air, mossy and raw, of the wet stone of the pavement, of the skies washed fresh after a shower, and the water still dripping from the canopy of trees above him, he recognised immediately; it was a feeling of old. But Baron's Inn? He remembered the name of the apartment complex he had seen on the outskirts of the city, he couldn't quite remember where—a West Chester Apartments. These names puzzled him. West Chester. Baron's Inn. How had people chosen these names?

He pulled his mobile phone out of his pocket. His brother-in-law had neither called nor messaged. He wondered how long he should wait on the pavement before going back to his hotel room, and lying low. He was beginning to feel hunted, like a whistleblower, confined to a room, waiting to decode instructions locked with passwords.

His brother-in-law had located Chotu. It had taken him several days to locate the right corporator who had led the way to the agent who could ferret out Chotu. Chotu was not answering his mobile phone, and the adult education centre where he had enrolled for classes had no address or other phone number for him; only the number of his sponsor, and that was Aprameya.

Chotu lived at the edge of the city, in a settlement of migrant workers who worked at a waste segregation unit. The settlement was built on land leased from a landlord whom Keshav Rao knew, but about which he had to be discreet—discretion, that was the code word in the city—for the man neither acknowledged his ownership of the land nor the existence of the settlement. And he operated only through his agent. There was no question of approaching him directly.

A woman came out of a building on the opposite pavement, robust and vigorous-looking, dressed in 'male attire' as his mother would have put it, carrying a cardboard box and she made for the kerb, probably to cross the road. He felt a weariness come over him, and he rocked on his feet, standing on the pavement. He had a letter from Tim, excited about moving to his farm, asking about his plans. The owner of his apartment wanted to know how long he planned to be away. And Chef Ganucci had sent him an email saying his new building was almost ready and the new fine dining restaurant was opening soon. They would be in business by Thanksgiving. Did he want his old job back? And there was the house. There was Neel Kamal, his fortune, the millstone round his neck, the thing that had almost got him killed. He still had to meet Rajagopal and get his will registered.

A car drew up to the pavement. It was Keshav Rao and the agent. He got into the front seat, next to the driver. They drew away from the kerb, from the red wash of Baron's Inn, which stained the pavement like a pool of blood. He could not recognise the streets through which they drove—the lights, the throngs on the pavement, the buildings, the roads, the cars and the shops, the darkening sky, gave up nothing to the fleeting glance, to the brief glare of the headlights. And he was one among them, nothing more. As was Keshav Rao, who had fallen silent in the back seat, and Aprameya, wherever he was, and his sister, and Thippy, and his niece who had called him to say how unhappy she was since her friend Chandan Bala had gone away. The road stretched ahead unending, and in the swiftly descending darkness, the tail lights of the vehicles looked like a string of fireflies, motionless, flickering.

They were driving through a glade, a thicket of bamboo, the headlights sweeping an arc through the thorny undergrowth.

We are taking the road through Cubbon Park, his brother-in-law said.

They emerged from the park. On the other side of the roundabout there should have been a white building, elevated by a ramp, a ramp leading up to the foyer and further on to a high-ceilinged hall with tables and chairs, and attendants in white uniforms taking down orders in their notebooks. The last time he had been there, so many years ago, he remembered sitting under a chandelier, at a table covered with a white table cloth, looking at Thippy's composed face, marvelling at her refusal to be overawed by her surroundings. It was her first time out to such a place surely, and yet she was prepared for it—she had been wearing a 'proper woman's dress', a half sari with a gauzy veil that threw a soft light on her face. He had watched her eat—he remembered her dainty fingers, the sliver of dirt under her finger nails, her small even teeth, and the way her mouth moved. The memory was fresh in his mind, as if he were there, at the table, in the glow of the chandeliers again.

As the car emerged from the park and approached the circle, he saw that the building was gone.

There used to be a restaurant here. Tiffany's ...

Long gone. Pulled down—his brother-in-law all but snapped, irritated perhaps by his irrelevant preoccupations.

*

The settlement was a small shanty town of dwellings with tin-sheet walls and roofs covered with blue plastic tarpaulin sheets, held down with old bicycle tyres. It was at the edge of a slum, in a plot of land enclosed with compound walls, a gated community. The plot with about a hundred such hutments was lit up at either end by a tall cluster of lights, like a football stadium or a prison. The lights threw a harsh piercing white light on every corner of the settlement, but the hutments themselves had no electricity. Some of the houses were dark, some had single lamps flickering inside, throwing shadows on the walls; he was reminded of the distant light of the folk tale, the sole flickering lamp in the landscape, that welcomed the weary traveller, looking for shelter for the night.

Shadowy figures emerged to take stock of them, as they stood at the gate. The agent had a low-voiced conversation with a few men in broken Hindi and they were led between rows of houses, on a rough dirt pathway, to the back of the settlement. This was where Chotu lived. The door to his house had a curtain, unlike other doorways they had passed, which were open, offering a clear view of the small rooms, with floors of hard-packed mud. The houses or hutments rather, were low-roofed, it would be impossible for a fullgrown person to stand upright and not hit the ceiling; only a child could walk in it, adults would have to crawl. Chotu's house was in the last row of houses, just a few feet away from the tin-sheet boundary wall. There were three people in the house—three pairs of slippers lined up outside the door. A hinterland of plastic discard lay behind the hutments, heaps of old plastic mats, bottles and milk sachets, separated into piles.

By the time they reached Chotu's house, there was a small crowd of men behind them, the young men in jeans, two of the older men in lungis and kurtas. One of the older men, Rashid, acted as the spokesperson, speaking only to the agent. The other men looked on, watchful, saying nothing.

As they waited outside, Rashid spoke to the agent who laughed and patted him on the shoulder. Rashid was assuring the agent that they were above board, a legitimate colony of waste collectors and separators; their papers were in place. This land, the cycle rickshaws the men hired to drive to the garbage heaps and cart back the plastic, were leased from authorised owners—they must know Babu surely—and their waste was pledged to five agents, who in turn sent the maal to Delhi. Just that morning they had sent off three truckloads. They worked with a 'madam' who had a contract to receive and segregate wastes from the corporate offices—seven of them—sorting out the plastics and the cardboard packing cases. They could even handle the more complicated waste—the e-wastes and the electrical equipment, the innards of computers, televisions, refrigerators, floppy discs, printed circuit boards and tubelights. He said that with a certain amount of professional pride, while behind him, the men looked wary.

A woman came out of the house carefully straightening the curtain in the doorway. This was Manju, Chotu's mother. Her skin gleamed copper-gold in the football-stadium lights, her curly hair stood like a halo round her head. Her sari was drawn round her shoulders. When she spoke they could see that her front teeth were black.

She looked frightened when they asked for Chotu. And when they asked where he worked, she just looked at them, saying nothing. The agent spoke to Rashid who said something to her in turn, in Bengali. She replied in a low voice, her lips barely moving.

She says he sometimes spends the night out, with friends.

Tell her I know her son, He comes home sometimes, when my son has his classes on our terrace, Keshav Rao said. My son is his English teacher.

She smiled bashfully at the ground, and said nothing

Before they left, the agent tried to push some money

into her hand but she backed off, refusing to take it. Back in the car the agent said he had the information they wanted. Chotu seemed to have found a job at a second plastic factory in an industrial estate at the other edge of the city. He has caught a lucky break, the agent said. Few could break into the carefully guarded territories. He had Chotu's new cell phone number. They could meet him in the morning, before his shift began.

*

Keshav Rao had started a cold. The silence in the car was broken by his constant sniffles. The agent took out his cell phone and began to talk continuously on it, telling each caller that the connection was bad and that he could not hear him clearly.

They were making their way to the industrial estate at the edge of the city, to a small factory that turned plastic waste into new plastic objects. This part of the estate was the preserve of industrial plastics and polymers. The agent had the name of the particular unit where Chotu worked, in this oasis of smallscale industry, on the road to Mysore, at one time a distant suburb, and now very much part of the city.

In this maze of plastics and polymer units, they had to locate Chotu. The railway line ran along the road, the highway on which they were travelling, and a pylon stood at a distance, an atlas holding up a mountain of cables. At some point they saw the river—the industrial estate had made good the promises of the Founding Fathers of the nation, led by Nehru, that the smallscale unit be included in the economy. It should have been a picturesque sight;

river, road and railway line—nature and man—running hand in hand, but the river was a black thick stream whose foul-smelling vapours assaulted them; it could be mistaken for a sewer. The river had a name, the Vrishabhavati, the agent reminded him (Keshav Rao was dozing with his handkerchief spread over his face)—now a thick stream of industrial effluents—and the smallscale industries made free use of it to send their wastes out in the hope that it would reach the vast ocean and mingle with it, a veritable drop, safely out of their sight.

Chotu had begun on the lowest rung, rooting through mounds of garbage, hovering round the collection points where the tipper autos would bring small loads of household waste and dump them into large trucks to be taken away to landfills, waiting to pick up discarded plastic bags and bottles, and anything of waste value, perhaps a bonanza of clean, not-much-work plastic, to fill in his sack and pedal his cycle rickshaw to a kabadiwala's yard—every sackful earned him a hundred rupees. While most young men from his settlement were content to make the one trip in the morning and sleep for the rest of the day, Chotu made several trips. And when his kabadiwala's yard was in danger of closing down, because the area where the yard was located had suddenly become sought after, on the verge of being transformed from slum to middle class respectability with organised housing, he had come to see Mr Jagadish, the agent. Mr Jagadish had been a supervisor in the ward where Chotu collected garbage, so he knew the workings of the waste disposal mechanism minutely. Chotu had been full of ideas. He wanted to start his own sorting yard, he wanted to enter into an agreement with a factory to receive the sorted plastic wastes, he wanted a loan for a baling machine to compress the waste so that transporting it would be easier and he could send more waste per trip to the factory.

The agent, Mr Jagadish, dressed in a white full-sleeved shirt and white trousers, with a large gold-strap watch on his wrist, was full of grudging admiration for Chotu's spirit of enterprise. Can you beat it, a stripling who had no papers, no rights of any sort, and he wanted a bank loan, wanted to start his own yard! Of course, the loan would have to wait ... in the meanwhile, Mr Jagadish got him a job at Shri Shakti Thermoplastics, a middling size plant whose owner, Pratap Singh, Jagadish knew. The unit recycled waste plastics into a number of new goods—there was a picture of smiling buckets, bottles and garbage bags, plastic sheets, pellets and film on the board mounted on the compound wall. Chotu would be on the lowest rung here—loading and unloading trucks as they arrived with waste and departed with finished goods. As one of the many casual labourers he would not feature on the rolls, or the records; he would be truly part of the 'informal' workforce.

They went up a narrow flight of stairs to the first floor where a large open space was separated into sections with different machines. Closest to them was a shredder, looking much like a coffee grinder. A woman was feeding sawn halves of plastic jerry cans into the funnel-shaped chute on top, while a man stood on a platform guiding the large pieces into a narrow aperture fitted with a rotor blade. From the other end, through the bent tube, the machine discharged small coarse flakes of plastic into a bin. The floor around the bin was littered with bits of green and yellow hard plastic.

Pratap Sir would be at the pelletizer—the man on the platform pointed to a large machine that seemed to be performing a complicated series of procedures. The flakes of plastic, fed through a chute, passed through a chamber where they were heated and were then extruded through a die, emerging as strands of yellow-grey plastic spaghetti, which in turn were fed into a long trough of water.

They peered behind a metal partition. A young man in a white tee shirt and bouffant hair whistled as he fed blocks of what looked like thermocol into one end of yet another machine. From the other end there emerged waves of pink-grey plastic, with the consistency of halwa, folding upon themselves in thick gleaming sheets.

I really love this place, agent Jagadish said, as if reflecting on happier times. Nothing is wasted here.

Sir, Jagadish—Keshav Rao said testily. Have you forgotten why we are here. Let's find your Pratap Singh and Chotu.

Pratap Singh was found in the hottest, darkest room of his factory, training the new boy at the injection moulding machine.

New boy?

They were just in time to see the new boy fire up the nozzle and then feed a pellet of blue plastic on to a mould. It passed through the heated barrel and pumped out a blue plastic bucket. The new boy opened a glass-fronted door in the chamber, pulled out the bucket, trimmed a plug of blue from the bottom (the part of the bucket that always gave way), inserted steel handles into the sides, all in one swift continuous motion and set the bucket on a platform for the boss's inspection.

The new boy was learning fast. When he took off his protective mask, they saw that it was not Chotu.

We have no new people, no one by that name, Pratap said. Maybe a temporary hand to load and unload the trucks, maybe help in the assembly. They would go down to the godown to check.

And there, in the godown, was Chotu.

You said your name was Kumar, Pratap Singh said.

Yes it is. Both ...

Agent Jagadish wants to speak to you. Make it quick and get back to your work.

He had not seen Aprameya, he did not know where he was. Yes, he had been at his house that evening, yes, Aprameya was teaching him English and maths, yes, he had enrolled at the weekend adult education centre, yes, he met Aprameya on the terrace of his house sometimes, but he knew nothing. He would let them know if Aprameya got in touch with him. How had they found him? What? They had questioned his mother?

When they left, Chotu was standing at the top of the steps leading down into the godown, punching numbers on his (new) cell phone.

Well—agent Jagadish said when they reached the car. I'll take leave of you now.

He lingered by the car. Keshav Rao took out his wallet. A long blast of sound, a familiar foghorn startled them. They hadn't realised that the railway lines were so close to the factory. A train trundled by, its blue coaches rattling. It took its time going past and they watched till it went out of sight.

Tippu Express from Mysore. Late today, agent Jagadish said.

He pocketed the notes Keshav Rao handed him and left. Ashwath was sorry to see him go. The train had given them pause, it had taken them out of themselves, into a larger than life moment, as if they were together in a shrine, in the presence of a god. Now it was just the two of them, he and his brother-in-law, all the way back in the car.

Seven

One morning, when he was sitting at Suchi mama's place, the devotional programme sponsored by the Nivarana Ashram was playing. The station played bhajans and chants that were part of the ashram's festivities and ceremonies. He could recognise Savitri's voice in the lead. In between songs, Savitri dispensed advice. People sent in anxious queries about jobs, their marriage prospects, persisting ailments, and she replied on behalf of Sundari Amma, reading out the answers which one of the volunteers at the ashram had taken down. They heard Savitri's pious and grave tones, and Suchi mama said—Would you believe she was capable of quarrelling over property? I am glad your parents are not here.

That was a risky statement, even for Suchi mama.

He had smiled, and said nothing.

Suchi mama, my father was not as tough as you are, he said at last. Though he was the older brother.

Suchi mama looked pleased at that. He would begin again about the house, Ashwath knew, urging him to settle the matter before his sister's family carved off chunks of it. But Suchi mama did not proceed on his usual tack that morning.

Your father died an unhappy man. Lonely ...

Savitri was by his side, and my mother, Ashwath said.

That may be, but not his son. You were not there. Why does a man long for a son? He could not bless you with the last gifts a father is supposed to hand over to his son, along with his earthly possessions—the blessing of divine speech which grants him his heart's wishes, a steady, happy state of mind and unfaltering breath.

They are with me, Ashwath said. I consider the blessing given.

*

They were on the way to the ashram, he and Savitri, for an audience with Thippy, to ask her to divine where Aprameya was and to send him home.

Savitri looked exhausted. There were deep lines around her mouth. She had been keeping up a punishing routine of fasting and prayer. It was the month of Shravana, well into August, the month of self-mortification and denial.

At the gate of the ashram, they parted company. Savitri had duties to perform as a member of the ashram, and he was a guest, one of the few invited to view the divination ritual, where Sundari Amma would answer questions. But the rules were the same for everybody, even those who were part of the ashram. The 'questions' and the identity of the questioner were known only to Amma and the questioner had to take a chance on whether it would be answered.

The gates to the ashram were closed. Too many curious

visitors, Savitri said. They have no respect, only curiosity. We restrict our visitors. We have nothing to hide, we often have visitors—serious people, doctors, scholars, researchers—but this is not a tamasha, a spectacle. We don't allow visitors to take photographs—this is a healing session.

He knew the routine from his previous visit. He was frisked and patted down at the security kiosk and relieved of his mobile phone. He was handed a token and told that he could retrieve his phone on his way out.

There were people waiting at the Reception, other guests with whom he would share his buggy ride to the temple. The assembled group was in the middle of what appeared to be an animated discussion. He looked for a seat away from them, but the only place vacant was on the sofa, which he had to share with someone else, and he was perforce part of the group.

Right in front of him, sitting close together, was a couple with their child, a boy of about seven or eight. The man and woman were looking straight ahead, their faces frozen. They did not appear to be part of the conversation. The boy looked solemn and was unnaturally still for a boy his age. They seemed bound in a cocoon of private misery.

Next to him on the sofa was a distinguished-looking man with delicate hands which he was using to punctuate his speech. He was speaking to a woman sitting opposite him. From their conversation Ashwath gathered the man was a doctor and the woman a journalist or a researcher. With the ease of long experience of addressing people and dispensing advice, the doctor drew Ashwath in to their conversation.

I have just been telling Malini here that I have been

monitoring Amma's blood pressure, the physiological changes she undergoes, since her very first episode. Her pulse rate slows down, she breaks into a sweat, and when she speaks it is with great effort. She is exhausted afterwards, and it takes her some time to recover. I find that her bouts of uneasiness are increasing. I have told her, and her personal physician Dr Nachiketan about these symptoms.

Episode—you call it an episode, you speak of it as a physical ailment—the young woman, mother of the silent boy, who had been shunning contact with everybody burst out, as if she could not hold herself back any longer. It was then that Ashwath realised that she had been part of the conversation in the group and getting progressively angrier, holding herself back by force.

What she is, the woman continued, her voice hoarse with feeling, is a channel of grace. She puts herself on the rack so that she can take on our pain. For that moment, the grace of her chosen deity descends upon her ...

And how do you think she does that, the woman the doctor had just addressed as Malini asked. Her accent was decidedly American. On hearing her speak, Ashwath felt that he had met her before. Perhaps a similarity of experience had produced a type—razor sharp, confident of her entitlement, her brain snapping at every opportunity, ready to squeeze every moment to the full. She was documenting cases of possession disorder from all over the world, she said. She had just come back from Spain, and before that she had been to Mexico. No, she wasn't interested in exorcism, she shook her head rapidly, she was studying oracles, healers. She nodded at the young mother, who had turned her back on them again. So Malini addressed the doctor with the delicate hands, Dr Roy. It's interesting, but in most of the cases I have studied, the demographics of the women who are divine channellers or oracles is very similar. They are not very educated and they come from poor families ...

The young mother continued to turn her back, now stiff with anger, on them.

Your studies may be right, your numbers correct. But I don't think they take into account that above all, she has to be a good person, pure of heart. Divine grace does not come calling on just anybody.

It was a new voice that spoke. An elderly man with a flowing beard, dressed in white, with the look of a sage, had joined them. The sage-like man introduced himself as Nachiketan, Amma's physician and head of the Ayurvedic section of the ashram. He was in charge of guiding and overseeing all the herbal preparations. The doctor in the group, the one who had said he had been monitoring Amma's condition right from the beginning, greeted this newcomer respectfully, with a deep bow and a namaskar. The flyer described Nachiketan as an Ayurvedic doctor from a long line of practitioners and an expert in astrology, one who had an authoritative knowledge of the Prasna Marga.

You have to have a blemishless heart, an open mind, an almost infinite capacity for compassion towards all beings, Dr Nachiketan continued. The mother of the young boy unbent and turned towards them again.

Amma is given the gift, the diksha of speech by Vac Devi, the goddess of speech herself, temporarily, for a period of time. According to the scriptures, there are other qualifications too for divine grace to descend upon you, so that you can help others. Equanimity of temperament, calmness of mind, love of austerity—one who does not require much sleep or food, who steps lightly on this earth, has little bodily waste, yes, one who does not sweat much, has not much urine, faeces or flatulence, and also someone who is naturally sweet-smelling and whose face is a lotus in bloom. You will agree that it is a tall order—Dr Nachiketan smiled at Malini—it is not enough, how did you put it, to belong in the right demographic bracket, to be just poor. He spoke to her as if he were cajoling a child.

But, Dr Roy interjected, coming to Malini's aid in a sense, you said yourself, Nachi, that it has become difficult for her since the—incident—he lowered his voice so that only the other doctor could hear him. I heard she has gone on a fast, she keeps to herself, spends most of her time in the garden.

And you—the sage-like Dr Nachiketan addressed Ashwath suddenly. I know the others, but why are you here, what do you want from Amma?

I have a question for her, like everybody else, Ashwath said.

The very day after Aprameya's disappearance Savitri had sent all the birth details of her son, of the 'question', to a volunteer who did the weekly aggregation of questions—his date of birth, the star under which he was born, and the nature of his 'ailment'.

The buggy is ready,—a volunteer came in and announced, and led them out.

How will we know, Malini said clutching the volunteer's hand in a panic—How does Amma answer our questions?

So, thought Ashwath, she too had a question, a problem to be solved, possibly beyond her case study.

You will just know, Dr Nachiketan said. Sometimes Amma speaks after the ritual, sometimes she doesn't say anthing but you will find a sign. Or when you wake up in the morning you will find that you have the answer you were seeking.

The buggy took a different route from the last time he had been there. When it stopped, they were at the edge of a grove of trees. In the fading light it looked thick, like a forest, and there was a narrow beaten path leading into it. A tall tree stood at the head of the path and the air was full of the sweet milky fragrance of the akasha mallige, the Indian cork, which held its flowers in bunches high up in the sky, allowing them to fall on the ground rather than be plucked.

As they walked down the path towards the temple, the group fell silent. Suddenly, he noticed that Savitri was by his side. He could not fathom the look on her face, her expression was questioning in part and also withdrawn.

*

The path and the darkness ended. The temple in the clearing was not the old stone structure of his imagination, but a modern building, with a granite façade and marble flooring. They entered a courtyard paved with stone, with an altar in the centre and built-in seating arranged around it, like in a stadium, but on a much smaller scale. There was a pattern drawn and filled with coloured powder on the altar, a yantra or a symbol of some sort, representing the goddess to whom the prayer was offered. In the middle of the yantra was a clay pot, dressed in flowers, vermilion and turmeric, from which a plume of smoke still uncurled. A little to the side sat a drum, the gong at rest by its side, as if it had done speaking. A pair of brass cymbals, one cup turned up and the other face down lay next to the drum, its chimes still lingering in the air.

They were to wait there, in this altar chamber, till they were summoned one by one, to put their question to Amma.The young couple with the silent child went in first, to an adjoining room, the sanctum where Amma was promised. He and Savitri were next. He recognised the smell as soon as he entered, the rough smoky fragrance of the resin that had always burned in the outhouse when he had been a boy, the garden full of its fumes. The room itself was in darkness, except for a ceiling light that was directed at a large brass pan, an uruli filled with water or it could be oil. A brass lamp was placed next to it. The water in the brass pan was still and heavy, reflecting a white curtain. He could hear a low murmur of voices in the room. They sat on the cane chairs arranged in front of the brass pan—this was a modern temple, civilised in its amenities—watching the curtain.

There was a low chant, a prayer was recited, and the curtain was pulled aside. They could see her reflected in the clear pool of liquid. She was sitting in lotus pose, her upturned feet resting in her lap. The folds of her white sari were gathered loosely round her and her hair lay in thick waves over her shoulders and her back. Her face glistened, pale despite the bright vermilion and sandalwood paste on her forehead. She sat still and calm with her eyes closed, as still as the water in which she was reflected. Her face had grown thinner, her cheekbones more prominent and her skin stretched over them as tight as a drum. She looked starved, he thought, as if she hadn't eaten in days. It was the last thing he noticed, those silver protrusions on either side of her cheek, which he first thought were the pendants of her earrings, but were actually the two ends of a small spear, the shaft protruding from one end and the silver head from the other. On her it looked like an ornament. There was no sign of blood, of a puncture or a tear on her cheeks.

Someone came up and whispered something in her ear. For a long moment she sat still. Then her brows contracted, her eyelids pinched further into themselves, and then she began speaking, in a laboured voice, strained and high pitched.

Not your child—he could barely make out. *Not your child ... Another unfortunate ... another unfortunate ...*

And then the water in the uruli rippled, the curtain was drawn and their turn was over.

*

Back in the car, he sat back, exhausted. In his hands he held the prasada from the ceremony—flowers, dried leaves and ash from the ceremonial fire and an incense of herbs to be burnt for the next few days.

We are lucky, Savitri said. Of late it is becoming more difficult for her to speak. She is taking longer to recover from each session. The doctors are worried. They say she will have to stop.

Could you make out what she said?

Her answers are never direct. It is not our child alone she has in mind, but all children. She feels for every one of them ...

Savitri was calm, as if the burden of finding her son was no longer weighing upon her.

I remember the time when she first came to see me. Savitri's eyes were closed. She was speaking softly, more to herself.

I was alone at home that day. I had been alone for so many days that I felt the house could well be my tomb. Aprameya was—how old? I can't remember. And Shweta was a baby. In those days I used to be constantly in pain. The doctor said everything was normal, there was nothing wrong with me. She prescribed calcium tablets. It did me no good. It was Thippy who did her trick of healing. She just passed her hands over me, like a wand or a baton, and rested them on top of my head, right here. Immediately, I felt better.

She spotted the pipal tree in the garden and she cleaned out the dry leaves from its base, and asked me to care for it. That was the first sign to me that you would come back—for the ashwattha is your tree, is it not, planted firmly in the yard where her house had been? And also that attachments are not so easy to root out, whether it was my husband or you or her.

Then we walked in the garden, hand in hand, like sisters, and she showed me the plant right there in our backyard, the sweet flag reed by the cement tank at the back, you know the one with the tall fragrant leaves and seed like a small corn cob, and asked me to make a decoction of those leaves. That would calm my nerves she said, and drain out the sorrow and the anger from my heart. The incense that I burn is the one that she gave me. I still remember the first time I lit it in the house and how its fragrance spread, it smelt sweet and was acrid in the throat when I breathed it in. I could smell sandalwood and taste the neem on my tongue. It reminded me of the days when she was in the outhouse and the whole backyard would be swathed in those same fumes ... This is His way of setting the balance right I thought, for the injustice we had done to them.

Within a few days, I felt much better. The acid in my stomach settled, I didn't feel so anxious.

Savitri babbled on, but he had stopped paying attention. He thought of Thippy's feet, upturned on her lap in lotus pose, the soles still edged with dirt, the toes as he remembered them, lumpy, like gooseberries, and her face, contorted, unrecognisable. He closed his eyes and breathed deep, feeling his breath sough through his constricted throat; he would not see her again, he knew that for sure. That thread in his karmic weave had reached its end, the colours already faded. The woman he had seen bore no resemblance to the girl he had known.

Savitri, he said. I have closed that door behind me. There is no more Thippy. Make your peace with Sundari Amma.

The phone in his pocket beeped, as if on cue. It was a message from his niece.

He is back, dude. So chill. Went on a college trip it seems.

A sense of relief spread over him, a rippling of pins and needles over the entire length of his skin. He felt he could not move, could not take another breath without rupturing his ribcage.

I know, Savitri, sitting at his elbow, said softly. I know.

She reached out for the phone to call her son.

Aprameya, she said, you're back? Good. Check the

water in the sump and switch on the pump. Time it for three minutes.

They sat back and watched the meaningless road go by, a jumble of lights and shops, and cars and buses and two-wheelers, and people. The car was cold—the driver had been a little too enthusiastic with the air conditioning; moreover there was a strong smell of sweat in the car.

*

Savitri, he said. Why did you do it?

She made a movement of surprise, looked at him and looked away quickly.

I've known it all along. That scatter of lead was meant for me ... She still said nothing, continuing to look out of the window.

You've been wanting to do that since your NCC days I know—ever since I persuaded them to pull you out of the NCC. You had your chance and you missed ...

I could have got you if I wanted—She rose to his bait and then retreated, realising the import of what she had admitted. We aim to shoot into the ground, she said quietly. It's the noise that matters. It scares off the monkeys.

The monkeys, of course. Interfering beasts—

There must have been something in his tone to rile her for she reared up, like a snake with its hood raised. They were back on the terrace again, mortal enemies, best friends, siblings who breathed as one, each reading the other's mind even as a thought was formed.

It's taken me so long, twenty-five years, to make good for the life you disrupted, the people you abandoned, to put the house together again—her voice choked on a slurry of spittle and pent-up emotions. She cleared her throat and swallowed, wiping her hair back from her forehead as if to punish the wisps for escaping from their regimented knot.

When she spoke again, she was calmer, almost ruminative. Do you remember a saying that Amma would keep repeating to us and we'd laugh at her—consider what falls to your lot as ambrosia—*palige bandaddu panchamruta*. I know it's not the best, I can hardly claim to have panchamruta on my plate but in the middle of the mess I've settled down to some order. I have made a life, however ragged it is. And then you had to come back and disrupt it again. To claim the house that I had saved and held together—your property!

In that moment, her sack of worries was opened and laid bare to him. Her fear, that her husband may have raised loans against the house or even tried to sell it, that it was the only means of binding her difficult son to her, or that he might make a deal with the ashram and cut her out, and that ultimately, if he asserted his right to the house, they may well be homeless.

They wilted after you left, Savitri continued, her voice beginning to rise again. And you wouldn't visit, even after they passed. She never gave up hope that you would come back and get married—that was what kept her going, even when you would not reply to her letters. A beautiful bride for the apple of her eye. She made me put aside the jewellery for her in the locker and made me promise that I'd keep the house in trust for you.

Look Savitri—he interrupted her dam burst of anger—it's started raining again.

Her hand rested on the seat next to him, knuckly and veined, unguarded. He covered her hand with his and said, We never much cared for that panchamruta if you remember—gooey stuff. They couldn't believe that the gods could have cared either for the viscous mix of milk, honey, yogurt and bananas that their mother would try to get them to eat.

He recalled the day of the telegram, announcing the news of his father's death. It had been a perfect summer's day; the sun, brilliant, dazzling, friend to all, who moved across the sky removing darkness and spreading light, had anointed the day with an overspill of his offerings. Ashwath had wandered about aimlessly, swathed in darkness on a blindingly bright day, when the air was so crisp that it could be folded and put into your pocket, amidst happy, holidaying crowds, grieving for a life gone awry.

Savitri, he said at last. We've come to terms now, you and I, with what we have and that will have to do. I can give no explanations, but I can tell you this much. By the time I come back next year, the lawyer will have the papers ready. And we'll take a decision on the house. You and I together. Nothing else matters.

The sound of a popular song burst upon them. The driver had switched on the FM radio. They were reminded that they were not alone.

Where now, the driver asked. What route should I take?

Go left, take the flyover, Savitri said. And switch off the air conditioner, will you.

He forced himself to close his eyes. He rolled his eyeballs downwards, resting them on his cheeks; he felt the crunch of movement in his forehead. He sat back and tried to relax. They had a long drive back home.

*

When he had just arrived, perhaps a few weeks after that, they had all gone to a music concert. It was the first time he had seen his sister's family together, and though he didn't know it then, it would be the only time. The month-long music concerts were part of the Rama Navami celebrations, the festivities to celebrate the birth of Lord Rama. The concerts organised in the grounds of a nearby school were famous. His parents and Suchi mama's family used to wait for these concerts every year and Suchi mama would get season's tickets for all of them. Keshav Rao was active in organising the concerts and it was Savitri's ambition to be invited to sing at one of them.

One part of the vast grounds was cordoned off and an open-air stage was set up with covered seating for the audience. The rest of the grounds had been barricaded for parking. All along the sides of the compound wall were tea and bajji stalls for 'light refreshments' as the organisers put it in the programme leaflet.

He had bought tickets for all of them from a well-meaning but woolly-headed volunteer at the booth, who had taken several worried minutes to calculate the amount and then given him the wrong change, and then they had picked their way through the slush to the seats under the shamiana.

The tickets had cost him fifty rupees a piece and they were barracked off right at the back. Usually there was a big audience for these concerts and the organisers had made room to seat several hundred people. But that evening, most of the seats were unoccupied. In front of them stretched row upon row of stockades fashioned from rough raw logs, tied together with coir string. There were a few people in each section, most of them elderly. He was surprised when Shweta and Aprameya agreed to accompany them, but they were sitting a little away, with their friends. Shweta, who took music lessons, sat with the girls from her music class, and Aprameya with Shankar, who was musically inclined, and Chotu, who just did not want to go home.

The stage, a raised wooden platform covered with durries, seemed quite distant from where they were seated, and the figures of the performers were rather indistinct. In their direct line of vision was the idol of Sri Rama, clothed in a fresh white dhoti and angavastra, garlanded with jasmine. A faithful Hanuman knelt at his feet. Right in front of the stage, in the first section, were the cushioned seats and sofas for the donors and the friends and relatives of the organisers. The lower stalls like theirs had white plastic chairs which shifted noisily every time someone stood up or sat down.

When they came in, the preliminary concert, the first round of performances had just got over. The two singers were twin sisters, middle-aged, well-established vocalists—singing like this since they were girls in two plaits—now they wear saris and do up their hair in a bun—Savitri said—not married, parents are no more—summing up their life in a sentence, setting it in stone. The two sisters were getting off the stage with their accompanists, stepping awkwardly to avoid the ruts in the coir matting; one of them stepped heavily and almost fell.

*

An important man, possibly a big donor, in a light-coloured safari suit, is being ushered in to the front seats, by an organiser. The possible-donor is accompanied by two women dressed in silks, with thick ropes of jasmine coiled round their heads. Their diamond nose rings wink at the audience as they sit down. Just as his group has to crane their necks to the right to look at the singers, the VIPs will have to tilt their heads upwards to look at the stage. People keep coming and going in to the stands. There is a noisy shifting of chairs. An elderly woman lurches past them, sits down on a plastic chair and turns the one in front round so that the seat faces her, and puts her feet up. She smiles apologetically at them as if to say, What to do, age catches up with the best of us ...

Aprameya hands out bajjis from a greasy newspaper packet. The bajjis are oily but very tasty—Ashwath is eating ridge gourd bajjis after years. He is amused too that a stickler like his sister is dipping her hand into the packet; she would never have tolerated such casual behaviour at a music concert.

A cool breeze has sprung up. It may begin raining again. But the shamiana is very well sprung. It also looks very aesthetic. Along the sides are frills of multi-coloured satin, and there are overhead fans at regular intervals, and tube lights on the ceiling and mounted on poles in the aisles.

On the stage, before the next singer comes on, the mangalarati is being performed. A priest lights a lamp and waves it in circular motions in front of the idol and rings a small bell that he holds in his other hand. They all stand up for the mangalarati which is very low key. A junior priest is dispatched with the lamp on a brass plate, into the gathering. Meanwhile, the next performer and his accompanists are settling down on the stage, testing the mics and their instruments. The sound system is somewhat primitive, but it will do. Ashwath recognises the singer. He is Savitri's contemporary, and Keshav Rao's former student, now far advanced than either of them, a vidwan or maestro in his own right. He begins with the raga Hari Kambodi, a song in praise of Lord Rama. Ashwath recognises the raga and the song.

Savitri leans across to him.

He smiles. You were taught this song, I remember. But they haven't said a word to each other.

The singer's style is brisk. He punctuates his notes with gusto, with short barks almost. The mridangam keeps up with him. The mridangam player is a very young man, this might well be his first concert. He is Aprameya's friend and student, which explains why Aprameya is there with Shankar and Chotu. The mridangam works up a crescendo of beats, it sounds like an approaching storm. He is backed by the staccato beats of the ghatam, which is, in effect, a large pot. The violinist follows note by note, close on the heels of the singer.

The song is over. The applause is desultory, perhaps because of the size of the hall and the scattered audience. The singer begins on another composition, hums the first tentative notes. It is the raga Mohana, the first one Savitri was taught. He catches her eye and smiles. They are back on Nanda Talkies road on the way to her music class. The summer air is hot with the fragrance of roses.

The breeze outside has grown stronger. Any minute it will rain. Halfway through the song, the 'light' insects start drifting in. In a matter of minutes, they multiply, coming in swarms, flapping into people's faces as they weave their crazed paths to the lights, fluttering round them, bumping into them like demented lovers, in futile suicidal acts of devotion.

There is a mild agitation in the audience. People stand up. They must turn off the lights, someone says. Keshav Rao takes charge. He makes his long way to the front and the booth on the side where the organisers are. The lights are swiched off—only the stage and Lord Rama are lit up. In the audience, people's heads are silhouetted in the darkness, and their hands as they hold up their fingers to keep the beat.

The insects have already begun to fall to the ground. A feast for the crows in the morning.

The junior priest with the mangalarati lamp has been weaving his way through the aisles and has now reached them. The naked flame should have been tossed in the breeze, despite the priest's protective hand around it, carrying with it the ripple of anxiety that it may go out but when the lamp reaches him, Ashwath sees that the flame has been capped with a hood, a perforated shield of thick plastic which keeps it burning steadily upwards. It is a simple thing. A neat device which does the trick and keeps the flame from blowing out. The young priest waits patiently as the coins clatter on the plate, and people crowd round to warm their hands on the flame.

That evening he had felt the joy of homecoming, that he belonged here, with the people he was with, and had also felt acutely a sense of what he had lost. This could have been my life, he had thought. This is what I could have had.

You could still have a life here ... your life back—Savitri says. She could well have heard him think.

I have a life there and a job to go back to ...

Suchi mama still has hopes for you and Malati—the imp of mischief is back in her voice.

Savitri, he says, you are making fun of me.

Then he catches his sister's spirit and replies—Who knows? I am a colossus now. I have to straddle two worlds.

It was true. He had written to Chef Ganucci, accepting his offer of a job at the new restaurant. And to his landlord, telling him he wanted to renew the lease on his apartment. It was a nice apartment, small, with a balcony that looked out to a quiet leafy street, a street full of parked cars. The heating worked and the manager was a pleasant, business-like man. He must remember to take a present for him. He would most probably arrive at the best time of fall, when the trees were aflame, and the view from his balcony would be uplifting. There was a beautiful ginkgo—the oldest tree in the world—just outside his balcony, with its fan-shaped leaves turning golden in the fall, all of them, and he waited for that each year. He must remember though, not to bring the seeds of the ginkgo in; he would never be able to get the smell out of his apartment.

Savitri is speaking again. Suchi mama is getting a Mrityunjaya homa done. For you. He wants to ensure that you live long.

He is familiar with that hymn, he knows it by heart, the salutation to Rudra, the three-eyed one, fragrant, beautiful, the granter of prosperity, and the appeal to Him for grace, to be loosened from the bondage of death as gently and as naturally as a cucumber from its stem, but to be granted immortality, to live forever. He likes the cadences of the shloka, and its imagery, that it combines the lofty with such a precise natural detail. He notices the stress on the senses, the nod to worldly strife, and the final encompassing beauty of the metaphor of release.

Author's Note

As in a work of fiction, the reflections of events and places in the novel are impressionistic; the details and chronology are not intended as historical records, and the novel takes some liberties to suit its fictional purpose.

Details of the works quoted in the book are as follows—

The epigraph is from Philip Larkin's *The Daily Things We Do: Collected Poems,* The Marvel Press, 1979, and Faber & Faber, 1988.

The imagery in Chapter Three, Part IV, is from *Pattupattu, The Ten Tamil Idylls,* and the lines quoted are from the poem 'Porunarattrupadai', translated into English by J V Chelliah, The South India Saiva Siddhanta Works Publishing Society, Tinnevelly, Madras 1, South India. 1962.

The lines quoted in Chapter Three, Part V are from the poem, 'To be in Love' by Gwendolyn Brooks; Chapter One, Part VI, has lines from 'The Harbor', Carl Sandburg: Chicago Poems; the lines from Martin Luther King Jr.'s speech that appear in Chapter Five, Part V are from the speech delivered at the New Covenant Baptist Church on 9 April 1967.

The work of installation art referred to in Chapter Six, Part VI, is modelled on Jitish Kallat's Public Notice 3, at the Art Institute of Chicago, 2010-2011.

The theatre performance in Chapter 6, Part VII owes, among other sources, to the Jogeerata performed by Manjumma Jogti and Group at the Theatre Festival in Ranga Shankara, Bangalore, in 2010.

I acknowledge with thanks the invitation from the International Writing Program, University of Iowa to participate in their programme. My stay at the residency between August and November, 2011, facilitated the writing and research of this novel.

Finally, I thank Ravi Singh, Publisher, Speaking Tiger, and Renuka Chatterjee, VP (Publishing) for her guidance and immersive editing of the manuscript.

ALSO IN SPEAKING TIGER

TIBET WITH MY EYES CLOSED STORIES

Madhu Gurung

A collection of vivid and deeply emotional stories ... [that] deals with issues of identity and belonging, allowing one to experience the hope, pain, and remarkable perseverance of a people and region that are at risk of being forgotten.' —Shashi Tharoor

In this collection of short stories, heart-breaking and heart-warming in equal measure, the lives of displaced Tibetans building new homes in India are chronicled with rare nuance. The eleven stories are divided into the five colours of the Tibetan prayer flag: in Blue (Sky), 'Zinda' is the name of the Tibetan village which a child has to escape after Chinese occupation, returning only as a young man to this unfamiliar motherland after a bittersweet surprise. Mariko, the former monk protagonist in White (Air), shatters expectations by becoming a beauty icon and dancer. 'In the Footsteps of Buddha's Warriors' from Red (Fire) tells the story of the Chushi Gangdruk, the forgotten Tibetan guerrilla group which fought bravely from Nepal for an independence which never arrived.

Madhu Gurung writes evocatively and with deep empathy about the Tibetan community's struggles and success, despair and hope, and the fabric of family and identity that stretches and dissolves and knits itself back in new configurations.

Page Extent 272 pp | Price ₹350

ALSO IN SPEAKING TIGER

BODY AND BLOOD

Stories on Breaking the Ten Commandments

Urmilla Deshpande

What would happen if one did steal, commit adultery, covet one's neighbour's goods, even murder ... and break all the rules we were taught to live by?

Each story in this first-of-its-kind collection takes you into a realm where people are prompted by love, desire, jealousy, hatred and, at times, a strange compassion, to throw out the old, conventional rules, and make their own. The title story, 'Body and Blood', is a macabre revelation of how far one can go when one loves someone before all others, even God; in 'Honour. Or Not', a young girl abused by her father since the age of thirteen finds a shockingly unexpected way of 'honouring' him when he dies.

In a lighter vein, the protagonist in 'Sunday Snow Job' asserts that working girls have to work, even on the Holy Sabbath, while Gomes in 'Heart of Gold' finds it is possible to covet your neighbour's wife and get rich too. 'Wakulla' raises the question: can stealing be an act of compassion, and not a sin? In 'Fall', Srinivas discovers that one can make love to one's best friend's wife without actually committing adultery. And coveting your neighbour's goods is fine—as long as they are the right ones, as 'Elegy in a Churchyard', the tenth story in this riveting collection, teaches us.

Written with panache and by turns erotic, tongue-in-cheek and shocking, this is a collection of noir and black humour at its best.